KU-570-017

CHILD OF SIN

When housemaid Lizzie Burton falls pregnant, stony-hearted Agnes Ridley turns her out with only the clothes on her back. If it weren't for Debbie, who follows her into exile, Lizzie would be friendless as well as destitute. The girls meet big-hearted Sadie Trent, who takes them in and cherishes them, but even Sadie cannot protect them from the vicious Abe Turley, who is determined to take his pleasure – and then his revenge; and from Fleur Masson, who hides an evil trade behind the respectable façade of a fashion house. Can there ever be true happiness for a child of sin?

C8000000109880

Loan
not
at

CHILD OF SIN

CHILD OF SIN

by

Meg Hutchinson

Magna Large Print Books
Long Preston, North Yorkshire,
BD23 4ND, England.

British Library Cataloguing in Publication Data.

Hutchinson, Meg
    Child of sin.

A catalogue record of this book is
available from the British Library

ISBN   0-7505-1723-9

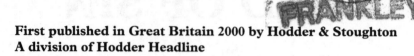

First published in Great Britain 2000 by Hodder & Stoughton
A division of Hodder Headline

Copyright © 2000 Meg Hutchinson

Cover illustration © Kevin Tweddell by arrangement with
Hodder & Stoughton Ltd.

The right of Meg Hutchinson to be identified as the author of this
work has been asserted by her in accordance with the Copyright,
Designs and Patents Act, 1988

Published in Large Print 2001 by arrangement with
Hodder & Stoughton Ltd.

All Rights reserved. No part of this publication may be reproduced,
stored in a retrieval system, or transmitted in any form or by any
means, electronic, mechanical, photocopying, recording or otherwise
without the prior permission of the Copyright owner.

Magna Large Print is an imprint of Library Magna Books Ltd.

Printed and bound in Great Britain by
T.J. (International) Ltd., Cornwall, PL28 8RW

All characters in this publication are fictitious and any resemblance to real persons, living or dead, is purely coincidental.

From early childhood I have loved writing and telling stories, so much so it became my regular reason for 'misbehaving' at school. This book is for those teachers at St James's Church of England School, Wednesbury, who turned a blind eye to a young girl's ruse yet at the same time never failed to encourage her in her writing. To those women I send my gratitude. Never will I be able to say thank you enough.

Chapter One

'You realise, of course, you can no longer stay in this house? What you have done is unforgivable, a wicked thing. You have brought disgrace upon yourself and shame upon my house.'

Head bent, fingers twitching nervously at the corners of a snowy white apron, Lizzie Burton remained silent, the tears stealing gently down her cheeks the only evidence that she had heard the harsh words of her employer.

Cato Rawley glanced over the top of his rimless spectacles, taking in the trembling figure before him, its trim shape somehow accentuated by the lace-edged apron, a matching cap setting off her shining chestnut hair. The girl was downright pretty. It was easy to see how a man might lose his head over her.

Removing his spectacles, he rubbed them with a fine lawn handkerchief, coughing to disguise the fact that more than his mind was disturbed by this scene.

'Well, girl!' He replaced the glasses on his nose. 'Have you nothing to say?'

Lizzie's chestnut hair swung, catching the light that flowed into the quiet room.

'This man – what's his name?'

His question met only by silence, Cato followed it with another. 'You *do* know his name? You weren't so foolish as to allow some fly by night...?'

9

'No, sir.' Lizzie looked up, speaking for the first time since being sent for by the master of the house.

'That's something at least. I take it then that you will be marrying as soon as possible?'

Hearing the sob that escaped her, he frowned. 'This man, whoever he is – he has agreed to marry you?'

'Yes.' The word was squeezed out between lips that barely moved. 'He has agreed to marry me.'

'Then the sooner it is done the better.' Rawley leaned back in his luxuriously padded chair. 'However, the fact that you are to marry, that this man is to give his name to the child he has fathered, does not in any way excuse the wrong you have done. Carnality can be forgiven by none but the Lord. I hope, child, that you will pray to Him, both earnestly and often.' He fiddled again with his spectacles, not looking at the girl standing facing his desk. 'This is a painful duty but one I cannot shirk. It might have come more gently from your mistress but since she is absent...'

He looked up then, the sight of that pretty face streaked by tears bringing a familiar ache to his loins. The girl *was* lovely, it was a pity he had not noticed it before. 'The sin you have committed is abhorrent to me. I cannot expose my wife to such a taint. However, I must also exercise Christian charity. I will instruct Mrs Ridley that you be paid your wage to the end of the month, but you will leave this house first thing in the morning.'

Deborah Hammond carried the last of the

supper dishes into the scullery. Leaving them unwashed on the board set alongside the shallow brown stone sink, she returned to the kitchen. Glancing at the girl sitting at the big scrubbed table, her head sunk on her chest, she felt a quick surge of compassion mixed with anger. Compassion for her friend and anger at the man who had seduced her.

Going to sit beside the trembling figure, she asked gently, 'Have you seen the master?'

Lizzie nodded, the words she struggled to say catching in her throat.

Touching a hand to the girl's shoulder, Deborah asked softly, 'What did he say?'

'What do you expect?' Face flushed from the heat of the blazing fire, the housekeeper swung around to face the two girls. 'He's told her she's to go, and it's no more than she deserves, dirty little slut! Eh, what a thing to bring on this house!'

'Is that all you can think of?' Deborah's eyes flashed green fire. 'This house? What about Lizzie?'

'What about her!' Agnes Ridley's mouth curled like the crusts of week-old bread. 'Didn't nobody here push her into bed with a man. What she did was off her own bat, and now she has to pay for it she's snivelling. Well, she can go *on* snivelling, she'll get no sympathy here. She can't expect the master to keep her on.'

'But where will she go? She has no parents, no family. You know that and so does the mistress.'

'But the mistress don't be here.' The house-keeper's mouth curled again in triumph. 'For

11

myself, I've no idea where the slut can go and I don't care.'

'How can you say that?' Deborah's brows drew together in disbelief. 'Lizzie has been in this house for eight years. You have known her since she was a child. In all that time she has never done anything wrong or unkind...'

'So we were led to think!' Agnes snapped. 'But now we have the proof – proof that she's no better than the trollops who flaunt themselves along of the North Western, waiting for men getting off the trains.'

'Lizzie isn't like that.' Deborah felt a tremor beneath her hand, heard the other girl's soft intake of breath. 'She would never do anything so brazen.'

Crossing to the range gleaming by the yellowy light of the gas mantles, Agnes picked up a ladle, dipping it into a large saucepan bubbling gently on the hob.

'If she's not like that then how come she's carrying some man's bastard?'

'What she did was wrong, and Lizzie knows that.' Deborah slid an arm about the silent girl. 'But she needs help. You can't just turn your back on her after eight years.'

'Eight years!' Agnes answered acidly. 'Eight years of having a good home, a clean bed and regular meals. And how does she thank the master for that? By bringing shame to his house. Well, he's given her his answer and I'll give her mine. She'll get no help from me. "As ye sow, so shall ye reap". That was what my mother always told me.'

12

Withdrawing her arm from Lizzie's heaving shoulders, Deborah stood up, her face resolute. 'In that case,' she said quietly, 'you should pray for your harvest to be long in ripening for you will have a deal of reaping to do.'

'Why, you!' Ladle in hand, the housekeeper whirled round, narrow eyes bright with fury. 'You dare talk to your betters like that, and I'll speak to the master about you!'

'And enjoy the telling, as doubtless you enjoyed telling him of Lizzie's predicament. As for speaking so bluntly to my betters, that is one thing I could not possibly stand accused of when speaking to *you*. And I doubt very much I would be doing so in speaking to the master either.'

Colour deepening in her face Agnes Ridley dragged air into lungs held tight by anger. 'You'll be sorry for that!' she hissed. 'Sorry for letting your tongue run away with your common sense. I'll have you dismissed too. You can go with your trollop of a friend!'

'Don't say any more.' Lizzie looked up, her reddened eyes imploring. 'Don't say any more, Deborah, or you'll lose your position. Apologise before it's too late. Tell Mrs Ridley you didn't mean what you said.'

Keeping one hand on the other girl's shoulder, Deborah fixed her eyes on the older woman's flushed face as she answered.

'But I *do* mean it. My tongue did not run away with my senses Mrs Ridley. Quite the reverse, my tongue has held my senses in check for years, but no more. And now I'm going to say what common sense has told me for years: that you are

13

a spiteful, vindictive woman who delights in nothing more than venting your frustration on those ill equipped to strike back. You gain pleasure from making the lives of those who serve in this house a torment to them.'

Across the kitchen Agnes's breath was expelled in an audible gasp and her narrowed eyes stared at the girl facing her so bravely.

'The master shall hear of this!'

'And when will you tell him?' Deborah's head lifted defiantly. 'After you have left his bed, or while you are doing the very thing you both condemn Lizzie for doing? You are right in one thing you say. There is a trollop in this house but that trollop isn't Lizzie – it's you!'

On the other side of the table the housekeeper's thin lips folded even further inward giving a sharp fox-like point to her narrow features. Fingers tightening about the ladle, she glared at the girl who for the first time since coming to Portland House had dared to answer her back. Another of them! Thoughts savage as whipcord flicked through her mind. Another girl half her age; another pretty face to take Cato Rawley's attention from her, another young body to entice him away. Oh, she had seen the looks he had cast in the direction of such girls; looks that clearly indicated it would be to her own benefit if they could be got rid of. Now fate had given her her chance, and she would make certain no pretty young thing came to serve here as maid again.

'Don't you dare say that to me!' Always quick to surface, Agnes's temper flared again.

'Why not?' Deborah kept her own anger under

14

control though the contempt she felt for this woman rang clear in her voice. 'It's true. I've heard you, night after night, going to the master's room whenever his wife is away. And that's very often, isn't it, Mrs Ridley? You see to that with your lies and insinuations. You goad the poor woman until she's glad to go.

'You saw yourself in her place, as mistress of this house, but that was before Leonie Elliott came on the scene. Now she has taken Cato Rawley's fancy and he no longer wants you. That's the poison that is festering inside you, the sickness eating away at you, the frustration that drives you to lash out at every opportunity. But all your spite will not alter anything. You have lost your dream. Cato Rawley will never take you for anything more than a means to satisfy his lust.'

The ladle dropping from her hand to clatter noisily on the flagged floor, Agnes Ridley stared at Deborah, white-faced in shock. She had been so careful! All these years she had been so careful, waiting until long after the maids were in bed before going to the master's room. Yet all the time they had known … *they had known!*

Leaning heavily on the table, she stared into eyes cool with derision while her brain whirled, trying to piece together a reply. She must not admit to what this chit of a girl accused her of; she must not admit to being Cato Rawley's mistress.

'The master shall hear of your wicked lies,' she pronounced. 'He will hear of them and you will be sent packing tonight.'

'Yes, he will hear, but telling him is one delight

you will not have, and nor will he have the pleasure of dismissing me. I am going to see him right now … to give in my notice.'

'You can't do that.' Narrow eyes widening, showing the venom pictured in them, Agnes straightened. 'You can't go upstairs now, the master has company.'

'Then they too shall hear what I have to say.' Deborah turned towards the door leading to the main part of the house.

Her tightly laced corsets creaking as she moved, the housekeeper edged around the table to stop her.

'Don't try being cocky with me!' She glared. 'If I say you don't go upstairs, then you don't!'

Deborah watched her hand rise menacingly, her own gaze unflinching as the open palm began its downward swing; then, calmly and coldly, she said, 'I wouldn't do that if I were you, Mrs Ridley. You have slapped both Lizzie and myself for the last time!'

'I'll show you whether I've slapped you or that slut for the last time!' Agnes took her hand back above her head, eyes half closed as she drew in her breath sharply. 'I'll knock that old buck out of you! By the time I've finished you won't be able to talk for a week. You don't backchat Agnes Ridley and get away with it!'

The sounds of Lizzie's chair scraping against the stone floor and frightened cry did not distract Deborah's attention from the palm already resuming its previous sweep toward her. Bringing her own hand sharply upward, she caught the older woman's wrist and with a strength she'd

16

never known she had, forced it slowly down against Agnes's skirts before releasing it.

'If the truth sounded like impertinence then that is unfortunate,' she said quietly, 'but it is no less the truth. You will never beat Lizzie or myself again.'

Breath coming in swift gasps, the housekeeper took a step back. Though her hand remained still her eyes darted quickly from one girl to the other.

'Get your things together, the two of you, and get yourselves away. There'll be no place for you come morning. No place anywhere once folk get to know what you are.'

Slowly untying the straps of her apron and folding it neatly, Deborah laid it on a corner of the table which years of dedicated scrubbing had rendered almost as white. Then removing her lace-trimmed cap set it on the top, all the time her eyes holding fast to the woman whose words had been law to her for so many years.

'What would that be, Mrs Ridley?' One hand smoothing her dark skirts, she regarded the housekeeper with a derogatory look. 'Just what will folk find Lizzie and myself to be?'

'I'll tell you what they'll find.' Agnes Ridley's voice cracked with rage, her carefully cultivated mode of speech slipping back into the dialect she tried so hard to disguise. 'They'll find you be a smart-arsed big mouth wi' nothing the back of 'er 'cept a one up, one down slum of a home and a father never out of a public house long enough to care. As for 'er…' she tipped a sideways nod toward the still trembling Lizzie. '…they'll find

17

'er to be slut, same as I 'ave. A no-good stinking little whore who don't 'ave sense enough to know when to keep 'er legs closed.'

'Then that is something we will have to learn to live with.'

'Arrh, it is!' The other woman sneered. 'But you won't be learning 'ere. You'll both be out of this 'ouse tonight.'

Stepping once more to Lizzie's side, Deborah pulled the other girl gently to her feet.

'Go and get your things.' She smiled into the anxious tear-strained face turned towards her. 'I'll not be long, then we'll leave together.'

'You get yourn an' all. That is, if you've anything to get.' Agnes smirked. 'The things you 'ave on your back belong to the master and I doubt he'll give you leave to keep them after what that slut's done!'

'You have no need to worry.' One arm supporting Lizzie, Deborah walked her to the door. 'I will inform Mr Rawley that anything he has paid for has been left behind … and that includes his whore!'

She had assured Lizzie everything would be all right and so it would have to be. Shawl pulled tight against the night air, one arm linked with the younger girl's, Deborah felt the same rush of trepidation she had felt when standing outside the master's room. She had felt nothing but anger during her exchange with Agnes Ridley and was not sorry for it or for choosing to stay with Lizzie; yet at the same time she felt a sense not just of trepidation but almost a fear, the same feeling that had followed the death of her parents, taken by the cholera.

'Where will we go, Deborah?'

Swathed in a shawl, Lizzie's face was made paler by the moon, the eyes darker with fear.

Giving a squeeze to the arm linked through hers, Deborah forced a smile. She had asked herself the same question on leaving Rawley's sitting room; she'd had no answer then and she had none now, but Lizzie was scared enough without hearing that.

It was a question Rawley's visitor had also asked. Perched elegantly on a brocade-covered chaise-longue she had listened to their conversation, intervening only as Deborah had turned to leave. A picture of that woman crept back into her mind now. Dressed in a violet taffeta gown, its neckline cut just above her breasts, the amethyst stones of her necklace and pendant earrings matching exactly the colour of her wide almond-shaped eyes, while the creamy skin of her face contrasted attractively with the curious brown beauty spot on her left cheek. But it was her hair, pale and golden as fresh-grown wheat and shining like silk, that had caught Deborah's attention. The woman was undeniably beautiful. And she smiled as she asked her question, the warmth of it sliding into those wonderful eyes. Then, receiving no answer, she had glanced at Rawley.

'There is a place, Cato,' she had said, her voice soft and strangely musical. 'They could go to Father Travers – he runs a refuge for fallen women.'

'I don't think so, Leonie!'

Deborah remembered her surprise at the sharpness of Cato Rawley's response and the sudden tightening of his mouth.

'Lizzie, of course, must leave.' He had turned to face Deborah and she had seen the stony glint in his grey eyes. 'And if you insist on leaving with her then I feel it would be best for you to find your own way from the start. The refuge could not house you for ever.'

Keeping her voice firm, Deborah had answered quickly. 'I am not a fallen woman, and as for Lizzie, she is to be married very shortly. It was kind of you to think of us but we will not need the help of Father Travers.'

The woman had smiled again, her lovely eyes playing over Deborah's face. 'Once she is, my dear, and should you find you require a position, then you may come to me at Bayton Lodge. We will find you something there, I'm sure.'

'Tell Mrs Ridley to pay your wage to the end of the month!' Cato Rawley's voice had cracked as he spoke and he looked angrily at his visitor, but she had continued to smile blandly.

'Where can we go now?' Lizzie repeated, chasing the memories from Deborah's mind. 'We have nowhere to go, nobody to turn to.'

'We have each other.' Deborah forced herself to smile. 'And in a few days you'll be a married woman. Until then we will find a room to share and we have money enough for food. Really, Lizzie Burton, I don't know what you're worrying over.'

'You, Deborah.' Standing there under the cold

light of the moon, Lizzie suddenly looked older than her years. 'I'm worried for you. What will you do, and where will you live? You shouldn't have left your job for me, it might not be easy to get another.'

'It won't be as bad as you think,' Deborah answered. 'I've already been offered a place. Mr Rawley's guest said she would find me something at Bayton Lodge.'

'Oh, Deb, that's marvellous! But where's Bayton Lodge? I hope it isn't so far we won't see each other after I'm married.'

'Of course we'll see each other.' Smiling to reassure her, Deborah urged the other girl onward. 'Nothing will keep us apart.'

Coming to a sudden halt, Lizzie caught at Deborah's free arm, fingers biting into the soft flesh, and when she spoke it was with an urgency that betrayed her inner fear.

'Promise me, Deborah ... promise me that whatever happens, you will always be my friend? Don't turn from me, please ... never turn from me.'

Catching the girl to her, Deborah hugged her, the tremors that ran through the slight figure echoed in her own.

'I'll never turn from you, Lizzie,' she murmured as the other girl sobbed against her shoulder. 'We'll be friends as long as we live.'

Lizzie answered, 'As long as we live,' her voice soft as she turned away and began to walk in the direction of the chimney stacks rising against the night sky, leaving Deborah with a fear she could not name.

Chapter Two

The two of them were gone and no other with a pretty face, or even the promise of one, would again find employment at Portland House.

Agnes Ridley sat at the kitchen table, staring into the fire.

He had as good as promised she would be mistress of this house. Each time she had gone to his bed, each time he had made love to her, the promise had been there; unspoken it was true but nonetheless there. And then that painted bitch had come upon the scene and from that moment Cato Rawley had hardly remembered her own existence.

Agnes, fingers twisted, her lips turning in on her teeth.

Her mistress, Delia Rawley, was almost at her end with consumption.

Her end!

Finger nails biting deep into her palms, Agnes felt none of their sting. Bitterness and hatred cut far sharper as her thoughts ran free.

No more than a month or two, that had been the doctor's last diagnosis, and Delia Rawley had gone home to spend a few of those last weeks with her parents. At her departure Agnes had walked every inch of the house, touching each stick of furniture, every delicate ornament, seeing herself as the proud wife of Cato Rawley.

As she still would be!

She rose to her feet, the caustic gleam in her hard eyes bringing no smile to her tight lips.

The woman upstairs with him now might well have ideas of taking Cato for herself, but she had reckoned without Agnes Ridley.

Her movements mechanical, she fetched the bucket of slack from the scullery, throwing the chippings of coal on to the fire and banking it for the night. She returned the bucket to its place beneath the sink, rinsed her hands and dried them on the square of huckaback hung over a thin rope stretching across one end of the room.

Returning to the kitchen, she removed her long white apron, her eyes resting on the one still lying folded on the corner of the table. She had got rid of those two girls and by God she would get rid of Leonie Elliott!

Walking gingerly over the rough ground, heart beating rapidly at the thought of the open mine shafts that riddled this wasteland, Deborah again remembered the assurances she had given the girl clinging to her hand. But that had been bravado. True they had their wage. Cato Rawley had proved as good as his word there and had paid them to the end of the month. That, together with what she had saved, lay tucked inside the pocket of her skirt. It was not much to show for years of labour in that house, labour made no lighter by Agnes Ridley's quick hand and sharp tongue. The money would buy them food and lodging but for only a limited time; Deborah had to find work, but at least Lizzie

23

would be well cared for. She felt the other girl's fingers twined in her own. It was a pity things had gone as they had, that Lizzie's fiancé had not waited until the marriage certificate was signed before taking the privileges of a husband. Her friend had talked so happily of a wedding gown and Deborah as her flower maid, but now...

She pushed the thought away as Lizzie came to a standstill, her glance on the sky above the small town huddled at the foot of a natural incline.

'It's almost beautiful, isn't it, Deborah?'

Her own glance following that of the younger girl, she nodded.

Overhead, sweeping halfway across the darkness to meet the horizon, the sky was painted pale gold with moonlight. Against it the chimneys of the terraced houses were lined like regiments of dark-uniformed soldiers, whilst beyond them winching wheels of the several collieries rose stark and black to the heavens, as if carved from ebony.

It was beautiful, Deborah agreed silently. Spread before them, it looked like some magnificent canvas painted by an unknown artist.

'Who would believe the dirt and the heartbreak it hides?' Lizzie went on, her voice hushed. 'Such beauty hiding the truth of the hardship and toil that make folks' lives so hard to bear. Is all of life like that? Fleeting moments of beauty that blind people to reality, hide the truth from their sight?'

Many lives perhaps, Deborah's heart made answer. Especially those whose existence was tied to coal mines such as those giving life to

Bloxwich. But Lizzie's would not be one of those lives. She had said very little about the man who had taken her heart but one thing at least she had divulged; he did not earn his living in the mines.

Catching the girl's hand tight in her own, Deborah walked on. Lizzie would marry her man. He would provide her and their child with a good clean home that would harbour none of the fears the colliers' wives suffered every day.

'You should take care, walking this way by night.'

Unseen by either of them until he stepped from the rim of the shadows fast deepening as the moon folded itself in clouds, a man of stocky build, a flat cap pulled low over his eyes, blocked their path.

'Short Heath be a dangerous place by day. At night it can be lethal.'

Coming to Deborah's side he fell into step with them as the girls moved on, his face hidden by his peaked cap and the encroaching darkness.

'There's many a one been swallowed by mine shafts hereabouts an' never found again neither...'

His voice was harsh and tight as though blocked in his throat. Deborah felt her pulses quicken and the blood run cold in her veins.

'Thank you.' She forced the words through tight lips. 'We'll take care.'

'Can't say as I've seen you afore.'

He turned his face and Deborah caught the flash of his eyes reflecting the moonlight.

'Where are you bound? You coming to visit somebody?'

Feeling Lizzie's fingers tighten on her own, Deborah knew she must not let her own nervousness transmit itself to the girl pressing close into her. Giving way to fear now would do neither of them any good. And why should they be fearful? The man had not shown them any animosity.

'No, we're not paying anyone a visit.' She tried to sound relaxed though it was a struggle. 'We ... we're looking for somewhere to stay.'

'Lodgings?' He turned his glance away, looking towards the houses huddled together under the night sky. 'Be you looking to stay in Bloxwich, or is it just a night or two you want lodgings for?'

Deborah did not want to answer. She did not want this chance met stranger to know their business. Her free hand tightened on her shawl, pulling it closer about her as if it would protect her against this man who had brought a tingle of fear to her spine, despite her efforts to remain unaffected. But not to answer might cause him to take exception; he could view it as rudeness and become angry.

'We're not sure.' Unwilling to risk unpleasant-ness, Deborah forced herself to reply. 'That depends upon whether we ... I ... can find employment.'

'Employment, is it?' He glanced at her sideways again and then just as quickly away. 'Well, many of the families in this place work in the bitties and tackies, though for the most part the younger men have taken work in the coal pits.'

'Bitties and tackies? What are they?'

He gave a low gravelly laugh, the sound like

26

gravel stones rubbing together.

'It be the name that's given to the making of awls, needles, nails and saddle blades. They're made in the outbuildings at the back of each house. The men hand forge the blades, which are polished by the women and girls while young lads work the bellows. But I doubt you'll get taken on by any of them. The businesses provide barely enough to keep their owners as it is.'

Deborah walked on in silence. If there was no work for her here, and none for a woman in the collieries, then she must go elsewhere. She would stay long enough in Bloxwich to see Lizzie married and then leave. But to go where?

'So you need lodgings until you find out whether or not you can get work? Well, I can help you there. I know one or two with a room to spare.'

'We thought of a hotel.' The answer came to her lips quickly this time, at some inner prompting. A feeling of unease strong inside her, Deborah halted, lips trembling as she faced him. 'Thank you for offering to help us find a lodging but that will not be necessary. We prefer to do it for ourselves.'

'Just as you like.' Once again his eyes caught the moonlight, the flash of them washing over Deborah like a dash of cold water. 'But you need money for hotels, I reckon. They don't come cheap.'

Instinctively Deborah's hand left her shawl, going instead to the pocket that held her savings. 'We have money.'

A slight movement of his head showed he had

27

not missed her gesture.

'That's very fortunate.'

He laughed again, the harsh sound echoing in the shadows, and Lizzie whimpered, pressing herself so close that Deborah almost stumbled.

'Fortunate for me, that is.' He thrust out a hand. 'Give it over!'

'No!' Deborah's fingers clenched the coins in her pocket. 'I won't! I...'

His hand shot out, grabbing the collar of her blouse, yanking her forward so that her heels left the ground and her face was drawn almost level with his.

'You will if you know what's good for the pair of you!'

It was little more than a snarl, the stench of his foul breath in her nostrils adding to the sickness of fear now thick in her throat.

'All I want right now is your money. Make me strip you to find it and could be I'll be in the mood to take more. Ain't often a man has a pretty young thing like you beneath him on the ground, let alone two.'

He was threatening rape, and it might be all too easily carried out. Terrible enough for her but Lizzie was expecting. What if he should attack her? What would that do to the child she carried?

Her hand trembling, Deborah withdrew the coins, holding them out to him.

'Now that's what I call being sensible.' He grabbed the money, shoving it quickly into a pocket of his jacket, then caught roughly at Lizzie. 'Now yours!' He pulled her towards him, ignoring the cry of terror that came from her.

'Come on, little lady ... give!' He shook her, forcing her head back on her neck. 'Or is it that you'd like the other? P'raps you fancy a man between your legs?'

'Leave her alone!' Aware only of his rough handling of Lizzie, Deborah struck out at him, feeling her hand connect with his cheek. Then she was sent reeling backwards from a blow to her mouth.

'Don't be greedy!' He laughed cruelly. 'Your turn next, but first this one!'

Hitting the ground with a jolt that forced the breath from her lungs, Deborah lay stunned as Lizzie's screams rang out across the deserted heath.

Her head still spinning from the blow that had knocked her to the earth, Deborah forced herself to her feet.

'Lizzie?' She blinked and tried to focus her eyes as the world swung dizzily around her. 'Lizzie, are you all right?'

Breathing deeply, the fresh night air filling her lungs, clearing the mist from her eyes she looked to where Lizzie had stood.

'Lizzie!' she called again, in a voice that was cracking with fear. 'Lizzie ... Oh, God, Lizzie ... where are you?' Feeling the blood in her veins turn to ice, she stared into the shadows but they held no sign of the familiar slight figure of her friend. Lizzie was gone.

Where had he taken her? What was he doing to her? Fear turned to panic and sent Deborah running in circles, her screams ripping into the night.

'Lizzie! Lizzie! Answer me. Oh, please answer me...'

'Stop that! Stop your screaming!'

'Liz–' the last word fell away into a sob as Deborah felt herself caught and held in a firm grip.

'What have you done with her? Where is she – where is she?' Her body shaking with sobs, the question came again and again.

'Look at me!' The voice was rough and the quick shake he gave her was anything but gentle, but this was not the threatening stranger who had questioned and robbed her.

'What have you done with Lizzie?' Deborah glanced up at him but the face danced with the tears half blinding her.

'Who the hell is Lizzie?' Her shook her again, more gently than the first time. 'And what's a woman doing out on the heath at night? Have you no sense at all?'

An instinct of self-preservation set Deborah trying to twist free but his hold was too strong. 'He took our money,' she sobbed, unable to release his grip on her. 'There was no need to ... to...'

'No need to what?' The voice was softer now but still as firm. 'What was there no need to do?'

'Money could have bought you the rest!' Suddenly Deborah was angry and with anger came strength. Twisting violently she broke away. Stepping backward, her eyes flashing fire she stared at the man who had grabbed her. 'But that wasn't enough for you, why spend money on that you could steal; even if that money was not yours to begin with. Why spend it buying a prostitute when you can rape an innocent girl?'

'So that's it!' The voice that a moment ago was soft now was razor-sharp with cynicism. 'You came out into the heath at night with a man, then scream blue murder when he takes that which you obviously came for. Some innocence!'

Angry as she was the words forced themselves past its barrier, echoing in her mind ... *you came out onto the heath at night with a man...*

Frowning she tried to dig beneath the rage still holding tight to her mind. The words ... somehow the words were wrong, with a *man,* but he knew that she and Lizzie had been alone.

Thoughts of her friend returning the awful fear she pushed the words aside. What he said now was the least of her worries, it was what he had done, where he had left Lizzie must be her prime concern.

'Just tell me where she is.' She murmured, her shoulders sagging. 'Tell me where you have left Lizzie.'

'I don't know anything about a Lizzie!' It was contemptuous, cold as the breeze springing from the heath.

'But you...'

'No, not me!' The answer cut into her like a knife. 'Don't saddle me with the blame for the troubles your own filthy games have brought on you. If you have to go whoring you should choose your ground more carefully if not your man. You deserve all you got! Now I suggest you go back to wherever you came from before anything else happens.'

Watching him turn away, the sudden burst of moonlight silhouetting in perfect detail the height of him, the broadness of his shoulders, the head free of any flat cap, Deborah realised her mistake. A cap could be removed, thrown away in the darkness, but this man was taller by a foot, his frame less stocky, and the voice, that had been hard with anger but there was none of the scrape of gravel in it, nor none of the sourness in his breath.

'Wait … please.' She called after him. 'I am sorry, the darkness … I made a mistake … I thought…'

Walking toward him as he turned she lifted her hands then dropped them to her sides.

'Forgive me.' She spoke softly, her anger gone, but the fear trembled in her voice. 'I … I thought he … the man who attacked my friend and I had come back to…'

'You really were with another woman?'

Deborah nodded, her mouth clenched to hold the trembling of her lips.

'You did not come onto the heath with a man?'

The release of breath through his nostrils sounded loud on the hushed air as she nodded again.

'Then I must be the one to apologise, I am sorry. I should not have spoken as I did. But the question remains, just what *were* you doing out on the heath at this time of night?'

Still stifling her sobs, Deborah related what had happened, words tripping over themselves in their hurry to be told. Standing there in the moonlight, the man listened in silence, not speaking until she was done.

'No wonder you thought I was this man. You must have been terrified. If you'll trust me, I'll take you down to the village. Someone in Elmore Green will give you a bed and tomorrow you can see the constable.'

'No.' Deborah pulled her shawl determinedly about her though her voice still trembled. 'I must find Lizzie, I can't go without finding my friend.'

She was clearly telling the truth thought Clay Gilmore staring through the masking shadows at the face whose pain he could see highlighted by the moon. It would take real talent to lie and weep so convincingly. He hadn't seen a more convincing display at Wood's Picture Palace in the High Street but somehow he felt this was no lie. As for the other one, the friend called Lizzie could be anywhere on the heath. If their attacker had raped her then chances were she was already lying at the bottom of an old mine shaft. Lord knew there were plenty of them around. Any one of them would easily hide the evidence of what her attacker had done.

'Thank you for your offer,' Deborah broke in, 'but I must find Lizzie.'

She turned away but Clay moved quickly to catch her arm. 'You don't know the heath, and it's pitted with shafts. Best I come with you.'

Taking her silence for agreement he fell into step beside her. 'This man,' he asked, 'have you seen him before? Do you know who he was?'

'No.'

'Could you identify him in any way?'

'Not really. I only know he was less tall than

33

you and quite stocky. He … he wore a cap but the peak was pulled down too low for his face to be seen clearly.'

Holding on to her arm as she stumbled on the uneven ground, Clay questioned her again. 'Well, was there anything else about him. Some peculiarity in his walk or posture?'

Clutching her shawl beneath her chin, Deborah shook her head. 'No … Well, one thing. I thought his voice sounded strange. It was very rough and tight, sounded like he had a sore throat. But never mind him!' Panic sent her voice rising. 'I don't care about him, only Lizzie. I must find her!'

Listening to her call the other girl's name, Clay Gilmore's mouth set in a hard line. She might not care about the man who had robbed them, the man who was clearly capable of rape and possibly murder, but Clay cared, and what was more had a pretty good idea who he was!

Chapter Three

'There you go, Sadie, a pint of best ale.'

Sadie Trent spread four halfpennies on the counter of the outdoor hatch of the Spring Cottage public house.

'I 'ope as it don't be all 'ead.'

Scooping the coins into one hand, the other wiping a cloth over the narrow ledge from which women and children were served, the landlord smiled.

'It 'as a head on it as good as your own, Sadie.'

'Arrh, but mine ain't all froth, an' if this beer don't be the same you'll be gettin' it back.'

'Go on with you, Sadie,' the bewhiskered publican remonstrated genially. 'That be as good a pint of pale ale as you'll get anywhere in Bloxwich and well you knows it. That be why you comes here every night … or could it be as you comes to see me?'

'Huh!' she laughed, taking up her jug and drawing her shawl over it. 'The only time I comes to the Cottage just to see you, Jos Chapman, will be when they carries me in … in me box!'

Turning sharply, she walked back along a corridor so narrow her skirts brushed both sides of it, a corridor she had never known to be lit in the forty years she had been coming here.

Stepping into the cold night, she paused, easing her heavy shawl over her head. As she did so she watched a man walk slowly along the road carrying what looked to be a woman in his arms while another walked beside him.

'Hey up, there's Clay Gilmore.' She smiled as he drew level with her. 'Be that what your pit master be payin' with these days? It might put a smile on your face but I knows many a wife in Elmore Green who won't be smilin'.'

'Evening, Mrs Trent.' Clay hitched the silent figure higher in his arms. 'The women need have no fear. Not of the pit master paying wages such as this anyway.'

Catching the grimness in his voice, Sadie peered more closely at the bundle in his arms.

'What be wrong with that one?'

'These women were robbed on the heath.' He hitched his burden higher. 'And this one...'

'Where do you be taking them?' Sadie walked beside him as he set off.

'To our house. There's nowhere else will take them without payment.'

'Your mother won't be able to find room for two more. The woman has a heart of gold but there are limits even to her charity. You'd better bring them to me. For one thing my place is nearer, and for another the sooner you set that woman down the better for you. You be puffin' and blowin' like a brewery hoss.'

Quickening her step, Sadie turned left into Green Lane. Passing the first block of houses separated only by a narrow entry, she stepped beside the second darkened archway.

'Up there, lad, the door be open.'

Following him along the roughly cobbled entry,

Deborah waited at the doorway to the house until Sadie shooed her inside.

'Put her there, on the settle.' Setting the jug in the hearth, she whipped off her shawl and hung it from a nail hammered into the door. Bending over the still form as Clay moved aside, she placed a finger at the base of Lizzie's throat. 'There be a pulse, which means her ain't dead, but it don't mean her won't be if you stands there like a mawkin, Clay Gilmore! Get a move on and fetch Doctor Wilson. Tell him Sadie Trent says for him to come. And you, young woman...' She turned her glance to Deborah. 'Snivelling be doing no good to her or you. Get yourself upstairs and bring a blanket from the bed while I build up the fire. We needs to keep this wench warm.'

'Thank you.'

Eyes full of tears, Deborah repeated her words of gratitude later as she followed Sadie down the stairs after helping her put Lizzie to bed. 'I'll repay the doctor's fee, I promise.'

'Arrh, well, there be time enough for that once you be in a job. Right now what you need is a meal inside you.'

'It's very kind of you...'

'Hush, wench.' Lifting a dish from the dresser that filled the whole of one wall and ladling broth into it from a pot on the fire, Sadie set it on the table. 'What be life if you can't do a body a kindness now and then? "Do as you would have others do to you" was what my mother taught me, and I reckon it be good enough for me. Now

37

eat that broth and then you can get yourself up to bed. A night's sleep will soon have you feeling better.'

'I ... I thought Lizzie was dead!'

Unable to hold back the tears she had fought for so long, Deborah pressed her face into her hands, her shuddering sobs a testimony to the fear that had overwhelmed her.

'I thought ... he said...'

'You don't have to tell me anything.' Sadie pressed one hand to the girl's heaving shoulders, her voice tender with pity. 'You be under no obligation to Sadie Trent.'

'I think it might help,' Deborah said as the tears subsided. 'I told that young man...'

'Clay Gilmore.' Sadie went to a chair drawn well into the fireside, settling herself into it. 'He be a fine man, be Clay. Ain't no way he would 'arm a woman nor turn his back when folk needed help.'

'He was very kind.' Deborah dabbed her eyes with a handkerchief. 'I don't know what I would have done had he not come along when he did.'

I think I do, Sadie thought, thrusting a metal poker into the heart of the fire. You'd like as not have found yourself a bed at the bottom of a pit shaft.

'He heard me screaming.' Deborah toyed with her spoon in the dish. 'It was he who found Lizzie. I told him what had happened but I didn't tell him everything...'

'Like the fact that wench upstairs be carryin' a child!'

'How ... how did you know?'

After taking the poker from the fire and blowing ash from its glowing tip, Sadie plunged it into the jug.

'Give me credit for summat,' she answered above the hiss of beer bubbling in the jug. 'I've seen a few carryin' women in my time, I don't need no doctor to tell me when I be looking at another.'

'Lizzie *is* with child.' Deborah stared at her bowl of broth. 'That's why we were out on the heath. We had to ... we were looking for new employment.'

The old story! Holding the pottery jug in both hands, Sadie took a long drink before setting it back in the hearth and wiping her mouth with the back of her hand. A wench lets a lad get a bit too free, then afore you know it there be a child on the way and she's shown the door. It had gone on since Eve and would go on as long as there were men walking the earth.

'But you ain't carryin'.' She squinted through the dim light of an oil lamp set on the dresser. 'There were no call for you to be put out.'

'I chose to leave.' Deborah shook her head, declining the implied offer of beer from the jug.

Sadie leaned back in her wooden chair, her gaze suddenly fixed on the glowing heart of the fire. They said history had a way of repeating itself, like a wheel going round and round. Resting in her lap, her fingers tightened. Hers, it seemed, had just come full circle. As she stared the flames faded, giving way to a picture of two young women, one half carrying the other who was heavily with child. Behind them rose a large imposing house, its door firmly closed.

That had been the way she and Emmy had come to Elmore Green. Emmy had borne the child the man of that house had refused to own, carried it in shame and suckled it in sorrow.

'I'll take Lizzie away tomorrow,' Deborah said softly.

At a stroke the pictures in the fire vanished, leaving only flames dancing in its place. 'To go where?' Sadie reached for her jug.

'I ... I'm not sure. Anywhere.'

Swallowing the mulled ale, feeling the warmth of it in her throat, Sadie felt the memory of tears prick her eyes. Hadn't she said those very same words to Emmy? *We'll go anywhere, but we go together.* It had not proved as easy as it had sounded. They had walked miles, day after day, working for a meal here or a crust there; sleeping under hedges or in hay barns. But in every village it had been the same: no place here for whores and bastards. Finally they had come to the outskirts of Walsall where they had been allowed to stay, sharing a byre with the cattle. They would be safe there, she had told Emmy. After all, the Holy Family had shared a cattle shed. And that was where Emmy had given birth, but hers had been a girl child, one they had both loved dearly until...

'Anywhere can be a long way,' Sadie blinked away the tears, 'an' it can take a deal of finding. You be welcome to settle here, until that girl upstairs be fit enough to go on any road.'

The lump that rose to her throat almost choking off the words, Deborah answered, 'I will pay you, Mrs Trent. Tomorrow I'll see the constable. He will find the man who robbed us and get our money back.'

Pushing herself to her feet, Sadie collected Deborah's dish and spoon. 'Don't go putting no faith in that,' she said dryly. 'Young Colly Latham be too lazy to get up off his arse long enough to scratch it, even had he brain enough to work where the itch was, which he ain't! I reckon any poor fool they has locked up in the daft house could do as well as him. Save your breath, me wench, and face it – you've seen the last of whatever you had in your pocket. Just give thanks to the Almighty that whoever the swine be, he took no more from you than money.'

'But Lizzie...'

Reaching the curtained alcove that led to the tiny scullery, Sadie glanced at her. 'You heard the doctor's words. The girl were knocked about the face but her weren't raped. Money you can manage without! It has been done before. Life is hard without it but it can at least be lived. And the wench upstairs will live, God be praised.'

Going into the darkened scullery, long practice directing her unerringly to the shallow sink, Sadie dropped the dish into it, hands gripping the cold stone as she leaned against it, eyes closed tight against the memories. She had knelt long hours in the darkness of that night, whispering almost the same words as Emmy fought for life... *'You will live, Emmy. You have to live...'*

Opening her eyes, she rinsed the dish and spoon in water fetched earlier from the yard, drying them on a scrap of cloth taken from a string drawn from wall to wall.

But Emmy had not lived. Life had proved hard, too hard, as it might well prove to be again.

'No, my dear, I must go home. I'll see you again soon.'

'Very soon, my love. It has to be very soon.'

Standing outside the sitting-room door, Agnes Ridley's lips pressed hard over her uneven teeth. They would not be spending the night together? The bitch played a clever game: a kiss here, a touch there, and then away home; she played Cato Rawley like a fish on a line.

'It will be, my darling.' The words were followed by a throaty laugh.

'When? When will I see you?'

Agnes smiled grimly. He sounded like a drowning man. Tonight he would want *her.* Leonie Elliott would not share his bed so he must make do with Agnes Ridley. Well, so be it ... she too could fish, and she would be the one to land the catch!

'I said soon, darling. You must be patient.'

'How can I be patient?'

The words rushed out, on a tide of passion. Agnes had experienced that same passion, felt his hot breath against her skin. Yes, he would ask for her tonight. Her smile remained hard and fixed as the low sultry voice reached her again through the door.

'You must learn, my darling. We will be together, I promise, together for always. Until that time...'

'I know, I know.' Cato's despairing groan seemed to press against the door, the strength of it adding to Agnes's satisfaction. 'But that doesn't make parting any easier. If only Delia ... if only I were free.'

'It cannot be long now, my love. Have you heard from her?'

Even beyond the closed door, Agnes heard the rasp of greed underlying the silken show of sympathy. Alert as she herself had been for years to the prospect of becoming the second Mrs Rawley, she recognised unerringly the same aspiration in Leonie Elliott.

'Not from Delia herself.'

The conversation continued to drift into the corridor.

'I got a letter from her mother. It seems the doctors there are of an opinion with our man here. The consumption has almost destroyed her lungs. They do not hope for a recovery.'

Neither does Leonie Elliott. Agnes's smile remained cold. But she must not condemn her for that when she herself had harboured the same hope.

'Will you go to her, bring her home?'

'I asked the same thing over the telephone,' Cato answered, 'but her mother begged me to let her stay a little longer.'

'And you, of course, agreed?'

Agnes pressed closer to the door as the sultry voice was lowered. 'How very considerate of you, my darling, denying yourself precious time with your wife when all you have to replace her is me.'

'You are a bitch! A cold-hearted, beautiful little

bitch. But I love you … God help me, I love you.'

In the silence that followed Leonie's triumphant laugh Agnes turned away, making her way to her own rooms. She knew what lay beneath that silence; mouths clamped hard together, hands groping flesh heated by desire. Well, let them enjoy their passion while they could, for when Delia Rawley's life ended so would Cato's affair with the lovely Leonie!

Agnes had waited too long, put too much effort into her plan to abandon it now. She looked around the sitting room that went with her post as housekeeper. It was comfortable enough but hardly satisfactory. She wanted the whole of Portland House, to be its mistress. Nothing else would do.

Sinking into an armchair drawn close to the cosy fire, Agnes stared into its depths.

She had planned it all so carefully, ever since she had seen a poor vagrant woman die. Malnutrition and hard soul-destroying labour already had her half dead so that when the fever struck it was over in hours, but not before her ramblings had revealed an interesting story.

Coals settling deeper into the bed of the fire sent a shower of sparks flying upward into the dark void of the chimney. Agnes remembered listening to those fever-ridden whispers, storing away secrets. Soon afterwards she had resigned her post as nursing sister at Walsall's Sister Dora Hospital and come to Elmore Green, where she secured for herself the position of housekeeper to Cato Rawley. She had quickly become more. Deprived for months of the comfort of his wife's

44

bed, he had found comfort in hers whilst Delia Rawley, already showing signs of the sickness now ready to claim her life, came to depend on Agnes's sympathetic ear and nursing skills – though in fact her medical knowledge had done more to accentuate rather than to alleviate the disease destroying her mistress's lungs.

Delia had taken to visiting her parents' home more and more often, staying longer each time. Agnes watched the last spark, the tiny jewel of light, flare defiantly in the blackness before dying. It was like Delia Rawley's life. Her visits home signalled brief stands against the encroaching illness, but the spark of resistance those visits ignited soon died on her return.

Her simple trust that all was being done was for her own benefit made it so easy, thought Agnes, staring deeper into the fire. No one questioned the care she gave her mistress or detected any lack of it. The doctor, knowing the inevitable outcome of such an illness, expected no more than a process of gradual deterioration and therefore looked no further. Growing ever more weak, Delia Rawley offered less and less resistance to suggestions she should spend time at her parents' home, free from the dust-laden air of the mines and the smoke of furnaces operating in the outbuildings of almost every house in Elmore Green drifting across with the faintest breeze, could only be beneficial to her recovery. Suggestions Agnes made with utmost subtlety.

And with each successive absence she had seen herself become more secure in her ambition; seen the prize of becoming mistress of this house draw nearer. And now Leonie Elliott...

But she would not take that which Agnes Ridley had worked so long to achieve! Agnes's fingers twisted together painfully. There would be no prize for Leonie Elliott!

If only she had stayed a little longer, eased the pain of love she brought so alive in him.

Cato walked restlessly about the room.

Leonie could be cruel in her kindness; cruel to leave him and go and help others. But he would not want her any other way. He paused in his wanderings, her gently smiling face still vivid in his mind. Such a beautiful face. Could he truly be blamed for falling so madly in love with Leonie Elliott? He had not wanted to, God knows he had not, nor would he ever willingly hurt Delia.

Delia! The memory of a lovely smiling face and beautiful golden hair faded from his mind and he pictured instead the pale, life-weary face of his consumptive wife. While there was yet a breath left in that thin body he would not hurt her, never turn from her. But Leonie? He could no more turn from her either. She aroused a passion in him he could not master, a need no other could satisfy.

It had been this way since their first meeting. Until that time his housekeeper had seen to his needs, both in and out of bed. But then Leonie Elliott had arrived, the exquisite Leonie, and all strength of will had drained from Cato. She had claimed him for her own, and though he knew what they did was wrong, he had not the strength to resist.

Tonight he had begged her to stay as he so often did, but her answer was the same as on those other occasions. She had some poor woman coming to the house whom she simply must help.

Darling Leonie. Her nature was as beautiful as her face. But her soft yielding kindliness had left an urge that refused to be ignored. Until she returned it must needs be satisfied in other ways.

Reaching his hand to the tasselled bell rope that would summon Agnes Ridley, Cato gave it a quick sharp tug.

Tomorrow Deborah would go back to the heath to search for the bundles both she and Lizzie had dropped in their fright.

Shivering from the bite of the cold water in which she had washed, she slid into a voluminous calico night gown borrowed from Sadie. The woman had been so very kind. Removing the pins from her hair, Deborah watched it fall like black silk, flowing over her breasts. Taking up the large bone comb set on the washstand, she drew it slowly through the heavy strands. Her mother had loved brushing her hair. What was it she used to say? Staring into the mirror above the washstand, Deborah looked back into the past. She was once again a small girl dressed in a pretty yellow organdie dress tied with velvet ribbons, matching bows fastened to the ends of her thick dark plaits.

'You're so pretty, my little girl.'

The words came softly from a long-gone yesterday.

47

'One day you will be a beautiful woman, and this will be your crowning glory.'

Deborah's breath held in her throat as she seemed to feel the touch of her mother's lips on her head.

'You will be beautiful, my little darling, and one day I will dress your hair with rosebuds for your wedding.'

The memory seemed so real, the picture of her mother so clear, that Deborah reached out to touch her, breath breaking on a sob as her fingers met cold glass.

After braiding her hair she climbed into the small iron-framed bed. Blowing out the candle she had carried up the narrow stairs, she stared at the moon-filled window, its light shimmering through her tears.

'... I will dress your hair with rosebuds...'

The long-remembered words seemed to brush her cheek with the softness of a kiss. But her mother would never again dress her hair for she was dead, worn out by hard work and a broken heart.

She should push the memory away, not dwell on the past. But that was what she would do from now on. The past would be her guide for the future – Lizzie's past. Her life could well be spent supporting the child some man had denied. She might pay long and hard and in full measure for a moment's madness while he...

Blinking away the tears Deborah turned her face from the window. There would be no rosebuds for her hair, no wedding for Deborah Hammond. 'I will stay by you' she had told Lizzie, and that was a promise she intended to keep. She would never desert her. Her friend's marriage would be the only thing to separate them, and if that was not to be...?

Closing her eyes, her lips pressed firmly together, Deborah repeated her promise in her heart. It was one she would keep.

Chapter Four

Clay Gilmore stood in the shadows of Clew's grocery opposite the Spring Cottage. He had been there an hour or more: waiting, watching. He had finished his shift at the mine, washed and left his home without taking a meal. He smiled as he thought of the pleased look his mother had tried to hide. She so wanted to see him wed and this in her opinion was obviously the lead up to such an event.

But he was not here to see a girl. The smile faded and in the shadows his eyes glinted icily. He was here to find the man who had robbed the two women.

Bloody fool! Clay drew a disparaging breath. He hadn't enough common sense to spend his ill-gotten gains in some other beer house, one where eyebrows wouldn't be raised at the way he was spending; but then, Abe Turley had never been heavy on brains.

He had been standing at the bar, hangers-on at both elbows, but they would fade away when the money ran out or at the first hint of trouble, whichever came sooner.

The talk and laughter increased. Clay straightened up, watching the door with its etched glass panel swing open, a swirl of tobacco smoke following the man who stepped into the street. It wasn't Turley. Clay relaxed once more, leaning against the shop door. Turley had been in the beer house most of the afternoon judging by the way he'd looked when Clay had called in on his way home from the pit. He was there still. It was just a matter of time.

Had that girl, the one who'd walked beside him last night, already left Sadie Trent's house? The question that had plagued Clay through the night and during his shift quickly returned to mind. And what if she had – of what account was that to him? All he wanted was to return their stolen money. Clay shifted his weight from one foot to the other, pit clogs scraping against the tiled floor of the doorway. That was all it *should* be, yet somehow he felt there was more to it than that.

An image of her had stayed with him after leaving her with Sadie. Wide eyes the colour of meadows in summer, a mouth softly pink against a skin white as first milk, and hair black as a raven's wing.

In the depth of the shadows, Clay felt warmth rise to his face. If his mother got wind of this she would say he'd been struck by the moon.

The bar room door swung open once more, wider this time, a man's shout following the figure that staggered unsteadily into the darkness. Clay pushed himself upright, hesitating as Abe Turley turned to throw an answer back towards the smoky room. Watching the stocky figure set off along Elmore Green Road, Clay felt a touch of guilt at what he planned to do. It had never been his way to confront a man not fully in control of his senses, and Turley had obviously had more than the odd pint; but then again, the longer this business was left undone, the less money Deborah Hammond and her friend would see returned to them.

Making no attempt to keep to the shadows Clay followed Turley, his long sure stride soon bringing him level with the man ahead. He had no desire to hide what he was about to do. It was high time Abe Turley was given a fright.

'Abe!' He called the name loudly yet had to repeat it a second time before it seemed to register and the man turned.

'Eh … who!' Abe Turley peered at him. 'Oh, it's Clay Gilmore. If you be wanting a drink with me you should have come sooner, but I'll be glad to stand you one…'

'I don't want a drink, Abe.' Clay Gilmore halted, the man's sour drink-laden breath hitting him like a sledge hammer. 'I just want to know how you came by your good fortune?'

Away from the light shed from the low curved bay windows of the public house the alarm in Abe Turley's eyes remained unseen but Clay recognised the sudden tensing of the man's stocky body. Turley may have been drinking much of the day but he was not drunk. Clay felt a sense of relief. If it came to it he would not be beating money out of a man too intoxicated to fend for himself.

'Good fortune?' Abe blinked. 'What mean you by that?'

'Standing drinks for the men in the Spring Cottage. That isn't your usual style. It's more your line to be begging drinks from them.'

'I don't cadge from nobody!' Abe answered hotly.

'Well, not tonight certainly.' Clay remained cool. 'Tonight it's been your turn to play the Good Samaritan. I wonder, where did you get the money? You have no employment apart from running shady errands for them who don't want to get their own hands dirty. So who have you been dealing with this time? It must be someone with plenty for him to pay so much you can afford to throw it around.'

'I ain't done nothing! Nobody's paid me!'

'Well, well!' Clay smiled coldly. 'And there has been no rainbow of late so your pot of gold didn't come there. So where, Abe? Just where did it come from?'

'You always was an interfering bugger, Clay Gilmore. Well, this time I'm telling you – it ain't none of your business where I gets my money from or who pays me, so just sod off!'

Turley turned away but Clay was already standing in front of him.

'Like it's none of my business two women were attacked and robbed coming over Short Heath last night, one of them being slapped almost senseless?'

'So what?' Abe answered truculently. 'Ain't none of my doin'.'

'Wasn't it, Abe. Are you certain of that? I know you never did take top prize for thinking but make a little more effort before you answer for even you must know I am to get the truth either willingly or I beat it out of you.'

'You put a finger on me, Clay Gilmore, and I'll...'

'What?' Clay challenged him. 'You will do what?'

'Have you for assault. I'll have you up before the Magistrate.'

'Using who for witness?'

'Same bugger you got to witness that I robbed them women.'

Clay straightened his shoulders, the earlier hint of aggression deepening to threat as he felt the imminence of victory.

'Ah, but you forgot, I don't need any witness, Abe. I don't intend bringing you before any bench. I intend to act as Judge myself and, if need be, executioner.'

Abe's breath caught, the sound loud in the quietness of the evening street. Clay smiled grimly. The bravado had soon disappeared.

'What's it to you?' Abe spluttered, breath escaping raggedly. 'What's it to you what happened to them women? Be one of 'em special to you, is that it? Then if so I advises you to look round for another one. Any self-respectin' wench wouldn't be out on the heath at night.'

Patience ebbing, Clay shot out one hand, grabbing Abe by the lapel and jerking him off his feet. 'Self-respecting or not, no woman deserves to be robbed and knocked senseless. You did that, Turley. The fact you're throwing money around like water bears testimony to it. Make you feel big, did it, hitting a woman? Make you feel like a man? Well, you are not and never will be. You are scum and will never be more than scum! Now hand over whatever's left.'

'They be lying.' The words came out awkwardly, the hand that held the lapel of his coat lodged against Abe's wind pipe. 'If ... if they say it was me stopped them up on Selman's Hill, then they be lying.'

Releasing the lapel, Clay gave him a shove, sending the stocky figure, reeling, to end up with his back against the wall of Goodwin's shoe repair shop.

'They didn't tell me where they were accosted,' Clay ground out, the last of his patience dissolving into cold fury. 'One of them never mentioned where; the other one couldn't for she were barely conscious. Yet Selman's Hill was where I found their belongings this morning – that is, just their clothes tied in bundles. How strange you should know the exact place when you were not there – when you were not the man who robbed them. How do you explain that, Abe?'

'Were nowt but a guess.' Knowing he had made a mistake, Abe strove to cover it. 'Anybody coming in that direction would pass over Selman's Hill. It be a straight drop into Elmore Green.'

'So you know where they were coming from.' Clay's voice was ominously soft. 'It seems you have the gift of second sight, Abe. You should use it to make a living instead of robbing innocent women.'

'You found their things, their … their bundles. They must have lost their money, tripped in the dark and dropped it. It be easy done.'

'Oh, yes, Abe, very easily done,' Clay agreed in the same soft, dangerous tone. 'But not so easily as having it taken from them after a man's fist struck them in the face. Yes, I found both bundles but I didn't look for their money and we know why I didn't, don't we? We know where it went and it wasn't on the ground of Selman's Hill.'

'Well, I don't bloody know where it be! Most like they be lying over that an' all. Like as not they had no money in the first place. Probably made the whole thing up between them. They had their arses kicked, turned out probably for thievin', and thought to get money from some poor bugger by claimin' he gave them a hiding and then robbed them. Well, it ain't going to be me!'

Along the street the door of the Spring Cottage swung open and the sound of voices carried on the night air. 'Don't try, Abe!' Clay warned softly. 'You'll be unconscious long before they reach you!' Then as the men lumbered off in the opposite direction he went on, 'If it was not you then that should be easy to prove. Just tell me where you got the money you've been spreading so freely?'

'Piss off, Gilmore!' Abe spat viciously. 'What you hoping to get out of this? Promised you a free go, 'ave they? Hope to get yourself a night with one of them, or both, is that it? You get a good time with a pair of prostitutes and Abe Turley pays the price. Well, you picked the wrong bloke this time.'

'Wrong as always, Abe.' With one swift movement Clay's hand fastened beneath the flabby jaw, lifting the other man several inches from the ground. 'I've been offered nothing by those women, and even if I had I could not morally accept a second payment.'

His teeth forced together by Clay's grip, Abe's question came out in a strangled gasp.

'You're asking how it would be a second payment?' Clay laughed quietly, a sharp intimidating
sound. 'The first is the pleasure I'm going to get
from breaking your neck.'

Feet still dangling in the air, Abe forced one
hand into his trouser pocket. Withdrawing it, he
shoved the closed fist against Clay's chest,
gasping as he was dropped to the ground.

'Take it ... take the bloody money!' he
wheezed. 'Do your knight errant bit, and give it
back. But I hope they *do* give you a reward. I
hope they opens their legs wide for you, Gilmore,
and I hopes both of them has the riff ... I hopes
they give you the clap!'

Taking the coins held out to him, Clay dropped
them into the pocket of his coat.

'I'm sure both of them will be grateful to you at
least, Abe. But in case they don't see you again,
let me thank you for them.'

Drawing back his arm, Clay drove one bunched
fist hard into the other man's face, then turned
away and walked in the direction of Sadie Trent's
house, closing off the words Abe Turley had spat
at him; but he could not close off the feeling of
disappointment, almost of pain they had
aroused. Could the girl with meadow green eyes
be what Abe had said? Was she a thief, and worse
... was she a prostitute?

He told himself he would return the money and
that would be the last he would see of her. It
wouldn't matter to him after that what the girl
was. But raising his hand to rap on Sadie's door,
Clay knew that was a lie.

'I couldn't think where else to go, Father, 'cept the poor house, and I would sooner Molly and me went to the grave than take her there.'

'I can understand, Mary Ann. It's a sorrowful place, that I will not deny.'

'I've tried every place.' The woman's voice caught in her throat, 'but there be nothing. Nobody wants any help. I be at my wits' end...' As tears fell, the woman dropped her face into her hands.

'Now, now, Mary Ann.' The priest touched his hand to her shoulder, voice soft with sympathy. 'Be sure we'll find something. Come, take some tea and we'll talk.'

'Don't think I haven't tried.' Mary Ann accepted her drink with shaking hands, glancing sideways at her fourteen-year-old daughter. 'But since my Joseph were killed down the pit things 'ave just got harder and harder.'

Handing tea to the young girl, Father Philip Travers ran his eye over the thin drawn features, the pale hair that shone from regular washing, the dress that was clean despite its many patches. Poverty had not yet reduced them to living in squalor. Despite her situation Mary Ann had kept herself and her daughter clean, and despite her drawn look the girl was pretty; a few good meals and a different dress and she would surely secure a post in any of the large houses in the district.

Taking his own cup and saucer in long tapering fingers, the priest sat back in his comfortable velvet-covered wing chair.

'Times are hard, Mary Ann.' He spoke gently his voice almost musical. 'But we can trust in

God to help.'

'I've been trusting!' The words blurted out, the woman put her cup quickly on to the chased silvery tray the housekeeper had carried it on. 'But it seems heaven has turned its back on me. Prayers comfort the soul, Father, but 'tis bread comforts the body. Me and my Molly needs bread.'

'And you shall have it.' He set his own cup beside hers on the tray then rose to his feet.

Mary Ann watched the black robe swing about his legs as he crossed to the fireplace to tug on an embroidered bell pull. He was a handsome figure of a man. Not so tall as to tower over a woman, nor so broad as to threaten her. He would make a husband any woman would feel proud to have. She watched him turn away, running one hand through his thick brown-gold hair. A fine-looking husband. Thoughts swept through her in a quick tide as she glanced at the finely cut features, marked only by the red bloom of a spot high on one cheek. What a waste! For no woman to know his touch, for him not yet knowing the sweetness of a woman's body...

'You and Molly will stay the night here.'

Mary Ann felt a tinge of colour creep in to her cheeks as he looked at her, a smile in those jewel-bright eyes. Had he guessed the thoughts that had run riot in her brain?

'Then tomorrow we will see about finding work and a home for you both.'

'The Lord bless you, Father.' Mary Ann slid one arm about her daughter as the girl stood up. 'You'll have our eternal thanks, and if there is anything me and my Molly can do for you...'

'I want no payment.' Philip Travers smiled as his housekeeper entered the small sitting room. 'And your thanks must be given to God, for if we find you a place, it will be through his guidance and not mine.'

Glancing at the middle-aged woman, a crisp white apron almost covering her dark, severely simple gown, brown hair drawn tightly back from her brow and braided into a knot on the nape of her neck, he spoke again.

'Ah, there you are, Mrs Bailey. Will you be so kind as to take Mrs Sanders and her daughter and give them supper in the kitchen? They will be staying the night with us so if you...'

'I know, I know, there's no need for you to go telling me.'

The housekeeper turned her attention to the women whose clothes seemed held together by faith rather than thread. Two more to drain the strength from the man who gave it all too willingly, who too often tramped the town and its outskirts trying to find a place for the homeless and the destitute. But he would go on doing it despite her remonstrations; would go on until he wore himself out.

'I know the routine well enough,' she went on, hands folded across her stomach, 'and why shouldn't I? The number of people who have knocked on this door and not one of them been turned away! You take on too much. I swear you'll be making yourself ill...'

'I'm sorry, Father.' Mary Ann Sanders drew her daughter closer. 'My Molly and me, we didn't mean to be a nuisance. We won't be a burden, not to you nor to nobody. Thank you kindly for the tea.' Glancing towards the housekeeper she drew herself up, summoning the last remnants of her pride. 'Thank you for allowing us in. You'll not be bothered by us knocking on your door again.'

'Mrs Bailey didn't mean any unkindness.' Smoky eyes gleaming softly, the Reverend Travers stepped quickly into the breach. 'She's solicitous of my welfare – a little too much so at times, I fear, but she did not mean any slight to you, I am certain.'

'Course I didn't.' The woman smiled and there was warmth in her brown eyes. 'It were just me trying to knock some sense where there's none. But there you go, you can't go growing crops on stone! And that is what this man's brain is made of: stone!'

'So you are always telling me, Mrs Bailey.' He laughed, the sound low and musical as his speech. 'But even stone can be broken if you keep at it long enough.'

'It will take more than a sledge hammer to get through to you! But what can't be cured...'

'And no one endures better than you, Mrs Bailey.' He laughed again, his glance going to the young girl, her eyes lowering as they met his. A pretty girl. The thought returned as he watched mother and daughter follow his housekeeper from the room. A very pretty girl. There should be no difficulty in placing her.

Going into the study, he picked up the telephone. Finding a place for Molly Sanders would be no trouble.

No trouble at all!

Chapter Five

'I was wondering, Sadie. Be those two women still with you?'

Sadie Trent ran a sharp eye over the man standing at her door. Twenty-seven and wedded to no woman. And why? Why was Clay Gilmore not wed? There was many a wench in Elmore Green would have jumped at him, arrh, and let him jump on her just to get his ring on her finger, but he seemed interested in none of 'em.

'Well, you can stop wondering, Clay Gilmore,' she said, noting the well-scrubbed face and boots freshly blacked. 'The answer be yes, they still be here.'

'Oh!' he began, then stopped, his glance dropping from hers.

'Oh, what?' Sadie was enjoying the embarrassment she knew was flooding him. This lad needed a bit of teasing, to draw him out of himself.

One hand gripped the bundles of clothing he had recovered from the heath. Clay thrust the other into his pocket, drawing out a fistful of coins and holding them out to her.

'Would you return these? Tell them...'

'Tell them yourself,' she interrupted crisply. 'Come you indoors 'less you want the whole street to know your business. Chances be they knows it already. Folk hereabouts have ears the size of furnace stacks and noses to match – and them forever being poked where they ain't wanted!' She stepped aside, leaving the way clear into the small space that served as sitting room and kitchen.

'It be Clay Gilmore,' Sadie introduced him, drawing a long chenille curtain across the closed door as he spoke. 'He be here to see you.'

'Good evening, Mr Gilmore.' Deborah laid aside the cloth she had been stitching. 'I was hoping to meet you again before Lizzie and I leave Elmore Green. I wanted to thank you once more for helping us last night.'

His mind had not played him false. Clay stared at the girl sitting at the far side of the table, the light from the oil lamps spilling pale gold over hair as black as midnight; reflecting the brilliance of eyes that gleamed like gemstones. The image that hung over him as finally he fell asleep in the small hours of dawn had stayed with him deep in the bowels of the earth as he hacked away at the coal. It had been true to life. It was not his imagination, the girl was truly beautiful. Too beautiful. She would not have time for an Elmore Green man, a collier with nowt to his name.

'Well, answer the wench!' Sadie's words were intended to goad him into speech yet still he could not find his tongue.

'You be standing there like a mawkin!' This time Sadie's words were sharp. 'Do you want the wench to think you nothing but a fool!'

'I know that's not true.' Deborah smiled. 'Mr Gilmore, it was very kind of you to do what you did last night. Lizzie too would wish to thank you but...'

63

'She is all right?' Natural anxiety released Clay's tongue. 'She is … she wasn't…?'

'No.' Deborah's smile faded, eyes clouding a little as she answered his unspoken question.

'Lizzie's face was badly bruised and she is still rather shaken by the experience but the doctor assures us that rest and quiet will have her well in a few weeks. I hope you will forgive her for not thanking you herself but she is sleeping and I would rather not disturb her.'

Ain't no need to wake Lizzie, Sadie Trent thought as she turned to the kettle beginning to whistle on its bracket over the fire. It be my guess Clay Gilmore be talking to the one he *really* came to see.

'There's no need for thanks from either of you.' He smiled briefly. 'I only did what any man would do.'

'Any man bar the sort as knocked that young wench senseless.' Sadie poured water into the enamel teapot, replacing its lid with a bang.

'Well, there'll be one less of his kind in the world, or will if he knows what's good for him!' Clay held the bundles and the coins out to Deborah. 'I brought these back. I don't know if anything be missing but these will be better than none.'

Deborah looked at the coins glinting in his open hand. 'Where did you find them? Were they on the heath?'

'Don't matter where he found them.' Sadie brought the pot to the table, bridging the gap in the conversation. 'You got your money back, or most of it judging by what be in his hand, and that be all that matters.'

'But we have not yet spoken to the constable.' A tiny frown registered on Deborah's brow. 'We were waiting until Lizzie felt a little more able to answer his questions. How could he have known we were robbed?'

'It doesn't pay a man to throw his money around in Elmore Green,' Clay answered quietly. 'Especially a man who normally has none.'

Clattering cups on to the table, Sadie caught Clay's eye, her own full of silent knowledge. 'It be a case of a full pocket makin' for an empty brain. Needed no great search to find the culprit, eh, lad?'

'I reckon you're right, Sadie. That one was found easy enough. Colly Latham's to be congratulated.'

'Arrh, Colly Latham has his uses.' Sadie nodded but her expression showed what she really thought. Colly Latham might have his uses, but none of them were as constable. It was not he who had recovered these girls' belongings.

'I must see him tomorrow,' Deborah exclaimed.

'That will have to wait,' Clay said quickly. 'Magistrate Rawley saw your attacker at Portland House this morning and had Latham take him off to the Assizes at Wolverhampton for trial. It will be a week or more afore he gets back. That be why Colly allowed me to return the money to you. He said you would like as not have need of it.'

'There be no call for you to go pitying the man.' Sadie saw Deborah's fingers clench and the way her mouth tightened at the mention of Portland

65

House. She covered it before Clay could ask any questions. 'He be a rogue and deserves to be sent down the line, and for a lot longer than a twelve month an' all. The Assizes be best place for that swine!'

'Lizzie and I have cause to be grateful to you once more, Mr Gilmore.' Deborah took a bundle in each hand, leaving Clay to place the coins on the table. 'Please will you accept...'

'No!' Dark eyes deepening to black, his mouth instantly firming, he refused what instinct told him was to follow. 'Your thanks be enough for me. I'll take none of your money.'

'Then perhaps you will take a cup of tea?'

'I take the offer kindly, Sadie.' He turned towards the door that gave on to the communal yard. 'But I promised to get back. Mother had the meal on the table before I came out.'

'Then I can understand your rushing away,' she answered, placing the teapot back on the hob. 'A good meal be like payment, best taken at once.'

'I'll say goodnight to you then.' The door open, he turned a last look toward Deborah. 'And to you, Miss Hammond.'

'That be a fine lad.' Sadie secured the heavy chenille curtain after he had gone, blocking the draught that found its way through the badly fitting door. 'A wench would be a fool to look past him.'

'He's certainly very kind.'

Watching the girl place the two bundles in the corner against the stairs, Sadie felt a tinge of disappointment. She had hoped there might be some trace of interest in the girl's answer or in her eyes when looking at Clay, but there had been none. When Deborah Hammond looked at Clay Gilmore she saw nothing, but a friend. But it was not friendship Sadie had seen in Clay's eyes. Turning to the fire once more, she picked up the heavy enamel teapot. Yes, a wench would be a fool to look past him. She smiled sadly at the thought. Just how many fools had already looked past Clay Gilmore?

'You're certain you are well enough?'

Deborah looked anxiously at Lizzie who was doing up the last of the buttons on her brown wool dress. It was the only one decent enough to wear outdoors. The blouse she had worn on leaving Portland House had been torn to pieces by... She pushed the thought away, the fear of that night strong enough still to have her trembling.

'Mrs Trent has said we can stay until you are truly strong enough to travel.'

'I am strong enough.' There were still bruises on Lizzie's face though they were yellowing now. 'We have to go sometime, or at least I do, but there's no need for you to leave. You could stay in this place. Perhaps Mrs Trent would rent you a room on a permanent basis. But I have to go back, Deborah.'

'Go back? To Portland House!' Lizzie's night gown half folded in her hands, Deborah stared in disbelief. 'You can't. You know Agnes Ridley would never take you on again.'

'I'm not going to ask for employment, I'm going to see if ... if my baby's father has been for me.'

Deborah noted the pause. Not once had Lizzie said the name of the man who had seduced her. But why? Why had she never told even her best friend who he was?

'Don't you see?' Lizzie went on. 'He'll not know where I have gone, and Mrs Ridley won't be able to tell him unless I go back...'

'But they won't take you into Portland House, and where else would you stay? You can't sleep in the fields!'

'I'll find somewhere.'

Deborah had heard that tone before. Lizzie might be young but she could be very determined. Deborah placed the folded night gown on the few clothes waiting to be retied into a bundle. Reason would be her only weapon. She must see if she could talk Lizzie into following a different path. But which? She tied the corners of the cloth covering the bundle. Lizzie was right, of course, her fiancé would not know where to look for her, but then again they were not a thousand miles from Portland House. Surely he would realise they had to make for the nearest village? Yet in the two weeks they had been here there had been no man asking after Lizzie. Every day Deborah had asked when she and Sadie had sat alone, after Lizzie was asleep, and every day the answer had been the same. There had been no man enquiring in Elmore Green.

'You do see, don't you, Deborah?' Lizzie said softly, her brown eyes imploring. 'I have to go back, for my child's sake.'

'Yes.' Deborah nodded. 'I understand, and I'll go with you.'

Each carrying their bundle, the two walked down the bare wooden stairs.

'There you both be.' Sadie glanced up from the pot of porridge she was stirring. 'Breakfast be ready so sit yourselves down.'

'Mrs Trent.' Deborah halted, suddenly not wanting to say the words that must come next.

'I know, I know. You be leaving. My eyesight ain't so poor I don't see what you be holding in your 'ands. But you ain't in such a rush you can't take a bite afore you go?'

Rattling the spoon against the pot, she filled three dishes, setting each on the table which was covered with a spotless white cloth.

'Have you decided where you be going?'

'We're going back to Portland House.'

Her hand jerking as she spooned sugar over her porridge, Sadie sent a shower of tiny sparkling crystals over the cloth. 'You be going back there? But you said they put you out. You told me that housekeeper and the master both turned you out on to the road! Was that the truth?'

Deborah met the older woman's eyes. 'Yes, Mrs Trent, it was.'

'Then why in the name of God be you going back there?' The spoon came down with a bang. 'If they've chucked you out once, what makes you think they'll take you back?'

'I shan't be asking them to do that,' Lizzie broke in quietly. 'I want only to know if … if anyone has called at the house asking after me, and to leave word where I have gone.'

'Even though you don't know where that will be!' Sadie's tone was crisp. 'How can you tell how

69

far you will have to travel afore you find someone who'll take you in? Could well be you'll find nobody. Folk who'll give a home to a down and out, especially one who is carryin' a fatherless child, be few and far between.'

'My child is only fatherless because … because he cannot find me. We are to be married, the banns will have been called by now.'

Again that pause. Deborah pushed away her dish. Once more Lizzie had put no name to the father of her child.

'Perhaps he has called at the vicarage?' She pressed her hand over that of the younger girl. 'We'll go there first. Maybe there's a message there for you.'

'If you ask me, I say you ain't in any fit state to go traipsing back to that house. That babby ain't so tight in the womb it won't fall afore its time. You would do far better to wait.'

'For how long?' Bright with tears, Lizzie's eyes fastened on the lined face of the woman who had helped them. 'A month … two or after my child is born? I can't do that, Mrs Trent. I can't let it be born in shame. My baby must not be a bastard.'

'It won't be, Lizzie, it won't be.' Jumping up from her chair Deborah put her arms about the other girl, feeling the sobs that wracked her thin body. 'We'll find your baby's father. You will be married.'

'And I will dress your hair with rosebuds.' Deep in Deborah's heart the promise was made to another this time.

'I be going into Wallington Heath today.' Sadie looked at the girls, one comforting the other, her

70

throat tightening as memories rushed in on her. 'I'll call in at All Saints and the Wesleyan Chapel and I'll ask at Bayton Lodge – the cook there be a good friend. If there's been any talk of a man asking after you then she'll know.'

Bayton Lodge! Deborah felt a little more hopeful. That was the home of the woman who had been visiting Cato Rawley the night she and Lizzie had left, the one who had promised to find her a position once Lizzie was married. If there had been any talk of a man enquiring after their whereabouts, maybe she would have carried word to Portland House. And if so then Agnes Ridley would certainly know of it for that woman never missed a single thing that was done or said between those walls.

'You'd far better bide here another day,' Sadie called after her as she carried dishes and spoons into the scullery. 'It will save you a long walk and the news will be the same at the end of it.'

'Mrs Trent's right, Lizzie,' Deborah said gently. 'The heath isn't the easiest place to walk, and waiting one more day will do no great harm.'

Pulling herself free, Lizzie looked up, her eyes red from weeping. 'Do you think she will?' she whispered. 'Do you think she will call at the vicarage and at the other chapel?'

'I believe that if Mrs Trent says she will do a thing, then she will do it,' Deborah whispered back. But the rest of her thoughts stayed locked in her heart. She believed Sadie Trent could be trusted with their lives.

Leonie Elliott touched one finger to the face

reflected back from the mirror of the dressing table, amethyst eyes narrowing in the search for wrinkles. But there were none ... yet. The fingers moved over the flawless face, exulting in the touch of supple flesh, then dropped away to rest on the table top. Young and beautiful, in both face and body, but for how long?

Picking up a hairbrush and drawing it through the heavy strands of pale gold hair falling over ivory shoulders, that worry reflected in the lovely face.

Cato Rawley was infatuated, but infatuation had been known to fade as quickly as it blossomed. He must be secured by more than infatuation, but how whilst his wife still lived?

Brush catching on a knot Leonie pulled sharply, the frustration of weeks at that angry tug. With Cato Rawley for her husband, a secure home and wealth were guaranteed; and both were needed quickly if the present life-style was to be maintained. True, Leonie Elliott *seemed* possessed of a fortune, and had been once, but the remnants of it were fast disappearing. Entertaining in style did not come cheap, and neither did gowns from Fleur Masson, to say nothing of the cost of running Bayton Lodge.

The eyes staring out of the mirror smiled secretively.

Fleur Masson! The woman's real name was Florrie Marston, but who cared so long as she supplied what was expected? And despite her background Florrie had a definite flair for supplying her exclusive clientele with just that.

Which was what was needed. Leonie threw

down the hairbrush. A visit to Madame Fleur Masson for a new gown perhaps? Coiling folds of silken hair with expert ease, pinning it high, those lovely amethyst eyes gleamed with renewed interest and enthusiasm. There might well be new gossip to be gleaned, but even if not the diversion would be most welcome.

Today a new gown. Leonie rose slowly to her feet, eyes following every line of the sleek, naked body. And tonight a new game. A smile that was slow and sultry spread over the faultless painted mouth. Cato Rawley would soon be even further enmeshed.

There had been no word left at the Vicarage of All Saints and none at any other church house Sadie had passed on the way to Wallington. She had even tried St Peter's, the Roman Catholic place on the High Street, though she did not know whether the man promised to Lizzie followed that faith. But follow it or not, there was no word of him there. Sadie hitched the basket that weighed heavily on one arm as she juggled the large paper parcel she held beneath the other. She could have had the carter bring what she needed, but she did not want cloth smelling of Auntie Sally. As a disinfectant there was none better, but as perfume... She hitched the basket again, muttering as a carriage rolled past, spewing tiny chunks of mud against her skirts.

It had been the same story those months she had stayed in Walsall. The town had trams and a railway station, and now long years later this transport had come to Bloxwich. But for her, and many more in Elmore Green, it made no difference. Folk like her didn't have money to spare for riding on trams or trains. Sadie snorted. It was 1902 and the world was no easier a place than it had been centuries before. It was still a case of the rich man shall ride while the beggar man walks. Shanks's pony would be her mode of transport all her life long, and right now her particular pony needed shoeing. She winced, feeling a sharp stone bite through the paper-thin sole of her boot. But just like everything else she needed, boot repairs would have to wait. Besides she ought not to grumble. She watched the carriage dwindle into the distance on the long stretch of Stafford Road. Now that wench lodged in her house, the one carrying a child, *there* was one with cause to grumble. The bloke who had lain with her should have claimed her afore now. She should be settled with a ring on her finger.

Setting down the basket with the paper parcel balanced on top, Sadie fished a handkerchief from her pocket, wiping it over her face. She had called at every rectory, read the notices on every church gate along her way, enquired in the house of every friend where she'd stopped for tea and a chat, but none could give her any news. She pushed the handkerchief back into her pocket, glancing away to her left across the wide stretch of fields and heathland. Maybe he thought the wench had made for Little Bloxwich. Maybe he thought she would feel less embarrassed in that small village. Certainly there were fewer people there to stare and point the finger, no more than a dozen houses, a tavern and a tiny school house.

Fewer people to snigger, yes, but also to offer a helping hand.

Maybe she still had time to go there. Sadie glanced at the sky. Judging by the sun it was already late in the afternoon. It would be well on by the time she was returning, and none but the moon to light her way. It would be taking a risk; one slip on the heath and there would be nobody to hear her cry.

Perhaps the farm at Selman's Hill then? It was only halfway but the folk there might have news. With the parcel under one arm she lifted the basket, almost immediately feeling the bite of the handle on her arm. Selman's Hill was only halfway to Little Bloxwich... She stared across the deserted fields again. It might after all, be better to go some other time.

The sun had long set and Sadie's feet were dragging in a tired shuffle as she passed the entrance to the park. She could go in there and sit for a while on a bench, let the blood flow back into arms numb from carrying basket and parcel. Sadie let out a long sigh at the tempting thought, but knew that once she sat down then a king with all his army wouldn't get her on her feet again. Best to push on. She would ask Deborah to fetch her a jug of beer tonight.

Deborah... She clutched the parcel, forcing her tired legs to carry her on. And the other wench, young Lizzie, they were two well-mannered girls; such as she might have had if only... She quickly blinked back the tears that clouded her eyes. There would be no daughters for Sadie Trent. She would never know that love.

Chapter Six

'Hey up! Going for a drink, are we? You come with me, darlin', I'll fill your jug for you.'

Deborah flinched at the burst of laughter that followed, averting her glance from the youths following her along the road. 'You'll have no bother,' Sadie had told her, counting out the price of a pint of best pale. 'Nobody takes any account of a woman going into the outdoor. Just you tell the landlord who the ale be for and he'll ask no questions.'

'Let me carry that for you.' One lad stepped quickly in front of her, the others flanking her to each side.

Deborah's heart jolted. She had never had to deal with a situation such as this before. In fact, other than the gardener and the stable hand at Portland House, she had hardly ever spoken to a man. Agnes Ridley had kept both her and Lizzie too strictly tied to the house for them to come into contact with any. Yet Lizzie had, somehow. If only he would come! Deborah held the jug, clutching it close as the man in front tried to take it from her. If only the father of the child were to find them and Lizzie could be married, then all of this could be put behind them. Deborah could find a new place of employment...

'Come on.' The youth snatched again at the jug while the one on her right pulled the shawl from

Deborah's head. 'We all know what you be out after and it ain't Jos Chapman's ale!'

The one who had pulled off her shawl laughed, a high-pitched scraping sound. 'What do it be, Cal?'

'I won't be saying.' The one called Cal handed the jug to the other, his face lit by a shop window showing a wide leer. 'But you can watch and learn, Ben. You can both watch and mebbe give the lady a bit more of the same. Really fill 'er jug, if you takes my meaning.'

'Mebbe you will let me watch too, Cal. I'm always ready to learn, no matter who the teacher.'

Trembling, Deborah tried hard to hold back the cry of outrage rising in her throat. These men were probably only teasing her, making a game of her for their own amusement, probably they played it regularly with the village girls, but to her it was frightening.

'Go on, Cal.' The fourth man kept to the shadows. 'Show us what it is we can all give the lady.'

''Twas only a bit of fun.' Cal Morris stepped back, bravado melting like mist in the sun. ''Twas only fun, we were doing no harm.

'Oh!' Clay Gilmore stepped into the light spilling from the grocer's window, a smile on his face. 'And there was I thinking you were tormenting the girl.'

'No, Clay. Like Cal told you, we were just having a bit of fun.' The one holding the jug thrust it back at Deborah.

'Then I'm ready to join in with you.' He glanced back at the taller of the three. 'Come on,

Cal, I'm waiting for you to show me what it is we can all do.'

'We were only...'

'I know!' Clay Gilmore's voice was harsh. 'It was only a *bit of fun*. Well, if you see tormenting a girl as fun, I'm sure you'll see my pummelling the three of you in the same light!'

'Ain't no need for fighting, Clay.' The one who had snatched the shawl dropped it and was already running as he spoke.

'Tom be right.' The second man stepped cautiously away from Deborah's side. 'There be no need for fighting.'

'Seems they don't go along with my idea of fun.' Clay set himself squarely in front of Cal. 'How about you? Or would you rather finish your game with the girl first?'

'We ... we never touched her.'

'Fortunately for you, Cal Morris, or it would not be a hiding you would be getting – they would have found you down one of the old shafts and you would be in no condition to say how you came there. So no more of your games in Elmore Green. Save them for the Goose Fair over at Walsall – that is, if you have the courage to try them there. Now get yourself away before I really start having fun!'

Having watched the three of them out of sight, Clay turned to Deborah, taking the jug from her shaking hands.

'You'd better let me carry that,' he said gently, 'Sadie's had it for as long as I can remember. I can't see her being overjoyed if it gets broken.'

Hand as gentle as his voice, he draped the

78

shawl back over her head.

'They wouldn't have hurt you. They're just lads and full of themselves. They were merely bragging, showing off to each other, it won't happen again. Believe me, you'll be safe now. But if you wish I'll see you back to Sadie's house.'

Twisting her hands in the shawl, Deborah made an effort to hide their shaking but the tremor in her voice refused to be hidden.

'I ... I would appreciate your company, Mr Gilmore.'

Looking down into her face, seeing her eyes still clouded with fear, Clay felt his insides twist. He should have given those louts the hiding of their lives! Watching the tremor of her lips he knew his threat to kill Cal Morris had not been an empty one. He would kill, and gladly, any man who harmed this girl; a girl he hardly knew but who already filled his heart.

Stopping beside the Spring Cottage, Clay pointed to a wooden bench just visible beneath a tree, its branches heavy-leaved and drooping.

'Wait here.' He set her gently on the bench. 'I'll get the ale. You've taken enough teasing for one night, and Jos Chapman be a rare one for his jokes.'

Wrapped tight in her shawl as she waited, Deborah glanced at the sky. The clouds were gold-edged by the glow of the moon. Why had all this happened? Portland House had never been a happy home but at least she and Lizzie had been safe there. And Lizzie's promised husband ... why this doubt, this feeling that he had not searched for her, that he had not called at the house or anywhere else?

Did Lizzie feel that too? The thought brought Deborah up with a start. No, she couldn't, she must not be allowed to think that way! Suddenly the fear inside Deborah was not for herself, the tears coursing down her cheeks were not from the jeers of those young men but from fear for Lizzie; she was too young to be left with such a responsibility, too defenceless to bear the brunt of carrying a fatherless child, to have the rearing of it alone. That man must come to her ... he must!

'Miss Hammond.'

She had not heard Clay come to stand beside her and, lost in her own fears, did not see his mouth harden at the sight of her tears glinting in the moonlight. Rising to her feet, Deborah fell silently into step beside him.

They were almost at Sadie's door before he spoke and then his words had a stilted, almost forced sound to them.

'Will you be leaving Sadie Trent's?'

Deep in the misery her mind had conjured, Deborah did not hear the softly spoken question, so when his apology followed she was surprised.

'I ... I beg your pardon, Mr Gilmore, I confess I was not listening. What did you say?'

Leaving it a moment while he drew a long steadying breath, Clay repeated the question.

'Lizzie and I will be leaving in the morning.'

Each word a blow to him, Clay's fingers tightened on the handle of the jug.

'We would have left today but Sadie suggested we stay on while she made enquiries in Wall-ington...' Deborah broke off quickly, realising the slip of the tongue she had made. He would be sure to ask what enquiries and that was Lizzie's private business. 'I ... we thought that maybe there would be work for us there.' The lie tasted bitter on her tongue. This man had shown her only kindness and in return she must lie to him.

'There be nothing at Wallington Heath except for farm labourers' cottages.'

Listening to his answer Deborah felt the same warm guilt touch her face. If he recognised the lie, and somehow she felt he did, then he hid it well.

'The folk there have little enough to support their own families, except for her at Bayton Lodge. Perhaps Sadie thought to ask there. I hope she got you a post.'

Deborah swallowed hard, forcing herself to continue with the lie. 'They told her that no staff were wanted.'

He should not press the point, it was no business of his, yet despite himself the words spilled out.

'Then where will you go tomorrow?'

'We have not decided that yet.' Deborah felt relieved to be speaking truthfully again.

Following her along the entry that gave access to Sadie's house, one hand resting on the latch of the door, Clay looked at the pale face turned up to his. 'If ever I can help in any way, Miss Hammond, promise you will ask?'

Taking the jug, Deborah smiled up at him, moonlight reflecting on the tears still filling her eyes and turning them to golden pools. 'I will, Mr Gilmore,' she whispered, 'I promise.'

'Don't go talking so crackpoticall!' Sadie plunged the hot poker into the jug. 'You can't go trawling a wench in that condition here, there an' everywhere! 'Sides, if you keep moving on, how do you expect that man of hers ever to catch up with her?'

'But we cannot go on imposing on you, Mrs Trent.' Deborah sank into a chair pulled opposite Sadie's at the fire.

'Inwhating?' Sadie looked over the rim of the jug. 'If the words means you be putting on me, then you ain't. Don't you fret, wench, you wouldn't get very far if you tried that. Sadie Trent be nobody's fool and her don't be nobody's rubbing rag neither! I'll tell you when it be time for you to quit this house, and that time don't be here yet!'

Taking a drink from the jug, she set it down in the hearth, wiping her lips with the back of her hand. Then, leaning back in her chair, she regarded Deborah with a steady gaze. 'Young Lizzie be a wench with more than a full belly, her heart be full as well – full of fear and full of doubt. She won't be up to travelling the road on top, take it from one who knows. One who stood where you be now. One who saw her friend die of heartache.'

Turning her glance to the fire, Sadie watched the old pictures flicker in the flames. 'Emmy had a child,' she whispered softly. 'We were girls together in Essington, lived within a stone's throw of one another, our parents working for a farmer. Then at sixteen Emmy got herself in trouble. Her parents demanded to know the name of the man and when Emmy refused to tell them they threw her out. So she came to us.' Sadie drew in a long breath, using it to hold back the tears always waiting for a chance to flow.

'She came to us but my parents were as hard as her own.' The breath emerged slowly, bringing the words with it. 'The said it was no more than she deserved, that they would not take her in. When I said I would not leave Emmy to go alone, they said I was no better than she was, a trollop they would no longer house.'

In the bed of fire a coal settled, sending a shower of sparks into the chimney. Deborah watched as one by one the tiny pinpoints of light lived out their short existence. Had Emmy been like one of those sparks? Living so short a life before the light of it was snuffed out, darkened by a man who took so much and gave nothing in return? Was that the story Sadie was telling?

'We left together,' the old woman went on, speaking softly, her eyes on the fire as though addressing some unseen presence at its centre. 'It was winter and the going was hard. We were given a meal here and there in return for a day's work but we were never allowed to stay. We slept, whenever we could sleep for the cold, in hedgerows or sometimes a barn. I wasn't familiar with the area beyond Essington village and as a consequence we found ourselves going round in circles. It took us weeks, with Emmy growing weaker by the day. I remember we passed a place known as New Invention, going on into Bentley before finally arriving on the edge of Walsall town. It was there in a cattle byre, that Emmy gave birth to her child, a girl. The farmer's wife helped in the birth but would not allow Emmy into the house. I begged of them to give her a warm place to rest and recover her strength but they refused. The next day we were made to move on. It was a week before we found a place. A woman in the town let us have a room in exchange for our labour. I don't know which was the more damp, the room and its bed or the laundry where we both slaved from dawn to dusk. The child was no more than three months when Emmy fell ill of fever. I took her to the hospital and there I stayed in the waiting room all night, praying she would recover. I never saw her again.'

Sadie paused, a sob rattling in her throat. In the silence that followed Deborah waited.

'I had no money to bury her.' Her voice almost soundless, Sadie went on painfully. 'They said she would be given a pauper's burial that wouldn't even include a coffin, just a sheet wrapped about her against the earth. I could not face seeing that even if they had told me when and where the burial would take place.'

'And the child ... Emmy's daughter?' Deborah's whisper was soft, coming when it seemed the older woman would not speak again.

'We called her Beth.' Sadie smiled into the flames. 'She was a beautiful child. After her mother died I would leave her in the neighbouring house. An old woman there looked to her while I worked in the wash house. A month after that I lost her.'

Eyes widening with pity, Deborah could not speak. To lose first her friend and then the baby – how had Sadie stood up to such pain?

Taking the poker, the old woman thrust it into the fire, waiting until the tip glowed red before plunging it once more into the jug. As the liquid hissed and sizzled she spoke again.

'The child did not die. It were one Saturday evening. I had gone to the market for food. Late in the evening was the only time I had free. The weather was not yet warm and it would have been awkward carrying the swaddled child in one arm and a basket of meat and vegetables in the other, so I left her with Sissy Cooper. The woman minded her whenever I needed to go to the market. While I was gone a smartly dressed woman with an educated voice turned up and said she was Emmy's sister and had come for the baby. Seems from what Sissy told me when I got back that this woman had names and papers to back up her claim. Needless to say she took the child.'

'Did you get her back?'

'Don't think I didn't try!' Sadie placed the poker back in the hearth then took a drink from the jug. 'But even could I have found where that woman had taken her, how could I prove she was not a sister to Emmy? Her parents would never have backed me, they would not have owned a bastard child. In the end I came to Elmore Green and here I stayed, but I never forgot Emmy or her child.' She looked up, her glance fastening on Deborah's face.

'That's why I be offering you and that girl

sleeping upstairs a home here in this house, for as long as you will stay. I could not rear Emmy's child but if it comes to it I will care for this one that be coming. If it be the Lord's will the child is to have no father, then it will have three women to love and mother it.'

A home for them both? Deborah stared at the woman who was awaiting her answer. A place where Lizzie could have her baby if the father did not turn up. A place of safety and understanding.

Reaching out one hand, she touched it to Sadie's. 'Thank you,' she muttered. 'Thank you from both of us. But Lizzie *will* have a home of her own, she *will* be married. The man that...' She hesitated, the fear that haunted her returning now. 'He will come, Mrs Trent, he will ... won't he?'

Sadie Trent turned again to the fire, giving way for a moment to memories of yesterday, hearing those same words, watching them come from another girl, her face twisted with misery.

'I can't answer that question,' she said, watching the vision of torment melt into the flames. 'Only the Lord can do that.'

'But you–?' Deborah felt driven to ask, desperate to find some vestige of hope for Lizzie. 'You believe he will, don't you?'

Sadie reached for the jug finished the last of the mulled ale. Wiping her mouth, she rose to carry the empty vessel into the scullery. In the kitchen Deborah shivered as a sudden coldness touched her spine. Sadie had deliberately not answered her. But why?

'I didn't tell you it all.'

She looked up as the woman returned to her chair.

'Tonight, when I got 'ome, I didn't tell you all that passed today.' Light from the fire and the one lamp burning on the dresser etched the lines deeper on Sadie's face, illuminated the shadows of sadness in her eyes. 'I let Lizzie go up to bed without saying all that I found out. That might have been wrong of me but I make no apology. To my mind that wench be bearing enough burdens without my giving her more. But my heart tells me that keeping my mouth shut will be of no help to her in the long run.'

'What do you mean? What else did you find out?'

''Twas what I *didn't* find that troubles me, wench.' Sadie shook her head. 'I told Lizzie I called at every church and chapel house I passed and that were the truth, but what I couldn't bring myself to say was that I read every notice pinned to gate or board and not one of them spoke of any marriage for her.' She leaned forward, the frown on her brow adding to the sadness in her tired eyes. 'You see what that means, don't you? If no askings be posted then no banns have been called.' She sank back into her chair as if those last words had taken all of her strength.

Stunned by what she had heard, Deborah could only stare. Above her on the mantelpiece the battered tin clock ticked rhythmically. No banns called! It rang like a tolling bell in her mind. The father of Lizzie's child had had no banns called!

'I couldn't bring myself to tell the wench,' Sadie

said softly, pity echoing in every word. 'How could a body tell her such? That man has given no notice of marriage anywhere in this parish which means he never had any intention of marrying Lizzie.'

'No!' The cry rang out across the room and both women caught their breath as they turned to see Lizzie pitch forward down the stairs.

Chapter Seven

'I have been looking for a way to help you, Mary Ann.'

Father Philip Travers smiled at the woman sitting in his study, hands meekly folded over skirts that were a kaleidoscope of neatly sewn patches. 'I have found something, though I do not know if it will prove acceptable to you.'

'Beggars can't be choosing their charity, Father.' Mary Ann reached out to the girl sitting beside her. 'Me and Molly will be grateful for anything.'

'It will be no charity.' The priest too glanced at the young girl. A night's sleep in a warm bed, combined with his housekeeper's good solid cooking, had already brought a bloom to those pale cheeks. 'The work will not be light.'

'That won't worry me none.' Mary Ann smiled, bringing a sudden sparkle to her faded eyes. 'Just so long as me and my wench have a roof over our heads, I will work my fingers to the bone.'

Which would not take a deal of doing. Philip Travers glanced again at the thin hands then the drawn face of the woman who had asked for his help.

'There will be a roof and food and clothing.' He paused for a moment as if loath to say what must come next. Then, an apologetic frown drawing together his dark, well-defined eyebrows, he went on, 'You see, Mary Ann, I couldn't find any place that would take both of you.'

The woman's smile faded, leaving that hopeless defeated expression once more. 'You mean, me and Molly would be parted … that I would lose my daughter?'

'Not lose, Mary Ann.' The priest looked at the stricken face, touching his hand briefly to the thin rough ones twisting together in the woman's lap. 'Molly would not be far away – you could pay her visits.'

'But … but her ain't never been parted from me afore!' Mary Ann's lips trembled. 'Her ain't much more than a babby. I can't let her go – how would her fare without her mother?'

'I knew it would trouble you, Mary Ann.' He pressed her fingers comfortingly. 'I will tell them you cannot take the positions. Maybe in a few weeks there will be something else…'

A few weeks! Mary Ann Sanders looked at the daughter she had trailed around every house and workshop in the town. Molly was already half starved. The bones stood out on her body like beacons. A few more weeks of what she had suffered for a year or more could see her under the ground.

'No.' Taking one more glance at her daughter, she turned her eyes back to the priest. 'No, Father, we will not be refusing. If you tell me my wench will be looked to properly…'

'She will,' Philip Travers cut in quickly. 'You have my word, Mary Ann. Molly will be very well taken care of.'

'Then that is all I ask.'

'But I don't want to go anywhere without you!'

90

Dropping to her knees, the girl buried her head in her mother's lap.

'Hush, my baby.' Mary Ann touched a hand to the pale yellow hair. 'It seems a moment since I called you no more than that, but you are a girl grown, well old enough to be making your own living.'

'I can do that, Mother,' the girl sobbed. 'But I want to do it with you!'

'We are not always given what we would have, Molly.' She stroked her hand over the shining hair. 'But we must take what the Lord sends and be grateful.'

Looking across at the priest, the sadness in her heart showing in her effort to smile, she asked, 'Where would these positions be, Father?'

'Not here in the Pleck, I'm afraid, nor anywhere else in Walsall. As you yourself have found, there's no work to be had there.' Seeing the woman nod, he continued, 'I spoke to a friend of mine, a Mrs Elliott. She has a house in Bloxwich. She thought at first to offer you a post herself, but now she has secured you one as laundress with a friend of hers – a Mrs Cato Rawley. However, it was stipulated that one person, an older woman only, would be accepted. Have you any objection to working as a laundress, Mary Ann?'

As the woman gave a brief shake of her head, he glanced at the girl still kneeling beside her.

'As for your daughter – I found her a position as scullery maid. It is not much, I know, but I was assured that should she prove satisfactory in her work, then she could well rise to become a parlour maid.'

'Parlour maid,' the woman whispered, her daughter's head nestled in her lap. 'You would like that, Molly. Just think of it: parlour maid. Wouldn't that be something, my girl a parlour maid? You'll look so pretty in a clean dress with a fancy lace pinny and a cap with frills on it! And when you come to see me, you can tell me all about the lovely things you will get to see in the house, and I will be so proud of you.'

'What do you say, Molly?' the priest asked.

Rising to her feet, the young girl wiped one finger across her wet cheeks. 'If my mother thinks I should take the job then I will, and I thank you kindly for the trouble you have taken.'

'That's settled then.' He smiled, reaching for pen and paper. 'I will give you both a letter of introduction then we will see about getting you started on your way.'

Her daughter held close to her, Mary Ann Sanders listened to the pen scratch busily across the paper. Inside her heart felt close to bursting. Today her girl would be gone from her. First her husband had been taken by an explosion in a coal mine and now her only child was separated from her by poverty. Taking the finished letter in her hand, she glanced down at the words she could not read. What else could life do to her? What was there left to take away?

'We should have taken more care.' Deborah poured soup into a dish then placed it on a wooden tray alongside a hunk of bread and a spoon.

'Be no use in blaming what happened on carelessness!' Sadie's retort was sharp. 'There be no weight to that girl. Listening for her tread would be like listening for a feather settling on grass. We both took it her was sleeping.'

'I should have stayed in the room with her.'

Sadie tutted and let the cloth she was sewing fall to her lap. 'I've just about heard enough! That fall was no fault of yourn nor none of mine, so give over maudlin' and take the wench her dinner.'

She had been more of a misery than a help, Deborah admitted to herself as she climbed the stairs. Mrs Trent had tried again and again to reassure her that Lizzie's accident was no fault of hers. But as she passed into the bedroom and saw that pale face, the purple bloom of shadows circling the closed eyes, she felt again the sharp sting of guilt.

'I've brought you some soup.' She smiled at Lizzie's eyes fluttered open. 'It will help you feel better.'

Almost immediately her face crumpled. 'It isn't soup I need – it's him. Oh, tell me that what Mrs Trent said wasn't true? Tell me he will come, Deborah. Tell me he will!'

Setting the tray on a small table alongside the bed, Deborah gathered the weeping girl in her arms. 'Mrs Trent said she had seen no notification on the churches she passed but that does not mean none has been given. She did not visit every church in Bloxwich, just those in Elmore Green.'

'But that means no call has been made.'

'No, it does not,' Deborah soothed her. 'It only

93

means no banns have been called in Elmore. There are plenty more churches we have not tried, and should we find none here then Bloxwich is not the only parish.'

Pulling free, Lizzie turned a tearful face to her. 'You mean ... you mean he might have posted them in some other parish?'

'Of course.' Deborah smiled, inwardly praying she showed a confidence she did not feel. 'Now eat up and when you are completely well we will look for those churches together.'

'You are a good friend, Deborah.' Lizzie leaned back against the pillows. 'If my baby is a girl I want her to have your name, and I know ... I know her father would agree.'

The father would agree! Closing the bedroom door softly behind her, Deborah stood with her eyes closed against the awfulness of her thoughts. They had to find him first. And with a twist of the heart she acknowledged it would not be easy.

'She's resting and seems easier now,' Deborah answered Sadie's querying look at her as she carried the tray into the scullery. After drying dish and spoon, and throwing the cloth over the line, she visualised that pale face, the marks of bruising still clearly showing on it, the furrow to the forehead as the eyes closed. Lizzie's body was now at rest, but her mind...?

'Mrs Trent.' Deborah took a deep breath as she re-entered the cramped front room, which was littered now with cloth and ribbons and laces.

'Sadie.' The older woman did not look up from her sewing. 'I can't get used to hearing you say Mrs Trent. I would rather you call me Sadie,

94

same as my friends do. Same goes for Lizzie too.'

This carried a deeper meaning than mere words expressed. They were no longer just girls she had taken in temporarily, she acknowledged them as her friends. A lump rising to her throat, Deborah took a moment to answer and when she did so emotion throbbed in every syllable.

'Sadie, I … I don't know how to say this…'

'Then don't!' The answer was sharp but beneath the words lay a care of gentleness.

Picking up a length of peach satin she had been helping to sew with small glass beads, Deborah bent her head to the work, not wanting Sadie to see the sudden upsurge of tears. But that did not hide the huskiness in her voice. 'I … I just want to say that not since my mother died has anyone really had time for me. Except for Lizzie, no one has ever seen me as a friend. It was always more a case of the work I could do and never the person I was. But you are different, you see the girl as well as the servant.'

'You won't never be nobody's servant as long as you bides in Sadie Trent's house!' She jabbed her needle fiercely into the delicate cloth. 'And neither you nor young Lizzie will be without a friend so long as I be here.'

A tap on the door putting an end to any reply of Deborah's, the older woman glanced up, squinting from the fine work.

'I'll go.' Glad the emotion of the moment was broken, Deborah laid her own work aside. Opening, the door, she stood back as a woman dressed in an expensive grey cashmere day suit trimmed with black fur tippets, a fur-trimmed

95

bonnet set atop her piled-up hair, brushed unceremoniously past her.

'Sadie.' The woman settled unasked in a chair, her glance sweeping over Deborah as she closed the door.

'Florrie!' Sadie's brusque reply revealed that the woman's fine clothes and expensive-smelling perfume in no way impressed her.

Removing grey calfskin gloves, the woman opened the rather large bag she had carried in, taking out a length of palest blue silk voile. 'That lemon gown you brought me last week ... the bead work was exquisite...'

Feeling her presence to be an intrusion, Deborah went towards the stairs.

'I would like something along the same lines for this.'

'Arrh, well, you'd best ask Deborah about that,' Sadie answered. ''Twas her hand did the sewing.'

'You sewed that gown?'

Turning her head, Deborah nodded.

'Whose 'ouse be you tied to?' The woman looked again at Deborah, a hint of interest lighting her eyes.

'Her ain't tied to no 'ouse, Florrie Marston. The wench be her own mistress,' Sadie answered for her.

'Mmm.' Crowned with its fur-trimmed bonnet, the woman's head nodded speculatively. Any attempt at disguising her natural dialect completely forgotten, she lifted one hand. 'Come over 'ere, wench. Sit you down. There might be a bone we can pick on together.'

Taking a chair, Deborah sat beside her. The

96

woman's clothes spoke of wealth and a life-style very different to that of Elmore Green, but the way she spoke and Sadie's attitude towards her indicted that she was not so very far removed.

'You sews a neat hand,' the woman went on. 'I could use another seamstress, especially one as good as Sadie. Have you done much in the needlework line?'

'Nothing like the work I have seen Mrs Trent do. I was employed as a parlour maid, but whenever there was household linen to be repaired it was passed to me.'

'You never made no gown?'

'No.' Deborah touched a hand to her cheap brown cotton skirts, half hidden beneath one of Sadie's aprons. 'I made my own things though I would not call any of them gowns, but I was sometimes given one of the mistress's to repair.'

'An' who might that be – your mistress?'

'Mrs Cato Rawley.'

'Portland House? Comfortable place!' The woman raised one perfectly pencilled eyebrow. 'So how come you left it?'

'That be of no more concern to her and it certainly be none of yourn!' Sadie laid aside the cloth garment she had been working on, pushing herself to her feet. 'If it be the business of stitching you've come about then you be welcome, but if it's poking your nose you be set on then there be the door. Close it after you.'

'I meant no offence, Sadie.' The woman raised her hands in denial.

'Arrh, well, I won't say there were none taken.' Sadie's tone was tart. 'In my 'ouse a woman's

97

business be her own, and not open to any Tom, Dick or Harry with a mind to ask! The fact be clear. Her no longer works for Rawley. Let that be an end to it!'

As Sadie turned her attention to the kettle steaming above the fire, the woman laid the silk voile on the table. 'Do you think you could sew that?' She smiled as though the short sharp spat had never taken place.

Deborah touched her fingers to the delicate fabric, feeling its softness fold about them like the touch of petals.

'I will dress your hair with rosebuds...'

The long-cherished memory returned. How often after her mother had kissed her good night she would dream of a gown as soft as this – a gown she would wear to her own wedding. But that was all it could ever be: a dream.

'I reckon Deborah could.' Sadie rattled cups in their saucers. 'But only should her want to.'

'The work would need to be perfect. The Salon de Fleur Masson sells no inferior garment.'

Looking up from the delicate blue cloth, Deborah answered quietly, 'I cannot guarantee perfection, but any work I do would be of my very best. I do not believe in shoddiness.'

'That gives you your answer, Florrie Marston!' Sadie grinned, pouring out freshly brewed tea.

Accepting the cup, the woman inclined her head briefly. 'Judging by that lemon gown, I reckon her best be good enough.' She glanced across at Deborah, her hand withdrawn now from the lovely silk. 'But the beadwork ... was the design yours as well as the stitching?'

98

'No,' Deborah smiled up at Sadie as she took the cup from her. 'That was done mostly by Lizzie. She is very good with a pencil. She can draw anything.'

'Afore your nose gets to twitchin' again, Florrie Marston, Lizzie be another friend of mine – and her business be her own an' all.'

Ignoring the rebuke, Florrie drank her tea then set the cup aside, turning once more to touch the fabric lying on the table.

'If I give you an idea of what I'm wanting this made into, do you think Lizzie would draw me a sketch, showing the design she would put on it?'

'I could ask, but I'll set no promise as to the answer,' replied Sadie.

'And you.' The woman glanced at Deborah. 'Will you take on the making?'

'Only if the pay be fair,' Sadie interrupted as Deborah nodded.

'It could be none other with you around. You don't get no easier to deal with, Sadie Trent!'

'And no easier to fool neither.' Sadie set her own cup aside. 'Now, how about paying for the last frock afore you gets to talking of the next?'

Again feeling her presence to be an intrusion, Deborah stood up. 'If you don't mind, I'll go and look in on Lizzie.'

Watching her go, Florrie Marston ran an appreciative eye over the girl's slender figure, the neatly combed hair shining blue-black. She was beautiful, and she would make a welcome addition to the Salon de Fleur Masson.

But sharp as her eyes were, Sadie Trent's were a match for them. She noted the other woman's interest and as Fleur turned to count out some coins, Sadie knew that from now on her own eyes would need to be sharper still.

'The wench be well enough, doctor reckons the fall did no harm to the child.' Jug in hand, Sadie stood by the opening that led to the outdoor counter of the Spring Cottage.

Clay Gilmore seemed to have taken to the habit of waiting there for her, though he tried to make their meetings seem coincidental.

'That be good to hear.' He shifted his weight, uneasily, uncomfortable at the silence Sadie allowed to drop between them.

'Arrh, it does.' She turned into the dimly lit passage. 'And if you still be standing here when I comes out, you can say what you really wants to ask.'

Smiling to herself, she collected her usual pint of ale, answering the usual banter of the tavern keeper.

'So, Clay Gilmore.' She looked up at him as she stepped out on to the street. 'You still be here then? Well, lad, you had the courage to come. Now have the courage to admit it. It were not Lizzie Burton you was wanting news of, though I don't say you don't be pleased to hear the wench be mending.'

'There be no selling you half measure, be there, Sadie Trent?'

'No, lad, I wasn't born yesterday,' she chuckled, 'I got my full share of wits and a few to spare. Enough to know you don't happen to be outside the Spring Cottage at this time every night by

100

accident. Am I right?'

Thankful for the evening shadows that masked the warm blood in his cheeks, Clay's answering laughter held a self-conscious ring. 'As always Sadie.'

'And be I right in thinking it be Deborah Hammond you really wants news of?'

'Will they ... will *she* be leaving?'

There was an almost painful longing, yet at the same time fear, in his words. He wanted to know yet feared the pain it might bring. Sadie's fingers tightened about the jug a she remembered feeling such pain herself. She had wanted to know, kept on asking and asking the nurse at that hospital; she had wanted to know, would Emmy live? And the pain their answer had brought haunted her still.

Did Clay Gilmore realise what he risked in harbouring such a feeling for Deborah Hammond? For not even the deepest shadows of night could hide from Sadie the fact that he did harbour feelings for the girl.

Turning to him, she thrust the jug into his hands. Striving to rid herself of shades of the past, she pulled her shawl closer about her head. 'If you be going to pick my brain, Clay Gilmore, then you can at least carry my jug.'

Shortening his stride to match hers, Clay fell into step beside her.

'I offered both them wenches a home with me. They ain't said they're staying in so many words, just a thank you and a confirmation that Lizzie will be married. What Deborah Hammond will do after that none can say but Him above.'

'The man Lizzie is to wed, he's turned up then?'

'I only wish he had, for the girl's sake. Truth to tell I think her has seen all her is going to see of that one!'

'Could be the man can't find where she has gone.'

'Tchah!' Sadie spat contemptuously. 'And could be pigs might fly which they won't! I've tried every church house from 'ere to Wallington and never a word of no wedding and never a word of Lizzie Burton. Poor little bugger! The only wedding night her is like to know has already passed under a hedge somewhere and the bridegroom buggered off!'

'So what will she do?'

Reaching the entry that led to her door, Sadie stopped. 'If he has left her with any sense at all then her will stay here in this house. But sense don't count for much when your heart be breaking, and if one goes then they both will. And you don't want Deborah to go, do you?'

Standing there in the shadows, Clay felt his whole being answer. No, he did not want the girl to leave Elmore Green yet he could not ask her to stay. He had only spoken to her a couple of times.

With a smile he could not see, Sadie took her jug.

'You need to give me no answer, Clay Gilmore, for I can see for myself. Tomorrow be Sunday. You come here as soon as you be able. Could be you could help the wench.'

'You know I will if I can, she has only to ask.'

Sadie sniffed derisively. 'Oh, arrh, you think her

102

will do that, do you? Well, my guess be her won't, no more than you have asked her what it was you've been wanting to ask. That wench be a woman of pride – pride such as ain't often seen. That one will ask nothing and take less unless she pays for it. So you do as Sadie Trent tells you and get yourself up here tomorrow. Could be I knows a way of keeping Deborah Hammond in Elmore longer than her expects.'

'Sadie Trent is very kind. So different from Agnes Ridley. Whenever I think about that woman, I get the shivers.'

'Then don't think about her.' Deborah pulled the bed covers over her friend, tucking them beneath the mattress.

'I can't help it. The way she would sometimes look at me … as if I was a calf, being raised for slaughter.'

'Lizzie Burton!' Deborah laughed. 'The ideas you do get, where on earth do they come from!'

Lying back against the pillow, Lizzie's face wore a troubled expression. 'I don't know where they come from, Deborah, I only know they have always been there in my mind, right from my earliest memory. They terrified me then and they frighten me still. She would come to that house … only twice a year, but she would come. I would be scrubbed clean with a frock to match for that visit, every effort being made to present me as a well-cared for child. She would look me over, every inch carefully scrutinised, and then that gleam would come into her eyes. It was almost as if she were already counting the money

I would bring her. I don't know which of these two frightened me most: the eyes of one or the sharp slaps of the other.'

'Well, neither of them will frighten you again.'

'Only you ever treated me well,' Lizzie said, catching Deborah's hand. 'Treated me like a friend. I used to pray every night you would not go away. That you would not leave me with Agnes Ridley.'

'I would never have left you, Lizzie, and I will not leave you now. At least, not until you marry.'

Against the pillows Lizzie's hair lay like a cloud of brown silk, her eyes glinting with the softness of tears. 'You think he will come, Deborah ... you really think he will come for me?'

To speak a lie would be heavy on her conscience but not to speak at all would be worse. Her silence would say it as clearly as any words, say what she truly thought: that the man would never come looking for Lizzie.

'Yes, I do think he will come.'

For Deborah the lie was the lesser of two evils and she spoke it with a smile as she tucked the other girl's hand beneath the blanket.

'Don't go yet, Deborah, stay with me a little longer.'

Lizzie's face wore the same expression it had as a child when she had pleaded not to be left alone. Deborah felt her heart twist. Damn Agnes Ridley! Damn that other woman who had reared a child in unhappiness and misery! Damn the world for hurting Lizzie!

'Just a while longer, then you must sleep. You will need to be wide awake when you design that beadwork. We must give only the best to the Salon de Fleur Masson.'

Their eyes meeting, both girls dissolved into giggles.

'Are you sure that's the name she used?' Lizzie asked, wiping her eyes.

Stifling her last giggle, Deborah nodded. 'That is what she said. "The Salon de Fleur Masson sells no inferior garment".'

Lizzie's face crumpled again. 'It sticks to the tongue like something you might get from the herbalist! Fleur … it sounds like a posh way of saying flower. Do you reckon that's what it really means? A posh name for a clover or a dandelion.'

A grin spreading over her thin pale features, a roguish gleam in her wide eyes, Lizzie was for one brief moment the mischievous laughing child she had become in those rare times they had played together. Suddenly the doors of memory swung wide and Deborah stared into a world long past, but one that she would never entirely lose.

Two girls, one a few inches taller than the other, raced across the lower meadow below Portland House, dull brown skirts flapping about bare ankles, hair flying in the breeze.

'Watch me, Deborah!' The younger one cartwheeled, white bloomers displayed like pennants, then laughed with delight as the other pretended she could not manage the same and collapsed in a heap on the grass. One pulling the other to her feet, they ran hand in hand to the shallow brook that wound through the fields.

'Will she come if I call her?' Her face earnest,

the younger child looked into the smooth water. 'Will the water nymph come, Deborah?'

'Maybe she will be too busy.'

'But she never comes.' Lizzie's mouth dropped. 'Why does she never come, Deborah? You said the water nymph lives in the brook.'

'So she does.' The taller of the two smiled gently. 'I also said she has many other streams and rivers she must visit. But I am sure if you leave a gift and tell her what you want to say to her, then when she returns she will know.'

'But I don't have a gift, I don't have anything.'

'This could be your gift.'

Picking a violet-petalled marsh orchid from a clump near the water's edge, the older child gave it to the younger.

'But this is a flower. Flowers don't talk. How can this tell the water nymph what I mean?' Lizzie's mouth dropped further.

Dropping to her knees and drawing the other down beside her, the older girl smiled again. 'Have you forgotten, Lizzie, that the water nymph is a fairy and fairies have magical powers? We may not be able to hear flowers speak but she will. Whisper the words into its petals and it will hold them there until she comes.'

Trust shining in her eyes the child smiled, the droop gone from her mouth. 'Water nymph,' she whispered, 'take Deborah and me away from Mrs Ridley. Take us to a place where we can be happy, and won't ever be beaten again.'

It had taken many years but it had happened at last. Deborah watched the figures melt back into the past, fading away as dreams always did. It might not be the way a water nymph would have done it but they were free of Agnes Ridley and no one would ever again beat Lizzie.

'Truly though, Deborah,' she was saying now, 'that can't be the woman's name. Not unless she's a foreigner. Is she, do you reckon?'

'No.' Deborah shook her head. 'The name is foreign-sounding but the way she spoke was very much as Mrs Trent speaks. Also she called her Florrie ... Florrie Marston.'

'Then why call her gown shop the Salon de Fleur Masson?'

'Who knows?' Deborah shrugged. 'Perhaps the women who buy there feel they are getting something special, something they would not get from plain Florrie Marston. But Sadie was having none of it.'

'I like her.' Lizzie was suddenly serious again. 'She seems like a woman who would always speak the truth. I don't feel she would ever hurt us, Deborah.'

'No, Lizzie, I don't think she would either.'

Catching again at Deborah's hand Lizzie's question was soft, almost pleading. 'We will be all right, won't we, Deborah?'

Hearing the pain and uncertainty behind her question Deborah sank to the bed, taking her friend in her arms. 'Yes, we will be all right,' she murmured. 'Sadie has said we can stay here for a while. When you feel up to it we will look for a place to rent until you are married.'

Drowsy now, her voice thick with sleep, Lizzie smiled as Deborah eased her back on to the pillow. 'He will come, you see. But I don't mind staying here until then. Sadie … you know, Deborah, each time she looks at me it seems as if she knows me … as if she has known me all my life.'

Pushing herself from her seat on the bed, Deborah stood for a moment, looking down at the girl with her eyes closed.

'Dream, sweet Lizzie,' she murmured. 'For when dreams fade, all we have is reality.'

Chapter Eight

The woman did her job well.

Agnes Ridley inspected the linen pegged on the washing line strung along one side of the vegetable garden, out of sight of the rear of the house.

She worked well and joined in none of the tittle-tattle of the others, silently eating her meal at night then going straight to her room. All she had said was that Leonie Elliott had secured this post for her.

Leonie Elliott! Agnes's jaw clamped tight. That woman was moving staff of her choosing into Portland House, she obviously already saw herself as mistress here. But that she would never be. This house and all that went with it was to be Agnes Ridley's by right!

Cato had asked for her again last night, asked her to come to his room as he had so often done before that woman came on the scene; and she had gone to him, lain naked in his bed while he made love to her. Only it was not love. Agnes turned towards the house, her glance taking in the long graceful windows, the deep red brick. No, it was not love. All trace of that, if it had ever truly existed, had fled with the coming of Leonie Elliott. But his love she could live without; this house was her real love, and it *would* be hers.

Entering the rear door into the scullery she

took a duster, passing with it along the passage that gave on to the main rooms. She had not replaced the two girls; she would manage the cleaning herself until she took her rightful place as mistress. Where had they gone anyway? Picking up a Staffordshire figurine, Agnes dusted it carefully. Was that little slut still carrying her child? Had the man responsible kept his promise and married her?

Replacing the dainty figurine, Agnes smiled acidly. It would be something of a miracle if he had. Lizzie Burton must have been six months gone. A man didn't leave things that long unless he meant to leave them altogether. But she would make enquiries, discreetly of course. It might be useful to her in the future, knowing where the girls were.

Flicking the duster over furniture and ornaments, she worked quickly until she came to Delia Rawley's room. Then, laying the duster aside, she opened the wardrobe, running her hands over the gowns hanging there, revelling in the touch of silk and lace, hearing the satisfying rustle of taffeta. Most of them had never been worn, Delia these days always feeling too ill to go out or to entertain visitors to the house. Nor would they be worn until she, Agnes, wore them. They too would be hers along with the jewellery.

Going to a heavily carved chest of drawers, she opened one drawer, taking out a carved wooden box that was covered over by petticoats. Cato had told his wife to take her jewellery with her to her parents' house but at the last moment Delia had handed it to Agnes, asking for it to be hidden in

110

that drawer. Opening the box, Agnes lifted out a necklace of square-cut amethysts. Holding it to her throat, she twisted and turned, watching the light dance from the purple hearts of the stones, flickering on the heavy gold settings. She would wear this on her wedding day, the day she became Mrs Cato Rawley.

Returning the necklace, she replaced the box then closed the wardrobe doors, leaving the room exactly as she'd found it before walking slowly downstairs. Each day brought her closer to becoming mistress of this house, and when that day came Leonie Elliott would never again enter its doors.

'It be a bit early yet to be setting off.' Sadie Trent looked at the tin clock on the mantel. She had thought Clay Gilmore would be here by this time. He couldn't have changed his mind, surely? She put the thought aside. That man wasn't one to go letting folk down. If he said he would come, then he would come. 'Services won't be finished yet. Give yourself another half an hour. That way the vicar will have said his last Amen and folk will have got away home. There'll be less of 'em to stare.'

'I think it wiser to go now.' Deborah took off the apron that reached down to her feet, folding it neatly before slipping it into a drawer of the dresser. 'I want to be back before dark.'

'I still think I should go with you.' Lizzie started up from the chair set close to the fire.

Moving quickly to her side, Deborah pressed her back into her seat. 'No, Lizzie. I know how

111

you feel but look at things sensibly. You're still not quite over that fall. A long walk will tire you out, and that won't help your recovery. I don't want to be unkind...' she smiled, giving the girl's hand a squeeze '...but I can get along so much more quickly on my own.'

'That's just it!' Lizzie caught the fingers between her own, her brown eyes bright with anxiety. 'You will be on your own. You don't know the way, it could be dangerous. You know what happened the last time we crossed the heath.'

'Stop worrying.' Deborah forced confidence into her voice. 'I'll be all right. As for knowing the way, Little Bloxwich can't be that difficult to find.'

'The place be easy enough got to,' Sadie chipped in. 'It be the coming back. The heath be bad to cross in the dark for them that knows it well, never mind one who don't know it at all.'

'That settles it!' Lizzie threw off the rug Deborah had placed over her knees. 'I'm coming with you!'

'Lizzie. I...'

A rap at the door interrupting her, Deborah turned to open it but Sadie was there first.

'Well now, Clay lad. I never thought to see you here, not on a Sunday. Come you in.' She stepped aside for him to enter, smiling ingeniously as though she had not the slightest knowledge that he was expected.

'Mother asked me to bring this along.' He held out a fresh-caught trout. 'I got two this morning. This will go off if it's not eaten right away. I hope you don't mind?'

Taking the paper-wrapped fish, Sadie beamed. 'Mind! I'd be a fool to mind a bit of fresh fish. Give your mother my thanks, lad.'

Turning to Lizzie as Sadie carried the fish into the scullery, he smiled. 'I'm glad to see you recovered, Miss Burton.'

'That makes me sound so pompous.' Lizzie's answering smile was immediate. 'I would be much more comfortable with just plain Lizzie.'

'Lizzie I will agree with, but plain ... not in anyone's eyes.'

A tinge of warmth touching her pale cheeks, Lizzie's eyes glowed at the compliment. 'I have not yet thanked you properly for helping Deborah and myself that night on the heath. It was very kind of you, Mr Gilmore, we're both very grateful.'

'It's hardly kind of you to go on calling me Mr Gilmore, when I am to call you Lizzie.'

'Clay then. How do you do, Clay?'

Deborah watched as the girl held out her hand, seeing for a brief instant the mischievous child she was only months ago. Then the brief spark was gone, lost once more in the depths of a sadness that would not leave her.

Deborah reached for her shawl, draping it about her shoulders as Clay turned to glance at her. 'Lizzie speaks for us both, Mr Gilmore. We're very grateful.'

'Grateful enough to call me Clay?'

'Yes.' Deborah's smile lit up her face. 'Enough for that.'

'That be a lovely fish, it'll make a good supper

supposing you finds your way back.' Sadie bustled into the room. 'Though you'll need more than luck to do that if you be caught on the heath after nightfall.'

'I said not to worry.' Deborah finished knotting her shawl.

'But I do worry!' Sadie returned crisply. 'And so would you if you knowed the heath like I do. It be treacherous. There be more pit shafts scattered over that ground than there be currants in a roly-poly pudding.' She turned to Clay. 'You tell her the risk her be taking, setting off for Little Bloxwich by herself.'

So this was the reason Sadie Trent had asked him to call! She wanted him to take Deborah Hammond to the village. But how would that help keep the girl in Elmore Green?

'It would be safer not to go alone.' Clay took his cue perfectly. 'The heath is no place to be if you don't know it.'

Throwing the rug aside once more, Lizzie got to her feet, the sudden movement causing her to sway dizzily. Moving quickly he caught her, lowering her gently to the chair.

'Lizzie, please!' Deborah's eyes were dark with concern. 'You're far from well. If you won't think of yourself, then think of...' She checked herself quickly. '...then think of me.'

'But I won't let you go alone.' Lizzie stared at her, eyes wide with defiance. 'You might as well get used to it, Deborah. We both go together or I follow after you set off.'

'Sadie...'

'No use you looking at me.' She dropped into

114

her chair by the fire. 'I've tried talking but to no effect. The pair of you be more stubborn than Turner's donkey, and even a pit boot to the backside don't set that creature to changing its mind once it's set.'

'Excuse me for interference.' Clay addressed Deborah. 'If you're set on going to Little Bloxwich, I could take you there and see you back safely.'

'Eh, lad, that would take a weight off my mind! I wouldn't want to see the wench meet with an accident.'

'I'll not meet with any accident,' Deborah protested, colour mounting to her cheeks at Sadie's obvious manoeuvring. 'Thank you, Mr Gilmore, but I could not put you to so much trouble.'

Stepping over to the door, he raised the latch before looking straight at her, his clear gaze betraying none of the pleasure he was feeling. 'It's no trouble. I like a walk on Sundays, it helps clear the pit dust from my lungs. Little Bloxwich way is as good as any, though if you stand and argue much longer I doubt you will be there before dark.'

Deborah knew she was trapped. It was the only way to prevent Lizzie from carrying out her threat. Folding her hands beneath her shawl, she walked out into the street after him.

'Really there is no need...'

Clay halted abruptly, his tone cool. 'Look, Deborah, or Miss Hammond if you prefer, I have said I will go with you and I intend to keep my word to Sadie. However, if you have a dislike of

115

my company then I give you my word I will not speak or approach you in any way again.'

He thought she was taking exception to his company. Guilt at her own thoughtless words flooded Deborah's cheeks. She should have given more heed...

'If we hurry I can get you there in under the hour,' Clay said briskly. 'We can by-pass Selman's Hill. Then once your business is finished I can bring you back here. It could all be over...'

Self-reproach and apology clear in her eyes, Deborah touched one hand to his arm. 'It's not your company I take exception to. It's your spending your free time on our concerns.'

'My time is mine to do with as I wish,' he said, the hint of coldness fading from his voice. 'And there's nothing I wish more than to help you.'

Shyly averting her glance she walked on, a feeling almost of happiness washing over her.

Passing St Peter's church, Clay branched off to the right. Harrison Street would lead straight on to Cemetery Road. Once on that there would be no houses to pass before reaching Little Blox-wich itself. It would be easier for Deborah with no folk to gawp as they passed.

Stretching away to either side the heath was dotted with wild flowers, flaunting their colours in the May sunshine, and as they walked birds fluttered indignantly into the air, only to settle again and resume their songs once the intrusion was past.

It was all so beautiful. Deborah loosed the knot of her shawl, letting it slip free of her head. So wild and beautiful and so very peaceful; it was hard to see how anything so wonderful could hide a darker side.

But wasn't that too often the way of things? Weren't there many darker sides? Lizzie's man friend must have seemed so wonderful, but the promises he'd made had revealed a darker side. If not, why in all these months had he not come to claim her?

Watching the frown between her brows, Clay felt his pleasure in the moment drain away. Was there a man in Deborah Hammond's life, someone she could not forget?

He turned his head, fearing his own emotions would show as clearly as hers. A few feet from them a small bird broke cover, uttering a shrill anxious cry as it rose into the air.

Her attention caught, Deborah watched the bird drop again to the ground as if hurt.

'Shh!' Clay whispered. 'It's a ruse, she isn't hurt. It's all a pretence to draw you away from the nest. Come, I'll show you.'

Taking her hand, he guided her carefully to the spot from which the bird had risen and, dropping on to his heels, gently parted the rough grass.

'Here.' He held the grass aside so she could see. 'The children are all at home.'

Deborah caught her breath with pleasure at what she saw. The nest, set in a shallow hollow in the ground, contained four eggs, their greyish-white shells tinged with purple and mottled with brown, like tiny freckles.

'Skylarks.' Clay settled the grass back in place. 'Another week should see them out of the egg.'

'They're so pretty,' Deborah said as he rose.

'My father used to say larks had the most beautiful song of all.'

'I agree with him, they make good parents too. Just look at that hen.'

Glancing at the bird, Deborah felt a stab of alarm. 'Are you sure she isn't hurt?'

'It's a favourite trick,' he answered softly. 'She will pretend an injury to her wings, hoping to draw you to herself and away from the nest. Then, when you have almost reached her, she will take off another few yards.'

Deborah smiled, relieved the bird was unharmed. 'How brave, but I think she deserves to come home now.'

'You said your father "used to say"?'

Beside him Deborah nodded. 'My father was killed in a mine explosion when I was eight years old. He often took me walking in the meadows before that, though he never showed me a skylark's eggs. Perhaps he knew I would be unable to resist touching them.'

'Most kids couldn't, myself included. But I'm glad he did not show them to you. That way the pleasure was mine.' Clay glanced sideways, seeing the colour rise high in her cheeks.

'Where were these meadows?' he asked, breaking the short silence that followed.

'Somewhere on the outskirts of Walsall if I remember correctly, a place folks called the Pleck. But my mother left there almost immediately after Father's death. The house was tied to the colliery and we had to go. It was less than a year later that she died and I was sent to the poorhouse.'

Clay remained silent. She would tell him more if she wanted to; if not it would make no difference. He already knew all he needed to about Deborah Hammond.

'I was there almost a year,' she continued quietly, feeling relieved to speak of it, to let it out after years of holding it inside. 'Then I was told a woman was offering me a good home where I would be well cared for, though I must work hard to please her.' She paused as her voice caught in her throat. 'I worked hard and God knows I tried to please, but there was no pleasing Agnes Ridley. I fell asleep many a night begging God not to let me wake the next morning, and I know Lizzie did the same. She was brought to Portland House at the same time as me. I remember thinking how thin she was. I was almost afraid she would break. To this day I find myself wondering why – why choose two such young children to work in that house? Why, when there were so many older and more capable of the work who would have given anything for the chance to leave that institution? But now we're both free of Agnes Ridley and Portland House, and I will never let Lizzie go back. Never! Not even if…'

She broke off and Clay did not urge her to go on. The pain he had heard in her voice was raw and deep, too deep for it all to come out at once. But he could wait, and if given the chance maybe he could help with the healing of it.

'There be little Bloxwich.' He pointed to a huddle of houses away in the distance. 'If you can say whose house it is you're wanting, I'll point you to it.'

119

He deserved to know the truth. Deborah glanced at the face of the man who had surely saved Lizzie's life and also brought back their belongings. Somehow she felt her friend would not mind his being told of her plight.

Covering the last of the distance to the village, Deborah told him why they had had to leave Portland House, neither gilding the truth nor leaving anything out. Only when she had finished did he speak.

'This man? You have not said his name.'

'That's because I do not know it. Lizzie has refused to tell me.'

'Then what does he look like?'

Hitching her shawl on to her shoulders, Deborah gave a slight shake of the head.

'I don't know that either, I have not seen this man. In fact, I didn't know he existed until ... until I found out about the baby.'

'Why all the secrecy?' Clay sounded puzzled. 'Unless he's married already.'

'Oh, no!' The cry was sharp, almost desperate. 'He can't be, he wouldn't...'

'How do you know? You say you have never met him, and even if you had you wouldn't know unless he chose to tell you.'

It was true. Deborah felt stunned. She had never once thought of such a thing. Now it was brought to her attention it was mind-boggling. Lizzie expecting a baby by a married man! Oh, God, it mustn't be!

'So if you don't know his name or his face, how come you know him to be here in this village?'

Her brain still whirling, Deborah shook her

head. 'I ... I don't. I came to ask if perhaps a man had made enquiries after Lizzie, and to see if there was a notice of marriage on the church gate. Mrs Trent tried all of the ones in Elmore Green and those along the way to Wallington but she did not come here so I had to, for Lizzie's sake. She's so afraid. At first she was certain he would come but now she is afraid. And sometimes when I look at her, when I see the desperation in her face, then I am afraid too. Afraid of what she might do.'

For several moments Clay said nothing, then when he looked at her it was with a set determined face.

'Deborah.' He tried to smile but his lips refused to perform the service. 'I appreciate your telling me what you have, and I would like to go on helping in any way I can. But with or without your say so, I intend to help Lizzie. If it is at all possible I will find the man who has put her through all this, and when I do he is going to pay!'

The happiness that had washed over Deborah as they had left Sadie's house faded suddenly, leaving a cloud over the day.

MY TIME IS MINE TO DO WITH AS I WISH, THERE IS NOTHING I WISH MORE THAN TO SPEND IT HELPING YOU.

The words filling her mind, Deborah turned toward the half dozen houses clinging close together like frightened children. She'd thought he had offered his assistance out of feeling for her, but really it was Lizzie he'd wanted to help. There was no jealousy in the feeling that settled

121

like a stone in her stomach, only sadness. Clay Gilmore had called at the house with the bundles he had recovered, he had carried the jug of beer walking her home from the Spring Cottage, they had walked together but only now did she realise … she was falling in love with him. But Clay Gilmore was already in love. He was in love with Lizzie.

In the shadow of a doorway a pair of watchful eyes narrowed. He had watched them go, watched the way one looked at the other. Now he waited for them to return. He had suffered the laughter and taunts of the men in the tavern. Unconsciously his tongue pressed into the gap where once he'd had teeth. But she would not laugh at him. He would hear her scream, watch her beg, and then he would…

He leaned forward, peering at the figures silhouetted against the coming night. It was them. Breath hissed between his teeth like an angry snake's. They were together now but they would not always be. That wench, the one who had caused all the amusement in the tavern, she would be alone sooner or later, and when she was … then would be his turn.

Pressing deeper into the shelter of the doorway, wrapping himself in the shadow he listened to the sound of footsteps and muted voices, holding his breath as the two people passed the doorway. His eyes had not deceived him. Clay Gilmore he could recognise easily but the girl could have been any in Elmore. Only this wasn't any village wench, it was her, the one Abe Turley wanted, the one he intended to have; and when he did she would have no need to speak quietly for there would be none to hear except himself and he would not want her to speak quietly. Fingers bunching into fists he let the picture he conjured so often return, drawing air deep into his lungs as his brain feverishly painted every lurid detail.

Yes, he would want her to scream, to cry out as he ripped away her clothes, beg him to stop as ... but he would not stop, he would drive into her body as Clay Gilmore's fist had driven into his mouth. Yes, she would pay and the only amusement would be Abe Turley's. And when he was done then that wench would be left to remember him; remember long and slow as she died from starvation in an abandoned pit shaft!

Chapter Nine

Philip Travers smiled as he accepted a cup from the nun seated opposite him in the warm room.

'Ah, this is pleasant.'

'As it is for us. The day of Blessed Communion is always pleasant, Father. It helps us in our faith and in our work to receive the Body and Blood of Christ.'

'And the work you do pleases Him, of that you can be sure.'

Mother Joseph, Superior of the Convent of the Little Sisters, crossed herself devoutly. 'That is all we pray for, that and the health of the Church.'

'Speaking of health, how is yours bearing up?' He smiled kindly, warmth filling his extraordinarily blue eyes. 'You should not take so much upon yourself, the convent cannot afford to have you ill again.'

'I am well enough, Father.' The nun smiled, pleased at his thoughtfulness. 'As for the work of the convent, I do only my share. The sisters here are most caring. But for all we do it is you must take the most credit. You are the one helps our young people to find work once they leave us.'

Letting the cup rest in its saucer the priest looked down at it, his smile gone. 'I can help so few of them ... if only I could do more. It seems so very little.'

'What seems so little to you is a great deal to us,

as it is to our girls. Without your splendid efforts we would be unable to place them at all.'

'Now there you go again, Mother Joseph, reminding me of what I had almost forgotten.' Returning cup and saucer to the tray laid with a spotless white cloth, he took a small leather-bound notebook from the pocket of his long clerical robe. Flicking over several pages he looked again at the woman shrouded in black, her lined face closed around with a heavily starched white wimple. 'I have a promise of a post as assistant housemaid at The Poplars, supposing the girl be acceptable.' He thumbed to the following page. 'I also persuaded Lee's Farm to agree to take on some help in the dairy. Do you think you have any suitable girls?'

Mother Joseph's tired face beamed. 'The Holy Mother bless you!' she said, her head moving slowly from side to side. 'It is a wonderful thing you do, Father, a wonderful thing. And just when I was thinking there would never be a place for another one of them. Two girls … two more to give thanks to God for the help of Father Travers.'

'They have yet to be accepted, Mother Joseph, don't forget that.'

'Oh, they will be, I am sure they will. We will have them both looking like bandboxes.'

'Well, no one could have them scrubbed cleaner or looking smarter, that's for sure.' He closed the book but did not put it away. Instead he seemed to muse for a moment as if thinking deeply. 'Tell me, Mother Joseph…'

He paused as a tap on the door heralded the

arrival of a white-gowned novice, her smooth un-lined face a testimony to her youth. Waiting while the Mother Superior gave permission for the tray to be removed, he nodded to the novice, waiting again until the door clicked softly behind her.

'Tell me,' he said again, 'the girl brought to you a few months ago … what was her name?'

'Eve? Do you mean Eve Randle?'

'Eve, of course.' He lifted one hand absently, fingering the red mark high on his left cheek. 'That's a name I should remember, eh, Mother!'

The nun heaved a deep sigh. 'She has the name and she has the character. The wife of Adam was not given to listening to the word of the Lord and neither is this one. I fear we will have trouble finding anyone to take her, and heaven knows she is not cut out for life in a convent!'

'Hmm.' The priest continued to finger his cheek. 'A problem without a doubt. However there may be a way.' He glanced at the elderly nun. Hope was already blossoming in her eyes. 'I make no promises but there might just be a way.'

'The Holy Mother and all the Saints be praised!'

'Now, now, Mother Joseph. Like I said, I can make you no promise.' Reopening the notebook as the woman crossed herself piously once more, he glanced at a page. 'Tell me truthfully, as I know you will, can the girl use a needle?'

Her faded eyes lit as though the hand of heaven had touched them. Reverend Mother let loose the breath she had been holding in. 'She can that, Father,' she said, thankful to be able to speak the truth, adding no polish here or there to brighten

126

it. 'That is one saving grace the girl is blessed with, she has a fine hand with the needle.'

'Good, good.' He nodded. 'I happen to have heard of a gown shop whose proprietor is looking for someone capable of putting the finishing stitch or two to her creations.'

'Eve Randle could do that, I'm sure.'

Getting to his feet, he crossed to a heavy oak desk set beneath a high window, he raised eyebrows enquiring if he might use it.

Nodding her assent, the nun watched as he wrote quickly, copying from the notebook.

'Then have the girl go to this address.' Folding the sheet of paper, he handed it to the nun. 'I needn't tell you that her obtaining such a position will depend not only on her presentation but on her manner. She must be polite and civil, there must be none of her namesake in her attitude, she should listen and speak only when asked.'

'I will tell her, Father. The Lord bless you for your help.'

'He blesses us all, Mother Joseph, He blesses us all.'

Picking up the hat he had removed on entering the room, he placed it on his head, pressing it firmly over golden-brown hair; then, making the sign of the cross over the nun's bowed head, he walked from the convent.

'There was nothing, was there, Deborah?' Her brown eyes brilliant with tears, Lizzie watched her friend hang her shawl on the nail hammered into the back of the door.

127

'Give the wench a chance to get herself in.' Sadie tried to smooth the tension she had watched build in the girl all afternoon.

'He hadn't been to that village, had he?' Lizzie brushed aside the older woman's efforts. 'Nobody had seen him, had they? Nor were there any banns posted to the gate of the church.'

'There was no church.' Deborah went quickly to the other girl, sinking to her knees and taking the thin hands in hers.

'And no word.'

Glancing across at Sadie. Deborah saw the glint of warning in her eyes. Lizzie was near to breaking point.

'He wouldn't have thought to go there,' Deborah reassured her. 'It is such a small village, no more than six houses. He must have known we would get no work there.'

'Did he?' Lizzie asked, her voice completely devoid of hope. 'Or did he knew we would come here to Elmore Green and so deliberately avoided it?'

'Don't think that, Lizzie. You know it isn't true.'

'Do I?' Pulling away, she stood up and went to stare out of the window that overlooked the street. 'Or do you know that it is! Six months and more is a long time, Deborah. Long enough for a man who has no desire to face his responsibilities to disappear.' Touching a hand to a stomach that still showed little sign of the child within it, she stared into the darkened street. 'He will not come, there is no use in pretending any more. My child will be born and raised a bastard.'

'You mustn't say that!'

128

Turning at Deborah's cry, Lizzie smiled gently as if all of a sudden things had been made clear to her.

'It doesn't matter,' she said softly. 'It doesn't matter any more. We'll manage alone, the baby and me. We will always be together.'

'You won't be alone. I will always be there too.'

Her smile leaving sadness in its wake, Lizzie crossed to the door to the narrow stairs. 'Yes, Deborah, you will be there ... to the end.'

She ought to have known! Lizzie climbed the stairs slowly, her mind on a handsome smiling face. Agnes had sent her to collect blackberries for a pie and they had met against the hedge in the top field. Coming from Little Bloxwich, he was on his way to Walsall to find work as a carpenter. But gazing into smiling eyes she had not listened, other than to his softly asked, 'Can we meet again this evening?'

That was the only time he had told her of himself and she had never asked again. In love from that first moment, she had trusted him completely.

'We will be married Lizzie, you will be my wife.'

Remembering those whispered words, she felt her heart twist. Had it all been a lie? Did he never have any intention of marrying her? Reaching her room she leaned against the closed door, sobs breaking from her as a handsome face burned behind her tight shut eyes.

'Come back my love,' she murmured, 'please come back.'

Catching Deborah's hand as she went to follow the other girl to her room, Sadie shook her head.

'Leave her be.'

'But she's upset.'

'Arrh, I knows that,' Sadie answered quietly. 'But her be facing the truth and that be what you have to do.'

'But there are other towns…'

'Deborah, accept it!' Sadie's tone sharpened. 'You can look 'til you be blue in the face but it be my bet you won't find him. But should you do so and he denies being the father, what then? You can't force him to marry Lizzie. You'll just bring the wench more misery than her's got already.'

'But the child …. To grow up without a father. And Lizzie … what will the shame of it do to her?'

Her tone softening as Deborah slumped into a chair, Sadie shook her head. 'No more than it has done to many a one before her. As for the child, it will be cared for. Between us it will have not one mother but three.'

The love of three women. The ceiling of her room its canvas, the moon splashed patterns of soft yellow light across it. Eyes wide Deborah watched them change with each passing cloud. That love might be enough for a child but what of Lizzie? She deserved more, deserved the love of a man she could rely on, one who would love and help her in return. A man like Clay Gilmore. *I want nothing more than to help you…*' He had meant those words for Lizzie. He was already attracted enough to give her his help but would he give her his love?

Her eyes closing, Deborah felt the same quick surge of emotion she had felt earlier in the evening, that same sudden flush of sadness. But why should she feel sad? If Clay Gilmore did fall in love with Lizzie it would be the most wonderful thing in the world. The end of all her friend's problems.

Clasping both hands together Deborah whispered into the silence. 'Please God, let it be so. Let Lizzie find happiness.'

'I want it to be something special. This is too ordinary.'

Leonie Elliott waved her hands dismissively. The pink organdie would have been quite pretty, if one were a sixteen-year-old girl. The lemon silk was beautiful ... but Fleur Masson was too shrewd to show the best first.

'I'm afraid they will not do. Perhaps I should try some other salon.'

Clapping her hands quickly as her client made to rise from the small gilt chair, Fleur Masson adopted her business smile, an accommodating curve that lifted her mouth but lent no warmth to her eyes.

'Perhaps, *madame*, something like this...'

Lifting one well-manicured hand she gestured towards a curtained alcove. For several seconds there was no movement, then with dramatic slowness the velvet drapes were drawn aside.

Standing beside her customer's chair Fleur heard a quiet intake of break and smiled deep inside. This one had caught the attention of her customer. The purchase would be made but the buying price would be high.

By the muted light of gasoliers set at intervals

131

about the room, the gown's shot silk taffeta darted tints of green and blue, of red and amber, colours flashing and withdrawing like flames in a fire. The whole gown was embellished with hints of silver as tiny beads caught and reflected the light.

'This is my most recent addition.' The owner of the salon gestured with her hand, urging the gown to be brought forward, but the girl wearing it ignored her. Keeping to her own deliberately slow pace, knowing the impression she made, she eyed the figure on the dainty chair.

'The beadwork was specifically designed for this gown,' Fleur went on. 'It is an exclusive design – one that will not be repeated.'

Coming almost to the chair the mannequin stared full into the eyes that watched her, then, her own eyes the last to slide away, she turned slowly. Coming full circle she stood perfectly still.

The smile inside Fleur Masson deepened. She could already feel the money in her hands, and this particular creation would bring her plenty. It had been a master stroke, putting this girl into the gown. Her red hair shone like silk velvet. A pretty mouth, rouged and pouting, was a perfect foil to a complexion like cream, while long lashes were lowered alluringly over deep-hued almond eyes. This latest addition to her salon was a shrewd investment; Eve Randle was truly beautiful.

'Perhaps *madame* would care to see a further selection?' She waved her hand, dismissing the girl.

'Wait!' Leonie reached forward, touching the stiff silk with long fingers. 'The gown is exclusive?'

'Completely.' Fleur nodded. 'And this is its first showing. No one has seen it except for *madame*.'

'But the trimming?'

Watching Leonie's hand follow the line of the beautifully cut waist then touch the crystal beadwork of the bodice, Fleur answered, 'That was done on different premises, the gown then being put together by my own seamstresses.' Not all the truth, but what the eye don't see the heart done grieve over! Beneath the acquired exterior the old Florrie Marston raised its head.

Leonie's hand felt the softness of flesh. There was no whalebone beneath the taffeta. That too was her preference.

'Very prudent.' The hand dropped away as the girl began another slow turn.

'It is wise to guard one's business, *madame*.' Fleur waved gown and mannequin away. 'There are always those ready to steal one's assets.'

'No doubt.' Leonie watched the girl's figure glide slowly towards the curtain alcove, red hair glinting in the light, the lovely gown echoing its shade. Yes, that was what she wanted. This purchase would prove entirely satisfactory.

'The price? But not here.'

'Of course.' Fleur waited as her best client rose to her feet. 'My office?'

Inside the holy of holies set at the back of the salon, Leonie refused a chair.

'How much?' She was terse and to the point.

'This one is special, and so is the price!' Here in the privacy of her inner sanctum Florrie Marston came into her own, and was very much on a level with the woman who faced her. Here the client-

133

proprietor relationship no longer applied. Leonie Elliott wanted something only this salon offered. There would be no subservience, no bending to the customer's will. It would be pay or lose the prize.

Eyes the colour of amethyst, and cold as the stone, stared at the dressmaker. The Marston woman was becoming over confident, thought Leonie. She looked down at her gloved hands. But where else would she find quality such as this establishment offered? And what she had seen in that showroom was of the best. It would be difficult to find its equal. Keeping her thoughts to herself she posed the question again, this time in icy tones.

'So what exactly is the price of something special?'

It would be worth trying. Florrie was not for an instant duped by her client's air of disinterest. If this one balked at what was asked then there would always be another; maybe the profit margin would be lower, but then bricks weren't made without using straw. If you didn't ask, you didn't get.

Smoothing her hand over her own elegant mauve gown she met her client's cold stare, her own equally cool. 'Three hundred,' she said firmly. 'The price is three hundred pounds.'

In the quiet of the tastefully furnished private office Leonie's swift intake of breath was clearly audible. Three hundred pounds! It was a staggering sum to ask. She opened her mouth to say as much.

'Before you do refuse,' Florrie Marston read

134

the signs, 'remember this model will not be easily beaten. It is a totally exclusive design, and you have been the first to view it. But should you think the cost too high,' she shrugged her shoulders eloquently, 'then of course I must offer it elsewhere.'

Three hundred pounds! Leonie ran the price over in her mind. But the effect was breathtaking. The picture it had made in the salon... A stunningly beautiful picture, returned swiftly. This would sell on for ten times what was paid to Florrie Marston.

'Payment in the usual manner?'

Triumph masked by a bland nod of the head, Florrie watched the cheque being signed.

'When would you like delivery to be made?'

Smoothing gloves back over her long fingers Leonie turned towards the door. 'Friday ... in the afternoon. Make sure it arrives.'

'*Madame* need have no worries.' Florrie was once again the polished Fleur Masson. 'It will arrive safely. Like every other purchase *madame* has been gracious enough to make.'

Holding the jug beneath her shawl, Deborah walked along Elmore Green Road, her boots tapping a rapid rhythm on the roughly laid setts. She had taken to fetching Sadie's nightly pint of ale, the older woman pleading it was a pleasure to have someone fetch it for her. But the pleasure was hers. Deborah felt a tingle at her nerve ends. Clay Gilmore had been there outside the Spring Cottage every night from the day they had gone to Little Bloxwich, and every night she found

135

herself looking forward to seeing him again.

'Miss Hammond.' He stepped from the lee of the building adjoining the tavern, inclining his head slightly as she looked up at him. 'How is Lizzie?'

His first words were of Lizzie! Her pleasure mingled with a swift dart of disappointment and Deborah found it difficult to separate the two. She was pleased at the interest he continued to show in Lizzie yet disappointed there was none shown in herself, not even enough for him to address her by her given name.

'I fear our finding no trace of her fiancé in that village has thoroughly disheartened her.' Deborah loosed the jug into his hands. 'Nothing makes her smile any more. She goes about her work in the house, the little that Sadie will allow her to do, but she rarely speaks. I really am worried for her.'

'It's understandable she's depressed, but Little Bloxwich isn't the only place to look.'

Pulling the shawl over her head as Clay called good night to a man passing by on the other side of the street, Deborah answered him.

'Lizzie has forbidden us to look any further. She is convinced now that the man never had any intention of marrying her.'

'Does that mean you will be leaving Elmore Green?'

Deborah could not help but hear the anxious note underlying the question. Was he afraid of losing Lizzie?

'Sadie has offered us a home for as long as we want it,' she replied, not looking at him, 'and I have some employment sewing for the same woman as she does. I think we should stay, at least until the child is born.'

'It would make more sense than tramping the country from one place to another, and Lizzie would find no better friend wherever she went. Sadie Trent be the salt of the earth, you'll find none fairer no matter where you go.'

Sadie had been more than fair. Waiting for the jug to be filled, Deborah remembered the woman's refusal to take more than fifteen shillings a week bed and board for herself and Lizzie. She had pushed back the sovereigns she had been offered from the money Clay had returned, saying that was all she would take, and even when Deborah was paid for her sewing, Sadie would accept no more.

'You say Lizzie will have no more searching for the man who seduced her?' Clay Gilmore fell into step beside her as Deborah began to walk back to the house.

She nodded. 'I wanted to talk her out of it, or at least try, but Mrs Trent said to let it go. Continuing to search and most likely finding nothing would only cause Lizzie more misery.'

'But you don't agree?' Clay Gilmore looked at the girl walking beside him, the shawl partly hiding her face. But he did not need to see it to know every line. It had been etched on his heart ever since their first meeting.

'I don't disagree,' Deborah replied. 'All I really know is that I want Lizzie to be happy. I want to see her smile, to hear her laugh again. I would do anything for her to be her old self but I know she won't be so long as her child is without a father.'

137

She would do anything. Reaching the entry, that gave on to the door of the house that was only one of many joined together in a line that edged the length of Elmore Green Road, Clay handed back the jug.

'Sadie and Lizzie have forbidden you from going on with the search,' he said quietly, 'but that does not include me. I shall go on looking.'

Glancing up, Deborah stared into his strong face. He thought so much of Lizzie, so much he would go on searching?

'But … you said it yourself. Without a name or a face he will be impossible to find.'

Clay smiled and with one finger gently touched her cheek. 'Should I let that stop me? Would it stop you had not Lizzie spoken as she did?'

'No.' It was only a murmur as Deborah shrank from his touch.

His smile fading instantly, his hand falling away from her face, Clay took a step back, widening the space between them. The word had been as much a denial of his touch as it had been an answer to his question.

'Then I shall go on looking, but to spare Lizzie any more heartache I ask your help.'

'Of course,' Deborah answered quickly. 'Anything.'

That word again! Clay smiled grimly to himself. She would do anything for her friend but bear his touch.

'I will not tell Lizzie what I am doing,' he went on, ignoring his own hurt. 'But if you will continue to come to the Spring Cottage of an evening, then should I have news of the man I

138

will pass it on to you.'

The jug in her hands, Deborah watched him walk away. For one wild moment she'd thought he would ask her to accompany him on his search. But why would he? She turned into the dim passageway between the houses. It was not she but Lizzie that Clay Gilmore was interested in.

Chapter Ten

Closing the door behind her Deborah set the jug in the hearth before removing her shawl. Lizzie and Sadie had been sitting by the fire when she went out, the girl sketching; it was a thing she had done more and more often as the days had passed, using it to withdraw into her own closed world.

She glanced towards the alcove that gave on to the scullery but the curtain was in place; neither of the two women was there. Hanging up her shawl, Deborah reached a plate from the dresser, balancing the jug to keep out sparks or dust from the fire. They must be upstairs. She glanced across the room, only now noticing that the door to the stairs stood slightly open. A tiny frown creased her brow. Why were both of them upstairs? Lizzie was capable of putting herself to bed.

Staring at the door, she felt cold fear touch her spine. Had something happened to Lizzie? A cry stifled in her throat, she fled up the stairs.

'There you be, wench.' Sadie looked up from where she stood bent over Lizzie's bed.

'Lizzie!' All her fear, all her pent-up worries, came out in that one cry as Deborah looked at the girl, her face white as the night gown she wore. 'Oh God, Lizzie, are you all right!'

'Nothing to be worried for. The child has

staked its right to be born, nothing more natural than that,' Sadie reassured her.

Sitting beside Lizzie on the narrow bed Deborah took the girl's hand in hers, the fear in her friend's large brown eyes catching at her heart.

'It shouldn't be coming yet!' Lizzie gasped, clutching at her stomach as a stab of pain robbed her of breath.

Holding tight to her hand, Deborah threw a glance towards the older woman.

'You can never put no set time to a child's coming.' Sadie smiled reassuringly at Lizzie, but when Deborah met her eyes she read the worry flickering in the depths. 'There be many a woman in Elmore Green will vouch to that. Babbies come when they 'ave a mind, not when you do.'

'But there are weeks yet.'

'Did you write the date each time the man lay with you?' Sadie asked sharply. 'Less you did so you can hardly be certain which time the seed was sown. But the harvest comes in its season and that child be ready despite what you think.'

A fresh spasm catching Lizzie, Deborah looked helplessly at the woman who had taken them in. She herself had never seen a woman in childbirth, had no idea of the true nature of the pain that went with it, but somehow she realised Lizzie's suffering had only just begun.

Waiting for the pain to subside, Sadie laid the girl back against the pillows.

'Listen to me, Lizzie, wench,' she said gently. 'You've only just started. There be a long road to

141

tread afore you be done. The pains you feel will come more regular; when they do, try to breathe deep and in between rest if you can. Deborah and me will be with you. I've seen this many times and I tell you it is the way of nature. Trust me, wench. Trust old Sadie Trent to keep you safe.'

Glancing at Deborah she became matter-of-fact. 'Go you downstairs and build up the fire, then set the kettle and a pot to the boil. You'll find clothes in the lower drawer of the chest next to the settle. Bring them up here.' Touching a hand to Lizzie's she went on, 'While Deborah be doing that I will be busy finding wrappings for the child. You're not to fret, we won't be long.'

Leading the way she halted at the door to her own room, a finger to her lips in warning to speak softly. 'I reckon the child do be coming afore its time,' she confirmed. 'Seven months be the worst time of all but the wench must not know it. I'll do all I knows how but should it be as my skills don't be enough then you must go for the doctor. You know which be his?'

Worry striking her dumb, Deborah could only nod.

'Good!' Sadie turned to her room. 'Now get that water on to heat.'

The worst time of all! The worst time of all! It beat in her brain, over and over, as Deborah fed coal to the fire then filled kettle and pot from the pump. The worst time of all! Pulling open the drawer, she snacked out the several pieces of white cloth folded there. Holding them to her she raced up the stairs.

142

Following Sadie's brisk instructions she laid the cloths on the small chest that was the room's only piece of furniture apart from the iron-framed bed, then folded the blouse and skirt Lizzie had been wearing, slipping them into the chest.

'Them can be taken for washing.' Sadie indicated the girl's underclothing with a brief nod. 'They won't be needed for a day or two.'

It was a way of preventing her from dwelling on her worries, Deborah knew. She understood and appreciated Sadie's efforts as she carried petticoats and bloomers to the tiny wash house in the yard. The woman thought keeping her busy the best way to hold the fear inside her; but how long could she hold it, how long before Lizzie's pain had her crying out too?

But she must not cry! Screwing up her fingers, she let the nails bite deep into her palms. For Lizzie's sake she must not give way. 'Oh, God!' Dry sobs carried the words she had meant to say only in her heart. 'Oh, God, help Lizzie! Help us both.'

Beyond the window the sky was black as pitch. Sadie listened as the clock on St Peter's spire chimed. The girl's pains had been coming thick and fast for six hours and now there was no interval between. They ran together in one constant stream of agony yet still the child showed no sign of nearing birth. Since the first spasm had struck she had feared that something was wrong. Now she was sure of it.

Wiping beads of perspiration from Lizzie's face, holding her as her body convulsed with

143

pain, she looked across the bed to Deborah.

'There be nothing for it,' she mouthed, Lizzie's screams drowning her words. 'You must go for the doctor. Tell him Sadie Trent says to come quick.'

Casting one more glance at the figure writhing on the bed, Deborah ran from the room. Giving no thought to her shawl she raced into the street, the tapping of her boots on the setts the only sound in the silence.

Clay Gilmore had pointed out to her a large house standing alone amid the fields, and told her it was the doctor's. But where was it? Breath painful in her chest, her heart thumping, Deborah ran on. He'd said it was the doctor's house, they had passed it together, but where ... where?

She did not know! Oh, God, she did not know! Panic rose inside her and in a moment her brain ceased to function. All around her darkness pressed in, folding her in its welcoming embrace, shutting out the pain, shutting out reality.

Somewhere at its edge a dog howled, the long mournful note barely registering in her brain. Deborah smiled. She could sleep now, there was no more worry, no more pain, she could rest. Leaning against a wall, she let the delicious sensation sweep over her. Then the dog howled again, following it up with a series of loud barks.

Somewhere in her sheltered cosy world, Deborah felt rather than heard the sound. Travelling through the darkness that held her mind it seemed to be calling to her, telling her to return.

Once more the dog vented its irritation, its barks shattering the last of the bonds that shackled her mind, bringing Deborah back from the chasm that was threatening to swallow her.

The doctor's house ... she had been going to the doctor's house. But she did not know where it was.

You do! Once more in control of her senses she spoke sharply to herself. You do know where that house is, you only have to think. She had been walking with Clay. Forcing herself to regain her calm, she analysed her movements going back one by one over the days.

Away to the left an owl hooted. Deborah's startled glance turned towards the sound. The park. Trees only just discernible in the darkness jolted her memory. Returning from Little Blox-wich they had followed the lane past Selman's Hill. It was in that lane he had pointed to the doctor's house and minutes later they had emerged opposite the park. Sure now of the direction in which to go she began to run.

Running and walking, not knowing which hurt more, the pain in her side or her laboured breathing, Deborah drove herself on, sobbing with relief when at last she saw the solitary light of a lantern shining through the blackness.

No breath left with which to shout, the banged her first on the heavy door. When there was no answer inside the house to show she had been heard, she sank to the step. Sobs accompanying every movement of her fingers she fumbled with the buttons of her boot, eventually dragging it, still fastened, from her foot. Pushing herself

145

upward she used the heel as a hammer, the blows echoing in the surrounding stillness.

Come! Oh, please, come! Too breathless to speak aloud, Deborah prayed for deliverance. But despite her fervour she found no answer.

The purchase made at the Salon de Fleur Masson had been delivered. Leonie Elliott's smile was one of pure satisfaction. The telephone had rung at three precisely that afternoon, the resale price already asked being promised without question. It had proved a lucrative transaction. Fabulous amethyst eyes gleamed back at her from the mirror. But trade could always be better! Why be satisfied with one supplier when there were so many others with whom to do business? Unpinning the blue feathers fastened to her pale gold curls, sliding them sensuously over expertly painted cheeks, Leonie's smile deepened. The business of the evening had gone equally well. The bracelet Cato Rawley had given her sparkled on one slim wrist. Dear Cato … or should it be poor Cato? Leonie smiled secretively. Either way, what did it matter? Cato was besotted, and that way he would stay.

They had eaten supper together, taking the meal beside the fire in his bedroom. Leonie's long fingers peeled off the round black beauty patch, laying it in a tiny silver box set alongside jars of creams and bottles of expensive French perfume.

Cato had finished off a bottle of claret, following it up with several large brandies. Leonie touched the trace of Gum Arabic left behind by the beauty patch then, reaching for a jar of cream, spread it liberally over the spot.

It was so easy it was becoming boring. Wiping away the cream with a piece of soft gauze, the bracelet glinted in the light of the gasolier and the smile played around rouged lips. Boring or not the game must be played until Cato Rawley was irretrievably trapped.

Removing the bracelet, tossing it carelessly aside as if it had come from a tinker's tray, Leonie gazed at the lovely face reflected in the mirror.

'You are beautiful,' Cato had whispered across the supper table. 'A beautiful golden Satan.'

Satan. Full red lips stretched into a humourless smile. A devil that would claim its own!

Rising from the dressing stool, letting the gown already loosened slide to the floor, smoky violet eyes ran over a slim waist and curving hips on down the flat stomach, playing over the patch of golden brown nestling at its base.

A golden Satan. A soft exultant laugh rang out in the silence. What an apt description!

Desperation lending her strength, Deborah banged her boot on the door of the house, calling the doctor's name until at last a light showed inside.

'Give a body time ... give a body time!' The voice carried to her along with the sound of a bolt being drawn back.

'Please, you have to come! You must. It's Lizzie...'

The door opening under her hand, Deborah almost fell into the hall.

'Steady on, wench. Get your breath afore you speak.' A woman with her hair in grey plaits on her shoulders held a twin-branched candlestick above her head, the candles spilling waxy yellow light over a white flannelette night gown.

'The doctor,' Deborah gasped. 'Lizzie needs him ... the baby!'

Holding the candle still a little ahead of her the woman looked at the girl whose breath was coming in exhausted gasps then stepped out into the darkness of the porch that fronted the tall house.

'Be you by yourself?' she asked, coming back into the hall. 'Have you come down Little Bloxwich Lane at this time in the morning and nobody along of you?'

Deborah nodded.

'Have you no sense, wench?' the woman scolded. 'You should have sent a man.'

Pressing her hand to her side, trying to still the jagged pain, Deborah answered between gasps, 'No man ... no one but me ... please, get the doctor.'

'I can't do that wench, he ain't here. Doctor were called away just after supper. He be up at Field House, that be well past Wallington. The mistress there had started with her child. Could be he won't get home afore dinner time tomorrow.'

Tomorrow! Deborah's eyes widened with anxiety. But Lizzie needed help now, Sadie Trent had said she could do no more.

'Is there another doctor?'

The woman shook her head. 'Not in Elmore

148

Green nor nearby. Next I know of be in Shelfield. That be a tidy step from here and I doubt you would reach it before morning. And even so the doctor there ain't bound to be in neither.'

Deborah felt sick from the pain in her side and worry for Lizzie.

'Mrs Trent,' she said, teeth clenching after each word, 'she said ... she could do no more.'

'Trent?' The woman brought the candlestick closer shedding its light directly on to Deborah's face. 'Sadie Trent? You say she sent you here?'

Catching breath that still came short and hard, Deborah could only nod.

'If Sadie Trent sent you then it be something serious.' The doctor's cook-housekeeper seemed suddenly more sympathetic. 'Sadie Trent can handle most things, her don't go sending folk to this house lightly. But there be nothing to be done 'til the doctor comes back. You'd best bide her 'til morning.'

She could not stay. She would be needed in the house. Deborah shook her head emphatically and as she did the woman added, 'Be sensible, wench! You can't go traipsing back along that lane in the dark, it won't be safe walking alone at night.'

'I can't leave Lizzie.' Deborah straightened up, feeling the pull of a strained muscle. 'Thank you, but I have to go back. Mrs Trent will need my help.'

'Well, if you must.' The woman stepped to the door as Deborah left. 'But be careful, and don't take to the heath.'

Overhead the sky had turned to pearl tinged with

pink. Almost doubled over with the pain of the stitch in her side, Deborah struggled the last few yards of the lane that would bring her to the park. Resting for a few seconds against the wall of a building, she sucked in air between parted lips.

Ahead of her the High Street stretched stark and empty. A few more minutes, one last effort.

Pushing away from the wall, still doubled over by the insistent pain biting into her side, Deborah took a step forward then let out a cry as she felt a hand close roughly over her arm. Her boots grating on the cobbles, she was dragged backward off her feet.

Agnes Ridley lay in her bed, eyes fixed on the patch of sky she had watched change from black to purple and now to pearl pink.

She had come to this house again last night.

Acid, scalding and bitter-tasting, rose in Agnes's throat. They had stayed closeted in his room, taken supper there, the woman's eyes playing gloatingly over Agnes as she had carried in the tray.

'You can leave that until morning.'

Cato Rawley had dismissed her, his own eyes never leaving that woman's face.

Agnes swallowed the bile of anger, teeth gritted tight together.

She stood outside the door listening ... listening to laughter that had changed to soft moans. Heard him call that name, quietly and caressingly, then louder and louder as passion rose in him.

'Leonie ... Leonie!'

Beneath the sheets Agnes's fingers clenched into claws. That woman's hold on him became more marked with every visit.

If only Delia would die! Agnes glared at the lightening sky. It was going to happen anyway so why not now? If she died before that woman could worm her way any further into Cato's affections... But there was no real affection in his heart, no more for Leonie Elliott that he had held for Agnes Ridley; the woman was beautiful, that could not be denied, but she served only to fill a need in Cato Rawley's life, the same need Agnes herself had so often filled. She satisfied Cato Rawley's lust.

And she had satisfied it well last night!

In her mind Agnes heard again the soft teasing laughter, the quiet musical voice. The words had not come distinctly into the corridor but the sounds following them had spoken clearly enough.

Beneath the sheets, Agnes's finger nails dug deep into her palms. She had stood hidden in the recess of the doorway to the adjoining room until her legs ached, but still she had not left. She had listened ... and listened ... until there had been no more laughter, no more moans, only silence.

From the hall the faint sound of the long case clock chimed over the hushed house. It had chimed twelve before sounds came again from that bedroom. Cato's voice, pleading and imploring, and the other teasing and then gently rebuking. Leonie Eliott was leaving.

Agnes left the shelter of the doorway then. Her

limbs stiff from standing, she had made her way down the servants' stairs to the kitchen.

There she had waited, forcing her breath to come evenly, her eyes on the bell pull on the wall above the doorway.

But he had not rung.

Eyes stinging from long hours of staring at the patch of sky showing through the window of her room, Agnes pressed her lids closed.

When there had been no summons she crept along the passage that led from the servant's hall to the main body of the house. Gently easing the door open a few inches she had watched the two of them. Golden hair dressed with blue feathers had glinted in the light of the many-branched gasolier. A gloved finger had tapped teasingly against the mouth of the other whose grey-flecked dark hair seemed dusted with silver by that same light.

'Leonie, stay with me!'

Agnes had heard his words, desire heavy in every one. But the woman had only laughed a low musical refusal.

'Cato, my darling…'

Even through the tiny gap, Agnes had seen the pout of that painted mouth, the tilt of the head that allowed the eyes to smile up at him coquettishly.

'…you ask too much. I cannot stay.'

'But why?'

He had snatched her into his arms and immediately that slender body had curved itself seductively into his.

'Why will you not stay?'

152

'I will, my darling,' the velvety voice had replied. 'I will stay ... when you are a free man.'

Leonie Elliott's arms had lifted, going about his shoulders, one hand at the back of his head drawing it down to hers.

'Then I will stay. I will give you all you want, all you ask for, satisfaction you never dreamed of.'

With a moan he had brought his mouth down on those parted lips, his arms bringing her tighter against his groin.

Agnes's eyes flew open.

That bitch! She knew how to play Cato Rawley, how to keep him panting. She dangled her charms and he followed like a donkey after a carrot.

But let them play their little games, the outcome would be the same. Agnes Ridley would still be mistress of Portland House!

Chapter Eleven

Her feet sliding over the uneven cobbles, the cry still on her lips, Deborah was twisted sharply around, her face brushing against the rough cloth of a jacket, a man's voice harsh in her ears.

'What the hell are you doing out on the street at this hour?'

'Clay.' She fell against him, sobbing in relief on recognising his voice. 'Oh, Clay, you frightened me.'

'I damn' well meant to! What are you thinking of? Wasn't being attacked once enough ... do you have to risk the same thing happening again? The world is no fairyland, Deborah, despite your imagining otherwise!'

'I ... I have been for the doctor.' She kept her face pressed against his jacket, relishing the comfort it gave. She need have no more fears. Clay would help, he would know what to do.

'Alone!' He pushed her from him, holding her at arm's length. 'You went along the Little Bloxwich Lane alone?'

'I had to, there was no one else.'

'Lizzie? Is it Lizzie?'

Still breathless, Deborah nodded.

'Then why didn't you come for me? I would have gone to Field House.' His voice was sharp with anger.

The warm feeling that had spread over her like

154

a cloak on first realising who had grabbed her fell sharply away.

They were standing here discussing what she had done while Lizzie was lying in agony!

'What does it matter who went for the doctor?' she snapped, breaking his hold on her arms. 'What matters is Lizzie. Sadie can't help her and the doctor was out on another call.'

'You matter,' Clay said gently. 'You matter a great deal to me.' But Deborah was already several yards away.

Two rapid strides bringing him alongside her, Clay walked as she almost ran. Once inside Sadie's house he watched Deborah fly up the narrow stairs.

It could have been Abe Turley who had caught up with her at the end of that lane…

Going into the scullery Clay picked up the coal bucket that stood empty, guessing that in the circumstances it was Deborah who had forgotten to refill it. Lifting the latch quietly, he went into the yard and filled the bucket from the heap shovelled into one corner.

Standing feeding the fire, he turned as Sadie came down the stairs.

'Eh, thanks, lad.' She glanced gratefully at the fireplace. 'That be a help.'

'I saw Deborah by the park.'

'Arrh, lad, I guessed.' She held out the jacket he had thrown over the girl's shoulders.

'The doctor was out.' He came back from the scullery after once more filling the bucket with coal. 'Is there anything I can do?'

Shaking her head, Sadie glanced at the ceiling

as an agonised cry rang out from the room above. 'No, Clay, there be nothing you can do. Get yourself away to work. This be no job for a man, lessen he be a doctor.'

'Will I ask my mother to come?'

'Your mother would be the first I would ask, she be every bit as good at birthing a babby as I be myself, but this be no straightforward birth.' Sadie shook her head again. 'That wench be in a danger neither me nor your mother can deliver her from. 'Tis in the Almighty's hand whether they both live or die.'

At the top of the stairs she heard the latch click. It was as well Clay had gone. Crossing to the bed, she bent over the pain-wracked girl clinging tightly to Deborah's hand.

'It will be over soon,' Deborah was whispering, trying to comfort her friend. 'The baby is almost here, everything will be all right.'

Her head turning on the pillow, Lizzie opened her eyes, a smile of recognition and thankfulness spreading over her ravaged face.

'Yes, it will be all right now,' she whispered. But her glance had gone beyond Deborah, to the man standing framed in the doorway.

Downstairs, the kettle of water Sadie had sent her to fetch still in her hand, Deborah let the tears flow unchecked down her cheeks.

Lizzie's eyes had lit up when she saw that figure in the doorway, and Deborah herself had caught her breath with relief as she turned to look. His face showing all the signs of weariness, his bag in one hand, the doctor stepped quickly over to the bed.

In the quiet of the downstairs room Deborah murmured her thanks aloud. 'Oh, Lord, thank you ... thank you for bringing him.' She quickly climbed the stairs again, taking the kettle of water the doctor had asked for.

'I'll take that, wench.' Sadie took the kettle as Deborah glanced past her at the man swathed now in one of Sadie's voluminous aprons, a trickle of sweat running past his eyes.

'No!' Sadie stepped in front of Deborah, preventing her from going to Lizzie. 'Leave her. She be in the best hands. Leave her to Doctor Wilson. He won't turn away so long as there be the ghost of a chance. Get you downstairs, you be better there than here. I'll call should the doctor need anything.'

Throwing a last reluctant look towards her friend, Deborah shuddered at the sound of a long exhausted moan from the still figure on the bed.

Sadie edged towards the door, shooing her with a silent movement of her hands. Sinking to the floor, Deborah sat on the topmost stair, her head bowed on her chest, the fingers of both hands twined around each other. Her prayer changed to one of supplication, the words rising from the depths of her soul.

'Lizzie is very young and she did not realise the wrong she was doing. But she is not a wicked girl, please don't let her die. Please don't let Lizzie die!'

Crushed beneath a mountain of grief Deborah sat hunched on the stair. If only the man had come, if only Lizzie had been married! But though a marriage certificate would have spared her mental pain, it would have been no help against the agony her friend was suffering now.

'Deborah.'

Her own thoughts uppermost in her mind she did not hear the voice behind her, only looked up at Sadie's hand touched her shoulder.

'It be all over.'

What did those words mean? Fear stark in her eyes she looked up at the face above her. It was lined with weariness, haggard from worry and tension. Afraid to move, Deborah just stared.

'It be all over,' Sadie said again. 'The babby be born...'

'Lizzie?' All the fear of those long hours throbbed in that one word.

Sadie's mouth moved in a tired smile. 'Her be all right. The doctor has given her something to help her sleep. Now you go and make him a cup of tea. If any man has earned it this night then he has. We have him to thank for saving Lizzie's life.'

'And the baby?'

The smile remained on Sadie's mouth but in the light spilling from the bedroom Deborah caught the flicker of fear that sped across her eyes.

'We must wait and see. It be small and it be weak after the struggle it has had to come into the world. The cord was wrapped around its neck. But with help...' She crossed herself, a movement Deborah had not seen her make before. 'Now you see to that tea afore the doctor gets downstairs.'

Deborah performed the task automatically.

158

Lizzie's child was born and she had come through safely. Clay would be so happy.

'Is it Lizzie? Why didn't you send for me?'

His words and all the heartache they implied returned to Deborah then, and a little of her own happiness drained away.

'There be a pot of broth on the hob. Be sure and have Lizzie take some for her dinner. You too, my wench. You be no further through than a kipper between the eyes!'

'Then I'll have two bowls of soup!' Deborah laughed as the older woman folded the newly finished gown, wrapping it carefully in an old but perfectly laundered white cotton sheet.

'Be no laughing matter,' Sadie reprimanded, her glance travelling over the slender figure busy collecting sewing threads from a tin box gaudily painted with huge yellow pansies. 'You've shed too many pounds with running up and down them stairs. You should let me take more of a turn.'

'You do enough for us. I don't know what would have happened to Lizzie and myself if you had not taken us in.' Deborah looked up. All her laughter was gone, her lovely eyes were serious.

Reaching for her shawl, Sadie draped it about her shoulders, tying the ends together in a knot beneath her breasts. Taking up the parcel containing the gown, she gave Deborah a long look.

'That be what we be put on this earth to do, help each other, care one for another. Isn't that what you did for young Lizzie when you left

159

behind the only security you had? You left home and job to go with her. "Love thy neighbour as thyself". Those were the Lord's words and that be what you are doing. It won't be forgotten, wench. Though it don't seem much like it now, you will be repaid.'

'I don't want payment. All I did was leave a place I was unhappy in, while you are sharing your home with two people you know almost nothing about.'

Sadie hitched the parcel more comfortably on her hip. 'We don't go splitting hairs over who be doing what. Suffice it to say we both do what we can, but this much I will say. I have become fond of you two wenches. 'Tis a pleasure having you in my house.'

Looking at the work-worn face, Deborah felt a current of emotion surge inside her. Not since her mother had anyone except Lizzie expressed fondness for her.

'Sadie,' she murmured, 'I know Lizzie feels as I do for she has told me. Not since my mother died have I felt as happy or content as I have been here I this house with you. We have a great deal to thank you for and we will never forget that.'

Leaving the house before tears got the better of her, Sadie thought over the words she had said earlier. Please God she could care for these wenches longer than she was given to care for Emmy.

Madame Fleur Masson glanced up as a light tap sounded on the door of her private sitting room.

'It be Mrs Trent, *madame*.'

Her glance ran over the girl dressed in a dark blue dress and frilled apron, a lace cap set on hair the colour of fresh cut wheat. She was still too thin, but it was early days yet.

'Is that the way to announce a caller? Remember what I have taught you, Molly.'

'Beg pardon.' Molly Sanders bobbed a curtsy. 'Mrs Trent to see you, *madame.*'

'That is better, Molly.'

The girl smiled, china blue eyes reflecting her pleasure at her employer's praise.

'Will I show her to the office, *madame?*'

'No.' Laying aside the newspaper she had been reading, Fleur shook her elegantly coiffured head. 'Show Mrs Trent in here, and should anyone else call I will come to the salon.'

'That be a pretty wench.' Sadie smiled as Molly showed her into the room then withdrew. 'Though a bit more meat on her bones wouldn't come amiss.'

Fleur would rather have dealt with Sadie in some other place, one where her boots did not have to soil the expensive carpet. Indicating a chair, she tried not to wince as the other woman dropped on to its silk tapestry cover. But she had to take the good with the bad; the private office was no place for the sort of business she did with such as Sadie, but on the other hand the fewer ears heard the prices she paid for the work Sadie Trent did the better.

'She has only been here a short time,' Fleur replied to Sadie's comment. 'She'll most probably be leaving in a week or so. I found her a place as a favour to Father Travers. Seems her

161

mother was taken into hospital and he was anxious the girl should not be left on her own. There are always those would take advantage. But while she is here we will do our best to feed her and put the roses back in her cheeks.'

'Father Travers? Can't say I've heard of him, Florrie.' Sadie rested the parcel on her knees.

Annoyed at the use of a name she wished to forget, Fleur gave a scowl. Sadie met it with an amused glance of her own.

'Most likely not!' Florrie Marston answered her sharply, wanting the conversation done. It didn't do to say too much. The women of Elmore Green had sharp wits and long memories. They did not easily forget and it would take no time on their part to put two and two together.

'What parish be he from?' Sadie well knew the irritation her question would cause. Florrie Marston had always been close-mouthed; even as a child she never liked the rest to know what she was about.

Glancing at the parcel balanced on Sadie's knees, Florrie answered brusquely, vexation deepening in her eyes.

'Can't say as I know. Could be Walsall somewhere.'

Could be. Or then again it could be China somewhere, and Florrie Marston wouldn't let on! Sadie passed the parcel intro her out-stretched hands.

'Bit of a long way to send the wench, ain't it? From Walsall to Bloxwich. I would have thought he could have found a place for her nearer to her mother than that.'

"'E must 'ave had a reason, though what it might be I d'ain't ask. I thought it best to mind me own business!' Florrie's carefully nurtured mode of speech fell away like a shrivelled leaf in a gale.

Watching the other woman fold back the cloth that wrapped the gown, Sadie smiled inwardly. She always could get under Florrie's skin. 'You don't have to go round the Wrekin to tell me to mind mine, 'cos that be what you means.'

'Then we both know where we be standing!'

Getting to her feet, Florrie held up the gown. Draping it over the sofa she ran a critical eye over the bead embroidery, turning back the layers of tulle to inspect the delicate stitchwork.

Content to let the matter of the girl drop, Sadie watched. Florrie Marston would find no fault with the work but that would not prevent her from trying to pay a lower price.

'The design of the beadwork ... I expected it to be more elaborate. There could have been more crystals on the bodice and a wider use of silver thread on the overskirt.'

'The design be as you specified, same as the threadwork on the skirt. As for more crystals on the bodice, there be enough there to satisfy any woman's taste lessen she wants to look like a Christmas tree!'

Aware of the asperity in the tone but ignoring it, Florrie continued to inspect the gown.

'Might have been to the good to have that young woman bring this. Could have saved me a trip over to your place. I could have told her what I be wanting in the next.'

Sadie felt a touch of apprehension, a coldness creeping up her spine. She had never quite trusted Florrie Marston, but why she couldn't say. There was just something about her, a slyness Sadie could not come to terms with and something she did not want in proximity to Deborah.

'You can tell me what you be wanting.' It was crisply said, a no-nonsense inflection in her voice. 'The day I can't carry out what you asks be the day for me to pack it in. And you'd best look for another to sew your frocks!'

Smoothing the dress's layers of tulle, Florrie stepped back the better to view the whole.

'No need to take umbrage, Sadie. I just thought to save myself a journey.'

'If I can make it, then so can you!'

The wary note was still in her voice. Florrie turned to her, a conciliatory smiled doing nothing to hide her dissatisfaction.

'Of course. It was just a thought. Young legs be quicker than old.'

Arrh, they do! Sadie thought sourly. And old heads be wiser than young, and Florrie Marston's be wiser than most. The woman had shown an interest in Deborah when she had last come to Elmore Green, an interest Sadie did not wish to foster.

'Sadie Trent's legs be quick enough yet,' she said aloud, 'so pay what you be owing and I'll be on my way.'

Counting coins into the other woman's hand, Florrie Marston asked, 'The girl who does the designs for the beadwork – has her done any

164

more since I was at the house?'

Sadie thrust the sovereigns into a purse which was stowed deep in the pocket of her skirts.

'Some. Her has done some.'

Not exactly encouraging. Florrie detected the trace of animosity. But that would not put her off, and neither would Sadie Trent's protectiveness towards the one called Deborah; a girl as lovely to look at as that one would encourage spending and increase her profit, and profit was the religion by which Florrie Marston lived.

'I be interested in her work,' she said as Sadie rose to leave. 'I'll be taking a look at it, if that be convenient to you?'

'It be,' Sadie agreed, folding the sheet and tucking it beneath one arm.

'Next week then.' Tugging the bell pull that hung alongside the fireplace Florrie reverted to her more polished delivery, each word carefully modulated as the maid entered the room.

'Mrs Trent is leaving now, Molly. Please show her out.'

Watching the girl bob a curtsey, Florrie felt a glow of satisfaction. With a girl like that, hair gleaming like wheat beneath a summer sun, and the other as beautiful with hair black as a raven's wing, she could not help but reap a goodly profit. And despite what Sadie Trent intended, Deborah would come to the salon.

'Isn't he wonderful, Deborah?'

Propped up against the pillows Lizzie nursed her son.

'The most wonderful there ever was.' Deborah

smiled fondly at the picture they made.

'Is it right to call a boy beautiful?'

Bent over her sewing, Deborah smiled again. They had held this conversation for a week now, each time Lizzie's pleasure in her son clearly showed.

'I don't see why not. He *is* beautiful.'

'I said if I had a girl I wanted her named after you, but seeing as that was not to be, I'd like you to choose his name.'

Deborah kept her eyes on the satin she was stitching. She had thought Lizzie would give the child the same name as his father, but since the night of the birth there had been no mention made of the man. It was as if Lizzie had erased all thoughts of him from her mind.

'I couldn't do that, Lizzie,' she returned quickly. 'That privilege belongs to you.'

Tracing a finger over the downy head, Lizzie looked at the girl who had stood by her, choosing to leave both home and job to be with her.

'As you say, the privilege is mine. It is the one thing I have to give and so I give it to you. Don't refuse it, Deborah. I can never give you anything so precious again.'

Emotion filling her, Deborah kept her eyes lowered. It was such a lovely gift, one that would live in her heart forever.

Bent over the baby, Lizzie too felt the emotion of the moment. Deborah and Sadie ... both had given her friendship, both had given her love.

'It's all I have,' she whispered. 'If I only had money or jewels, I would gladly give you them.'

'Oh, Lizzie!' The cry breaking from her,

Deborah rushed to the bed, the lovely satin gown she was working on falling in a heap beside the chair. Tears clouding her eyes, she touched the other girl's hands as they held the child. 'Lizzie, don't think like that. Don't ever think like that. What you have offered, no jewel in the world could match and no amount of money could buy. How could it? In a way you are sharing your son with me.'

'Then you will name him?'

Deborah smiled through her tears. 'Only if you will share the task with me. You choose one name and I will choose another.'

Still showing the traces of her long painful hours in childbirth, Lizzie's drawn face relaxed into a smile. She looked down at the head nuzzling to her breast.

'You hear that, my boy? You're to have two names. You'll be like the gentry, won't that be posh?' Lifting her glance to Deborah she asked, 'What will you choose?'

Deborah stifled her tears and replied, 'I haven't an idea, I've never had to think of a name before. What about you? What have you decided upon?'

Instantly Lizzie's face clouded over, her eyes darkening. She looked quickly down at the baby. 'I ... I haven't thought.'

It was not the truth but Deborah realised that to challenge her would only aggravate the pain she knew was just below the surface. Returning to her chair, she picked up the gown from the floor, giving it a shake before resuming her seat. Pushing the needle into the fabric, she pretended to think.

'What about Marmaduke?'

'What!' Lizzie looked up quickly, disappointment clear in her exclamation.

'Or Sebulum? Or Baudric?'

Looking up then, Deborah revealed the teasing laughter in her own eyes.

'What about Aurelius?' Lizzie caught the mood. 'Or Uzziah?'

'What if we give him all five?'

'Hmm!' Lizzie pulled a pensive face. 'You don't think the gentry will find it a bit much to say: Marmaduke Zebulun Baudric Aurelius Uzziah Burton.'

Joining in the other girl's laughter, Deborah breathed an inner sigh of relief. At last Lizzie could smile again.

Chapter Twelve

'Poor little chap. He would need the strength of ten men to carry a string of names like that, not to mention the skill of a fairground pugilist to fight the battles they would cause when other lads teased him.' Clay Gilmore smiled down at the girl walking beside him.

'Well, what would you call him then?' Deborah continued the charade. Not by the flicker of an eyelid had she betrayed the fact that the names were just a joke between Lizzie and herself.

'Nice evening, Sam,' Clay greeted a man standing on his doorstep, tobacco glowing red as he sucked on a long-stemmed clay pipe.

'Well?' Deborah asked again. 'What name would you give Lizzie's baby?'

'Well, I wouldn't give him Marmaduke Wotsit Wotsit! Lord, Deborah, they don't even saddle a racehorse with a mouthful like that! Have some pity for the little fella.'

She wasn't sure when Miss Hammond had become Deborah, or Mr Gilmore had become Clay, but she felt more comfortable with the way it was now.

'Don't worry,' she laughed, easy now in his company. 'I was just teasing. Lizzie and I have no intention of giving her son such high-flown names.'

He gave her a sideways look, his answer holding a somewhat puzzled tone. 'Lizzie and you?'

169

Coming to the opening that gave on to the off sales counter of the Spring Cottage, Deborah halted. 'Lizzie asked if I would choose a name for her baby. I thought that the most wonderful thing for a friend to do. A real honour.'

Looking into her smiling face, Clay's heart caught inside him. Almost as wonderful as it would be if the girl could ever love him. But thoughts like that could lead to nothing. He must just be satisfied she accepted him as a friend.

'So what have you chosen?' he asked, forcing down the words he so wanted to say.

'We haven't.' She laughed again, a sound light as a falling petal. 'They get more ridiculous every time we try.'

The jug with its customary pint of best ale tucked beneath her shawl, she began to walk back in silence. Then, having passed the house where the man was still sucking on his clay pipe, she said, 'Have you managed to find any trace yet of that man, the baby's father?'

'Not yet. It's not easy. I didn't expect him to have left a trail behind him. It isn't very likely he will have given Lizzie's name even should he leave word where he might be found, and her name is all we have to go on.' He caught the dejected drop of Deborah's shoulders and added quickly, 'But I am going into Walsall come Sunday. Could be somebody will know something there.'

'Isn't it a big town? I remember Mrs Ridley one saying it was.'

'Compared to Bloxwich it is.'

'Clay.' She glanced up at him. 'I … I would like to go with you, if you have no objection?'

Instantly he glowed with a warmth that spread through every vein. Holding tight to the feeling he answered quietly, 'I have no objection.'

I have no objection! Deborah lowered her glance.

There had been earnestness in his answer, but no trace of eagerness; he had not even said he would enjoy her company. But then, she must not look for anything deeper than the friendship he already showed. Her fingers tightened on the jug as she strove to quell the feeling of disappointment his answer had evoked. His deeper interest was in Lizzie and that she must accept.

But as he said good night and turned away from her, Deborah silently acknowledged the true feelings in her heart.

'It be a bostin' cradle.'

It was very well made. Deborah laid the baby gently in the bed Clay Gilmore had made for him.

'He be a good lad, that Clay Gilmore.' Sadie repeated the words she had become fond of uttering.

'He has been more than kind to Deborah and to me.' Lizzie swung her legs down from the bed Sadie had made up for her on the wooden settle.

'That's more than I'll be if you don't get back beneath them covers.' Sadie's sharp eyes had caught the movement.

'But I have to get on my feet sometime.'

'That be as it may!' Sadie's reply was sharp. 'But that time ain't yet. You don't be over birthing the child, not by a long way.'

'It's been more than three weeks!' sighed Lizzie.

Turning to the fire, stirring a pot with quick ferocious movements of a wooden spoon, Sadie's retort was no less sharp than her first.

'I don't give a bugger! It can be three months, but you'll not be up and about 'til I deems you be ready.'

Straightening the covers over the sleeping child, Deborah turned to her friend. Lizzie's features were still far too thin and drawn, her heartache still visible beneath the smile that was too often forced to those soft brown eyes.

'A little longer won't kill you,' she confirmed.

Settling beneath the covers once more, Lizzie gave a wry grin. 'Oh, no?' Hasn't either of you heard the saying, "killing with kindness"?'

Tasting the contents of the pot, Sadie set the spoon aside. 'Won't make much different. The end result will be the same if you go catching the influenza.'

'Lizzie is going to do exactly as you tell her,' Deborah answered diplomatically.

'Then that be to rest and get good and strong again.' Sadie's glance was gentle now as she looked at the girl. 'You'll need all your strength, looking after a babby all day. It ain't easy…'

She stopped abruptly. Lizzie looked past her out of the window. The sentence had been left half finished, but she could add the rest. *'It isn't easy rearing a child by yourself'*, was what Sadie had been about to say. *'Not easy without the help of a father.'*

'Oh, my God!'

Arranging flowers in a bowl set on a stand in

172

the hall of Portland House, Agnes Ridley strained her ears to catch the voice speaking in the study.

'When ... who ... who did you say?'

Question followed rapidly on question. Agnes stood perfectly still.

'Why was I not called?' Another short silence. 'Yes ... yes, of course, forgive me ... what? Yes, I will be there as soon as possible. Yes, today. Goodbye.'

Her feet soundless on the thick Turkish carpet Agnes ran the few yards to the stairs, sprinting up the first half dozen. Then she turned and made as if to descend them as the study door opened.

'Ah, Mrs Ridley!'

Agnes glanced impassively at the man whose bed she had so often shared. Beige jacket and brown trousers, a gold Albert looped from the watch nestled in his silk waistcoat, Cato Rawley made a figure to command anyone's attention. He stepped towards the stairs, the afternoon light streaming through the glass-panelled door and catching the faint streaks of silver dusting his dark hair. His neatly trimmed side whiskers edged towards a firm chin which, unlike those of so many others who slavishly adopted the fashion set by the Prince of Wales, remained beardless.

'Mrs Ridley.' Standing at the foot of the stairs, he looked up at her. 'I have just received a telephone call from my wife's parents.'

Agnes's expression remained blank.

'Would you please look up the time of the next train there? I have to change.'

'Not bad news, I hope, sir.'

'My wife has taken a chill, it is feared it could

become pneumonia. I must go to her at once.'

'Of course, sir. I will get the train time now.'

It could be pneumonia! Keeping her face impassive, Agnes walked on down the stairs, but once past Cato she smiled. This would be the end of Delia, she would never survive pneumonia on top of consumption! Her lungs would not stand the strain and neither would her body, which was already far too weak. This would prove the end of the first Mrs Cato Rawley. Soon it would be Agnes's turn to fill that office.

Having made the call to the booking office of the railway station, she walked back into the hall as Cato, dressed now in dark jacket and trousers, cleared the last stair.

'There is a train from Bloxwich at four-ten.' Agnes spoke in a level tone, revealing none of her true feelings. 'The connection leaves Walsall at four-fifty. I took the liberty of reserving you a private compartment.'

'Thank you.' He brushed past her then turned. 'A bag, Mrs Ridley. Will you please pack me a bag?'

'Of course.' Agnes gave him a faint nod. 'I also asked that a hansom be sent from the railway station to pick you up, sir.'

'Yes, thank you.'

Watching him turn into the study, she smiled grimly. He could brush her aside now, but very soon he would not do it so easily. Making no move to do as he had asked, she listened as she had so often before, waiting for the sound of his voice.

'Leonie...'

Agnes's teeth ground together. She had known what he would do. Telephone that bitch to hear her purr over the good news. Only it wouldn't be so good for her. Leonie Elliott would never be his wife.

'Yes, I must go down there ... I can't tell until I see exactly what the situation is but I will return as soon as I can.'

Agnes waited, the lull in their conversation grating on her nerves.

'I know, my darling, I know, and I will miss you too ... Yes, my love, with all my heart. I want only for us to be together...'

The grim smile returning to her mouth, Agnes walked up the wide staircase. Cato Rawley had a hard lesson to learn, namely that you cannot always have what you want.

'It were the daftest thing. The times I've walked that heath and now I go and do this!'

'Thank goodness you were almost home before it happened.' Deborah changed the wet cloth draped around Sadie's sprained ankle for a colder one.

'You're right.' She winced as the cloths were changed. 'But it were a right trawl getting here, I can tell you.'

'Lucky those women saw you. Any further from the village and you could have been lying out on the heath for hours.'

'Arrh, wench, I could. But I felt a right Aynuk being pushed home in old man Perry's wheelbarrow!'

'Far better to feel foolish than limp home in

175

pain,' Lizzie said, concern in the voice but a well-guarded twinkle in her eye.

'That be easy for you to say. It weren't you perched in that barrow like a pig trussed for market. It just needed some noggy head to stick an apple in my mouth!'

'They'd need to have been foolish indeed to try that.' Collecting the bowl and spare cloth, Deborah carried them into the scullery.

'Now you are going to have to let me get up,' Lizzie was saying when she returned to the living room. 'Deborah can't do everything by herself.'

'I reckon you be right, Lizzie.' Sadie eased her foot where it rested on a low stool. 'But you take things steady. Ain't nothing needs doing so bad it won't wait a day or two.'

'Except perhaps brewing a pot of tea?' Deborah suggested mischievously.

Sadie glanced sideways at Lizzie, her own eyes bright with amusement despite the pain in her ankle. 'Listen to that, will you! And here's me thinking the wench had no brain at all.'

Accepting a cup, Sadie leaned back in her chair. 'Florrie Marston were right taken with that bodice you two worked, she said the design was quite unusual; you be very good at that, Lizzie. It could make you a decent living.'

'I'm glad it was acceptable.'

'Acceptable! I'll say it was. So acceptable that Florrie paid this for it.'

Balancing cup and saucer in one hand, Sadie reached into the pocket of her skirts, drawing out four gold coins. Holding them out to Lizzie, she smiled as the girl's eyes opened wide.

176

'She paid all that?' Lizzie gasped. 'Four sovereigns! Deborah, she paid four sovereigns.'

Sadie's glance travelled to Deborah whose own eyes were wide with disbelief.

'Arrh, Florrie Marston paid four sovereigns. But for the next her will pay more.'

'More!' Deborah's reply held incredulity. 'Surely no one would pay more?'

Tipping the coins into Lizzie's hand, Sadie sipped her tea, a satisfied smile playing over her lined face.

'Florrie Marston will. You just have to know how to deal with her. The profit her makes on them fancy frocks will be plenty if I knows anything. For years I have sewed for that woman, making barely enough from it to pay for my cottons, but you two ain't going to do that. Florrie Marston wants your designs and your beadwork, but her won't get them for pennies.' The smile faded to be replaced by a suddenly serious expression. Sadie put her cup aside. 'Look after your money, spend only what you must, and in a year or two you pair could be opening your own fancy gown shop.'

'A gown shop!' Deborah laughed. 'Lizzie and I open our own gown shop? I don't think so.'

'But I do!' Sadie retorted vehemently. 'You can sew, create your own designs, cut your own patterns – I've seen you do it all. On top of which you have a feeling for which material will suit which pattern and a flair for colour. What else do you need?'

Deborah stared at her. 'A dressmaking business? I … I wouldn't know where to begin.'

177

'Neither did Florrie Marston once!' Sadie snorted disparagingly. 'You be thinking you've never done anything other than the work of a paid servant. Well, Florrie never even did that. The times she tried for a position she was refused! Seemed they thought she didn't have enough oil in her lamp even to become a scullery maid. But that didn't stop her. She showed them folk in their posh houses just how much sense she really had, and now they be paying her not a servant's wage but pounds and pounds just for a fancy frock!'

'But would there be room for two gown shops?' Lizzie broke in. 'I mean, if Florrie's salon already has the custom of the gentry hereabouts, where could we find a following?'

'You see ... you see!' Sadie's smile returned. 'Already you be thinking like a businesswoman. 'Tis true Florrie had a following, but as time passes it will be *your* gowns, the ones you and Deborah have designed, *your* creations, that women will hanker for. Open your own place and they'll come to you.'

'But would that be fair?' Deborah looked doubtful. 'Would it be fair to try to take business from the woman who gave us work when we had none?'

'Florrie Marston gives nowt for nowt!' Sadie said caustically. 'That woman be sharper than the needles you sew with. She knows a good thing when it's there to be seen, and you two be that thing. Work for her no longer than you have to or you'll finish up the same as me – working for her for ever and being paid a pittance. You don't have to start up in Bloxwich, not if you feels that ain't right. There be other towns.'

'Do you think we could?' Lizzie glanced across at Deborah. 'Do you think we could set ourselves up one day?'

At the first flicker of interest she had seen in the girl's eyes for months, Deborah hid her own uncertainty. 'We could if we work hard enough, but...'

'But what?' Lizzie's hopefulness wavered.

'A French-sounding name, maybe. But ze accent...' Hunching her shoulders, Deborah lifted her hands expressively. 'Zat I do not 'ave, *madame!*'

Watching the two girls giggle, Sadie relaxed in her chair. The seeds were sown. With careful nurturing they might yet grow.

Leonie Elliott smiled, looking once more at the cheque lying open beside her breakfast tray.

It had been a most successful deal. Florrie Marston had charged a phenomenal sum for that beautiful creation, but Leonie had charged ten times that amount. There had been no quibble over the price. She smiled again, a slow almost lascivious smile, eyes playing over the amount written in a flowing hand on the slip of paper. So much for so little. Picking up the cheque and throwing her arms wide, Leonie laughed; soft and deep, the sound echoed in the silence of her bedroom. The buyers had made no demurral at the price asked, but then where would they buy such a beautiful creation except from Leonie Elliott?

Dropping her arms and letting the cheque flutter to the bed, her laughter pealed out again, quiet but triumphant. It had been the most profitable deal yet, one that might be repeated. But the people who paid such vast sums for an exclusive did not care to see their purchase reproduced; they would not stand for duplication in any form. Every deal must be totally new, both gown and model.

Teeth catching at her lower lip, Leonie stared into space. The red head had been lovely, but where there was one there would be others... A new gown and a new girl to display it. She just had to find one.

That girl she had seen in Cato's house ... the one who had given him notice so abruptly. She had not taken Leonie's offer of a position at this house, sadly. She pushed aside her tray. The girl had been beautiful, even in that drab uniform. Put her in an exquisite gown ... Leonie painted a mental picture. Jet black hair coiled high, a necklace of emeralds set about the throat echoing eyes the colour of damp moss, a faint smile on those lovely classic features... Now there was a girl who would generate a fortune indeed.

Throwing aside the covers, she went into her spacious dressing room. That was the kind of beauty needed to do justice to Fleur Masson's creations. But where was it to be found?

Bathed and dressed in deep ruby red velvet, a bonnet trimmed with matching feathers set attractively askew on her pale gold hair, Leonie smoothed supple Italian leather gloves over well-manicured hands. It was not prudent to be seen inspecting the line in the market place, even though there could be one among the women hoping to secure a day's work who might have the wherewithal beneath her patched clothing. Some such girls were comely enough, and given a few good meals … but comely was not enough. To attract the type of customer Leonie Elliott sold on to, the girl must be a beauty. A lovely face to set off a lovely gown, just as that flame-haired girl had done.

She had modelled well that day in the salon. Aware of her own beauty, she had carried the gown well. And Marston had said she had willingly agreed to accompany the dress to that other establishment, and to model it again. There had been no hitch after that. The asking price had been paid immediately.

In the carriage en route to the railway station, Leonie glanced at the evidence of coal mining and metal works: winding wheels and chimney stacks rising stark and ugly against the landscape; the tiny houses joined in long soot-stained rows like so many legions in hell. There would be girls in those hovels only too willing to model gowns at the salon but it would be too risky. Never play too close to home. The maxim had proved sound, and it would be foolish to abandon it now.

Alighting from her reserved first-class compartment, Leonie walked briskly from the station, a movement of her gloved hand calling a hansom. Walsall was a thriving town, one where most men and women were too busy earning their living to worry about their neighbours. This would be a more suitable gleaning field; here the leavings of society would be thicker on the ground.

Giving brief instructions to the driver, Leonie settled back in the carriage. The hotel in Bridgeman Street was a little seedy but it would serve her purpose ... and it was close to the Union Workhouse.

Chapter Thirteen

'But you can't go! That ankle is far too swollen. How far do you think you would get before it collapsed under you?'

'But Florrie said by teatime today or the customer would not want it. That jacket *has* to go today.'

'And it will,' Deborah answered firmly. 'Only you will not be taking it.'

'Of course I'm taking it.' Struggling to balance on one foot, Sadie winced with pain as she tried her weight on the other.

'You see, Mrs Sadie Trent!' Deborah pushed her firmly back into the chair. 'There is no way you are going to walk on that foot for at least another week.'

Seated beside the fireplace, Lizzie looked up from nursing her child. 'I could take the jacket. You need only tell me where the place is.'

Sadie smiled. ''Tis a kind offer, wench, but Blakenhall be a fair step away. Besides, you can't go. You haven't been churched yet. And until you have, you can enter no place other than this house.'

Folding the silk jacket with its heavy crusting of tiny crystal beads, Deborah wrapped it in a freshly laundered sheet then reached for her shawl.

'You ain't taking it!' Sadie tried again to stand

on both feet, snorting in exasperation as she fell back.

'Deborah, wait.' Lizzie settled the child quickly in his cradle, covering him carefully. 'I will come with you, I don't have to go inside.'

Picking up the cloth-wrapped parcel, Deborah looked sternly at her friend. 'You must stay here. Be sensible.' She saw the set of the other girl's lips and knew the arguments forming behind them. 'If the baby should need attention, Sadie can't give it. What if she tried to lift him and fell again? You see my point, Lizzie?'

The other girl nodded. 'But be careful, Deborah. I still have a mortal dread of that heath.'

'It's broad daylight. I won't fall down any mine shaft in the day.'

Meeting her smiling glance, Sadie looked serious. 'You take good care all the same.' Silently she finished the warning: There be plenty thought they knew the heath well enough. Plenty it took and never sent back!

Standing at the window, Lizzie watched her friend walk rapidly along the street with a feeling of misgiving. It was not so much the heath itself she feared, it was the man who had stalked it.

'The work is well done.'

'Thank you, *madame*.' Deborah watched the woman's close inspection of the tiny stitches.

'I had thought the jacket would not be delivered, it was getting rather late.'

'Mrs Trent suffered an accident on her way home last week and I did not know the way. I had

184

to ask directions several times I apologise...'

'Don't.' Florrie waved away her apology. 'It was very good of you to bring it. My clients are not given to waiting. Had you not brought it today then I'm afraid your delivery would have met with refusal.'

Holding the amber silk against her shoulders, Florrie Marston glanced towards a long mirror attached to one wall of the tastefully furnished room, then held out the garment to Deborah.

'Would you be so kind, my dear? It can be appreciated so much more fully when worn by another. I could have one of my girls model it for me but seeing as you are here...'

Deborah hesitated, something more than the woman's carefully erased local dialect telling her that all was not quite what it seemed here. She would rather leave at once but to refuse to comply with so simple a request would appear rude.

Slipping off her shawl, she stood still while Florrie eased the delicate silk over her arms.

'Very effective.' Florrie Marston stretched out one slightly plump hand, straightening the mandarin collar, then stepped back to admire the jacket. 'But perhaps over here ... the light in this room is not so good as in the salon.'

Leading the way to a tall window, she requested as Deborah followed, 'Would you turn round so I can see the back? Slowly ... slowly, my dear. Give me time to judge the line.'

Turning several times on the spot, Deborah listened to Madame Fleur voice her satisfaction.

'Beautiful, quite beautiful. Do you not think so, my dear?'

185

Slipping off the lovely jacket, Deborah did not see the look she directed towards a second window, half hidden by a curtained alcove.

Payment for the garment safely in her pocket, Deborah felt a strange sense of relief as the door of the salon closed behind her. It was a most elegantly furnished place, its rooms beautiful with their delicately shaded drapes of silk velvet, the deep piled carpets echoing the same scheme of apricot and pale blue, but for all its elegance the place seemed to hold a sense of threat.

You are being foolish, Deborah Hammond, she chided herself silently. But the feeling would not be so easily dismissed.

'Well?'

In the private room of the salon, Florrie glanced at the figure stepping from beyond the curtained alcove.

'Beautiful, as you said.' Leonie Elliott picked up the silk jacket. 'And the colour … it makes an excellent change. We must set it off to its best advantage. And the…'

Florrie raised a hand, stemming whatever was to follow. Once in her inner office, she closed the door firmly.

'It pays to be careful, Leonie. The less others hear, the less explaining needs to be done.'

Nodding her agreement, Leonie took the chair indicated.

'Have the jacket sent to Bayton Lodge.'

'And the model?'

A smile on her rouged mouth, Leonie gave a little shake of the head. 'None will be required, I have already seen the garment modelled. Though the girl who did it so demurely would, I think, make an admirable mannequin.'

'My own thoughts entirely.' Florrie too smiled but as quickly became serious. 'But that one will not be so easy to get as a workhouse girl.'

Leonie's thoughts flashed to the past, to a lovely raven-haired girl standing defiantly in front of Cato Rawley; the girl to whom she had offered a position at the Lodge. But the girl had never taken up on the offer. And now she was here, in Bloxwich.

'Why should she be more difficult to procure than a girl from the workhouse.'

Settling her slightly overweight frame into an elegant mock-Hepplewhite chair, Florrie answered, 'Because she lodges with Sadie Trent. She and a girl who recently gave birth to a child have lived with Sadie for several months.'

'So!' Leonie raised one perfectly plucked eyebrow.

'So ... Sadie Trent isn't a woman to pay no heed should the girl suddenly go missing!'

'She would not go "missing", as you put it. The girl would simply be accepting a position that offered better living conditions and prospects.'

For several seconds Leonie stayed deep in thought, her finger absentmindedly toying with the dark beauty patch stuck to one cheek, those brilliant amethyst eyes lifted to Florrie. 'Then we must secure her services some other way.'

'Meaning accidents are not exactly unknown in this little corner of the world. People have been known to fall into flooded pit shafts or long-forgotten gin pits; one more such disappearance would hardly give rise to a major investigation.'

Across the room Florrie Marston watched the superbly dressed figure smooth hand-stitched gloves over her tapering fingers. Leonie Elliott saw only profit, only the money to be made, while seeing none of the danger of this business in which they were engaged, one that involved more than the mere selling of gowns. But then, Leonie Elliott shared none of that danger. She had girls sent here from various places, as did the priest. While he knew nothing of what happened to them next, the Elliott woman knew it all; but if anything were to go amiss it would be Florrie Marston paid the piper. It was her salon they were employed in, and it was her sent them on.

'You don't know Sadie Trent, that woman ain't one to give up easily.' Florrie's cultivated speech slipped slightly.

'Neither am I!' Leonie's head jerked upward. 'Do you realise how much could be made with a girl like that? She has a skin like ivory and eyes a man could swim in. There are those would pay a fortune to have her!' Seeing the flicker in the other woman's eyes, Leonie pressed home her advantage. 'Dress her in white satin, trimmed with white tulle threaded with silver, coil that sable hair with silver ribbons, and present her as a bride. The three hundred pounds that last transaction fetched could become six.' Leonie hesitated, letting her words sink in. Florrie Marston wasn't one to let money like that pass her by.

'Six hundred pounds.' It was said more softly

this time. 'Think of it. When will such an opportunity come again?'

Maybe never. Florrie met those brilliant eyes. Money like that could not be refused. 'I think I can arrange something.'

'Make it soon.' Leonie rose with a rustle of her silken skirts. 'Meantime those twins I had sent across from the workhouse in Walsall ... their fair hair should look well against rose velvet.'

'Both of them?' Florrie frowned. 'One of them's a boy!'

'Our customers in the East have a penchant for fair hair.' Leonie crossed to the door before turning to smile at her. 'Some also have a predilection for boys!'

Listening to the door click softly behind her, Florrie felt a twinge of apprehension. White slave trafficking was a risky trade. Touching one hand to her immaculately dressed hair, she drew in a long breath. Going into the main salon, she smiled at the two childish figures holding hands as they practised walking down the centre of the long room.

A risky business indeed, but a profitable one!

It had taken longer than she thought. Deborah glanced at the sky. Already it was deep mauve darkening to purple. She should not have agreed to try on that jacket, or at least should have taken it off sooner, but the woman had been so insistent. Turn this way, now that. Pulling her shawl more tightly about her shoulders, she glanced back the way she had come. To calm Sadie's anxiety she had agreed to come to the salon via Harrison Street, taking the fork into Green Lane. But that had been such a distance, and returning that way would see it dark long before she reached Sadie's house. Crossing the heath would be quicker, and if she ran...

Not giving herself time to think better of it, Deborah hitched up her skirts and set off at a brisk jog, her boots making no sound on the grassy ground.

She had taken to the heath! Sheltered in the angle of a tall building the stocky figure of Abe Turley watched the girl, skirts flying in the breeze, run swiftly along the track towards Elmore Green. But she would not run far. He knew the heath, how its rough ground dragged at the feet. She would tire soon, and when she did he would not be far behind.

He had spotted her in the village and for once she was not with Clay Gilmore. Abe had followed at a distance, careful not to be spotted, then when she had turned into Green Lane he had guessed where she was going; everybody in Elmore knew Sadie Trent sewed for Florrie Marston. He had waited at the fork in the lane. She must come that way whichever route she chose to return.

And she had chosen the heath! A malevolent smile spread slowly across his mouth. Fortune was on his side at last.

Keeping a distance between them he began to follow her, using bushy clumps of gorse as cover. He knew exactly when he would take her!

Ahead Deborah slowed to a walk. It would not be sensible to run as she had the night she had gone for the doctor. To get a stitch out here on the heath was not a pleasant prospect. She would not tell Lizzie or Sadie she had returned by way of the heath. They would worry the less for her deception.

She thought again of wearing that lovely jacket. The silk had felt smooth and cool against her skin. It must be wonderful to dress in such lovely clothes. Lizzie should have clothes like that. She deserved better from life, better than to have been used by a man who obviously did not love her, then left to raise a fatherless child.

Feeling the bite of a stone in her boot Deborah balanced precariously on one foot as she loosed the row of tiny buttons. Removing the boot, she shook it, hearing the chip of stone clink as it fell to the rough trackway. Bending over to replace the boot she heard the crunch of a step behind her. Before she could straighten up a hand was twined savagely in her hair, yanking her back off her feet.

A scream only halfway into her throat died in a gasp as she was thrown hard to the ground, a thousand points of light dancing behind her eyes as the side of her head stuck an outcrop of rock. Then a sharp pain raced through her thigh as a heavy boot kicked it.

'Get up!'

Somewhere far beyond the blackness into which she was spinning the words were barked, harsh and gravelly, a sound redolent with threat. But it held no threat to Deborah, nothing could touch her in this soft dark world.

'I said, get up. You ain't hurt … yet!'

191

The voice came again. Barely conscious, Deborah moaned as she was grabbed by the collar and hauled to her feet.

'I knew I would get you sooner or later. You couldn't always be with that swine Gilmore, there had to come a time when you would be on your own. And I waited for that time, waited for months. Now it be here and you be going to pay.'

Suddenly she was being pulled back, drawn out of that safe comforting blackness, wrenched from its peace. But she did not want to leave, here she could rest…

'Don't go pretending with me. Abe Turley ain't so easily fooled as to think you're knocked out.'

Her head jerked violently back on her neck, Deborah moaned again as a sharp blow landed on her cheek, its stinging pain clearing the last of the darkness from her brain.

'That be more sensible.' Abe Turley shook her hard, bouncing her like a rag doll.

That voice, like stones rubbing together, and that breath, hot and rancid … it was the same voice, the same foul-smelling breath! Recognition lanced like a beam of light into Deborah's mind. It was the same man who had attacked and robbed Lizzie and herself the night they had left Portland House.

Forcing her eyes to focus she stared at the face leering at her from the gathering shadows.

'Arrh, it's me, Abe Turley.' He grinned, seeing the recognition in her eyes.

'But … but you … Clay said you had been taken to the Assizes? That you would go to prison.'

Releasing her abruptly, Abe Turley watched her reel backwards, hitting a boulder so covered with lichen as to be almost invisible against the gorse.

'Then Clay Gilmore be a liar. Abe Turley has seen no inside of a court, and nor will he!'

'I have money. Here, take it.' The beginnings of fear, cold and hard, rippling her nerves, Deborah reached into the pocket of her skirts.

Abe Turley watched the emotion reflected in her face. She was pretty, prettier by far than any wench in Elmore Green.

'The money would have been enough for me at one time.' The grin changed, becoming a lascivious leer. 'Now it ain't! I want more from you than money.' A sharp movement brought one of his hands level with his face, forefinger pointing to a gap where several front teeth were missing. 'I lost these because of you,' he grated, 'and you be going to pay for them.'

Blood oozing warm and wet from the cut above her temple, Deborah brushed at it with her hand, the other clinging to the rock for support.

'How?' she asked. 'How could I be the cause of you losing those teeth?'

'How!' It was a snarl, long and vicious. 'I'll tell you how. Clay Gilmore knocked them out ... and why? I'll tell you that an' all. It was 'cos he took one look at your pretty face and fell for you, fell so hard he wanted to kill the man who touched you. Oh, it weren't your money being taken that made Gilmore beat me senseless. It was the thought of my hands on you. He reckoned you belong to him. But he's reckoned without Abe Turley.'

193

'Please.' The fear mounting inside Deborah turned the word into a sob. 'Please, take the money. It … it's all I have.'

In the gathering gloom, Abe Turley ran his glance slowly over her slender figure and on up to the beautiful, frightened face. And smiled with pure sadistic pleasure.

'That ain't all you have, not by a long way.' He passed the tip of his tongue over flabby lips, leaving them moister than before.

Deborah felt her fear increase until she was fighting panic. Trying desperately to mask it, to prevent her own fear adding to his sense of domination over her she once more held out the coins. If she could get him to take them he might go, leave her alone.

'There … there are five sovereigns.' She bit her lower lip, using the pain to help distract her from the terror that threatened to engulf her. 'Take them and I promise to tell no one. I … I will say I fell and they rolled out of my hand. That I could not find them in the darkness.'

She watched the podgy hand reach forward, the same lascivious smile spread slowly over the wet mouth, and she wanted to scream. But she must not … she must not!

'I intend to take them.' His hand closed over hers, squeezing so hard the coins cut into her palm. 'And I intend to take *you*. Clay Gilmore will not have the woman he has set his cap at. He lost that hope the night he knocked the teeth from my head. You will pay dearly for that, not once or twice, but over and over again!'

Snatching her close to him, his free hand closed

over Deborah's mouth as a scream broke from her. Hoisting her so that only her toes touched the ground, he part carried, part dragged her in the opposite direction. Clawing at the hand clamped over her mouth, she struggled to release his grip, all the time watching the faint lights of Elmore Green dwindle away into the darkness.

Where was he taking her? And what did he intend doing with her? One after the other terrified thoughts ran through her mind. What did he mean, she would pay over and over again? With a feeling of dread she realised that was the one thing in all of this that she understood.

'He should have known...'

Trying desperately to break Abe's hold, Deborah heard the low, devilish laughter he could not suppress.

'...he ought to have guessed. The woman would be the one I'd go for. Take her and I've finished him, finished Clay Gilmore sure as chucking him down a mine shaft ... but he won't prove anything, there'll be nothing left to prove what he will claim. Abe Turley be too clever to leave anything lying around ... too bloody clever for Gilmore!'

As he laughed, Deborah felt his hand drop from her mouth and her feet once more touched the ground.

'Don't scream and don't run. Don't make me kill you here!'

By the light of the rising moon she saw the whites of his eyes flash, the smile with its dark gap among the teeth, and could almost feel the venom in his voice. Speechless now with terror that overwhelmed her, she sank to the ground, turning her face from him and covering her head with her shawl.

Lizzie and Mrs Trent would know something was amiss when she did not return, they would know she would not stay the night with Florrie Marston and would get the police to search for her. Deborah tried to still the fear inside her but as fast as a comforting thought occurred a negative one destroyed it. How long would they wait before raising the alarm? Searches took time, and time was something she did not have.

'Are you thinking Gilmore will find you?'

Abe's hand grabbed the shawl, snatching it away. 'You need not go setting your mind to that. Where I be taking you only the Devil himself would ever find you.'

He reached down, fastening his fingers in the neck of her gown to haul her upright. Despite her cry that pierced the silence of the heath, Deborah heard the tearing of the cloth and saw again the flash of his eyes as they fastened on her breasts.

'Perhaps I won't wait after all.' The tip of his tongue traced his lips again, leaving behind a wetness that glinted in the light of the moon. 'Perhaps I'll…'

But as he reached for her, Deborah's screams drowned out the rest.

'Marmaduke Zebulun Baudric Aurelius Uzziah Burton.' Lizzie laughed softly, stroking a finger tenderly over the fuzzy head of the baby sucking on her breast. 'It would serve you right if I did name you that. It might take away some of your conceit, young man. You already think you are the most important person in the house.'

The silk petticoat she had almost finished sewing resting on her knee, Sadie looked across at the girl sitting nursing her child. Young Lizzie Burton had been called upon to face a great deal of pain in her short years but the good Lord had rewarded her with a child, one who would give her the love that man had promised, only to turn his back. But Sadie Trent would never turn her back; this house would be home to both mother and child for as long as they wanted it, and with heaven's blessing she herself would be long gone to her rest afore they found another.

'What do you think, Grandmother Trent?'

Meeting the other woman's eyes Lizzie smiled.

'Should we give this self-centred fellow a string of names or will that only add to his fanciful ideas?'

Sadie's fingers tightened on the smooth fabric, the same thrill of emotion tingling along every nerve as it had when Lizzie had asked permission for the child to be brought up using that form of address. She had never known the joys and sorrows of motherhood and had long accepted the heartache of knowing no child would call her grandmother, but now God in His mercy had taken that heartache from her.

Smiling at Lizzie, she shook her head.

'I say we give him one more chance.'

Removing the nipple from the baby's mouth Lizzie lifted the tiny body, holding it against her shoulder and gently patting his back.

'There you are, saved by Grandmother Trent.

197

What do you have to say to that?'

A loud burp at that very moment set both women laughing.

Touching her lips to the small face, feeling the soft fluttering breaths against her cheek, Lizzie held her son, the same engulfing love that had swept over her on first holding him sweeping her anew. Closing her eyes, she breathed the warm clean smell of him, wanting only to hold him for ever.

Then, opening her eyes, she cradled the little form in her arms, her voice holding a note of mock reproof.

'Is that how you answer me? You have some apologising to do, my lad, and if you prefer to be just plain Thomas Burton then you had better make a good job of it.'

She held him out for Sadie to take, seeing pleasure sweep into her lined face.

'Plain Thomas?' Sadie beamed. 'He won't never be plain, he already be 'andsome as the day be long. This one will 'ave no trouble charmin' his way through life, an' the wenches will tumble at his feet.'

Just as she had tumbled at that man's!

Lizzie bent over the cradle, hiding the pain that filled her eyes. Not that, dear God, not that, she prayed silently. Don't let my son follow in his father's footsteps.

Chapter Fourteen

The Reverend Philip Travers closed the prayer book then raised his right hand, making the sign of the cross over the open grave.

'In the name of the Father...' he intoned over the quiet sobs of Delia Rawley's mother. Then, the burial service over, he turned back towards the church, the afternoon sun glinting on his white surplice, gilding his brown-gold hair. Standing at the open door he bade a quiet farewell to each of the small group of mourners, giving an extra word of comfort to the grieving mother.

'It is a hard thing to lose a beloved daughter,' he said, touching the woman's gloved hand in a gesture of compassion. 'But she is with the Lord. You must try not to grieve too much. He saw your daughter's suffering and took her into His care.' Glancing at the husband at her side, he added, 'Should your wife need help then the Church is always here.'

Watching them walk away together, the woman leaning heavily on her husband's arm, he turned as Cato Rawley, the last to leave the graveside, approached.

'You too must not grieve, Mr Rawley.' The priest took his hand, shaking it briefly. 'We must all bow to God's will.'

'God or His adversary?'

Cato replaced the black silk hat on his head,

eyes meeting those of the priest.

The musical voice dropped slightly lower but the eyes held Cato's. 'Which do you feel is the stronger, Mr Rawley? Whichever it is, only you have the power to break the bond, yours is the choice.'

For a moment Cato stared into eyes that smiled back at him. Then, in a voice that was almost regretful, he said, 'That is the problem, Father, I no longer have a choice!'

Agnes Ridley listened to the voices on the other side of Cato Rawley's bedroom door. That woman had lost no time in coming here! The entire week that Delia Rawley's body had lain in the house she had called daily, simpering at others who had called to pay their respects, always there, always supporting 'dear Mr Rawley'.

Dear Mr Rawley indeed! Agnes stifled her snort of contempt. He hadn't waited for his wife to grow cold before running back to that whore! She had listened to them talking together, watched them touch each other as they said goodbye. But they had not made love, she would have heard Cato's grunts and that woman's cries. At least he had shown his dead wife that much respect.

But tonight... Agnes glanced at the watch pinned to her blouse. Leonie Elliott had already been here several hours. Was she intending to sleep here?

'Do you think we might...?'

Quiet as they were the words caught Agnes's sharp ears.

'It is rather soon, my love.'

'What difference can it make now?'

Agnes stiffened, hearing the thickness of desire in Cato's reply. He had hardly looked in her direction since receiving the news of his wife's collapse, hardly spoken a word except to give her orders. True, she had not expected him to ask her into his bed, and that no longer mattered, but this ... bringing that woman here threatened what was Agnes Ridley's and *that* mattered.

'God, but I want you so much! God help me, I want you!'

The soft laugh that followed Cato's words preceded a silence that tormented Agnes. The more he made love to Leonie Elliott, the stronger the hold she would have on him.

No longer able to bear the thought she crept to the door bending to place one eye to the keyhole.

It was almost as if they had purposely placed themselves in her view. Agnes watched the other woman's hands slowly peel the clothes from Cato. First the jacket, then the waistcoat and trousers, finally the underclothing; and all the time she never dropped her gaze from his. Glued to the keyhole, Agnes swallowed the bile that rose in her throat as Cato drew the woman close, his lips pressing hard against that red smiling mouth. Then, eyes still locked with hers, he loosed the buttons of her gown, released the straps of a lace chemise, slid slowly to his knees, pulling silken petticoats with him.

Agnes watched his arms reach upward, reach for the naked body standing tauntingly over him, watched it sink slowly to the floor, twining itself close into the other.

A breath that was long and slow filled Agnes's lungs as she straightened up, a grim smile settling itself on her thin mouth, her eyes ice hard.

Let Cato Rawley have his moment. She could afford to give him that; but it was the last he would have. Tomorrow there would be no Leonie Elliott in his life. No woman other than Agnes Ridley!

Where could she be? Deborah turned her head, trying to see into the darkness that folded about her like a velvet cloak. Where had Abe Turley brought her? The cloth tied about her mouth holding in her frightened sobs, she tried to think. She had already been bound hand and foot when she regained consciousness, Abe Turley bending over her, the stench of his breath foul in her face. She had tried asking where it was he had dragged her but he had only laughed.

'Where nobody will think to look,' he had sniggered, 'not even clever Mr bloody Gilmore! They won't look here 'cos nobody remembers this place, they've all forgotten about it except me. But Abe Turley don't forget nothing, especially a beating.'

'But that wasn't my fault,' Deborah had tried protesting. 'I didn't ask Clay to do that to you.'

He had rounded on her then, eyes flashing in the light that trickled through a broken window, one finger jabbing at the gap where his teeth were missing.

'Oh, no, it wasn't *your* fault. My losing these was none of *your* doing. *You* didn't ask Gilmore to give me a hiding! But then, you didn't have to, did you? You only flutter your pretty eyelashes to get him to do it.'

She had turned her head away, trying to remove the hot rancid breath from her nostrils.

'I didn't tell him who it was robbed Lizzie and myself. How could I? I didn't know your name.'

'You didn't need to!' He had snatched her head sharply back, bringing his face closer to it. 'You had only to describe the man for Gilmore to guess who it was. And you did describe him, didn't you?' Her chin grasped in his hand, he had shaken her head, voice rising with his anger. 'Didn't you … didn't you?'

'Yes, yes.' The words were shaken from her on a sob. 'But I didn't mean for you to be harmed. I never thought Clay would…'

'You never thought!'

He had swung away then and Deborah had held her breath, willing him to leave, but he had stood with his back turned to her, stocky frame silhouetted in the pallid stream of moonlight filtering through the darkness, and when he spoke again his gravelly voice was doubly menacing.

'It would have been better for you if you had. Better to have kept your mouth shut! But it's too late for that now, the damage be done. All that remains for you to pay.'

He had heard the frightened intake of her breath and turned, staring at her intently.

'That's right, Miss Hammond, payment. And you be about to make it!'

He had stepped towards her then, his frame made heavier, more threatening by the gloom. She had tried to draw away, pressing herself back from his outstretched hand, but the chair to which she was tied merely scraped on the bare floor.

His hand had fastened on the dress already torn when he had hauled her to her feet on the heath. Now he snatched at it again, ripping it to the waist.

'Shh!' He laughed softly as a scream broke from her. 'We don't want to frighten the rats, do we?'

Deborah trembled, remembered how his podgy fingers had twisted around the straps of her bodice, the leer on his face as he ripped them away.

Almost sick with fear and shame she tried to erase the rest of it from her mind, but memory burned like a torch in her brain.

'Nice.' The word had been thick in his throat and the laugh like no other she had ever heard as she tried to twist away from the hand he trailed down her throat. 'Very nice.' It had moved to her breasts, stroking first one and then the other.

Pressing her lids tight over her eyes, Deborah tried to shut out the horror, but the picture remained, stark and vivid in her brain, and still that voice, harsh as gravel churning on gravel, invaded her ears.

'Has Clay Gilmore stroked these or is Abe Turley the first?'

It had sickened her then as it sickened her now.

'Am I to be the first to taste the other delights you have? The ones Gilmore hoped to claim?'

He had laughed then, throwing back his head, delighted with the torment he was inflicting on her; and there had been no way to shut out the coarseness of his words, no way to escape the vileness of what he said.

'Did you want him to be the first?'

He had gone on, drawing a kind of pleasure from her sobs. 'Did you want it be him took the virginity from you? Well, that be too bad, 'cos it will be me, Abe Turley. It will be me you will lie under, my flesh that will drive into you, and I will do it time and again, do it 'til you scream for me to stop. And then...'

He had straightened abruptly, hand falling away from her.

'But not yet. We must not have everything at once. "Keep a little for later" my mother tells me, and she's always right. I have an errand to run first but don't fret, I will be back.'

Then he had taken a cloth from his pocket, tying it about her mouth with a savagery that had the flesh stretched painfully. And he had gone.

But for how long? Deborah glanced at the scrap of a window. It was still dark, but then it could not really be so long since she had left the salon. It could only have been minutes before... She shuddered then caught her breath as a rustling sound came from a corner.

Rats! She shuddered again. Abe Turley had said not to disturb the rats!

Breath trembling in her lungs, she forced herself to listen. It was her imagination. Holding her breath, tears burning her eyes, she told herself it must be her imagination.

Her breathing steadying when the sound did not recur, she glanced again at the dull grey light beyond the tiny window. She had left the salon a little after six. She remembered hearing the soft chime of a clock from the mantelpiece in the room where she had modelled the jacket. It would have been no more than a quarter of an hour before Turley seized her, but how long to bring her to this place, and how long had she been unconscious?

There was no way of telling. Deborah felt sick with fear. Would those at the house already have alerted the constable? Had he set a search in motion? Would they find her before Turley returned? Would they find her before it was too late?

Abe Turley waited in the house adjoining the salon. This was where Florrie Marston lived, and where she kept the goods due for transport. Abe grinned to himself. She did not like to hear them spoken of in any other way. The girls who accompanied her fancy frocks and never one returning, they could only be referred to as consignments.

Consignments, pah! Where had Marston learned such fancy words? And the Salon de Fleur Masson! Where had that one come from? The woman had scarcely ever left Bloxwich or so his mother reckoned. But wherever the phoney accent and the fancy words had sprung from they helped proved her with an income to match, one which he intended having a larger share in.

His grin widening at the thought, he glanced about the room. Catching his reflection in a mahogany-framed oval mirror above the fireplace and seeing the space where once four teeth had been, the grin faded swiftly.

Gilmore! That bastard! Abe swore vehemently under his breath. He must have felt so pleased with himself, so righteous; thought he'd settled the score for the wench when he'd delivered that beating. Well, the score was *not* settled, but it would be soon, when Abe Turley took the wench...

Instantly his mind flashed back to the scene of an hour ago. She'd smelled so clean and fresh, like a morning in summer. There was no tang of the coal banks or the forge about her. It had been like twining his fingers in silk instead of hair, then the touch of her breasts, soft and smooth as velvet. The tip of his tongue flicked over his lips. God, he was going to enjoy having her!

Florrie Marston closed the door firmly behind her, waiting a moment before she spoke. When she did the glance she fastened on Abe Turley was bright with irritation.

'You took your time,' she snapped. 'Where the hell 'ave you been?'

The picture in his mind rapidly disappearing, Abe glanced at the woman facing him, her mouth tight with anger. Whatever had happened to the phoney accent? Meeting her stare, his own was insolent.

'Minding my own business. Same as you should do, Florrie.'

Her lips becoming so tight they thinned to invisibility, her eyes cold, she glanced quickly back at the door.

'How many times have I told you not to use that name!' she hissed.

'Why not?' He sauntered to the fireplace. Standing with his back to the fire, his legs set confidently apart, he smirked. 'That be the name you were given.'

'That don't allow you to use it.' The answer cracked back. 'You be too bloody cocky by 'alf, Abe Turley. But, remember. Sow enough thistles and one day you'll get pricked!'

'Be that a threat of some sort?'

Florrie looked at the man standing before her fireplace, for all the world as though he owned the house. He had been getting above himself lately. Abe Turley felt his foot on the ladder and was eager to climb it. Well, let him! The higher he climbed, the further he would fall. And she would push him ... hard!

'Call it advice,' she answered grimly. 'But don't expect too much of the same.'

The flush of triumph rode high in his veins. He had one woman where he wanted her, it was time he did something about this one. Florrie Marston should be made aware of just who she was dealing with. Abe Turley was no workhouse brat!

'It ain't advice I need from you, Florrie.' The smirk hardened to a sneer as he emphasised her name. 'It be a bigger share of the takings.'

She had warned him, advised him to listen to her warning but it was like talking to a brick wall. This was only the beginning, he would go on demanding if once she gave in to his greed. She had known that sooner or later he would have to be replaced. It had better be soon. Men like Turley were two a penny, finding another would be no problem, nor would finding one who would do away with him. But for the present she needed him.

'How much is a bigger share?' She walked to a safe set against the wall.

Abe's swollen confidence took a further leap. This had been easier than he thought. He glanced at the key she drew from her pocket. Should he ask for five pounds … or ten?

Florrie watched the greed flicker across the plump features. 'Well?' she asked again. 'How much is a bigger share?'

'Half … half as much again.'

'That would be thirty pounds.' Florrie twisted the key in her fingers. 'That's a lot of money to pay for a couple of hours' work.'

'Work you can't get no other to do. Work you can *trust* no other to do!'

She nodded but made no move to fit the key into the lock. 'You have been trustworthy, but then the money you are paid makes keeping your mouth shut well worth the effort.'

'It did … 'til now.' The gap between his upper teeth showed black as he grinned. 'But like everything else these days, the price of silence has just gone up.'

'Thirty pounds?'

Watching her lips purse Abe felt a twinge of doubt but as quickly it was gone. Florrie Marston couldn't run her little racket without him, and her could hardly chuck him aside for one word from him and it would all be over.

'I ain't doing the job for no less. Thirty quid or I'm off. And remember, that narrow boat won't hang about long after sun up.'

'I wasn't thinking of the thirty pounds.' Florrie allowed her features to relax, the ice to melt from her eyes. 'I was thinking it could be a hundred.'

''Undred!' Abe swallowed hard, his eyes

widening. 'Do you mean … a 'undred pounds?'

'That's exactly what I mean. But you have to earn it first.'

Abe shuffled his feet together, the mention of such a sum overriding everything else.

'The payment is high because this job will be slightly different.' Florrie slipped the key into the lock, turned it and swung the heavy door aside. Taking out a large envelope, she turned to face Abe. Her fingers ruffling the white five-pound notes she drew from it, she watched his eyes play over the money. 'Of course, you might not wish to do it.'

'What … do what?'

Florrie suppressed a smile, holding it beneath the surface. For half that money Abe Turley would sell his own soul.

'I have received an order for something special.' She ruffled the notes again. 'I have seen what I think would suit the client very well, but getting hold of it might be a little difficult.'

Abe's eyes followed the paper moving between the woman's fingers. Weren't nothing too difficult if it paid a hundred pounds!

Letting silence hang between them for fully half a minute, Florrie tapped the wad of notes against her finger tips. 'The commodity I have been requested is here in Bloxwich. In Elmore Green to be precise.'

'Then what be the difficulty?' he asked, his glance momentarily leaving the money.

There would be none now he had seen the reward on offer. Florrie pushed aside her own satisfaction. There would be time to gloat later, once the job was done.

'The difficulty is Sadie Trent.'

Abe's brow wrinkled into a puzzled frown as Florrie went on.

'What we need to fill our client's request is in Sadie Trent's house. A certain pretty, dark-haired...'

'Deborah Hammond,' he interrupted. 'You mean Deborah Hammond.'

'You know the wench?' Florrie's carefully cultivated mode of speech slipped again.

'We've met,' he answered.

Florrie watched the smile spread over his face. This might prove less of a problem than she had thought.

'Do you think you could get hold of her, bring her here to this house? Unseen, of course.'

His eyes going once more to the wad of notes, Abe held out his hand. 'The wench be as good as here. I've got her already!'

Counting out ten of the notes, Florrie placed them in the grubby outstretched palm.

'Fifty now,' she said as he looked sharply at her, 'the other fifty when the job's done.'

'And the money for the other little job, the delivery I was to make tonight? That be over and above the price of fetching you that wench.'

'Agreed.' Slipping six more notes free of the envelope, she added them to those in his palm. Why argue with him? This would be the last money he would see from her. In fact, it could well be the last he would ever see. Florrie Marston was not partial to extortion ... not unless she was the one doing it!

Chapter Fifteen

From the furthermost corner of her dark prison the rustling came again. The cloth about Deborah's mouth stifling her sobs, her breath escaped in short terrified spurts from nostrils dilated with fear. She had fought desperately not to give way to sheer terror, to try to think past the wall of panic that kept closing around her, tell herself that help would come soon and this horror would all be over.

The rustling came again, the blackness carrying it closer. Deborah felt the scream rise from the deepest part of her but the sound did not puncture the silence.

What if he did not mean to come back? What if he intended to leave her here? And where was here? Was it really a place only he knew about, a place no one else might ever find?

Again that quiet rustling from the shadows, sending slivers of ice through every vein, one terror chasing another from her mind. The sound must be rats ... it had to be! She shuddered at the thought of the creatures climbing over her, nibbling fingers and toes.

Oh, God, let him come back! The prayer blazed in her brain. Anything was better than the sheer cold terror of being left bound and gagged to be eaten by rats.

Her mind paralysed by a nightmare of fear,

drowning beneath wave after wave of it, the sound beyond the rustling registered. Not until the stinging slap of a palm against her cheek did Deborah realise the presence of the figure beside her.

'Don't leave me again, please, don't leave me here!'

Her cries falling hysterically from lips almost frozen with panic, Deborah's head jerked sideways as a second blow landed hard on her face. It dragged her back from the edge of the chasm.

'You mean, you don't like my little hideaway?' Bending over her, Abe Turley laughed. 'You ain't happy here? But I thought you would enjoy it, enjoy sharing the place with the rats. So you didn't? Now that's a shame 'cos this be where you be going to stay.'

'No!' Deborah lifted her head, beseeching him. 'No, you can't! You can't keep me here!'

'Can't?' He took a step backward. 'Abe Turley can do anything he wants.'

'Please!' Deborah was abject now, the terror of the past few hours only too vivid in her mind. 'Please, please, let me go.'

'Now that be a better way to ask. When little girls say please then they often gets what they want. Especially when they be as attractive as you.'

He bent over her once more, his hand pushing aside her torn bodice, closing upon the softness of her breast. Instinctively she stiffened but forced herself not to cry out. To antagonise him would only cause him to strike her again, or even

213

worse leave her alone in this place of horror. Just above her his breath came in shallow excited gasps that washed hot and sour over her face, but still she dared not shrink away.

He could take her now. In the darkness Abe Turley felt the intoxication of conquest mix with the fervid throb of passion. He could take what he wanted, what he had promised himself ever since Clay Gilmore had knocked out his teeth. The fingers closed around the soft mound of flesh and tightened, squeezing painfully as the flame glowing inside him burned brighter. He could take her now and no one would know. But Florrie Marston would. The thought dampening the fire, he dropped his hand. It would be the first thing she would ask and then he could kiss goodbye to the other fifty pounds. Florrie's clients didn't buy used goods.

But he had promised himself, gone to sleep nights thinking of how he would pleasure himself, how he would laugh seeing Gilmore's face when he learned the truth. Still, fifty pounds was fifty pounds. Reaching into his jacket pocket, he fingered the neatly folded notes. He could buy himself plenty of wenches for that much money. And Gilmore? Abe would still have the laugh on him!

Dropping to his haunches, he untied the rope from about Deborah's ankles. What did it matter which man took the wench, just so long as it wasn't Gilmore?

Drawing away as she felt the gag touch her face, Deborah sobbed. 'Please … please, I won't scream. Please don't tie my mouth again.'

Hesitating for a second, Abe thrust the neck cloth into his pocket. 'It don't matter,' he laughed. 'Where you be going nobody will pay any heed.'

'I can't think what be keeping the wench. I tell you, Clay lad, I be gettin' fair moithered and I know young Lizzie be worrying an' all. It ain't like Deborah to take so long running an errand.'

Sadie Trent's face showed the concern that had gradually been building in her since early evening.

'It takes time to walk back from that place. Following the road is a lot further than cutting across the heath.'

'Arrh, lad, it is.' Sadie looked at the man she knew had really called to see Deborah. 'But even given that, her should have been home afore now.'

'What time did you say she ought to have left that shop?'

'Must be a good three hours since.' Sadie glanced at the cheap clock on the mantel. 'Time enough to have walked back twice over, even following the road.'

'You think she might have taken to the heath?'

Sadie nodded, worry tightening her mouth. 'Arrh, I do that, and if her has…'

'If she has then I will find her. Don't worry, Sadie. She's probably coming up the street right now.'

'That be what Lizzie's been saying the last hour.' Sadie glanced at the girl laying her sleeping baby in the cradle set alongside the hearth. 'But

215

there's been neither sight nor sign of her. I know you both think I be worrying for nothing but I can't help but feel there be summat wrong!'

'I'll go now.' Clay turned, reaching for the latch, but was stopped by Lizzie's call.

'Wait, Clay! Wait for me. I'm coming with you.'

'No, Lizzie.' He caught her hand as she reached for her shawl.

'But I must. Deborah is my friend, I have to help look for her.'

'No.' His smile was gentle but his voice was firm. 'You have to stay with the baby.'

'But Deborah will think...'

'She will think what Sadie and I think. The baby must be your prime concern. She will know you wanted to go looking for her, Lizzie, and will think none the less of you for staying here.'

'You'll call back here?'

Meeting her troubled look, he smiled. 'I'll call back, Sadie. And I'll have Deborah with me.'

Abe had marched her across the heath, the occasional jab of his hand in her back sending her stumbling over the rough ground. But now they were back in the street she had left some hours ago. Deborah glanced to either side of her, recognising buildings she had passed that afternoon, their windows shuttered now against the night. Why had he brought her back here? Why had he not taken her to Elmore Green?

That was the shop where she had delivered the jacket, the Salon de Fleur Masson. Deborah did not need to read the tastefully painted lettering, recognising the bow-fronted windows that flanked each side of an imposing door. Was that where Abe Turley was taking her? But his hand once more shoving her forward they passed on, Abe pulling her roughly into a narrow passage that ran between two high buildings further along the street.

'Where are we going ... why have you brought me here?' she at last found the courage to ask.

Catching the rope still fastened about her wrists, he jerked savagely, pulling her almost off her feet.

'You don't ask anything!' he grated as her head bounced against his chest. 'And when we get inside, you say nothing about me except that I found you on the heath.' He twisted the rope, sending it biting into her flesh. 'You understand? Say one word of what happened and I will find you again. Only next time I'll kill you.'

Loosing the cord, he held it for a few seconds still twisted about her wrists. Over her shoulder, his voice was low and vicious.

'Don't think Gilmore will prevent me getting you. He didn't prevent it this time, did he? And he won't next. And you ... you will never know where I'll be waiting, nor if it will be just you I might take it out on. After all, that Lizzie be a pretty eyeful, not to mention her babby.'

'You wouldn't!'

Close to her ear his laughter was quiet and evil. 'Try it for yourself. All you have to do is open your mouth.'

Pulling the cord free, deliberately dragging it against her skin, he shoved her forward again, his hand between her shoulder blades.

Stumbling over uneven cobbles, Deborah walked on, the pain of her chafed wrists forgotten as a new, more insidious fear chilled her heart.

Stopping before a doorway set deep into the brickwork of a building flanked by outhouses, Abe knocked, a quiet surreptitious twice repeated sound.

'Remember.' His hand caught Deborah's hair, snatching her head back, his mouth so close against her cheek she could almost taste his rancid breath. 'Say nothing of this. Not if you want that kid to see its first birthday!'

Stepping to her side as the door opened he took her arm, nodding to a middle-aged woman in a white apron tied over a black gown.

'Florrie?'

The woman nodded, closing the door as they stepped inside.

'You know your own way, Abe Turley.'

Deborah glanced at the woman, her eyes signalling a plea for help, but was met by silence.

Holding fast to her arm, Abe propelled her along a dimly lit passage. Then, as they halted before yet another door, he pulled her close, one hand fumbling beneath the shawl and squeezing at her breast. His voice grated harshly.

'Lizzie will like this...'

His fingers tightened as she turned to look at him. 'That's right. I was telling you a lie. You see, it don't matter whether you tells Florrie Marston what happened or whether you don't. So long as your cherry ain't been picked she don't mind the fruit being handled. This way I get the prize both times. I get paid for you and then I get that little

218

friend of yours.'

The door opened abruptly, and Deborah was thrust inside a warm well-lit room, a glowing fire at one end of it.

'Miss Hammond … Deborah!' Florrie Marston was all concern. 'What on earth has happened?'

Glancing at Turley as she took Deborah's other arm, she added, 'Help me get her to the fire.'

Lowering her into a chair, she spoke to him over Deborah's bent head. 'What happened, can you tell me?'

'She ain't said much.' His eyes followed the slight inclination of the woman's head to where an envelope lay on a walnut bureau. 'Probably shock. She must have been on the heath some time. Most likely she tumbled, the ground be pitted with holes. Lucky she didn't fall down one of them old shafts. That way she would never have been found.'

'Yes, my dear.' Florrie patted her cold hands, ignoring the weals circling Deborah's wrists like scarlet bracelets. 'You have been very lucky. The heath can be so treacherous in the dark.'

'I didn't fall.' Lifting her head, Deborah threw a scalding glance at Turley and saw him slip an envelope into his pocket. 'That man attacked me!'

'Attacked you?' Florrie exclaimed on a small laugh. 'Oh, my dear, being lost in the darkness has you imagining things. Mr Turley did not attack you, he only helped you.'

'Does this look like he helped me!' Fear giving way to anger, Deborah held up both hands, the marks showing clearly on her wrists.

'I found her all tangled up in a bush. Broom be a strong plant and it was twisted tight round her hands and feet. It were all I could do to snap it.'

'There, you see.' The voice was kept deliberately soothing but its effect was lost on Deborah.

She twisted around in her chair as Abe spoke, her answer filled with loathing. 'He's lying. He attacked me and took me to a place where he left me bound and gagged...'

Florrie's laughter took on a sharper edge. 'You are in shock, my dear, just as Mr Turley has said. After you have rested you will see things more clearly.'

'I don't want to rest. I must go back to the house, they'll be wondering where I am.'

'Certainly you must return.' Florrie pulled on a bell rope beside the bureau. 'But not until you are cleaned up. Just look at your clothes! They're caked in dust and your poor foot is bleeding. You must have lost a boot when you fell. A warm bath, some clean clothes and a hot meal, Sadie Trent would not forgive me if I did less. Meantime I will send word that you are here and quite safe.'

'But why bring me here at all?' Deborah turned her glance to Florrie. 'Why did he not take me to Mrs Trent's house if he only intended to help me?'

''Twas nearer this place than Sadie's.' Abe Turley's reply was prompt. 'Made sense to bring her here. I didn't know whether it were just shock or if maybe her was hurt some other way.'

'You did the right thing, Mr Turley, it is better this way. It would be a shock to poor Mrs Trent seeing Deborah arrive home looking like this. You can leave her with me now, but perhaps you will call at the house on your way home and tell them that all is well?'

'No. He cannot be trusted. He will not tell Sadie where I am.'

Jumping to her feet, Deborah swayed dizzily, missing the sideways jerk of Florrie Marston's head that told Turley to leave, hearing only her request that a bath and a meal be made ready at once.

'Everything will be all right, my dear,' Florrie soothed her later as the middle-aged serving woman reappeared to say the bath was waiting.

'I tell you, I did not fall!'

'If you say so, Deborah, then of course I believe you. Go with Martha now and when you are finished bathing we will discuss this thoroughly. Tomorrow, if you wish, we will inform the constable of your experience.'

Turning to the woman who had answered her summons, Florrie went on: 'Some hot chocolate for Miss Hammond, please, Martha, and I think a little extra sugar. I believe it is very good for shock.'

Waiting until the door had closed behind them, Florrie took a key from her pocket, the same key she had used on the safe when paying off Abe Turley. It was a pity she had been obliged to send those twins earlier tonight but they had to be at the dock by Friday to be on the packet steamer for the East. Yes, it was a pity. She twisted the key between her fingers. Deborah Hammond was destined for the same place. A few hours earlier and she could have gone along as part of the same cargo. That way it would not have been necessary to pay for transport twice. But then Florrie Marston would not lose on the deal, it would all be added to Deborah's selling price.

Bending down, she inserted the key in the lock, a smile hovering about her lips. Drawing out a small blue glass bottle, she straightened up. Safes were useful for guarding more than money.

The bottle in her pocket, she kicked the door closed as the maid returned with a jug and a cup on a tray.

Waiting until she was alone once more Florrie withdrew the bottle, holding it up, admiring the depth of its colour as light from the gasoline danced through it.

Beautiful as a jewel. She laughed softly. Beauty to catch a beauty, one jewel to capture another.

Twisting out the cork, she held the bottle to her nostrils, then, her smile deepening, tipped several drops of colourless liquid into the cup. By the time this particular beauty awoke she would be well on her way to a new life. A life Sadie Trent could not even dream of!

Eyesight made keener by years of working in the kind of darkness contained only in the bowels of the earth, Clay Gilmore searched the inky space that stretched around and beyond him. Overhead the moon had withdrawn behind a sea of leaden cloud, denying the heath her soft luminous glow.

Standing still, he listened but the only sound to come from the stillness was that of his own breathing. He had searched and searched again every step of the path that led across the heath. Surely Deborah would not have been fool enough to leave its safety? Inside, the fear he had refused to recognise stirred again. Deborah would not have left the path willingly, but should she have been forced...!

Try as he might to dismiss the thought, still it persisted. And the more it hammered in his brain, the louder came the after thought. Abe Turley? Had he met Deborah on her way home from that shop? Was his hand at work somewhere in all of this?

But would he dare? The man was a coward. Would he risk accosting Deborah given the beating he had already taken and the worse one such a move would bring?

In the distance an owl hooted, its cry chilling in the blackness. Yes, Turley was a coward but he was even more of a bully. He would want revenge for that hiding, but he would take it from the weakest, the least able to fight back. He would take his revenge on a woman!

And if he had and that woman was Deborah Hammond, where would Turley take her? He could hardly take her to his own home, his mother's house. Yet it had to be somewhere fairly near. Turley could not carry a full-grown woman very far and Deborah would not go easily.

Clay would go on as far as Blakenhall, go to Florrie Marston's salon, ask what time Deborah had left. Then he would look for Turley.

Stepping forward, he felt his foot strike something on the path and glanced down at the ground just as the moon emerged, bathing everything in its sharp yellow light. Bending, he caught his breath. His foot had struck a boot. A small side button boot. A woman's boot!

Carrying it with him Clay walked on, eyes searching as carefully as before, ears attuned to the silence. But his mind whirled in a wild dance of speculation and thoughts of revenge.

Reaching the salon he stared at its darkened windows. He had sometimes walked here with Sadie Trent. As a boy he had carried her parcels of sewing for a lollipop or two ounces of Tigs Herbal sweets. Sadie had laughed once when he had said it must be lovely living in a house so big it had two windows. *Florrie don't live in there.* And Sadie had pointed to the shop then to the smaller building adjoining it. *Florrie lives there.*

Following the street, Clay turned into the short narrow alley leading to the rear of the buildings. He knocked loudly on the door he guessed to belong to a scullery or kitchen.

'I want to see Florrie Marston,' he said as the door opened.

A lamp in her hand, the middle-aged servant peered nervously into the gloom.

'Madame Fleur ain't...'

'Not Madame Fleur!' Clay snapped. 'I want to see Florrie Marston!'

Holding the lamp higher, its yellow light lending a saffron hue to her white apron, the maid looked keenly at the face of the tall man then at the woman's boot in his hand.

'It be young Gilmore, don't it? Cissie Gilmore's lad. I remembers you coming 'ere with Sadie Trent.'

'Yes, it's me, Mrs Vines,' Clay answered, glancing over her shoulder into the kitchen.

'How is Sadie? I heard as her met with some sort of accident.'

'A twisted ankle, but she's mending nicely.'

'Tell her Martha Vines be asking after her, lad; tell her I'll be across to see her soon.' The woman seemed to withdraw into herself then, voice falling to a mutter. 'It be time I went back to the Green. I've been here too long, seen too much…'

Clay shifted his feet impatiently as the woman's voice dropped lower and lower. He did not want to be rude but every moment he stood here could mean more danger for Deborah.

'Mrs Vines.' He spoke as gently as the worry inside him allowed. 'Mrs Vines, I have to speak to Mrs Marston.'

'Her be upstairs, lad. I don't know if her will see you. But come you in.' She stepped back, leaving the way clear. 'I'll ask.'

Listening to the maid's message, Florrie Marston's mind moved in quick circles. Clay Gilmore could only be here for one thing. He wanted to enquire after Deborah Hammond. To refuse to see him would only give rise to speculation that might rebound on her. Yes, wiser to speak to him. After all, there was no way he could link the girl to the salon. She had delivered a jacket then left. It was as simple as that. Nodding permission for him to be brought up, Florrie glanced rapidly about the room. There was no sign the girl had been here, and as for Martha and the others, they would say nothing. Jobs were hard to get anywhere in Bloxwich, harder still in the Blakenhall part of it, and here at the Salon de Masson it was easy to get rid of people who didn't know when to curb their tongue.

Deborah Hammond was in the little back room at the top of the house but as far as Clay Gilmore was concerned it might as well be the moon! Tomorrow the girl would be gone, there would be no more Deborah Hammond, but there would be more, other girls who would mysteriously vanish into the silence of the heath. They would leave no trace and no one would search for them. There would be a hue and cry about the one upstairs but the hunt would soon die away. The gin pits had taken too many in the past, too many for folk to suspect otherwise.

Settling herself into a beautiful brocade-covered chair, Florrie smiled. Let Clay Gilmore ask his questions. He would return to Elmore Green the same as he had left it ... none the wiser.

Chapter Sixteen

In her own comfortable sitting room Agnes Ridley sat staring at a small rectangular piece of card. It was yellow with age, the untidy writing on it faded to an insipid brown.

She had kept it for almost eighteen years and in all that time had never for a moment forgotten it. Tucked away in a cardboard box it had stayed with her, always near, always at hand; since coming to Portland House it had remained in her wardrobe, a constant source of reassurance. So long as she had that card, she had everything.

The wait had proved longer than she had hoped on first coming here but now it was over. Delia Rawley was dead and in her grave, and although Cato's remarrying so soon afterwards might cause a few eyebrows to be raised, they would be lowered again in time.

Agnes glanced again at the card. She had once thought it would not be necessary to use it, that Cato Rawley was in love with her, needing her almost nightly to feed the fire of that love. But her thoughts had proved wrong. The passion had been simply of lust. Any woman would have served Cato Rawley's needs and probably had done before. Agnes would have lived with that ... could have lived with that. But then Leonie Elliott had come.

From that moment he had changed. He no

longer wanted Agnes. Leonie Elliott satisfied him in every way. At the beginning Agnes had thought it a passing fancy; a new face, a pretty woman paying him attention, flattery turning his head. He was not the first man to be dazzled by such as Leonie. But as the months passed it became ever more obvious that what Cato Rawley felt for the golden-haired beauty was not mere infatuation. Maybe it was not love, Agnes turned her glance to the fire, but it was not enough to keep him from her!

They were playing the same game, she and Leonie Elliott, a game in which there could be only one winner, and Agnes Ridley did not intend to lose now. She had put too much into this to stand by while that woman took what was rightfully hers.

Cato had sent for her less and less, spending more and more of his evenings with his new-found paramour until he hardly recognised the fact that Agnes Ridley was alive. But it was a fact he was about to re-learn.

Pushing herself to her feet, Agnes stood for a moment, staring once more at the card. Then she scooped it up and returned it to the cardboard box, then the shelf of the cupboard that served as her wardrobe. It would be there for her, her insurance.

Leaving her room, she listened to the quiet house. Cato had left after luncheon and the only other person around was the laundry woman who never went further than the wash house or the scullery where she ironed. Agnes smiled. No, she would not be disturbed.

Nevertheless her tread was light as she went towards the room where for so long she had nursed Delia. Closing the door softly behind her, she glanced around at the ornate bed and heavy furniture. It had not been to her dead mistress's taste, she had sometimes said as much, but only to her housekeeper-nurse. Delia would never bother her husband by asking for new, never risk going against his wishes. But like so much else in Portland House, that was set to change.

Going to the tall wardrobes, Agnes flung the doors wide open, her gaze drinking in the colours of the beautiful gowns hanging inside. She would wear them all in turn. She ran her hands along the line of them, the pleasure of voile and lace, of taffeta and watered silk, bringing a wave of headiness.

Mauve! It was not every woman's colour but it had always suited Agnes. The mauve silk had been the last gown to be made for Delia Rawley. Agnes would wear that on her wedding day.

Taking it from its hanger she held it against her, admiring the way it picked up the colour in her eyes. Laying it aside, she loosed her hair, feeling it drop heavily to her shoulders. Taking up brush and pins, she dressed it high on her head, following the fashion set by the new queen. Smiling at the result, she reached for lip rouge and face powder. Delia Rawley had never used cosmetics. Agnes watched the dramatic change wrought in her own appearance. Perhaps Delia ought to have done.

Stepping out of her plain brown dress and cotton petticoats, she slipped into silk trimmed

229

with several layers of fine Brussels lace, the touch of it against her skin causing her to sigh deeply with pleasure. Reaching for the dress next she slid into it, fastening minute rock crystal buttons on sleeves and bodice.

Gazing at her reflection Agnes felt a huge sense of satisfaction. She had been an attractive woman in her youth, she was an attractive woman still. Only one thing remained to make the picture perfect.

Pulling open the drawer that held the mistress's jewel box, she took it out. The necklace of square-cut amethysts would set the seal on her finery.

Opening the box she stared. Slowly, surprise turned to anger then anger to fury.

The box that held the amethysts, held all of Delia Rawley's jewels, was empty!

'Florrie Marston says she left around six-thirty. She said she was not happy with the thought of Deborah coming back to Elmore Green alone, that darkness would have fallen before she was halfway back; said she offered her a place for the night but Deborah refused, insisting on coming home.'

Home! Sadie Trent felt the word pierce her like a knife. How many years had she longed for some voice other than her own to call this house home.

'You went by way of the heath?' It was Lizzie who asked the question.

'And back the same way,' Clay confirmed.

'Then could her have come by way of Green Lane after all? Perhaps her did and stopped off somewheres,' Sadie suggested.

Clay saw the hope in the older woman's eyes and could not bring himself to destroy it. Deborah Hammond had not been returning by way of the road but he would not say as much, nor would he show them the boot he had found on the heath. The fear and strain so evident on both faces said they were already suffering enough.

'That's what she must have done.' He forced a smile. 'You know how it is when you women start to talk, you have no mind for the time. Deborah is likely canting to somebody and has forgotten to watch the clock.'

That weren't Deborah Hammond! But Sadie kept the words inside her. True, she had not known the wench a lifetime, but she knew her well enough to know that cantin' wasn't her style. Wherever her was right now, or whoever it was her were with, the reason for it was not conversation.

'Arrh lad, you be right, the wench be cantin'.' Sadie nodded as she forced the lie from her lips.

'I'll go along Green Lane now.' With a brief smile to Lizzie, he turned for the door.

'Thanks, lad.' Sadie's voice could not quite hide the tremor she tried hard to quash. 'And tell her when you catches up with her, her'll have a fair tongue-bashing from me when you bring her back to this house.'

'It it's all the same to you, Sadie, if Deborah is to have a scolding then I won't be the one to tell her.'

Catching his glance Sadie read in it sympathy

231

for herself and Lizzie, but beneath the apparently flippant answer she recognised something deeper and more painful. Clay Gilmore was going through a hell of his own.

Following him to the door, Lizzie touched his arm. Unable to hide her own feelings, worry was raw in her eyes.

'Find her, Clay,' she whispered. 'Please find her.'

'I will not return to Elmore Green with that man!'

Deborah looked at the slightly plump figure of Florrie Marston, elegantly dressed in jade green velvet, brown hair carefully highlighted with henna piled expertly on the crown of her head, lip rouge touched to mouth and cheeks in a travesty of her earlier beauty.

'Of course you will not, Mr Turley has already left.'

Florrie Marston smiled soothingly at her.

Taking the towel from the servant who had filled the bath for her, Deborah went on angrily.

'I know you don't believe what I told you but it's true all the same. Abe Turley attacked me on my way home, and took me to a place where he bound and gagged me.'

She was telling the truth. Florrie glanced at the weal marks still harshly evident about the girl's wrists, the bruising beginning to emerge, dark and telling, against the whiteness of her skin; all signs of rough handling, even perhaps more. She felt a trace of alarm. Had Turley done more than bind the girl's wrists and stop her mouth? Was

232

the prize some foreigner would pay a high price for already tarnished?

'Why would Mr Turley do such a thing?' Florrie held back her concern as she flicked a dismissive hand towards the servant.

Murmuring her thanks to the departing Martha, Deborah wrapped herself in the towel as she answered.

'He attacked us once before, myself and Lizzie. He took our money and … and Lizzie was hurt. Mr Gilmore recovered our belongings and, according to that man, knocked his teeth out in the process.'

That Florrie could believe. Clay Gilmore was a different kettle of fish altogether. Turley was lucky he hadn't done more. Keeping her thoughts to herself, Florrie held out the satin robe she had brought with her.

'You say your friend was hurt? I hope it was nothing … nasty.'

The pause was eloquent, just long enough to convey a sense of concern but one that said propriety must be observed.

Taking the robe while at the same time holding the towel shyly about her body, Deborah recognised the implication. It brought a faint hint of colour to her cheeks.

'No, Lizzie was not…' She stopped, unable to bring herself to say the horrid word.

'That at least was one blessing.' Florrie loosed a long affected breath then caught one hand to her throat, the gleam of consternation in her eyes masking the truth of her real feelings: the fury that would be unleashed on Turley if he had taken Deborah. It was not the thought of his violating a young girl – he could do that as often as he wished, it would cause Florrie Marston no loss of sleep – but should he cause her loss of profit! Eyes wide with real horror she went on, 'And you, my dear. Did he do anything other than bind you?'

The colour in Deborah's cheeks took on a deeper hue. This woman could not have failed to see her torn clothing and must know it was not the result of a fall. Yet she had earlier denied what now she seemed to accept. It had been almost as if she had been defending Abe Turley. But why, when the ruined clothing and the marks about Deborah's wrists so clearly spoke of violence? She could not have believed his story about Deborah's being caught up in the broom. Deciding to say nothing of the doubts beginning to assail her, or of Turley's touching her breasts, she replied, 'I was not harmed other than the bruising you see.'

Florrie Marston's ample bosom seemed to recede six inches as she sighed her relief. The bruises would respond to a few dressings with Witch Hazel, fading within a week or so, and the marks about her wrists and ankles would be gone in the same period. It was no external mark that had caused her to worry, but Turley would answer for it just the same. He had let greed master his common sense, and now lust was driving him down the same path. It was time to be rid of Mr Abe Turley!

'The Lord be praised.' Florrie turned to the door that connected the bathroom to a bedroom.

234

'Now slip into that robe, then you must have the drink and meal I promised, and we will find you something to wear to go home.' Still holding the door ajar, she turned to smile at Deborah. 'Don't worry, my dear, I will take you to Sadie's house in my carriage.'

She would rather dress and leave straight away. The robe cool against skin flushed from the warm bath, Deborah tied the satin cord. Would it be too rude to tell the woman so? She had been kind, taking Deborah into her house, showing her hospitality. It would be churlish to refuse, she supposed. Walking slowly to the door that had closed on Florrie Marston, Deborah felt a sudden unease, a cold flicker against the base of her spine. She would accept the warm drink but plead a nervous stomach and refuse food. Churlish or not, she suddenly had a strong desire to be free not only of this house but of its owner.

Going into the other room, she glanced briefly at the bed with its soft peach covers, matching curtains pulled across the windows, glass-shaded lamps catching the warmth of the fire and casting it in a soft glow over polished wardrobe and dressing table.

'There you are, my dear.' Florrie looked up from the tray she herself had carried to the room. 'A hot drink will have you feeling better in no time.'

Pouring chocolate from the jug into the cup, she held it out to Deborah, the smile on her mouth reassuring.

'Drink that down while I see to it the carriage is harnessed. There are clothes for you.' She nodded to a dress and underwear draped over a wide armchair. 'Martha will have your own laundered in the morning and I'll have them brought over to Sadie's place.'

'This is all very kind...'

'Nonsense!' Florrie cut her thanks short. 'It's the very least any woman would do for a girl caught in the same circumstances. Now, drink your chocolate.' She raised her fingers, a smile hovering about the rouged lips. 'All of it, mind, or I will be very cross.'

Carrying the cup with her, Deborah stood before the fire, feeling the caress of its warmth through the thin fabric of the robe. But that cold touch still shivered along her spine. What was it about the woman that unnerved her? The charade of the Salon de Masson? The affected accent? No. Deborah sipped the hot sweet drink. The fact that Florrie Marston was pretending to be other than the woman she really was, pretending to be from some place other than Bloxwich, was not the cause of the worry that niggled at her mind or the fear that touched her spine. So what was?

Sipping the chocolate, Deborah stared into the heart of the fire. She had gone against Sadie's wishes by returning by way of the heath, but then she had gone against Sadie's wishes by coming to the salon in the first place. Why had Sadie not wanted her to come here? Was it truly because the road was unfamiliar to her, or was there another reason? Watching the flames dance on their scarlet bed, Deborah let the questions run wild in her mind. In all the weeks she and Lizzie

236

had lived with her, Sadie had not once suggested either of them accompany her to this place, and never had she left them alone with Florrie when she visited. Why? The flames leaped and whirled. Was Sadie Trent hiding something? Was Florrie Marston disguising more than her Elmore Green background?

Tipping back the last of the chocolate, its sweetness lingering on her tongue and in the back of her throat, Deborah tried to dismiss these thoughts. She did not want to think of such things now, wanted only to dress and go home.

Turning to place the cup back on the tray, the impression of the flames still dancing behind her eyelids, Deborah walked over to where the dress and underwear lay waiting for her.

Why had Florrie not sent for a constable? Why had she not had Abe Turley answer the accusation made before a policeman?

Loosing the robe, the flames rose higher behind Deborah's lids red, blue, purple and gold, leaping and whirling in a frenzy of colour. Why had...

But the question was lost as the colours danced frantically before her eyes and softly into blackness.

'I mind what you say, Bertha, but I still say enough is enough. That red-haired Eve Randle were nobbut a strumpet in the making. I have no objection to *her* being sent along Florrie's line. But them two little 'uns that went earlier tonight was no more than babbies!'

'You be most likely chafing over nothin'.' Bertha Johnson stirred the teapot. They had

237

worked for Florrie Marston for years and were getting old, too old to go looking for other jobs that didn't exist. And that was what would happen should Florrie catch a whiff of what was being said right now.

'I ain't chafin' over nothin'!' snorted Martha.

'You can't be sure that what you think be fact. We don't know what happens to the wenches as go along with them frocks.'

'You be right, we don't know for a fact.' Martha's reply was tart. 'But we knows that not one of 'em has ever been brought back.'

'Could be they find other jobs, better than the ones they had 'ere?'

'Oh, arrh!' Martha nodded her head disparagingly. 'A job easier than dressing up in posh frocks and swanning up and down a room while the gentry looks on! Some bloody job *that* would be! Only they don't get none such and you knows it, Bertha Johnson.'

Her glance anxious, Bertha looked towards the kitchen door.

'All I knows is we'll be in a fine old mess if her upstairs hears us. 'Tain't our business what goes on in that shop.'

'That were the song I warbled 'til them babbies was brought here. Now I've changed my tune.' Martha took her tea, carrying it to the fireside. 'You know as well as I do the life they've been sent into. Florrie Marston be selling more than frocks, her be selling folks – young wenches and now babbies – to them white slavers.'

'You can't be sure, Martha…'

'Can you be sure her ain't?' The reply was swift

and harsh. 'Why else would a wench be sent with a frock? Do you think that whoever it is bought a frock or such couldn't find a body to try them on? You been closing your eyes to what you know be going on, we both 'ave, and it ain't right, Bertha. It ain't right.'

Seated beside the fire, Bertha Johnson sipped her tea.

'Supposing it ain't,' she said, 'there's nothin' we can do. We can't fetch them babbies back. All we knows is that they got sent off from this house, but where they went from here, the Lord alone knows. I tell you, Martha, it be best we keep our mouths shut. Prison be a hard place and that be where we'll likely end up for it won't be Florrie Marston will take the rap.'

'Now you be talking daft!' Martha banged her cup down. 'We be naught but servants in this house. We can't be held responsible for what goes on in that shop.'

'Then if we can't be held responsible, why all your blethering?'

The question took Martha by surprise but only for a moment.

'Just 'cos the constabulary can't say I be responsible, don't mean I don't *feel* responsible!' she answered sharply. 'Wenches like that uppity little trollop Randle asks for all they get, but them little babbies be different. They hardly be old enough to know wrong from right. *They* be what I feels responsible for. I should never have stood by and seen them taken!'

'I know you feels bad, Martha.' The other woman laid her own cup on the well-scrubbed table. 'But like I says, there be nothin' we can do.'

Staring at the floor, Martha seemed to speak only for herself. 'So we has to sit by while that one upstairs be taken? And the next one will be young Molly Sanders. It be a wonder her ain't gone afore now. Eyes blue as a china doll and hair that shines like silk ... the wench be pretty as a oil paintin'. Florrie be grooming her for summat special but won't hold on to her much longer. Two or three days more be my bet and then her will go the same way as the rest. The wench will never see England again, that much I do be sure of.'

'No use fretting yourself, Martha. Even should we tell somebody what we fears, they most likely wouldn't believe us. Best get to setting the supper for upstairs and try to forget about it.'

One woman gathering the cups, the other stoking the fire with slack that would keep it alive overnight, neither of them saw the slight figure slip from the pantry and out into the corridor.

Florrie Marston be selling more than frocks...

The words still ringing in her mind, Molly Sanders ran up the back stairs that led to the servants' bedrooms.

...her be selling young wenches...

Eyes wide with fear, Molly stared at the door of her room as it closed behind her. What were white slavers? Why had Martha Vines's voice been edged with something like hatred when she spoke of them? It was true what she had said about girls going with some of the deliveries, and true none had returned since Molly's arrival here. Why – why did they not return?

240

...the next one will be young Molly Sanders ... Florrie be grooming her for summat special...

Her hands clutched together in front of her, Molly tried to still the tremors running through her. Mrs Marston had been nothing but kind to her, stopping every day to speak to her, asking had her mother contacted her, was she happy with the work she was given? Kindness, always kindness.

...two or three days ... the wench will never see England again...

Something like terror, something she did not understand, rippled through her, turning every vein cold in her slight body.

...the next one will be Molly Sanders...

She had to leave his house, not in the morning, not tomorrow but now, this very instant.

Reaching for her shawl Molly froze, a scream dying on her lips as the door opened and a plump figure stepped lightly into the room.

Chapter Seventeen

'You got the two of them on to that boat?'

Florrie Marston stared hard at the man recounting five-pound notes he had already counted several times. Abe Turley no more trusted her than she trusted him. But they were in this game together and one could not renege on the other without hanging himself.

'I told you I did. Went along quiet as lambs, they did. Pretty an' all, weren't they?' He squinted sideways at her. 'You must be getting a fair old price for them?'

'Shut your mouth, you bloody fool!' Florrie glanced quickly towards the door of the sitting room where Turley had waited. 'I've told you time and time again not to mention the business we do together. One day you'll open your mouth and somebody else will shut it for you. Permanently!'

Folding the notes Turley grinned, the gap between his teeth showing wide and dark.

'And what will you do then? Who will Madame de Masson get to deliver her special goods? Who will take her "gowns" across the heath at night for a pittance and then be told to keep his mouth shut? I'll talk as much as I want, Florrie, and as loud as I want. And right now I feel like talking very loud indeed.'

She had known this day would come, that Abe

Turley would become too avaricious. It was definitely time to look for a suitable replacement. Her eyes cold as pebbles in water, Florrie glared at him.

'You have been paid fifty and promised a further fifty, what more do you expect?'

Slipping the money into his pocket, he sauntered across the room to the sideboard, helping himself, uninvited, to a glass of sherry from a crystal decanter.

'I expect a lot more.' He lifted the glass high, admiring the sherry's colour as light from the gasolier played through it. 'And you, Florrie, are going to pay. Otherwise...' Holding the glass towards her, he grinned then tossed the contents into his mouth.

Anger stifling her, Florrie turned away. The dirty little snake was threatening her! But he wouldn't live long enough to do it again. Give him what he asked, get that girl upstairs safely delivered, then a drop or two from the small bottle still nestled in her pocket ... the canal was deep and wide, a comfortable enough bed for slime like Turley.

'Just what do you expect? Or should I say how much?' Florrie looked on coldly as he filled the glass once more.

'Half!' He lifted the glass as before, watching the play of light on the golden liquid.

Against her skirts Florrie's fingers tightened, but still the anger inside her remained controlled.

'Half as much again? Another fifty is too much. The consignment won't bring that much.'

Emptying the glass in one gulp, he slammed the

243

glass down on the sideboard, looking across at her with eyes narrowed to slits.

'Don't try that with me, Florrie!' he hissed, the gap between his teeth adding a slight sibilance to the words. 'This is Abe Turley you be talking to.' He waved his hand, indicating the room. 'I ain't fool enough to believe all of this and that fancy shop next door comes from selling frocks. Not here in Bloxwich it don't. I know where the money is *really* made and how much ... and it ain't bloody farthings neither!'

In fact he had no real idea how much she was paid for the women he took to that narrow boat. But Abe glanced sideways, seeing the mouth purse in the plump face. Florrie Marston couldn't be sure how much he knew. The only question was, would she put it to the test or would she fall for his lie?

'Fifty pounds.' Florrie winced as the fragile Stuart glass was banged down.

'I said half, Florrie.' Grin now entirely gone, he turned his back to the sideboard, leaning non-chalantly against it as he watched her. 'That didn't mean half again what you be willing to pay to have Deborah Hammond shifted, it were no fifty quid I was talking about. I want half, Florrie, and exactly that. Half of every penny you make; not just what you get for them twins or for the wench you've no doubt already drugged, but half of everything this racket makes or you go out of business!'

'Half!' Florrie's teeth seemed welded together with outrage. 'I'll see you in hell first!'

'Then we'll finish our conversation there.' He

stepped forward, the stink of his breath, made no sweeter by the sherry, floating before him in a warm miasma. 'Let's hope you have her out of this house before the constables get here.'

Rage choking her, filling her throat, Florrie watched him stroll to the door. How she wished she could kill him now, pour the whole of the contents of that bottle down his filthy throat! But she could not. Like it or not she must dance to the tune he fiddled. But then the dance must end. All she had to do was wait.

'There are others concerned in this,' she choked as his grubby hand fastened on the elegantly painted doorknob. 'I will have to consult them first.'

Hidden from her, his mouth stretched in that same mirthless grin, his small eyes gleamed. If this was the wine of victory he liked the taste; but it was not all drunk yet. Turning so slowly it was arrogant he gazed at the plump face flushed with rage.

'You talk to who you like, or pretend to, but it will make no difference. You see Florrie, from tonight I'll be the one them so-called clients will pay the money to. My hands will be the ones it's given into. That way I will be sure to see *all* that Salon de Masson makes. After all, we wouldn't want to cheat one another, now would we?'

Smile, you smug little bastard! Florrie thought viciously. Smile while you still can. You'll be dead long before you take Florrie Marston's business from her.

'Are we agreed?' His fingers tightened around the doorknob.

'Agreed!' She gave one brief nod. 'But tonight's job has to be finished first. Then and only then will I put anything in writing.'

In writing! He hadn't thought of that. Abe released the doorknob coming back to sit in a silk brocade chair.

'The *Midland Rose*.' Florrie took a chair across from him, folding her hands in her lap to still the angry quivering of her fingers. 'Has it sailed yet?'

Glancing at the lovely ormolu clock on the mantel, Abe drew his lips together pensively.

'Might have done, though it were dark when I got them twins to it.'

'Did Connors say he would sail tonight?'

'Connors said little or nothing, he was three parts cut.'

That sounded like the bargee who was forever drunk. Florrie tutted with irritation. Drunk or sober, daylight or midnight, the man was likely to sail whenever the mood struck him. But others would ask questions where he asked none.

'We will have to take a chance on his still being berthed alongside Hollands Bridge.'

'Be you sending the Hammond wench on tonight?'

'It has to be tonight,' Florrie answered him. 'It's too much of a risk to hold on to her. Sadie Trent and that Lizzie girl both know she came to the salon, and they also know she would go nowhere from here other than back to their house. Sadie for one won't take no for an answer, she won't easily give up. No, the sooner the girl is gone, the better. Once aboard that barge then nobody will find her and nobody will link her to me ... or to you, Abe Turley.'

Catching her meaningful glance, he nodded. For now he would follow Florrie's dictates, but only until he knew the business as well as her.

Leading the way, Florrie entered the room where she had left Deborah to drink her chocolate and dress. Waiting until the door clicked behind Turley, she went quickly to the figure lying unconscious on the floor.

Lifting away the underwear still caught between the girl's fingers and half draped across her naked body, Florrie felt a fresh surge of anger as her eyes noticed the red marks covering the small breasts. Abe Turley's work! She wheeled round catching his tongue sliding over his puffy lips as he stared at the girl on the ground.

'Those marks had best fade before this one gets to the end of the line!' she grated. 'Marked they fetch a quarter as much, which means three-quarters of our profit lost. That will come out of *your* share. Should it prove you've done more than squeeze her breasts, should it be you bedded her before the buyer, then the deal is off, null and void! Do you know what this means, Turley? It means more than no money. It means you might end up one night with your throat slit. The people we do business with don't like having faulty goods foisted upon them. Either they get what they pay for or you get dead! *That's* what null and void means.'

'I ain't touched her.' Abe dragged his glance away. 'No more than you can see anyways.'

247

Grabbing the rest of the clothes from the chair, Florrie dropped to her knees. 'Just make sure things stay that way. Now help me get her dressed. You can go by road. A carriage will be less noticeable travelling at night than the cart. If anyone asks, you're taking a lady into Walsall, but say no more than that.'

After watching the carriage drive away, Florrie turned back into the house. Tomorrow she would telephone Leonie Elliott to say the 'gown' had been dispatched. Then she would begin her search for Abe Turley's replacement.

Both hands pressed tight against her mouth, Molly Sanders stared at the woman quietly closing the door of the tiny bedroom.

'Shh!' Martha Vines touched a warning finger to her own mouth then stood for several moments listening at the door. Satisfied that no one was on the other side, she turned to the young girl still standing like a marble statue.

'Listen to me, wench.' Martha spoke in a hurried whisper. 'You don't know what be goin' on in this house … you don't know the things that be happening, that be waiting to happen to you 'lessen you leaves now.'

Martha paused to listen again, her eyes fastened on the frightened child-like face.

'There don't be time to tell you it all, you'll just have to trust old Martha. I want to help you, Molly. You be almost as much of a child as them two babbies who went earlier. God help their little souls. But you won't follow after, not if Martha Vines can do anything about it. But you

248

has to do your part, you have to be brave, wench, understand?'

Fear still striking her mute, Molly nodded.

'Then listen up,' Martha continued, her voice soft in the quiet room. 'If it's going to be done at all, it has to be done now. The mistress be busy about some business. It should keep her occupied long enough for what we want. Now, pass me your shawl. I'll hide that 'neath my pinny.'

Taking the shawl from the girl's shaking hand, Martha tied it about her ample waist, smoothing her long white apron over it.

'You spoke once of your mother,' she began again. 'Do you know where her be?'

Lips trembling as violently as her hands, Molly could not answer.

'Molly wench, pull yourself together!' Grabbing the girl's hands, Martha shook them hard. 'You has to think. Where was your mother sent?'

Nostrils widening on a long breath, thin chest heaving as she swallowed hard, Molly answered, 'We ... we went to a priest. He lived in Walsall. A placed called...' She frowned, trying to bring back the name.

'Where, wench?' Martha shook her again, a note of urgency in her whisper. 'What place?'

'It was ... the Pleck. Yes, he said the Pleck.'

'Be that where your mother was placed?'

'No.' Molly shook her head. 'He ... the priest said there was no work to be had there nor in any part of Walsall, but he had a friend who would find Mother work as a laundress.'

'Can you remember the name of the priest's friend?'

249

Thinking for a moment, Molly answered. 'It was a woman, a Mrs Elliott. Mrs Leonie Elliott.'

Hands dropping away from the girl's, Martha stared hard at her. She had seen that woman many times in the salon, and as many times wenches went missing from it. Gone to model gowns, Florrie Marston called it, but there was no codgin' Martha Vines. What Florrie said didn't fool her. Somehow or other the Elliott woman was deep in Florrie's racket and that meant young Molly couldn't look to her for help. But the priest ... if the wench could get to him...

'I ain't never heard of no Leonie Elliott,' Martha lied, 'her could well live many a mile from here in which case you might never find the place. But you said the woman got your mother a post with somebody else?'

Molly shivered as Martha held up her hand for silence, looking towards the door as she listened. Then, as the older woman nodded, she answered.

'Mother was told to go to a Mr Cato Rawley's house.'

Cato Rawley! Martha knew the name. But there might well be more than one man with the same!

'Where would this house be? Can you remember?'

This time Molly did not falter. Thoughts of her mother, of possibly going to her, melting the fear, she replied immediately.

'Bloxwich, and the house was Portland House. I remember 'cos Mother could not read the address on the letter the priest wrote for her. He had to tell her the name and the town.'

Cato Rawley. Portland House. Bloxwich. Martha almost smiled. It had to be the same man, the one she knew lived a mile or so from Elmore Green. If Molly could get there she would be safe, Rawley surely would not turn her away.

'Listen!' She took the girl's hands again in her own. 'It don't be safe for you in this house, don't ask me why for I ain't got time enough to tell. You must go … tonight. It will be frightening for you alone in the dark but you has to do it. Can you, Molly wench … can you do it?'

Seeing the girl nod, Martha fumbled beneath the shawl, tied beneath her voluminous apron, fishing out several coins from the pocket of her wide black skirts.

'Take this.' She pressed the coins into the girl's hand. 'But take nothing else. Should the mistress see you it must look as if you be about your normal duties. If her does come across you and ask what you be about, tell her I sent you to get my spectacles from my room but you couldn't find 'em. You understand, Molly? The mistress mustn't suspect. One little suspicion and I won't be able to help any more.'

'I understand, Mrs Vines.' Throwing her arms about the woman's neck and hugging her close, Molly whispered. 'Thank you.'

For a moment Martha surrendered to the pleasure of that contact. It had been many years … so very many years since anyone had hugged her.

'Now, wench, you must take every care.'

Reluctantly releasing the girl's hold, eyes bright with unshed tears, Martha gave her a last warning. 'You must not follow the road, Abe Turley will be going along that with Florrie's coach and we can't take a chance on his seeing you. The heath be too risky. It takes one used to its pit holes and mine shafts to cross that at night and even they have no guarantee of getting where they set out to be: but having said that we can't hide you not anywhere hereabouts, come daylight there will be folk about and one or another will be sure to see you and that means Florrie will fetch you back. Only way is for you to find a doorway or outhouse along of the end of the street and settle there, but at the first promise of light you get yourself away. Once you be clear of Blakenhall you can ask directions for Elmore Green ... got that, wench? Elmore Green. The folk there will show you the rest of the way, then you will be back with your mother.'

At the door Martha turned back, her glance taking in the girl's pretty face with its wide blue eyes, hair shining like a golden waterfall about her shoulders. She was beautiful. No wonder Florrie Marston had held on to this one longer than usual. The market for her would be wide and payment high. But, God willing, no foreign lecher would paw this lovely child.

'Can you count numbers?' The question was asked softly, Martha listening for more than the girl's answer. Then at Molly's nod she continued, 'Once I be gone from this room, you count each finger as many times as you have fingers on both hands. Then come down to the kitchen ... no

252

running, mind, it must seen you be doing nothing out of the ordinary! I will let you out of the back door but from there you be on your own. You understand what I say, wench?'

'Yes, Mrs Vines, I understand.'

For the last time Martha looked at the girl she was trying to help escape a dreadful future, her murmur even softer than before. 'May the Almighty hold you in His arms 'til your mother can.' Then, as quietly as she had come into the bedroom, Martha was gone.

Clay Gilmore wiped a hand across his eyes, brushing at the tiredness that stung them. He had left Sadie's promising to go by way of Green Lane, but that would be a waste of time. Deborah Hammond had not taken that route back from Blakenhall, she had gone by way of the heath. He touched the boot wedged deep in the pocket of his jacket. Almost every woman he knew wore the same side button boot but deep inside him he knew this particular one belonged to Deborah.

All night he had searched the track that led across the heath, going over ground he had searched hours before, but his diligence had met with no reward. He had found no trace of the girl.

Why had her boot been left on the heath? Had she stumbled and twisted her ankle, removing it to ease the pain? But that would not necessitate leaving it behind. Had there been a stone caught inside it? Maybe, but then again surely she would replace the boot after clearing it?

One after another the possibilities presented

themselves and one after another they were rejected; and always the same one occurred. Turley!

Screwing up his eyes against the tiredness, Clay scanned the heath, more visible now beneath a sky pearlescent with dawn. Another couple of hours and he should be going to his shift at the pit, but lose his job or not, he would not go until Deborah was found. He drew a long breath, the pain of her loss like a stone in his chest. Over the months he had fallen even deeper in love with the girl. Life without her now would be no life at all. He had not told her of his feelings – how could he? She would never accept his love, never give herself to him. But that did not mean he could not love her, take a delight in her lovely face or in her quiet voice. Yes, he loved Deborah Hammond and he always would no matter where she gave her heart. And should it turn out that Turley was responsible for her not returning to Sadie Trent's house then even God Almighty would not save his life!

Where would Turley hide her? Clay asked himself the same question he had asked before but this time he ran through the places more carefully in his mind. Turley had been sly and secretive as a boy, hiding things from others, concealing his activities while sharing theirs. Once he had stolen a rabbit from old Moses Hathaway, keeping it in a worked-out pit along of Sots Hole.

Sots Hole! Clay drew in a sharp breath. The lane there had been renamed Station Street since the opening of the railway line but to the folk of

Elmore Green it was still known by its old name; and it was still pitted all around by ancient coal and metal workings. That was where Turley would have taken Deborah, the places he could hide her there were endless.

Turning in the direction of the railway station, he caught a movement out of the corner of his eye. He scanned the ground which was dotted everywhere with clumps of gorse and taller bushes of broom. There! It was faint, no more than a shadow on shadow, but he caught it. A definite movement, a silent shifting from bush to bush. Dropping to his haunches, he crouched low to the ground, his breathing slowing almost to a standstill. It was no animal. The shape that flitted from bush to bush was human.

No movement betraying his presence, Clay watched the shape approach him. Saw the head hidden huddled in a shawl, the skirts where a man would have legs. The figure was that of a woman.

'Deborah?' The cry broke from his lips as he pushed himself to his feet. A few yards away the figure stopped, her startled scream ringing out in the dawn.

'Deborah, it's me – Clay.'

Two strides had him alongside the figure, his hands on her arms, his eyes on that white upturned face.

'You ... you're not Deborah.' He stared down at the silent girl, her violent trembling threatening to unbalance her. 'Who are you? And why are you here at such a time?'

Terror bubbling in her throat, Molly Sanders

could not answer, only her wide eyes reflected her terror.

'It's all right, girl.' Suppressing his own disappointment, Clay managed a gentle tone. 'You be in no danger from me, I won't hurt you. But how come you be on the heath at such an hour?'

The softness of his voice and the gentleness of his touch on her arms cut some way through her fear but still her answer was little more than a gurgle in her throat, causing him to repeat the question.

'I ... I thought you was him,' Molly sobbed. 'I thought the mistress had sent him to fetch me back ... Martha said she would. Martha said the mistress would fetch me back. Don't take me back ... please don't take me back to that house!'

'Nobody will take you any place you don't want to be, you have Clay Gilmore's promise on that.'

The name penetrating her fear, Molly sagged, all the remaining strength leaving her legs. Clay Gilmore was the name Martha and Bertha had used when talking of the man who had called to see the mistress. Not the same one who had brought the girl with him – Martha had called that one Turley.

'I don't want to go back. I don't ever want to see that woman again.'

Feeling the sobs rack her fragile body, Clay held her comfortingly. 'I've said you won't have to and I meant it. But what woman is it has you so scared, and which man did you think would fetch you back?'

She was crying so hard she could not answer. Clay waited for her to calm down. Somebody had this poor girl terrified.

'It's the mistress, Madame Fleur,' Molly managed to say. 'Martha said she would bring me back, and I thought you were that awful man...'

Madame Fleur! Clay felt his heart jolt. That was the fancy name Florrie Marston gave herself. Gently pushing the girl away from him, he looked into her tear-marked face. 'Martha?' he asked, careful not to let anger show in his voice, afraid the girl might see it as being directed at her. 'Do you mean Martha Vines?'

The girl nodded and the thread of hope inside him quickened. Perhaps she might know if Deborah had truly left the salon.

'The man,' he asked, 'the one you said would be sent to take you back, do you know his name?'

Molly nodded, catching her breath on a long shuddering sob. 'Mrs Vines called him Turley ... Abe Turley.'

His own hands shaking slightly, Clay drew in a long breath. 'Did you see a girl earlier today, one with black hair? She brought a garment to the salon, a jacket of some sort?'

Molly shook her head. 'I've not been in the salon, I worked as a housemaid in *madame's* private quarters.'

Clay felt the hope fade. This girl would not be able to tell him anything about Deborah.

In the strengthening light Molly caught the slump of his shoulders and the look of despair settle about his mouth. Somehow she was not afraid of him, it felt almost as if fate had sent him to help her. If only she could have given him the answer he so badly wanted.

'There was a girl,' she said tentatively. 'She came to the house early on last night. Abe Turley brought her with him. I only caught a glimpse of them from the pantry but it seemed to me like she didn't want to be there. He fair pushed her through the kitchen but I did see a little of her face. She was young, not so much older than me, and pretty – I might say beautiful – and her hair was black.'

Abe Turley ... and her hair was black.

Clay felt the blood surge through his veins, beating the rhythm of rage in his brain. His guess had been right all along. Turley had waylaid Deborah, but why take her to Florrie Marston?

'Did the girl leave with Turley?'

His breath catching in his throat. Clay waited for the answer.

Chapter Eighteen

Her whole body taught and stiff as a ramrod, Agnes Ridley lay in her bed, ears strained to a household now wreathed in silence.

They were still together, Cato and that woman, together in his room, in his bed.

He had returned home unexpectedly early last night, bringing his whore with him, and around her neck had hung the necklace of square-cut amethysts. *Her necklace!* It should have been Agnes's. It should *all* have been hers. Instead of which he had given it away piece by piece, given everything to Leonie Elliott.

First the solitaire diamond that had been Delia's engagement ring. Next had gone the ruby brooch; she had seen that a week later pinned to the shoulder of Leonie Elliott's gown. No more than seven days later she had seen the pearls. They had been Delia Rawley's wedding gift from her parents.

Beneath the sheets Agnes's fingers clenched, anger running fast in her veins.

She had served supper in the dining room, Cato and his trollop dining at the house before going out. She had seen the pearls draped twice about the woman's neck and as their eyes met Leonie Elliott's were laughing ... laughing at her!

Turning her face towards the window, Agnes was oblivious to the faint streaks of soft grey that foretold the dawn.

Each time she visited the house following that night, Leonie Elliott had worn one or another of Delia Rawley's jewels: garnet clips, emerald earrings, diamond fob watch, all of them rightfully Agnes's.

And last night it had been the necklace!

Agnes's fingers curled and uncurled, the memory of what had happened fanning the rage inside her until it bathed the whole of her body in heat.

She heard them laugh as they walked up the stairs, heard that low musical voice as they had gone into the bedroom. Leonie Elliott laughing at what had happened earlier that evening, laughing at her!

She had been in Delia Rawley's room when Cato had walked in, his words floating over his shoulder to the woman following behind.

'It will suit the stones perfectly, my dear...'

He had stopped abruptly, his gaze travelling over Agnes as she had turned.

'What the hell do you think you are doing?'

Grey eyes glinting like newly forged steel, he had barked the question as the golden-haired woman came to stand beside him, her smoky violet eyes mocking.

'Get that off at once. Get it off, do you hear? Tomorrow you pack your bags, you're finished in this house!'

'Cato, darling.' Leonie Elliott had placed a hand on his arm but her gaze remained on Agnes *'It's only a dress, why all the fuss?'*

'A dress ... a glove ... a bloody dishcloth. Who

cares?' he blazed, anger draining his face of colour. *'She has no right...'*

'I have every right,' Agnes had snapped, her fury more a reaction to the sneer in those smoky violet almond-shaped eyes than to Cato's outburst. *'Everything that was Delia's is mine as of right! I earned every one of these dresses – earned them by nursing a wife you didn't want, the same as I earned those jewels by coming to your bed every night, giving you what you wanted. I earned the right to be mistress of the house I ran for years. You will honour the promises you made while straddling my body, Cato, keep the word you gave while you drove yourself into me. You will marry me regardless of the whore you bring to this house. I will be the next Mrs Cato Rawley!'*

His features distorted with anger, Cato's voice had dropped to a low tone that throbbed with rage.

'Get that dress off. Leave this house first thing in the morning for if I see you again after you have received your pay for the year, I will have you arrested for attempted theft.'

'Cato, why be so cruel?'

The face Leonie had so carefully painted, the dark beauty patch high on one cheek adding to its remarkable attraction, turned first to Cato then back to Agnes, smiling.

'Let her keep the dress, I could never wear such a dowdy thing. Mauve is such a funereal colour, much better suited to the older woman. Take it, Agnes, it is definitely your style.'

It was a deliberate insult, a jibe sheathed in a smile but the thrust cut deep.

'*You think to take him for yourself.*' Agnes's lips could barely move for fury. '*You think your beauty is enough, but there is more to you than just a pretty face, is that not so, Mrs Leonie Elliott? More than either of you cares to admit. But I am not so reticent. I don't care if the world should find out that I shared Cato Rawley's bed, but if it were known that you had...*'

Beneath the cosmetics Leonie's face seemed to pale slightly but those eyes still held their mocking gleam.

'*Agnes, my dear,*' the musical voice had purred. '*Everyone knows a gentleman is allowed the services of a paid servant. As for a mistress,*' her creamy shoulders had lifted, '*once she becomes his wife...*'

'*And you think to be that wife?*' She had laughed at that, a short hard sound. '*That, Leonie, my dear, is something you will never be. You know that, Cato knows that, and if need be the whole world will know it...*'

'*Tomorrow morning in my study ... nine o'clock.*' His face the colour of well-laundered sheets, voice tight in his throat, Cato had swept out of the room.

Then Leonie Elliott's smile had disappeared. '*Don't try to be clever, Agnes.*' The words were just a breath on the air but the menace of them reached out like fingers of evil. '*I have no wish to see you harmed...*'

'Harmed!' Agnes remembered her own derisive laughter as she had stared into stone hard eyes. '*You are the one who'll be harmed if you think to take my place in this house. There's nothing you can do to me, but I ... I can ruin your life!*'

Hardly a muscle had moved in that seductive face, the voluptuous mouth wearing just a hint of a smile, the musical voice almost soothing as its answer was given.

'I doubt that, Agnes, I doubt that very much. No one of any consequence will pay heed to the ravings of a jealous woman. Too many of them have been plagued by the same. But I have friends, powerful friends in almost every county in the land. Play your hand against me and you will pay the consequences. I said I have no wish to harm you, but I will if I have to.'

I will if I have to.

It had been an undisguised threat, almost a cudgel standing there between them waiting for the first hand to take it up. Then Leonie Elliott had turned and left the room.

The rising dawn gently liberating her bedroom from the shadows, Agnes allowed herself to smile. In a few hours that threat would be gone from her life.

As Leonie Elliott would be gone from Cato's.

'Did the girl leave with Turley?' Clay's question hung in the air for a moment.

'No.' Molly Sanders shivered, the cold dawn biting at her thin body. 'Leastways I didn't see her go. Turley took her upstairs to *madame,* but he didn't come down right away as he usually does.'

'Usually?'

The girl shivered again and Clay recognised it was more from fear than from cold. Something had got deep inside this girl, something terrifying, and Abe Turley knew what it was.

'I've seen him bring others to the house, and then at night come and take them away again. Always at night, like he took the twins and like he took the Randle girl last week. It's always after dark he takes them and ... I heard Mrs Vines say none of them ever returns. And she also said I would be the next one to be sent.'

A coldness he could not rightly fathom closed about Clay's heart. Afraid of the answer yet needing to hear it he forced the question out.

'Where would you be sent?'

Pale light catching her eyes as she looked up at him, glistened on the fright lodged deep in them. Every word trembling, fresh tears coursing down her cheeks, she answered, 'Mrs Vines, her didn't say ... only ... only that I wouldn't see England again.'

Wouldn't see England again. Clay's blood turned to ice. He had heard tales of girls being picked up off the streets and sold off to whore houses or even abroad. But Florrie Marston wouldn't be involved in such schemes, she had a good business selling frocks, she had no need of white slaving. A good business? Clay considered this carefully. It certainly seemed very prosperous ... too prosperous for Bloxwich alone. There weren't many women with the kind of money it would take to buy frocks like she sold. There had to be more to the Salon de Masson than frocks, and now Deborah was almost certainly there.

'You won't let them take me, will you? You promised.'

Seeing her hands shake uncontrollably, Clay

knew that deep as his fears were he had to get this girl to safety. Every minute was sending her further into shock. In such a state she would never make it safely across the heath. But Deborah? Every moment she spent in that house she was in danger. What had the girl said? Turley only took them at night. But he had not taken Deborah, she was still there when this girl left; it must have been too late for her to have been passed on then. That meant the earliest she would be taken would be the coming evening. Clay had time to get this girl to Elmore Green and go back to Blakenhall.

Stripping off his jacket, he draped it about the spare shoulders, then with one arm supporting the quivering girl, began the long walk back to the village.

'Evie Randall was took last week...'

In the silence of the heath, Clay listened to the babblings of the girl stumbling along at his side.

'Mrs Vines said it were no more than she deserved, said that wench was no better than her should be, that her were a trollop. But them twins ... they wasn't trollops, they were only children, not much more than babies. Why let Turley take them? Why did Madame Fleur send them away?'

Children! The anger inside him set like stone. Was Florrie Marston not satisfied with young women? Was she dealing in children as well? He had thought to deal only with Turley but should this girl's words prove true then Florrie too would answer, and not just to him. There would be a very long prison sentence for the kind of filth she peddled!

'I was to be next. Martha said I was like to be sent next...'

Clay listened to her mutterings. 'But she helped me get away. Martha gave me money to get to my mother, said she was sorry, that she was responsible, ought never to have stood by and watched them twins be taken. But Bertha said nobody would believe them if they told, that it wouldn't be the mistress would take the rap. But Mrs Vines helped me ... she helped me.'

Off in the distance a vixen barked and a dog fox answered. Most likely calling to each other before taking the cubs underground to sleep the daylight hours away. Clay's arm tightened about the startled girl. If only all children received such care!

Beside him she fell silent but in Clay's head disturbing thoughts screamed as loud as the foxes.

He looked towards the village where a pall of smoke was already beginning to rise, lying over the houses as outhouse and workshop furnaces were rekindled, taking the place of the receding shadows of night. The 'Black Country' some wag had once called this heart of England and the name had stuck. But in this heart there beat a decency that smoke and grime from coal mines and metal workings, of furnace and puddling hearths, could not destroy. A living of any kind was hard enough to make hereabouts, a comfortable one something to be treasured. Was it any wonder Martha Vines had closed her eyes to what Florrie was doing? But Martha had risked hers to help this girl, and because of that she was also helping Deborah. Was there anyone could prove she had prior knowledge of the true business being carried on at that salon? No, that was all the doing of Turley and Marston ... and they would be the ones to pay.

Entering the village, Clay looked towards the house he shared with his family. His mother would look after the girl but then he would have to explain all over again to Sadie Trent. He could not go back to Blakenhall without telling her and Lizzie that Deborah was safe.

Safe! He smiled grimly to himself. Yes, she was safe now but the quicker she was brought out of that house the better.

'Thank God Deborah is safe, that she stayed at Madame Fleur's house after all.'

Madame Fleur! Sadie bent over the fire, hiding the scorn in her eyes. The airs and graces that woman had put on since moving to Blakenhall! But they didn't fool Sadie Trent, she wasn't taken in by them, nor by the tale told by that child Clay Gilmore had fetched to her. Molly Sanders reckoned Deborah to be still in Florrie's house but Sadie's innards seemed to be telling her different. If Florrie had found this little wench to be missing then it were a sure bet Deborah Hammond was already gone. Madame Fleur was too shrewd to risk having the girl found on her premises.

Laying aside the poker with which she had stirred the fire, Sadie swung the bracket with its soot-blackened kettle over the glowing coals.

'Arrh, the Lord shows His mercies,' she

answered Lizzie who sat on a low chair suckling her baby.

'It was good of Clay to search for her.' Lizzie looked up. 'He spent the whole night on the heath.'

Spooning tea into her ancient teapot, Sadie said nothing. Clay Gilmore would have spent as much time as it took. He thought nobody knew the agony this night had brought him but Sadie Trent knew, for it had brought her much the same.

Over the months since their coming to live with her the respect she felt for these two girls had deepened. It was no longer respect, though that remained, but what she felt for them now was more than that: it was love.

Lifting the infant to her shoulder, Lizzie patted his back with a gentle tapping rhythm, smiling as wind burped from his stomach.

'That girl he brought with him was badly frightened. It was lucky, Clay finding her as he did.'

'Arrh, it was that. Real lucky.' Sadie scalded the tea in the pot.

'You don't think she was attacked, do you? Out there on the heath, I mean.'

'No, I do not!' Sadie set the pot on the table with a bang. 'Bloxwich ain't riddled with bad 'uns like Turley, and he wouldn't try the same trick twice, not with the risk of having to face Clay Gilmore he wouldn't. It be more likely the wench has had words with her parents and run off in a temper, getting herself lost in the doing of it. Come morning her will like as not regret it and be ready to go home. Anyroad up, her was in no state to talk of what happened tonight, but tomorrow no doubt we will be told it all.'

Pouring tea into two cups, Sadie watched as the baby was settled into his cradle.

'That one be happy enough anyway.' She smiled as Lizzie looked up from straightening the covers. 'Let him bide there while you drink your tea then I'll help you carry him upstairs. You needs sleep, my wench, as much as that son of yourn.'

Coming to the table, Lizzie stood there for a moment, her brown eyes reflecting the feeling that rose suddenly to her heart. One of fear.

'Sadie,' she whispered, 'Clay was telling the truth, wasn't he … Deborah is safe, she is with Madame Fleur?'

Stirring sugar into her cup, Sadie lowered her glance watching the swirl of the liquid. Lizzie had the same thought that had played at the back of her own mind, thoughts she had pushed into the background. But now, as the girl spoke, they came rushing in, a tide of doubt and supposition that danced unchecked in her brain. But they were fears that must remain unspoken; Lizzie must not have more added to the sorrows still lodged in her heart.

'If Clay Gilmore says Deborah be safe in that woman's house then that is where her be, you can take that as gospel.'

Watching the tea circle in the thick pottery cup, Sadie felt the twinge the lie brought. She had known Clay Gilmore from a babby in napkins and could tell when the words he spoke were less than the truth; she had read the look on his face

269

tonight. He might believe Deborah Hammond to be in that house next to the gown shop, but he did not truly believe her to be safe. He had not gone home to his mother's house, she would stake her life on that. Clay Gilmore had gone back to Florrie Marston's.

Still standing beside the table, her wide eyes glistening with tears, Lizzie spoke again. 'If anything happened to Deborah, I think I would die.'

'Ain't nobody going to die!' Sadie's tone was tart, hiding the emotion that welled up in her. 'Now you get that tea inside you so we can get you up to bed. Being up most of the night don't mean we won't have a full day tomorrow, nor will that babby need less looking after. He will still be awake on time, wanting his stomach filled and his backside cleaned.'

The cradle carried to Lizzie's room, Sadie settled herself in the chair drawn close to the fire. She had looked in on the girl sleeping soundly in the bed she herself had given up. She were no more than twelve or fourteen years of age and belonged nowhere in Elmore Green. So where did she belong? She had said practically nothing, obviously shocked into silence, and Clay had said almost as little. But a body didn't need telling to know that wench had not run away from home: her reason for being on the heath at night were none of her parents' doing.

Poor little bugger! thought Sadie, staring into the fire. Her face told of more than fright, it spoke of sadness and of hardship. If told the same story as Lizzie's face had told and was still telling.

270

The father of her child had not been spoken of since the night of the birth, not since Lizzie's face had lit up as it turned towards the door, only to crumple as she saw the figure she'd prayed would come was not him but the doctor. But he had remained in the hidden chambers of her soul, remained to torture her with unkept promises.

Sighing loudly in the quiet kitchen, Sadie listened to the ticking of the battered tin clock.

Young Lizzie Burton smiled by day, but by night she cried for a child born a bastard, and a man who would never come forward to give his name to it.

Chapter Nineteen

Sure now that Deborah was nowhere on the heath, Clay had made good time in crossing it, familiarity lending speed to his feet. He would not wait politely for the household to waken but would hammer on its door until it was opened.

Within sight of the village in the approaching dawn he halted, his keen hearing catching the crunch of boots on the pebbly track. Sinking to his haunches, Clay watched from the cover of a bank of gorse.

Further along the track, a figure came towards him, head raised cockily, whistling loudly.

Abe Turley! Clay's hands tightened into fists. He would get his answers or Turley wouldn't reach home alive.

'Abe.'

He rose as the man drew level.

His whistle giving way to a startled gasp, Abe Turley stumbled a few steps backward, then as he recognised the man before him he snapped angrily: 'Christ Almighty, Gilmore! You bloody fool, bouncing up like that from out of nowhere. You could 'ave given me a heart attack.'

'Now that would have been a shame.' Clay stepped firmly on to the track. ''Cos I intend to give you a lot more than that.'

Getting over his shock at having a figure rise like a phantom in his path, Abe tried to smile.

'What do that signify, Clay? What have you that I be wanting?'

Clay took a step nearer. 'I did not say it was something you be wanting, Abe, but want it or not you will get it unless you answer my questions.'

'Questions?' Abe blustered, nervousness beginning to show. 'What bloody questions? You ain't asked none.'

Hanging loose at his sides, Clay's hands clenched again. If Deborah Hammond had been hurt in any way they would close round Turley's neck and throttle the life from him. Keeping the thought to himself, he answered levelly. 'Then I will ask them now. And be warned, Turley, I be in no mood for lies. Where is Deborah Hammond?'

He didn't know. Gilmore could not possibly know. Abe swallowed the nervous bile collecting in his throat. 'Deborah Hammond ... how the hell should I know where her is? You be the one following after her like a lost sheep.'

'You saw her early on last evening...'

'I ain't seen her at any time since...'

'Since you robbed her!' Clay's voice was tight. 'You lied about that and you're lying now. I found this on the heath.' Snatching the boot from his jacket pocket, he thrust it forward.

'A boot. Is that supposed to tell me summat?'

'It is, but just in case it doesn't, let *me* tell you. This isn't any boot, it's Deborah Hammond's boot.'

She had been bending over when he reached for her, bending over doing something with her boot. Abe did not need to look at the one in

273

Clay's hand to realise it must be the same.

'How the hell can you tell whose it is? It could be any woman's. But p'raps it had her name inside it,' Abe sneered, trying to hide the fact that he recognised the boot.

'Clever of you to guess, or did you see as much when you dragged it from her foot?'

Abe's nerves jangled but still he held on. Gilmore could be doing no more than making a guess. Nobody had seen him take the Hammond wench, nobody had followed them. Swallowing his rising apprehension, he answered brashly, 'I didn't take no boot from her.'

'No, you took *her* instead!' His movements slow, eyes never leaving the other man's face, Clay returned the boot to his pocket. 'I told you, I be in no mood for lies and you be lying, Abe. You caught Deborah Hammond on her way to Sadie Trent's house…'

'That be a bloody lie, Gilmore, and you knows it!'

'No, Abe, it's no lie. You see, Florrie Marston told me you took the girl to her house.'

'Her didn't! Florrie wouldn't say nothing!'

Softly, as if speaking to a newly awakened child, Clay answered, 'Maybe, maybe not. But *you* just have, and if you have any fancy to see another day you will tell me where you have taken her.'

The softness of his tone did not fool Abe Turley. He knew from experience the anger it could hide. He also knew the strength of those hands, what a beating from this man felt like; but the risk of that was preferable to losing the kind of money he would get as Florrie Marston's partner. Trying to keep his nervousness from showing, he gave a quick smile.

'You be making a mistake, Gilmore. I ain't taken the wench. If Florrie Marston told you otherwise then it be her doing the lying.'

Low on the rim of the horizon the sky blushed at the touch of the rising sun. Daylight was not far away. Clay felt cold fear along his spine. He did not know how or why but every one of his senses warned him that with it would come fresh danger for Deborah Hammond. One hand snaking out, he caught the other man by the cloth tied about his throat, dragging him upward until just his toe caps touched the ground.

'You never could take a telling, could you, Turley?' He twisted the cloth about his fingers, tightening it across the man's gullet. 'You always did have to have sense knocked into you. How many teeth must you lose this time before you tell me what I want to hear?'

'I ain't...'

Only half spoken the denial gave way to a grunt, Abe's head snapping back on his neck as a blow caught him in the mouth.

'Don't say I didn't warn you.' Following each word with a fresh blow, Clay let his rage surface. 'I gave you a fair chance which is likely far more than you gave the girl.'

Loosing the cloth, he stood over the figure that slumped to the ground.

'You lost your chance, Turley, but I won't miss mine. A beating is too good for scum like you, I have better in mind.'

'What be you going to do?' Abe's frightened

squeak echoed in the silent dawn. 'Gilmore, for Christ's sake…'

Bending to grab the neck of Abe's jacket, Clay left the track, setting off across the heath, dragging the protesting figure along on its heels.

'You're wrong, Abe.' He smiled grimly. 'I'm not doing this for the sake of Christ, nor for Deborah Hammond, I am doing it for myself.'

Hauled over the hillocky ground, unable to get a footing, Abe's answer was jolted from him. 'Doing what … where you taking me?'

'Not to Sots Hole. Not to the place you took Deborah Hammond. You did take her there, didn't you, Abe? You must have thought your little hidey hole long forgotten. But I remembered, Abe, like I remembered the rabbit you stole then left there to starve. Is that what you intend for the girl, have you left her to stave? But she won't. She won't be the one to die in fear – you will.'

Fear striking him, Abe struggled to bring himself upright, only to fall again as Clay jerked him easily from his feet. What did Gilmore intend … where was he taking him? Had he been to Sots Hole, already seen the girl was not there? Questions raced through Abe's mind. Had Clay truly been to the Marston house, and if so had Florrie told him? But she wouldn't, Florrie was too shrewd for that. But she might have said that he, Turley had taken her off somewhere; that was more like Florrie. Let some other silly bugger take the rap. That was it. She'd told Gilmore that the wench had been at the house but that Abe had taken her back to Sadie Trent's. It would get her off the hook. She knew Gilmore would like to do for him and if he did Florrie Marston would not be forced to share her business!

He opened his mouth to speak. It was snapped closed as he was bumped over the ground, his teeth meeting painfully on his tongue.

The sting of it together with the pain of being dragged so roughly bringing moisture to his eyes he shouted. 'Wait! I'll tell you – I'll tell you where the wench is.'

Letting Abe fall to the ground with a thud that rattled every tooth in his head, Clay stared down at him.

'I did meet the wench, out here on the heath … there was summat wrong with her foot, that must be why her shoe was off.' He tried to stand but a foot on his chest said otherwise. 'Anyways I couldn't carry her, not as far as Sadie Trent's place, and I couldn't leave her out here, not by herself, now could I?'

Clay giving no reply, Abe went on. 'We was nearer to Blakenhall by a half mile or so. That made it seem sensible to take her there, and so that was the way of it. Florrie Marston said her would keep her there for the night and get her back to Elmore Green come morning.'

'Sounds reasonable.'

'Of course it does 'cos it be the truth.' Abe Turley sounded relieved.

Hauling him to his feet, keeping a firm hold on his collar, Clay's stare was hard. 'For your sake I hope it is, because you are going to be with me when we knock Florrie up. I want you to hear why she has told me one thing while you have told me another. I want to see both your faces when I tell her I have a witness to Deborah Hammond being taken to an upstairs room in Florrie's house, a witness to your taking Eve Randle and some young twins to be sold to traffickers in white slaves!'

God Almighty, somebody had blown the whistle! Abe felt his knees buckle. It couldn't be Florrie, the woman would never put herself in the sort of stew would boil up from this coming to the magistrate's eye! But some bird had chirped, they had to have, that was the only way Gilmore could have found out.

'I ... I don't know anything about slaving,' he blurted. 'I ... I only takes frocks. The girls that went with them – Florrie said they was manne ... manne ... that they was going to model frocks for the buyers.'

'Models ... young children not yet grown?'

Scorn and disbelief clear in his reply Clay began to move, hauling Turley with him.

'I said the same.' Desperate at what might happen next, Abe lied. 'But Florrie said they were to model a special line in children's clothes.'

Jerking to a halt, Clay stared into the face of the man he was certain had taken Deborah; the man who even now was lying to him.

'Listen to me, Turley,' he said, the razor-sharp edge to his voice making the man squirm. 'I will ask one more time. Do you know where Deborah Hammond is? Should you answer with a lie I make this oath before God: you will never again see daylight, nor will any man ever find your body.'

Feeling the strength of the other man, the apparent ease with whicH he had hauled him along, Abe Turley felt his courage falter. He might have fooled Florrie Marston, got her to see things his way, but Clay Gilmore never would and the beating he had delivered before would be a pat on the head compared to what he would do this time; losing a few teeth on account of a wench was one thing, losing your life was another, and in this mood Gilmore could easily kill him.

'I'm waiting!' Impatient at the delay, Clay shook Abe, rattling his head rag-doll fashion on his neck.

'Her paid me.' The words shaken from him, Abe tried to wriggle free from the hand about his collar but it was useless. Clay Gilmore's years as a collier had given him a strength Abe's own hands did not possess. Giving up the struggle, he went on, 'Florrie Marston paid me thirty pounds to drive them twins, and another 'undred to drive Deborah Hammond.'

Eyes bright in the dawn light he stared into Clay's face. 'Think of it, Gilmore. One 'undred and thirty pounds for a few hours' work and all I did for it was drive a wagon and a carriage. A 'undred and thirty quid. You couldn't earn that much in three years, Gilmore, not if you dug half the coal in Bloxwich. But I did and I'll give half to you...'

Snapping him back and forth, Clay's answer was harsh. 'I don't want your dirty money and you won't ever get to enjoy it...'

'Don't be so bloody daft, Gilmore.' Desperation mounting, Abe tried again. 'There be no harm intended to the wench. Florrie said she'd just be delivering a frock, said her would be well paid as meself. And as ... as for what you fancied from her, with the money I offer you can have any number of pretty wenches. It be there ... in my pocket, the money Florrie paid me. Take it Clay. Take all of it.'

Clay's face twisted, dislike of this man and hatred of the trade he was involved in catching in his throat. 'Yes, take it, Clay ... I can always make more selling some other girl, some other child. That's the truth of it, isn't it, Turley? There are plenty of them on the streets, children and women willing enough to follow you for the promise of a shilling while you reap the Devil's reward. Well, the Devil pays his dues in more ways than money and yours will be paid before the next hour be over. He be waiting for you, Turley, and this time it will be me as makes the delivery.'

Twisting him about, Clay propelled him forward a few steps before Abe's knees folded.

'Wait!' he moaned. 'Wait, I'll ... I'll tell you where the wench be took.'

In silence Clay stared as the man dropped to the ground. What if he were not as scared as he seemed? If he really were involved with slavers, he might be more afraid of them, afraid their retribution would be more severe than the one he would meet at Clay Gilmore's hands. Keeping that fear to himself, Clay waited.

'I only drove the wench when Florrie Marston assured me her would be looked after, a good 'ome and all that...'

'Is that why she was taken at night, under cover of darkness?'

'Florrie said the business wouldn't wait 'til morning. The boat … it would be gone.'

The fear that had lodged all night in Clay's stomach turned to ice. A boat! Canals traced the Black Country like veins in a man's body. They connected and interconnected, one leading off another, following the country from end to end; and in between were a thousand different places where a cart or a carriage could wait. Deborah could be headed anywhere!

Fear and rage taking hold of Clay, he lashed out with his boot, hearing Turley's gasp as it found its mark.

'Which boat?' he grated. 'Where is it bound? Tell me, you bastard, and this time every word the truth!'

'I don't know.' Curled into a ball, Turley screamed as Clay's boot found his spine. 'It's true, Gilmore. Christ help me, it's true. I only know it were moored along of Hollands Bridge, the *Midland Rose* be the name of it.'

'The bargee?' White with anger, Clay let fly another jab with his boot.

Hands and arms covering his head, Abe Turley rolled sideways but Clay's foot stayed with him. His voice tight and high with tension, he answered, 'Connors, it be Jake Connors.'

The name was not familiar to Clay, but other bargees would know it, and if he had to he would question every one using the canal. Hauling Turley to his feet again, Clay's next words held all the threat of a rearing cobra.

'If that boat should not be there, then all the money in your pocket and in Florrie Marton's house won't help you.'

'You can't blame me if Connors be under way. It ain't down to me if he's slipped his moorings.'

'Like it wasn't down to you to take Deborah or those children to him in the first place?' Clay grimaced. 'You are as much to blame as Marston and I'll see the both of you pay!'

'Let me loose, Gilmore,' Abe protested as he was dragged along. It was nigh on a certainty the wench would not be found at Hollands Bridge, and even more of a certainty what Gilmore would do when he found the barge gone. 'Let me go to Elmore, I'll bring back Colly Latham.'

Clay's smile was grim. Turley would no more fetch the constable than fly in the air!

'How thoughtful,' he growled. 'But you stay with me, and if the girl is not found then neither will you be.'

Abe's body throbbed with real fear. It was still coming up to dawn; there would be no one on the heath as yet, no miners making for the pits. Gilmore could carry out his threat, kill him, and there would be none to see it done.

'The ... docks,' he stuttered. 'Connors carries stuff to the docks and the nearest be Bristol. If that be the port he be heading for, he'll go by way of Goscote Works, pass under the bridge. You ... you could catch him there, take the wench afore he has the chance to drop her off somewhere.'

And if Bristol was not the direction the bargee was taking? Clay thought of that possibility. But it was a chance he had to take.

YOU WILL HONOUR THE PROMISES YOU MADE.

Cato Rawley lay wide-eyed, staring into the shadows of his bedroom. The venom on Agnes Ridley's face had been plain to see, a venom that could soon turn to vengeance. He had been a fool to approach her, to take her into his bed; but the woman had been not unattractive and had been more than willing. He could not have risked taking a mistress from among Bloxwich society; talk might have filtered back to colleagues whose sense of propriety would have forbade their doing further business with him, while a woman with a well-paid post to protect...

But it was not to safeguard her post that Agnes Ridley had given her services. She had been stalking bigger game.

I WILL BE THE NEXT MRS CATO RAWLEY.

The words whipped at him like a lash. Mistress of Portland House was the prize she coveted.

THERE IS NOTHING YOU CAN DO TO ME, BUT I CAN RUIN YOUR LIFE.

The words had rung out after him as he walked away from that bedroom. Now they rang in his head and their warning was clear.

Turning, he looked at the face on the pillow beside him and his heart skipped a beat. Why had he met Leonie Elliott? What had the fates against him that they had set so beautiful a trap?

But they had met and he had fallen head over heels in love; and now they were both threatened by a woman's greed. Marriage to Agnes Ridley ... would it protect the one at his side? That required no further consideration. Cato knew it would not. Agnes was a vengeful woman, one who would not tolerate a rival.

IF NEED BE THE WORLD WILL KNOW.

Gently touching the sleeping figure, Cato stroked the velvet smooth shoulder. The world must not know. No one must ever know. Somehow or other Agnes Ridley must be silenced.

Chapter Twenty

Lizzie had blown out the candle.

Deborah stirred, a soft moan escaping her lips.

Why? Why had she blown out the candle? They kept a night light burning for Thomas's night feeds.

She tried to move but pain stabbed sharply through her temples and she fell back, hitting her head against something hard.

That was wrong. She did not share a room with Lizzie, not since...

Pain exploding like fireworks in her brain, she moaned again. Why this terrible headache? And her limbs, they felt as if she had been knocked down by a cart. She had been well enough last night. She had fetched Sadie's beer as usual, spoken for a few minutes with Clay, helped Lizzie bathe her child and...

No ... that was not right either! Confused and sick from the pain throbbing in her head she glanced about her, but the darkness was too dense for her to make out the furniture in her room. Easing her head slowly sideways she looked towards the window, then gave a silent scream of terror.

The window ... she could not see it! She could not see anything ... everywhere was blackness. She was blind! The pain in her head was not just a headache, it was some dreadful affliction that had taken away her sight!

Screams rose to her lips, fear running amok in her mind, drowning her senses until they almost failed her.

Then, the silent screams spent, she lay still. Eyes closed against the darkness, she dragged her thoughts together, fitting the broken pieces like a mosaic, watching the parts build slowly into a whole, presenting a picture that only increased her desperate fear.

Abe Turley had waylaid, bound and gagged her, leaving her in some awful place. Then he had returned only to take her to that house, Madame Fleur's. The woman had promised to help, providing her with a bath and a meal; but she had not eaten, had taken only a cup of chocolate... The drink! Realisation stunned her mind as fear had moments before. The drink must have been drugged. The woman had drugged her! But why ... for what reason?

It made no sense. Going over it again and again only brought Deborah to the same conclusion. There was no reason for the woman to drug her yet that had to be what had happened.

Slowly, her breathing harsh in the darkness, Deborah went over the whole thing again. She had been wrapped in a towel, had reached for the clothes that had been brought ... reached for them! She brought herself to a halt, considering the awful possibility. She had not dressed, was naked when she became unconscious. In the blackness she clutched at her body, sobbing aloud as her finger closed on cloth. She was dressed now, but Abe Turley had threatened to rape her. Had that woman given her to him? Had she allowed him to abuse Deborah before having her dressed and taken away?

Horror rose afresh, threatening to engulf her, taking every effort of her will to hold it back. If Turley had used her then surely her body would smart other than in the places she had been bruised when he caught her on the heath?

She tried to think past that horror. She was no longer in that room in Florrie Marston's house; the dank smell that invaded her nostrils with every breath she took was clear proof of that. But was she still in the house? Not unless it was moving! Unnoticed in the fear that had gripped her, only now did realisation dawn. Wherever she had been taken, whatever she was in, it was moving. Gently, soundlessly, almost like being rocked, but nevertheless moving!

From somewhere overhead a voice shouted and footsteps scuffled. Holding her breath, Deborah listened. Was it Turley, had he come for her again?

In the darkness a low sobbing was audible and Deborah pressed her knuckles against her mouth to stop the noise. But in the stillness it came again.

They were not her sobs! She held the breath tight in her throat, listening to catch the sounds over the drumming of her own heart. Wherever she was, she was not alone!

Footsteps shuffling once more above her head brought the sobs faster and louder, this time accompanied by a voice, itself trembling on the verge of tears.

Lungs aching from the strain, Deborah still refused to let go of the breath. Whoever it was in this place with her, did they know of her presence? Was someone else a prisoner, and if not why the sobs she could still hear?

The shout came again, followed by a bump that jolted her backward, bringing her head once more into contact with that same hard surface, forcing out the breath she had held. That sound from above was like someone walking in an upstairs room, but rooms were in houses and houses did not rock. Where in the world had she been brought?

Gingerly she stretched out a hand to each side of her. There had to be a way out.

'I'm frightened, Billy! I want to go home … I want Mother…'

Deborah froze, listening to the words carried on the sob. It was a child's voice. Somewhere in this hell hole there was a child!

'I'm here with you, Rosie. Try not to be frightened.'

The answer too was in the voice of a child. A boy and a girl. But why were they left in darkness?

'But I'm frightened, Billy,' the girl's voice cried again. 'That lady said we would be going to a nice place but we ain't … I want Mother.'

'You knows that ain't possible, Rosie.' The boy's voice trembled. 'You knows Mother be in the cemetery along of Father. But I be here, and I won't let nobody hurt you. Try to be brave. We can make a run for it once we gets where we be going.'

'Where do that be, Billy?'

In the blackness Deborah waited for the answer, but as the boy began to speak a sudden light showed itself. Instinctively she closed her eyes, forcing the breath into a long slow rhythm. If she could pretend the drug was still working her chance of escape might be better.

Seconds later the light fell full on her face, staying there for long moments, then it was turned away.

'You kids, stop your blartin'!'

The words were harsh and threatening, and Deborah heard a child's frightened cry.

'Stop your bloody snivelling or I'll throw you both overboard 'ere and now, and Turley's gaffer can whistle for his money. I gets little enough, it won't make no difference to me if you drowns 'ere. So unless you wants chuckin' in the cut, you'll keep quiet!'

Lifting her eyelids the merest fraction, Deborah peered into the gloomy light. A man stood with his back to her, a lantern held at eye level. The remains of the drug affecting her vision, or else being so long in the pitch darkness, she did not at once see the two small figures crouched with arms about each other; but as the man bent, holding the lantern forward, they came clearly into view.

Both tow-haired, one with its face buried against the chest of the other, two children were huddled in a corner, the boy lifting his head to the man who shouted again.

'You mind what I says! I hear one peep outta either of you and you goes over the side. 'Cept I

might keep that sister of yourn a bit of a while.
'Twould be a shame to waste the goods as well as
lose the profit. A man deserves a reward for his
labours.'

'Leave the child alone!'

Disgust thick in her voice Deborah pushed
herself to her feet, her hands reaching towards
the figure holding the lantern. But as quickly as
she had moved he had already turned, a leer
spreading rapidly across his face.

'So you be awake an' all?' One hand catching
hers, raised to strike him, he twisted it sharply,
carrying her arm up behind her back as she cried
out. 'Seems I won't be needing the kid after all.
Now ain't that fortunate for old Jake? Turley's
gaffer couldn't have given you as much poppy
juice as we thought. But Jake ain't complaining.
And given an hour of him between your legs, you
won't be complaining neither.'

Tightening the arm that held her, he snatched
Deborah hard against his body while lowering
the lantern to rest on a cupboard. The effort of
trying to push herself away, of trying to force a
space between their bodies, causing her words to
tumble out, Deborah sought to reason with the
man who had obviously been promised payment
for abducting her and probably these children
also.

'How much...' she gasped. 'How much is she
paying you? If you release me and the children
now ... I ... I will double it.'

'And how would old Jake be knowing that to be
the truth? Besides, right this minute it ain't
money I be interested in.'

Feeling his free hand close over her breast, Deborah felt panic begin to slide over her. Behind her the girl whimpered in terror. She had to hold on, had to keep her head if only for those children.

'Wait!' she gasped, drawing away as far as his hold allowed. 'Wait! Think of what you are doing, of what Florrie Marston will say if...'

'Florrie Marston?' The hand on her breast squeezed roughly. 'So Turley's gaffer don't be a man after all!'

He laughed, sending a cloud of beery breath into her face.

'But then neither is Turley. That one ain't worth a tinker's cuss. He was last in the line when brains were dished out. Tonight Jake is going to 'ave what he pleases, what *he* wants and be buggered to Turley and the woman who runs him.'

He snatched her closer to him, pressing his body against hers, the hand that had been on her breast beginning to claw away her dress. Deborah screamed. But it was drowned by thick throaty laughter as his wet lips closed over her mouth and she was forced down on to the floor.

The barge was there, moored just to one side of the bridge spanning the canal. Breath tight in his chest, Clay pushed the stocky figure of Abe Turley the final few yards to the towpath.

Midland Rose. The boat's name, entwined with loops of vividly painted roses, showed clearly in the pale light of morning.

'That be the one.' Abe glanced at the man still

firmly holding on to his arm. 'That be Jake Connors' boat. That be the one I drove the wench to. Her should still be there, Florrie wouldn't intend keeping her this close to Blakenhall so Connors shouldn't have put her off yet. I've told you all I knows, God's honour I have, now let me be off...'

'Honour!' Clay looked at him disparagingly. 'You don't even know the meaning of the word! As for God, don't count on Him for help.'

One hand still holding him fast, Clay used the other to free the buckle of the belt fastened about Abe's waist. Snatching it free he shoved Abe face down on the ground, using the belt to fasten his hands behind his back. Then, grabbing the cloth that had circled the thick neck, he tied it about Abe's feet.

Satisfied Turley was going nowhere, Clay glanced again at the boat, his blood curdling as he heard a woman's scream.

Deborah! With one leap he was on the barge and tearing open the hatch that gave on to the cabin, falling back as a sheet of flame rushed out at him.

The initial burst of heat and smoke receding, Clay jumped the few stairs that led down to the living quarters of the narrow boat, calling Deborah's name as he peered into shadows given life by the dancing flames.

'Clay! Oh, Clay, thank God!'

Beyond him a flurry of movement guided him to the spot where she lay trapped beneath a cupboard that in turn covered the heavy figure of a man.

Fire ran a glowing tongue over the wood of the cupboard, lapping at the trails of oil spreading across the cabin floor, devouring the man's clothing then reaching greedily for the girl's lifted skirts.

Heedless of the flames biting at his hands, of the already intense heat sucking the air from his lungs, he dragged the cupboard away, letting it crash against the cabin bulkhead.

The skin on his face feeling as if it were frying, he heaved the unconscious man aside, hauling Deborah to her feet and shoving her up the narrow steps to the deck.

'The children!' she choked, fresh air forcing the smoke from her lungs. 'The children, Clay. We can't leave them in there.'

Children! He turned. Flames spewed from the hatchway. Connors' children? Or were they the twins Turley had driven from Florrie Marston's house? No matter which, he could not leave them to die in that fire.

'Get to the tow path.' Giving her one push towards the side of the boat, he jumped back into the cabin.

Safe on the bank, fingers clasped together, Deborah stared at the hatchway, lost in the burgeoning fire. 'Oh, God, don't let them die,' she murmured. 'Please don't let them die.'

Standing there watching first smoke then flickering red flames lick along the roof of the cabin, every second was agony for her.

The man had grabbed her and was forcing her to the ground when the boy had seized the lamp, bringing it down across the bargee's head. The

293

boy had been trying to help her and now he was in danger of paying with his life, while she … she was safe.

A few feet away, still tethered to the bank, the boat was gradually being wreathed in thick smoke. She should not be here, not when those children were in danger. She had to help, she had to go back. If Clay and the children died, then she would die too.

Running the few feet, she climbed on to the deck of the barge, feeling the heat of the fire beneath her feet.

'Clay!' she sobbed, running to the hatchway as a figure emerged, clothes smoking, eyes streaming from the acrid sting of smoke.

'Take them, take them off!' Clay shoved the small girl into her arms then lifted the boy from his back.

'Clay, you can't go back in there!' Deborah's cry was pitiful as he pushed the boy towards her.

Looking into her eyes, dark now with new fear, he touched her face for just a second. 'I have to, Deborah, there's a man in there,' he said. Then, very quietly, 'I love you, Deborah Hammond. I love you with all my heart and soul.'

He loved! Deborah felt her heart leap. He loved her, not Lizzie!

The girl clinging to her neck, the boy's hand in hers, she led them to the bank. Her tears streaming unchecked, she sank to her knees, a child held tight in each arm. Clay Gilmore loved her as she loved him. But would he live to tell her so again?

'He has to live.' Unaware the words were

coming from her lips, she repeated them.

'He'll be all right, miss.' The boy's arms tightened about her as he tried to comfort her. 'You'll see, that man will be all right.'

Glancing down at the child's frightened face, Deborah tried to smile, only to scream Clay's name as the cabin roof exploded in a sea of flame.

The small white face of the girl hidden against her, Deborah's eyes closed. Clay Gilmore was dead, had perished trying to save her. He had said he loved her but now she could not tell him she returned that love. He would never hear her words.

Sobs shuddering through her, she buried her face in the girl's golden hair.

'Look, miss...'

Deborah felt the boy tug at her skirts but she could not look at that boat again, at the blazing fire that had ended Clay's life.

'Miss.' The boy tugged at her again. 'We 'ave to help them, miss.'

Pressing her face closer against the girl's hair, Deborah wanted to scream. How could she help, how could anyone help Clay now? He was dead and it was her fault. If only she had gone by road after leaving the salon...

'Keep a hold of my sister, please, miss. I'll help the man.'

Only on feeling the boy move did his words make sense to her. He was going back into that fire!

A cry of protest already on her lips, Deborah's

eyes flew open. He must not go, he must not die as well as Clay.

Scrambling to her feet, still holding the girl fast to her, Deborah watched the boy as he reached the tow path. Then, the sheer effort of it making her wince, she directed her gaze towards the boat.

'Clay!' she breathed. Then louder, so that it rang out over the crackle of burning wood, 'Clay!'

With that one word she began to run. He was alive. Oh, God, he was alive!

'Can you stay here with him?'

Safe on the heath a short distance from the burning boat, Deborah looked at the man she'd thought lost for ever. Tiny wisps of smoke still curled from his charred clothing, his hands were red from the kiss of the flames, his beardless face streaked with smoke, but he was alive.

'Can you stay with him?' Clay's eyes held real concern as he looked at her. 'I can't carry him back to Elmore yet and nor can we leave him here alone.'

Looking at the unconscious figure lying at her feet, Deborah felt her stomach curdle. This man had been about to force himself on her, he had intended to rape her. But he was injured. Those burns to his face and head...

Glancing back at Clay, she nodded. 'I'll stay.'

Reaching one scorched hand to her face, he smiled. 'I'll be back, I promise.'

Catching a wince of pain on his face as he lifted the little girl in his arms, Deborah's own face displayed the empathy she felt. She wanted to take Clay in her arms, soothe away the suffering this night had caused him, tell him of the love she held for him. But instead she could only watch him turn away, the boy close to his side.

'Hey!'

The shout detaining him, Clay hesitated.

'You ain't going to leave me here?'

His look more snarl than smile, Clay hitched the girl higher in his arms. 'Why not, Abe? You left these kids on that barge.'

'I told you, Gilmore, that were Florrie Marston's doing, it were her had 'em sent.'

'But it was you brought them.' Clay glared at Abe Turley, still securely trussed. 'That was your doing.'

'Gilmore ... Gilmore!'

But Clay only walked on.

The sun had gained a foothold in the sky but there was no warmth in its glow. Beside the tow path the flames had settled now, reducing the barge to a charred wreck. Deborah shivered, the chill of what could have been sending ice through her veins.

Kneeling beside her attacker she glanced at his terrible burns then turned her face away, stomach heaving. The boy had tried to help, he had struck the man's head with the lamp, but as it broke it had spread oil over him, oil the flames had seized upon.

'Hey!'

A few yards away, Abe Turley had twisted over on to his side and now lay watching her.

'Hey!' he called again. 'You'd better do something for Connors and quick, lest you want him dead.'

Connors. Was that his name? Strange, she had not thought of his having one; but then, she had not thought of him as a man, only as a beast ready to abuse a young child, ready to rape a young woman.

'Look at him,' Abe called again. 'That trembling of his body be more than cold, it be shock. You needs to keep him warm.'

Instinctively Deborah reached for her shawl. It was not about her shoulders, it must have fallen off.

She let her hands fall to her sides.

Her own state of shock slowing her senses, she stared absently at the shaking figure.

The wench was still dazed, still only partly aware of what was going on. Seeing what would probably be his only opportunity, Abe called again, this time taking care to keep his voice on a lower, more even tone. The last thing he could afford was to frighten her more than she was now.

'Listen to me, Connors is in a bad way, you 'ave to keep him warm...' He paused, eyes never leaving her pale drawn face. 'Deborah ... Deborah, you 'ave to help him.'

Gently, insistently, forcing himself to hold back the tension building in him at the thought of Gilmore's return, Abe repeated the words over and over.

'I can't ... I can't!'

The words came at last, bursting from Deborah on a flood of tears, Abe breathed a long sigh. The horizon was clear, he still had time.

'You can, Deborah,' he said soothingly. 'You can help. Just cover him with something warm.'

Her mind still clouded with fear, she spread her hands helplessly. 'I ... I don't have anything. My ... my shawl...'

Abe tried to wriggle forward but, damp with dew, the ground sucked at him holding him back. 'Use my jacket. Take it, Deborah. Put my jacket on Connors. Do it!'

Slowly, uncomprehendingly, she lifted her gaze to him.

'Come on, Deborah,' he urged quietly. 'Take the jacket.'

Her movements trance-like, she felt herself rise, her feet carrying her as though through a dream from which she could not waken.

'That's it, Deborah.' Abe lay perfectly still as she knelt beside him, her fingers fumbling with the buttons of his coat.

'I can help you.' He smiled at the puzzled frown that settled between her brows when, pushing the coat from his shoulders, it refused to fall free. 'Let me help you, Deborah. Untie my hands. The jacket won't come off if my hands are tied.'

Rolling forward on to his face he tried to hold his nervousness in check. The bloody wench was half asleep! If Gilmore showed now his chances were nil!

'Undo the belt, Deborah.' His voice was soft and quiet, soothing as a mother's blessing. 'Unfasten it so I can help you.'

Every movement distant, apart from her, taking place only in that same dream, Deborah loosed the buckle, unwrapping the leather belt that bound his wrists.

Sitting up, he snatched the neckerchief from about his ankles and was on his feet in an instant.

'You got away lightly once before.' Fist clenched, he raised his arm above his head. 'And you be getting away again, you bloody bitch! But you won't escape Abe Turley. I'll be back for you. And when I do you'll get more than this.'

Bringing his fist slicing down in a side swipe, he struck her full on the temple.

Teeth clenched together, words whistling through the wide gap in them, he looked down at her crumpled figure. 'I'll be back!' he grated again. 'No bloody twopenny wench makes a fool of Abe Turley!'

Chapter Twenty-one

'There be no more you can do now, Clay lad.' Sadie smiled into a face drawn with more than tiredness. 'Deborah be safe now, thanks to the Almighty and to you. Get you along home to your mother. She be sure to be fretting with you not in the house the night through. Go and get some rest, Lizzie and me will look to Deborah.'

'Arrh.' Clay nodded. 'I will that, Sadie.' At the door he turned, hand drawing the boot from his pocket. 'What do you reckon we should do with this?'

Taking it from him, Sadie ran a finger along the row of tiny buttons, all the fear of the past night returning to her.

'It be best burned lad, same as the fellow to it has surely been. Best burned and forgotten. That be, if any of we will ever be able to forget.'

'Well, Florrie Marston won't, not after the magistrate hears what Molly Sanders has to tell him.'

'It were an evil business. Lord knows how many that woman has sent into slavery. Wickedness and sin of that sort be deserving no mercy.'

No, she deserved no mercy. Clay set off down the entry. Nor did Turley, and if he and Clay met again it would not be the law meted out his punishment.

Closing the door, Sadie glanced at the two

children rolled in blankets, one sleeping on her old leather squab, her feet reaching only halfway along the worn sofa, the other curled on the pegged rug that covered the hearth. A year ago she had been alone in this house, now it was beginning to resemble an orphanage.

But she couldn't have turned them away, not even if there had been no Molly to tell her of what had gone before. Molly Sanders! Settling herself into the chair she had drawn to the fire, Sadie listened to the kettle singing quietly on its bracket. That child at least had a mother who loved her. Portland House was the name she had mumbled as she was settled into bed. Portland House. Sadie glanced again at the sleeping twins. The Lord in His goodness had made the mother of one child easy to find, but who would mother those two?

This house was too small to hold them all. Sadie turned her glance to the fire. With Lizzie and her child in one bedroom and Deborah in another, where could two more heads be laid ... where would the money be found to feed them? Resting her own head against the back of the chair, Sadie closed her eyes, a faint smile touching the corners of her mouth. This chair had served as her bed many nights after her man was took, it would serve again; as for feeding two more mouths...

He who giveth his bread to the poor, giveth it to me.

Words familiar from childhood deepened the smile on her lips. She had gone without before and survived. She would do so again.

'The master is closing the house, you will no longer be required!' Agnes Ridley held out two sovereigns to the woman employed as laundress.

'He has been generous in the money given you owing to the suddenness of his decision, leaving you with no time to look for a similar post.'

Mary Ann Sanders stared at the coins. The job was finished, she was being sent on her way. But where could she go, and what of Molly? Her daughter would think her still at this house.

'Take it, woman!' Agnes jerked her hand up and down, irritated by the woman's slowness. She wanted her gone from the house before facing Cato Rawley. There would be none here but her when she broke her news.

Taking the coins, Mary Ann held them in her hand. 'Mrs Ridley, mum,' she asked, 'when I was recommended for the post as laundress to Mr Rawley, was ... was mention made of my Molly?'

'Molly?' Agnes almost spat the name. If the woman didn't go immediately she would throw her out.

'My daughter, mum. That priest who found the both of us a place, he said a Mrs Elliott got me a post here with Mr Rawley but he didn't mention where my Molly was to be sent. I ... I thought maybe the master would know?'

'Why would the master know where your girl was sent!' It was more statement than question but Agnes's hand, already on the scullery door, tightened.

'I ... I just thought...'

'Well, he does not!' Agnes snapped. 'Had he known he would have mentioned as much.

303

Surely you asked the priest where your girl was being sent?'

'No, mum.' Mary Ann stared at the coins in her hand. 'I was that upset I didn't think, You see my Molly ... well, her don't be fully-grown, her be less than fifteen years and we'd never been parted afore, and I ... I didn't think.'

'Then you must ask the priest. You know where to find *him*, I suppose.'

'I knows the place, mum, it were the other side of Walsall town. The Pleck it were called.'

She had heard of the place. Many folk had come from there to the Sister Dora Hospital while Agnes had nursed. Most of them like this woman, down and out.

'Then go there and ask. Ask this Father...?'

'Travers, mum, he were Father Philip Travers.'

Agnes shifted her feet impatiently. She wanted this woman gone. 'Then go and ask him. Now off with you, I have to see to closing of the house.'

Leonie Elliott! Closing the door behind the departing woman, Agnes stood for a moment giving rein to her thoughts. It was not impossible there could be another woman of that name, but so close to Bloxwich? Again not impossible but highly improbable. Agnes Ridley knew every woman of consequence for miles about. Delia Rawley had had many visitors before becoming too ill and there had been no Leonie Elliott among them ... she had come later, and only to see Cato.

Crossing the scullery into the kitchen, Agnes stood with hands folded together, staring blankly at the walls.

304

Leonie Elliott was as self-centred as herself. A woman out for all she could get, and certainly not given to acts of charity. So why would she bother to find employment for Mary Ann Sanders? And a priest, a man of the cloth, that was the last sort of company Leonie Elliott would keep. It was a bit of a mystery, and one Agnes would look into after she was married to Cato.

Nine o'clock, Cato had said. Agnes glanced at the fob watch pinned to her shoulder. It was almost that now. In a few minutes he would be finished with breakfast. She had set that as usual; continuing her routine would speak as loud as any words. Agnes Ridley was here to stay.

Removing her apron she folded it neatly, her movements automatic as she placed it in a drawer of the large oak dresser. She had heard shuffling and footsteps in the early hours, the sound of voices. That would be *her* leaving. Had she taken those dresses after all? Agnes's fingers clenched at the thought. She would dearly have liked to go to the bedroom to see for herself, but Cato had relieved her of the keys and now the doors were locked. But no matter! She lifted her head, lips thinning. They would be replaced. Cato Rawley was going to replace many things.

The tightness still about her mouth, she made her way to his study.

'Normally I would have paid your salary to the end of the year.'

Cato had not looked up as she entered, nor had he asked her to take a seat. Watching him count a number of sovereigns from a box he proceeded to lock, Agnes felt the first slight flutter of trepidation but kept her features composed as he went on.

'But in this case I do not feel it is warranted, you do not deserve such consideration. Therefore I have paid simply the four months due from our last reckoning but I have written you no reference.'

If he had thought the last would cause her concern then he had badly misjudged. The ripple of nervousness she had felt a moment ago vanished completely and Agnes smiled.

'Of course not, Cato my dear. After all, as your wife I will have no need of any reference.'

Placing the coins in a neat pile before her on the desk, the movement unhurried, he glanced up at her. But calm as his movements had been, his eyes danced with anger.

'I had hoped you would have come to your senses by this time but it appears you wish to continue with this charade. I, however, do not. Take your pay and whatever else belongs to you and leave my house.'

'Leave your house?' The smile turned to a laugh as Agnes met his cold gaze. 'Oh, yes, you would like that, wouldn't you, Cato? That would suit you and your trollop very well, wouldn't it? Well Agnes Ridley is going nowhere, I am here to stay, to collect all you promised me when we lay together. You can forget Leonie Elliott. From now on she will be a figure of the past, someone you played with for awhile and have now discarded.'

'The only one I played with was *you!*'

The contempt in each word keen as a scalpel,

his voice bit into Agnes. She had not expected this, had thought her threats of last night would have brought him to his senses.

'...the one I am discarding is *you*. How you could ever have thought I would marry you is beyond me.'

'You implied as much ... you promised...'

Leaning back in his chair, Cato ran a slow deliberate glance over the woman who had so many times shared his bed, a woman he had never truly liked.

'I *promised*? I offered you marriage in return for the use of your body? How could I, a married man, say such a thing? But even had I not had a wife already, I would never have entertained the idea of making you such; you offered your services and were paid for them the same as any other common prostitute. That is what you were after all is it not, a common prostitute?'

'Maybe.' In her fury the reply fell softly into the room, but Agnes's eyes sparked. 'Maybe I am no better than the one to whom you gave those jewels. We are both out of the same mould and both want the same thing. But I told you before – Leonie Elliott will never be mistress in this house, she will never be your wife. You see, Cato, I have watched you together, watched you play your little games in the bedroom ... games I will tell the world about should you dare to go back on your word.'

Keeping his eyes on her, Cato shook his head slowly, a sardonic smile touching his mouth. 'And you truly expect anyone to believe you? A woman with ideas above her station, a blackmailer *and* a thief.'

'A thief!' snorted Agnes. 'Since when have I ever stolen!'

'Perhaps since years ago. Who can tell what happened to my wife's belongings? A husband does not always keep trace of such things. But since her death I have and I would say you *have* stolen, the most recent of your thefts having taken place only last evening.'

Agnes's nerves jarred. What was he up to?

'You see,' he went on, 'this morning I decided to remove my late wife's jewellery from her room to this safe. Needless to say the casket was empty. I immediately locked all of the upstairs rooms and those of the servants' quarters, then telephoned the local constabulary.'

Her voice trembling with fury, Agnes snapped, 'I have nothing of Delia's! I have stolen nothing.'

'That is not the view the law will take, not when the constable finds an amethyst necklace hidden in your valise, not to mention two of my wife's gowns in your bag!'

'That's a lie!' Agnes gasped.

'Is it?' Cato's smile was pure acid.

'You know it is. You gave that necklace to Leonie Elliott.'

'You're wrong.' The smile wiped from his face, Cato banged his fist on the desk. 'None of my guests was ever shown into my wife's bedroom. The only one apart from myself to have access there was you, and those gowns and jewels are in the luggage you have packed to take from this house.'

It was a ruse. He was trying to trick her, but it

would not work. There was nothing of Delia Rawley's in her bags. How could there be? She had packed them herself. Forcing the tremor from her nerves, Agnes met his eyes boldly.

'If you think to frighten me, Cato, then you are wasting your time and that of the constabulary. You know as well as I do that there is nothing which is not my own in those bags.'

'Nothing which is not your own.' He echoed her words sarcastically. 'But in your jealousy you believed them to be your own. You said as much last evening as Mrs Elliott will testify. Her word and the constable's findings will prove more than damning. You will be convicted of theft together with attempted blackmail; the gaol sentence for such a crime is many years' hard labour. Think of it. You are no longer a young woman and by no means pretty. Fifteen or twenty years down the line … you will be a sorry sight indeed the day you see freedom again.'

Somehow or other he *had* tricked her. She could see that in his face and in his eyes. But how?

'It was easy.' He read the question. 'While you have been here in this room, Mrs Elliott has been in yours. She has placed the gowns in your bag, the necklace in your valise. Now the door is locked and the keys safe in my bedroom.'

A flicker of triumph returning, Agnes replied, 'How will it look to the constable, finding that woman in your room?'

His hand lying where he had brought it down, Cato spread the fingers languidly. 'She will not be found in my room, nor in my house. Mrs Elliott has now left. But the constable will be told she left last night. After finding you in my late wife's gown and wearing her necklace, Mrs Elliott was too upset to follow through her kind offer of sorting those gowns for charity.'

'You bastard!' Agnes's cry spewed the bitterness in her soul as she stared into his face. Then as he smiled she reached into her pocket, withdrawing the card she had guarded for so long. It may not bring the reward she had desired, but now she cherished vengeance more, and this card would give her that.

'You think you have won, don't you, Cato?' She held the card to her breast. 'And so you have ... to a degree. The battle is over for me but yours is about to begin and it will be one you will fight to your dying day.

'Delia Rawley was barren. She could not give you the one thing you wanted most: a child, a son to carry on your name. And we both know you will never have a child from Leonie Elliott: nature does not permit a man to have a child by another man.

'Yes Cato, another man. I told you I knew, that I had seen you together, watching you kiss his body, take his genitals in your hands, press your face to them. I saw it all, Cato. Saw you roll on top of him as you would a woman, saw his arms close about you, watched as he got to his knees, as you entered him...' She paused, dragging in a long quivering breath. 'I watched you make love to another man, Cato, but it cannot bring you a child. As for marrying some other woman, that will never happen, you are too deeply enmeshed in Elliott's coils. You are the last of your line,

Cato, the very last Rawley. When you die so will your name. But the tragedy, Cato,' she laughed softly, viciously, 'the real tragedy is it need not have happened.'

The spread fingers closing, Cato looked at her. 'What do you mean?'

I'll tell you, shall I?' Agnes's smile was pure vitriol. 'I'll tell you. Do you remember almost twenty years ago, a girl called Emmeline Burton – Emmy? She was a pretty girl, with hair the colour of ripe chestnuts and eyes clear golden-brown like old brandy. *This* girl, Cato!'

Placing the card on the desk she stood watching as he looked at it, looked at himself smiling down at a young girl.

'You remember, Cato? You should, you seduced her. You seduced the girl in that photograph then turned your back on her when you found her to be carrying your child. Your child, Cato.' Agnes laughed wildly. 'The one you will never have!'

'It's not true.' He glanced up at the face twisted with mockery. 'It's not true.'

'Oh, but it is!' Satisfaction carried the words on a soft breath. 'Look at it, Cato, read the words written on the back.'

Turning the photograph in his fingers he scanned the words, the ink faded now to a pale brown.

Cato and Emmy, soon to be man and wife...

Then lower down, but equally old and faded, the words, *You will never know our child, Cato, the child we made together, but I will love it as I love you.*

'That's right, Cato.' Agnes watched the colour drain from his cheeks. 'The child you made

311

together, the child you turned from your house a second time.'

'What are you saying? How could I turn away a child that never was?' He looked up and she saw the flickers of uncertainty in his eyes. Belief beneath the doubt.

Leaning closer, Agnes smiled, showing teeth that were slightly crooked. 'Look at the face – at Emmy's face. Doesn't it remind you of another young girl? The one you dismissed from your service a few months ago? She was Emmeline Burton's daughter. *Your* daughter, Cato, *yours!* As it will be with her, so it will be with you. Madness will eat away at your brain, a madness that will destroy you!'

Her laughter echoing shrilly behind her, Agnes rushed from the study. Left alone Cato touched a finger to the face in the photograph then read the words again.

Had Emmy given birth to his child? And had Agnes Ridley known all along?

Was that the weapon with which she had hoped to hold him? But that was hopeless for a stronger power than that held him. Cato sat staring at the fire as he had since Agnes Ridley had slammed out of the room. Leonie did not whimper or cajole, did not demand as any other mistress might. In fact she asked nothing of him, but then she did not have to. Her beauty and delicate manner, her caring ways and willingness always to be at the beck and call of others not so fortunate, had enslaved him from the first.

He stared into the flames reaching into the dark heart of the chimney.

312

On the contrary it was he who did the asking, always wanting her to be there with him, his heart sinking when she said she could not come.

But soon ... he watched the myriad sparks shower from a coal falling into the hearth ... once they were together for always, her little kindnesses to other people need not entail her being gone from him. She could administer them from the home they shared.

She was so kind, so understanding. Leaning his head against the back of his chair, Cato closed his eyes, the question he had been asking himself rising once more to the forefront of his mind. How would Leonie take the news that he had a daughter? Would she be jealous, perhaps refuse to accept the girl at all? That would break his heart. But if what Agnes Ridley had thrown at him with such viciousness was true, if indeed he did have a daughter, then he would not turn his back on her a second time. He had not faced up to his responsibility where Emmy had been concerned but he would not repudiate her child. He loved Leonie Elliott there was no denying that, but that love could not be allowed to come before his own child.

Opening his eyes, Cato stared again into the fire.

But he would not be called upon to choose between them. Leonie was too kindhearted not to accept his daughter. First though, he must establish the truth of all this, must find the girl Agnes Ridley had spoken of, find her and talk with her. Then and only then would he tell Leonie of her.

'There be nothing else to be done, leastways not yet.' Sadie sliced determinedly into the potato she held in her hand, bringing away the peel in one long curling strip.

'But how will you manage?' Deborah sighed. The argument had been going on for an hour but Sadie showed no sign of giving in. 'With Lizzie and myself gone it will be difficult to feed three extra mouths, especially having no more work from Florrie Marston.'

'Don't talk to me about that one.' Sadie tossed the potato into a large cast-iron pot. 'I hope they sends her to the same place her was like to send you and where her's sent others before: off to the white slavers!'

'There's no real proof of her doing that.'

'Proof … you talk of proof?' Sadie looked up sharply. 'Ain't Molly Sanders' word proof enough? And what about them twins, ain't they proof?'

'A lawyer could argue otherwise.' Deborah topped and tailed a green bean. 'It could be as Clay says. Florrie has only to swear she told Abe Turley to bring me home, that she lent him her carriage to drive me here, but instead of doing so he handed me over to that bargee. Then she will appear quite innocent.'

'Oh, arrh!' Sadie continued peeling potatoes. 'And he did the same with them babbies, be that what her'll say?'

The last of the beans finished, Deborah gathered the bits and pieces, taking them to the fire. 'It would be feasible, especially with Turley

314

having bolted. There'll be no one to deny what she says.'

'So her will get away with it?'

'Clay seems to fear so, but at least one good thing will come of it. If Florrie were dealing with slave traffickers she certainly won't do so any more.'

'Oh, no?' Sadie gathered the potato peelings, wrapping them in old newspaper before wedging them beside the bean shreds Deborah had placed on the back of the fire. 'You don't want to be too sure of that, wench. Folk have short memories. A year or two and her evil doings will be forgotten, then it'll be back to the same old game. Anyway…' she turned brusquely as if only now had Deborah's earlier words registered in her brain '…what do you mean … you and Lizzie gone?'

Returning to the table Deborah picked up the heavy pot filled to the brim with potatoes, taking that also to the fire to hang from a bracket above the glowing coals.

'It's the only sensible way. Lizzie is well now and the baby is strong. We can find a place somewhere and that will leave room for Molly and the twins here with you.'

'You and Lizzie be going nowhere.' Sadie threw salt into the pot then glanced at Deborah with a look that was almost fearful. 'Least, not unless you *wants* to.'

'Of course we don't want to. It's just that Lizzie and I don't want you giving up your bed, not when we are capable of moving on.'

'And where would you move to?'

Hearing the hurt in the older woman's voice Deborah felt the sting of tears in her own throat. The last thing she wanted was to hurt Sadie, to repay her kindness with pain, but the fact remained that there was just not enough room for all of them here, and Sadie was too old to be sleeping in a chair.

'Not too far.' She tried to sound light-hearted. 'A couple of rooms somewhere in the village.'

Sadie took the pan of beans, scalding them with water from the kettle before placing them in the oven. 'Then that village won't be Elmore Green. I knows every family lives here and there don't be one has fewer in number than there be in this house. Besides, given a day or two young Molly will have found her mother, and that will be one less.'

Which would still leave the twins. Deborah looked at Sadie's lined face. She was kindness itself, could never bring herself to give those children over to the Parish, and neither would Lizzie or Deborah want that. It would be less trouble all round for them to leave.

'Sadie...'

'I know what you be going to say,' she interrupted. 'You be going to say 'twould be easier if you and Lizzie went. But it wouldn't be for me, Deborah.' Her voice breaking on a sob, she went on quietly, 'I don't think I could go on if I lost the two of you. I believe you were sent to me. For long, long years I prayed for children of my own, but none ever came. Then, as time wore on and I knew there would be no child in this house, I stopped bothering the Almighty. I reckoned He had made His ruling plain: Sadie Trent would go through life without knowing a child's love, or what it was to love one herself. It was hard and there were times I felt my heart to be breaking, but eventually I settled to what had been ordained for me. I forgot about having a child.

'But the Lord has not forgotten, He was merely biding His time and when it were full He sent me two. Two girls who, though not of my body, have become of my soul. I love you, Deborah, you and Lizzie both, more than my tongue has words to say. You are the joy in my heart, the sweet breath of heaven that nourishes my soul. You are the daughters of my hopes, the children of my prayers. The time will come when you have husbands, and at that time I know I will have to let you go. But don't let that time be now Deborah, don't take away my heart, don't let me lose you 'til it has to be.'

'Oh, Sadie!' Dropping the utensils she had gathered, Deborah threw her arms about her, warm tears on her cheeks mingling with those on Sadie's. 'You won't ever lose us, we will never go far from you. We love you, Lizzie and I. We love you very much.'

For long moments Sadie held the girl close to her breast, the warmth of love flooding through her. This was a feeling she had thought never to experience, never to hear a child say 'I love you'. That dream had faded when Emmy's child had been taken from her, but now it had returned, a dream fulfilled. Standing there with Deborah in her arms, Sadie murmured a prayer of thanks for a blessing she would cherish the rest of her days.

317

Chapter Twenty-two

'I ... am sorry, I suppose I am still nervous.'

Releasing Clay's arm which she had grabbed unthinkingly, Deborah apologised.

'That's to be expected.'

Clay glanced at her face, drained of colour now, then looked quickly away. He had told this girl he loved her, told her his feelings for her that morning by the canal side, but since then she had said nothing, given no indication of her own feelings. It was obvious why. She had no love for him, felt only friendship. By ignoring what he had said, pretending it had never been spoken, she was showing what she thought of his profession of love.

By his sides, Clay's hands clenched. He would respect her feelings and not tell her again of his own; if friendship was all he could have of Deborah Hammond then he would take that and gladly.

'It's silly of me to be startled by every little shadow.' Her hands shook slightly as they held the jug.

'It's not silly at all.' His voice was quiet and soothing. 'After what you were put through it's brave of you even to leave the house.'

'Sadie would rather I did not. She's more jumpy than I am, and Lizzie's as bad.'

'You can't blame them for that, they love you.'

318

Clay swallowed the rest of the words he wanted to add: As I love you Deborah.

She nodded. 'Yes, but life has to go on and I can't spend the rest of mine indoors.'

True. But you can take extra care. If you go some distance then be sure someone is with you.'

Reaching the Spring Cottage she halted, the look in her eyes one of veiled fear.

'The police haven't found him yet?'

'No.' Clay shook his head. 'Nor will they. Abe Turley knows the heath like the back of his hand.'

'Then you think that's where he is?'

'I wouldn't put money on that. It's my guess he's far away by now. He knows his life depends on it.'

'His life?' Deborah sounded surprised. 'Does ... does what he did carry the death sentence?'

For what he did to you it does, *my* death sentence. The thought locked inside him, Clay made no answer.

Taking his sudden silence for anger at her stupidity in releasing the man, Deborah dropped her glance.

'I didn't think what I was doing when I untied Abe Turley. The other man, the bargee, he was shaking so badly ... Abe said he would help.'

'Instead of which he knocked you senseless then ran off, leaving you and Connors. At least he didn't drop you into the canal but probably only because he was afraid of my returning before he could make this getaway.'

'But it's my fault he has got away. The policeman almost said as much. But I couldn't let that bargee die Clay, I ... I could not.'

319

'And you didn't.' Closing his hands over hers about the jug, he smiled. 'Abe Turley's one talent lies in fooling people. It's no shame on you that you were taken in by him. Just take better care in future.'

Her head lifting quickly her eyes displaying the state of nerves inside her, she asked. 'Do you think he will come back?'

'Not Turley. Even he has more sense than to do that.'

Waiting while she collected Sadie's pint of Old Best, Clay thought over his words to Deborah. He had lied to give her peace of mind, to hold back the fear that had been so plain in her eyes these last days. Turley was a coward and a bully, but more than that he could not bear to be bested. The fact that he had been beaten and cheated of a considerable profit all because of a girl would fester like a sore inside him, a little more each day, until it forced him to return. And when he did it would be Deborah Hammond at whom he would strike first.

Clay felt the blood in his veins turn to ice. He was caught between the Devil and the deep blue sea! No to go after Turley was to leave him free to return to Elmore Green, while to go in search of him was to leave Deborah unprotected. Whichever way he took could prove disastrous for her.

The walk back to Sadie's house passed mostly in silence, each of them troubled by thoughts they could not share. At the entrance to the passage set between the houses Deborah turned to him.

'Clay, I have not thanked you properly for what

you did for me. I owe you a great deal, I know that. I can never repay you...'

The hands he had held clenched at his sides during that walk, to prevent their touching her, now closed about her arms, the ferocity of the movement sending a little of the beer spilling over the sides of the jug.

'You don't have to thank me, Deborah.' His voice harsh, he stared down at her, moonlight icing his eyes. 'Nor do I need your thanks. I want only...' He paused, the words sticking in his throat. Releasing her, he turned his face away. 'I want only that you be safe.'

He had sounded almost angry, though Deborah, walking along the passage to Sadie's door. As if her thanking him had caused him annoyance. He had been abrupt with her since rescuing her from that barge. He had said he loved her then, that he loved her with all his heart and soul but from that moment he had made no further mention of it. It must have been a mistake, a slip of the tongue. In the heat of the moment, given the danger he knew he was facing by going back into that burning cabin, his mind had switched her name for Lizzie's. It was Lizzie he had meant to say he loved, Lizzie and not her at all.

He got on so well with Lizzie, Deborah mused, reaching for the latch. And he loved little Thomas, that was one fact he did not hide. So why his reticence in telling Lizzie of his love for her? Each time he visited Sadie's he laughed and talked with her yet did not ask her to walk with him. Was it old-fashioned reserve or natural courtesy on his part that warned he must give Lizzie time. Or was it simply fear she might refuse him? And Lizzie ... much as she talked of Clay, she had never once hinted at loving him. But she must, he was so kind and gentle.

'I will say good night here, Deborah.'

Her hand still on the latch, she turned back to him. 'But you must come in. Lizzie will be looking forward to seeing you.'

'Will you give her my regards, and Sadie too? There are things I promised my mother I would do.'

'Of course.' Deborah smiled to hide a swift pang of disappointment.

'Your mother has been very patient and I have been very selfish, letting you accompany Molly in the search for her mother when I could easily have gone with her.'

The urge to touch her too strong to master, Clay lifted his hand to her face, touching one finger to her brow. 'I don't think you have a selfish bone in your body.'

His footsteps fading quickly as he abruptly turned away down the shadowed entry, Deborah felt her heart crack.

I love you, Deborah Hammond, I love you with all my heart and soul.

The words returned to her, each one a sword in her breast. They were the words Clay had spoken. If only he had meant them.

'A young wench, you say?' Martha Vines looked at the woman who had stopped Bertha and herself with her question. 'And how long is it you have been searching?'

'A few days past, but I have seen no sign of her.'

Giving a swift cautionary glance towards her companion, Martha chose her words with care. Should the wench be one sold off by Florrie Marston it would be a sorrowful tale for her to hear, and by the look of her this woman had heard more than enough of sorrow.

'Be the wench your daughter?'

'Yes, my Molly. She's...'

'Molly? You say her name be Molly?'

Mary Ann's drawn features were lit by the hope that coursed through her.

'Yes, Molly Sanders. She was sent to be a house maid, but I don't be sure where.'

'How old would her be?' Martha directed a second glance at Bertha but put the question herself.

'Fifteen come lamastide and pretty as a picture though I say it as shouldn't, seeing as I be her mother. She has eyes the blue of a cornflower and hair pale as fresh-grown wheat...'

'Was the position the wench was given found for her by a priest?'

Surprise showing in her eyes, Mary Ann nodded as she answered, 'To be sure it was. Father Philip Travers over at the Pleck. I called to see him but he was away. His housekeeper said it might be a week or even more before he returned, so I have to go on looking and praying the Lord will help.'

'Seems He might have done just that. Bertha and me knows where there is a wench to be found who answers to your description.' Martha pulled her shawl close over her head. Village news always found a way of reaching her and Bertha.

'My Molly?' Hope danced like sunlight on water in Mary Ann's tear-bright eyes.

'We ain't said as much,' Bertha answered her cautiously. 'But the wench we speak of is called Molly. If you be of a mind to come along of Martha and me to Elmore Green, we'll take you along to where it is she will be.'

On the road that led to the village Martha and Bertha were careful to keep the conversation clear of what had sent the girl running from her place of employment; there would be time for that should this woman prove to be her mother, and if she were not then there had been no tales told out of school.

Passing the smithy that stood opposite the vicarage they were halfway to Elmore Green when Mary Ann stopped dead in her tracks, her mouth half open in a silent cry. Then, skirts flapping about her shabby boots, she began to run.

'I am sorry I may not be able to be of help for some time after this, Mother Joseph, but I have received news that my charitable acquaintance may well need to go away for some time. A rest cure, I believe.'

Looking over her teacup at him, the old nun's eyes were bright with sympathy. 'A rest cure, is it? I hope 'tis nothing serious.'

Father Philip Travers returned his teacup to the tray set beside his elbow on the desk. 'I am told not. But like yourself, Mother Joseph, our friend

324

Mrs Elliott drives herself too hard in the service of the needy. One person can only do so much as I have told her on many occasions, but like yourself she develops a curious malady of the ear whenever advice of that sort is given. Now it appears she is to be made to rest, her doctor has ordered it so.'

Fingering the cross hung about her neck, the nun tutted softly. ''Tis the way of the world, Father, the way of the world! Acts of kindness attract the attention of the Devil, who finds a way to put a stop to them.'

The priest nodded, silent for a moment, then continued. 'He is ever watchful, ready always to do evil. But with the help of Our Lord, he will be defeated.'

'Amen to that.' The nun crossed herself devoutly. 'Amen to that. And be sure that Mrs Elliott will be in our prayers, God grant she recovers soon.'

Eyes more violet that blue, Philip Travers smiled. 'She will be happy to receive your felicitations. I will give them to her when next we meet.'

Reaching into the pocket of his robe, he withdrew a small book bound in dark blue leather, holding it closed as a tap came on the door. Waiting while permission was given for the tray to be removed, he thanked the silent novice, her own white robes a startling contrast where accidentally they brushed against his black.

'All of the novices will take their final vows?' The question was put as he opened the book.

The old nun's face, peeping out from the stiffly

starched coil and wimple, became soft with pleasure.

'I am certain of it, Father. Heaven has smiled upon the four of them. In a month they will become fully accepted within the order of the Little Sisters, praise be to God. They will carry on the work of the Church when the older among us are called to the foot of the throne.'

'I do not wish to deprive the Almighty, Mother Joseph, but I hope He will not call you for many years yet.'

Her tired face crinkling deeply as she smiled, the nun leaned forward across the desk, a roguish note in her whisper. 'Sure, Father, and I have no wish to be going just yet. Do you think that selfish of me? For selfishness is a sin, I know.'

Violet eyes meeting smiling brown ones, he laughed. 'If it is selfishness wanting to keep you here among us for as long as possible then there will be a long line of sinners queuing for judgement and myself at the head of them.'

'Now I know that the Lord will look kindly on my wrongs for you of all the people I know could never be guilty of selfishness, nor hurt to anyone. If there be a crown in heaven then it is surely reserved for you for all the work you have done helping the children of this convent.'

Dropping his glance quickly, Father Travers thumbed through several pages as he answered. 'Speaking of which, I have an offer of a place for each of three girls.'

'The Holy Mother smile on you.' The nun once more crossed her breast reverently. 'Sure and you're a wonderful man.'

Lifting his glance from the book, he wagged one long tapering finger. 'We'll have no more of that, Mother Joseph, not unless you want me guilty of the sin of pride as well as that of selfishness. To work now, both of us, or it will be time for Evensong and me not at my church to take the service.'

'Forgive me.' The nun smiled. 'But I will take my chances with the consequences for I will think it all the same.'

Later, the outer door of the convent closing behind him, Father Philip Travers began the walk home, afternoon sun glinting on the brown-gold hair that peeped beneath his black hat.

Leonie Elliott had done well finding a position for three more girls. Mother Joseph had placed her records at his disposal and he had perused them well before choosing the most suitable candidates. Then the girls had been brought one by one to the Mother Superior's office. He had chosen well. He smiled, lifting his face to the warmth of the sun. Orphans from birth the three of them, they would work hard for the privilege they had been given.

'I worked up at Portland House. It were hard work with just me doing all the laundry for the household but I didn't mind that for it gave me a roof over my head and food for my stomach. The only hurtful thing was not seeing my daughter, not knowing if she was happy or pining; but now I have her here with me once more, thank God, and I won't part with her again 'til it be to give her to a good husband.'

327

'It were fortunate the two of them were along of Elmore Row when they were, or you might have gone right through the village and never 'ave known Molly was here.' Sadie placed the kettle she had filled for the third time on the bracket, swinging it across the fire.

'Bertha and me would have heard. Ain't much goes on in these parts we don't get to knowing. More folks than one travel to Blakenhall, Sadie Trent.'

If you were such a knowall, Martha Vines, how come you didn't know sooner about Florrie Marston's carryings on, or did you know but choose to ignore it?

Reaching for the teapot, Sadie kept the thought to herself, but it would not be forgotten. That and many more would be asked but not in front of strangers. The business of Elmore Green wasn't for spreading abroad; they knew how to deal with their own and Florrie would get her dues when the time was right.

Deborah placed cups she had frequently washed on the table then returned to the scullery for milk. 'We were going to come to Blakenhall on Sunday afternoon.' Catching Sadie's sharp lift of the head, she smiled. 'Clay Gilmore had offered to walk with Molly and myself.'

'But now I don't have to go there. Oh, Mother! I'm so happy to be with you again.'

'Hush, child.' Mary Ann touched a hand to the head buried deep in her lap, her own tears bright as the girl sobbed. 'We won't be parted, not if we never be given a day's work again.'

'Has your only work been as laundry woman?'

Smiling her gratitude as Deborah handed her tea, Mary Ann shook her head then answered Sadie. 'No. I spent most of my years at Mossley Hall at Bentley. I was needle woman there. But when the explosion took my husband, the master there closed the pit and the Hall. He went to live abroad and Molly and myself were among many others whose livelihood was taken.'

'You say you *worked* at Portland House? Does that mean you don't anymore. Have you given up the place you had there?'

Glancing first at her daughter as she lifted her head, Mary Ann answered Sadie's question. 'No, Mrs Trent. It would be truer to say it gave me up. Same as the master at Mossley Hall, the one at Portland House be closing it down and going elsewhere.'

'For good?' Sadie asked. 'Be he going for good? We have heard nothing of it in the village.'

'Neither had I before the morning I was told I had to leave. Agnes Ridley gave me a reference and the wage due to me then told me I had to go that very hour.'

Agnes Ridley! Deborah caught the glance Lizzie cast at her. The woman no doubt enjoyed doing that, but what of her own post? Was she to be one of the servants dismissed by Cato Rawley?

Taking her own cup, she went to sit on a stool beside Lizzie, listening as Mary Ann continued her story.

'Serve the old bugger right!' Sadie delivered her verdict. 'Now that one might find out what it be like to be put out on the streets, and if there be any justice at all her will find none to take her in!'

In its crib the child whimpered fretfully and Lizzie gathered him in her arms. Her head bent over his she looked across at Sadie. 'I will just take him upstairs.'

The woman nodded sympathetically, commenting among themselves that the room was probably too warm, or having so many people crowded into it could have a disturbing effect on the child.

'I'll go and check on the twins.' Deborah rose and followed Lizzie to the stairs.

'Be sure to tell that pair to behave themselves, my bedroom is no playground!'

The words were crisp but the smile that followed showed the softness of Sadie's heart. She was already devoted to the children. Having delivered Sadie's message to the twins, who were sitting quietly on the floor sorting a biscuit tin full of buttons, Deborah went to the room she had shared the last few nights with Lizzie. At the door she halted abruptly, a sudden chill running down her spine.

Lizzie sat on the edge of the bed, her face pressed against her son's tiny head, but instead of the gentle crooning she usually made when cuddling Thomas, long drawn out sobs dragged from her lungs.

'Lizzie!' Deborah flew the few steps across the cramped room, dropping to her knees before the other girl. 'Lizzie, what is it … what's wrong?'

'I don't know, Deborah.' She clung to her son. 'I don't know … yet somehow I do. Something is about to happen. I feel it, Deborah, I feel it in my heart and I am afraid.'

'Lizzie, nothing is going to happen.' Her arms around her, Deborah rested her head against that of her friend, feeling the fear that set her trembling. 'It's just your imagination after listening to that girl's awful story. But she's safe now and so are you and Thomas, safe with Sadie and me. Nothing is going to happen to either of you.'

'He is my reason for living...'

Resting back on her heels Deborah looked into brown eyes alive with fear. Whatever presentiment was in Lizzie it was real and it was dreadful.

Lifting the baby high on her chest, Lizzie touched her mouth to the soft face.

'You are my reason for living,' she murmured against the tiny head. 'You are the prayer in my heart, the song in my soul. You are the love I thought your father had for me, and you are the love I hold for him. We are both children of sin but yours was not your own and you will not be called upon to pay for it. You are my son, my child, and I love you, Thomas Burton. I thank God for giving you to me, and while I live nothing and nobody will ever take you from me.'

Chapter Twenty-three

'You're just over tired,' Deborah soothed her though somehow the fear that had set her friend sobbing had swiftly taken hold of her too. 'Let me take Thomas...'

'No!' Lizzie's head snapped up, her eyes terrible in their fear. 'No. I have to hold him. I have to hold him while I can ... it won't be long, Deborah. It won't be long.'

What wouldn't be long? Her arms going about Lizzie, Deborah held both her and the child. What was it that had Lizzie so terrified? What was this fear oppressing her as well?

Lizzie had been more than usually quiet since the churching; since the priest had stood before her speaking words that implored God's mercy, asking His forgiveness for her sin in conceiving a child.

Now holding her friend, Deborah thought back to the afternoon they had gone together to the church. The Reverend Hamilton had been sick of the influenza and so a priest from another parish had taken the brief service. He had come out of the vestry. Deborah remembered the light streaming from the window high above the altar, how it gilded his gold-brown hair, following the tall black-robed figure as he came towards them; but most of all she remembered the shudder that had run through Lizzie's thin body at that moment.

For a moment she had stared at him, at the handsome face marred only by a red mark high on one cheek. Then her stare had gone beyond him to the high altar and that long slow shudder had run through her again.

Perhaps it was to be expected, perhaps it was some sort of anti-climax after the worry of the past months; or was it that being here in the church, faced by a man of God, had brought back to Lizzie the enormity of what she had done, the dreadful wrong of bringing a bastard child into the world, a child no man would own to?

But the sin of that was not Lizzie's alone! In the quiet of the little room the girl's sobs rang out, each one twisting Deborah's heart. It took a man and a woman to make a child, a man and a woman to commit what the church labelled a sin. So why was the woman alone condemned? Why did heads turn and fingers point whenever Lizzie ventured outdoors? Why did the world vent its spite only on one and not the other?

But that priest at least had seemed to understand. He had smiled into Lizzie's frightened face, his voice soft and lilting as he spoke. It had been almost like a scene from the Bible. A white surplice over his long robes, the light from the tall windows shining about his head, he had raised his hand in blessing, a smile touching his mouth, a smile of forgiveness, a smile such as Christ must have given Mary Magdalene.

'Go ye and sin no more.'

Loud as Lizzie's sobs, the words still rang in Deborah's mind. They were a mockery. Lizzie had been a naïve child! She had known nothing of men or the sins of the world ... she was an innocent!

'You are not alone, my child, our Father in heaven is ever beside you.'

The priest had smiled as he said it but Deborah had felt it brought no comfort to Lizzie as she knelt in that church, and it brought no comfort now. If God was ever beside you, why had he allowed Lizzie to be treated as she had, and why allow Abe Turley to do what he had?

The priest had meant well. Deborah checked the pattern of her thoughts. Bitterness could do no good, it simply ate away at the soul leaving nothing but emptiness in its wake. An emptiness that lived and fed on pain, as now it seemed to be feeding on Lizzie's.

Maybe these thoughts were misguided. Deborah watched the younger girl, one tear-stained cheek pressed to her baby's head. Perhaps she had simply been surprised to see some other man in the Reverend Hamilton's place. He was unwell with the influenza, Father Philip Travers had told them, too poorly to officiate at the service. The old priest had been kind to Lizzie, assuring her he would not only perform her churching but also the eventual Christening of her child. Yes, thought Deborah, nodding to herself. The absence of Father Hamilton had upset Lizzie. Yet the other one had been pleasant enough, smiling down at her and wishing her well as they left the empty church.

But she had made no reply. It had seemed then that she was almost afraid. Why? Disappointed, yes, Deborah could understand that, but afraid

334

... of what? One priest was much like another, he could not be the cause of Lizzie's fear. Something else was troubling her, something that must go very deep.

Waiting for the other girl's sobs to die down, Deborah held out her hands to take the child. 'Let me have him, Lizzie. I won't take him away, I promise. I'll put him there on my bed where you can see him, but you have to rest. Besides, Thomas will get too used to being nursed. He won't want to sleep in his crib, will you young man?' She touched one finger to his head, now covered in bright down.

'I must not leave him, Deborah. I must not leave him!'

'And you won't.' Taking the child as Lizzie's hold on him reluctantly yielded, Deborah laid him on the adjacent bed then turned back to Lizzie, pressing her against her own pillows.

'Try to get some sleep,' she urged gently. 'Thomas will be safe there, no one will take him away.'

Holding the girl's hand, Deborah watched the shadows pass over that drawn face. What had gone wrong? What new anguish was tearing at Lizzie? It had all seemed to fade away directly after the birth of Thomas. The pain of the father's not coming to find her, the shame she had so obviously felt at carrying a bastard child, all of that had seemed to fade in the joy of having her son. And now it had come flooding back.

Lizzie's lids dropped and slowly she gave in to sleep. But it was not a peaceful one. Watching her face, the girl's hand still in hers, Deborah saw tears edge slowly from beneath the closed lids, and the fear that clutched Deborah herself tightened its hold.

Lizzie Burton had already suffered a great deal, but the pain on that sleeping face told Deborah it was nothing in comparison to the agony still raging in her heart.

She had seen the look on his face as he stared at that photograph and it had told her louder than any words the agony she had caused him. Her mouth set tight, a valise clutched in her hand, Agnes Ridley stared at the bare wooden floor of the third-class waiting room. She had walked to the railway station, the crisp April air blowing away none of the anger inside her but only fanning the fire of bitterness into a searing blaze.

How often had she herself looked at that photograph? At the smiling girl, that radiant face so different from the one of the girl Agnes had taken it from; a girl ravaged more by betrayal than the illness that had killed her.

The ward had been settled for the night. Staring into the cold empty fireplace, Agnes allowed the memories to return. Apart from just one nurse to assist her she had been alone when the woman was brought in. There had been no need to call for a doctor, the Sister Dora Hospital had seen too many of her kind for one more to cause a stir. Taken from the streets, ill and penniless, she should have been taken straight to the workhouse, but that institution would not accept one racked with fever; the risk of smallpox was all too real for them to find her a bed.

She had said nothing as the young nurse had stripped the clothes from her then stood her in a tin bath, washing her thin body with carbolic. But neither the harshness of that soap nor the long hard months that brought her to a state of collapse had dimmed the shine of her glorious hair. Damp from the scrubbing it had received, it had hung in glorious chestnut waves to the waist of the institutional calico night gown – hair so like that of the child brought years later to Portland House.

Outside the shrill sound of a whistle heralded the imminent departure of a train and around Agnes several passengers gathered their bags and baskets, but still she did not move. Eyes locked on to the empty grate she watched the unseen drama unfold silently in her mind.

The young nurse had tried to feed the girl soup but as it trickled unswallowed from her mouth Agnes had waved it away. Telling the nurse to pay no more attention to one more beggar who would be dead by morning, she too had made to leave the bedside. Then, catching the words that issued softly from that drawn mouth, she had turned back.

'*...you have to know, Cato...*'

Soft on her dying breath the words had been almost inaudible in the silence of that ward but Agnes's sharp ears had caught every one.

'*...please take our child, give her the inheritance due to her...*'

Inheritance. That one word had acted like a chain, binding Agnes to the bedside. The dim light of the one candle flickering on a central table touched her heavily starched cap and apron but left her face to the cold caress of the shadows. The woman was talking of an inheritance due to her child; the man who had left her in trouble was obviously no miner grubbing in the earth for a living but a man of consequence.

'*...take her, Cato ... give her the name that is rightfully hers...*'

Her rapidly failing strength making each word harder to hear, Agnes had sunk closer to the bed, bending close over the dying woman.

'*...she is your child, Cato. She is a true Rawley. She belongs with you at ... Portland House.*'

The woman had died with the last words still on her lips, but they had been enough. It had been easy to search the worn clothing, to find the photograph wedged deep in the pocket of that shabby skirt; easy to reckon the potential behind it. If the man were married, he would pay for silence. If he were unmarried his money would buy her future silence. But one way or another this dead woman's misfortune would pave the way to a better life for Agnes Ridley.

And so it had, until today. Beyond the open door people hurried along the platform, their footsteps mingling with the blasts of steam from the boiler and the clanking of huge iron wheels beginning to turn.

A woman had come with the dying patient to the hospital. Agnes had been told she was waiting in the lobby.

Deaf to the sounds around her, she was oblivious to all but the memories speaking in her mind.

'*Emmy has a daughter,*' the woman had told her, tears choking her every word.

'*A child not yet two months old, a child with no father to care for her.*'

Agnes almost smiled on hearing it. Fate was dealing her all the right cards. On her days off she had checked all that both women had said. Taking the train to Bloxwich, she had seen Portland House, double checking by asking if it was the residence of Mr Cato Rawley. It had all clicked so easily into place, as if it were meant to be.

She had traced the child, claimed to be its mother's sister and taken it from the old woman who minded it. That had been a stroke of luck for the younger woman, the one who had cried out on hearing of her friend's death, would not have parted with the baby so easily.

'The train for Birmingham be pulling in now.'

Agnes made no reply to the call from the doorway and after repeating it once more the uniformed porter withdrew, closing the door as he went.

She had taken the child to Palfrey on the further side of the town, paying two shillings a week to lodge it with a woman in Cobden Street. No one there would give a moment's thought to a child being taken in. One man's bastard was like any other. So long as they helped pay the rent and buy the gin they were welcome. Agnes smiled grimly, remembering the tiny houses, one tumbledown wall drunkenly supporting the next. The place was a warren of broken women and unwanted children. The one she had taken there

339

had raised no eyebrows.

Once every six months she had taken a day's leave from her post at Portland House, one she had found so easy to get, and taken the train to Walsall. She had visited the tiny house, telling nothing of herself or the child, merely satisfying herself of its welfare and handing over the next six months' money. Then with the girl's ripening she had thought to take her from the reach of the men who haunted the area and brought her to Portland House as a scullery maid. And in the years following she had told Cato Rawley nothing at all, never once breathed a word about the daughter who scrubbed his floors and washed his pots!

But now he knew! Agnes rose from the hard wooden bench. Cato Rawley knew of the child he had begotten almost twenty years ago, but she was as lost to him as ever she had been. Cato Rawley would live as he always had, without a child to succeed him, for Lizzie Burton had gone, vanished among the rest of the penniless, and Rawley would never find her again.

'I don't want to go, Deborah.'

Lizzie's face held the strange haunted expression it had worn since the afternoon of her churching, a look that pulled at Deborah's heart.

'But you promised.' She reached for her shawl. 'We both did. You can't disappoint Molly and the others, they're so looking forward to seeing you and Thomas.'

A tiny frown drawing her brows together, Lizzie shrugged away the shawl from her own shoulders.

'Tell them I'm sorry. It's wrong to break your word once it has been given but I can't, Deborah, truly I can't.'

'If the wench feels her can't go visiting all across to Blakenhall, then her can't go!' Sadie looked up from the petticoat she was stitching, the cloth spread like a silken pool over her knees. 'And that means you oughtn't to be going neither. I ain't as sure as you that Turley be gone from Elmore.'

'I'm not going alone.' Deborah smiled at the older woman. 'Clay is walking with me though I have told him there is no need.'

'There be every need!' Sadie repeated tartly. 'You might think that scum be gone for good but I knows Abe Turley, have known him from a sly little rat of a lad, and I won't be convinced you be safe from him 'til I see him carried into this village laid out on a door!'

Shuddering slightly at the thought, Deborah draped her own shawl about her as a means of not meeting the older woman's eyes. What Abe Turley had done to her was dreadful, her many nightmares proved just how dreadful, but to see him dead...

'There be a basket of pies and such in the scullery.' Sadie laid aside the petticoat. Pushing herself stiffly to her feet, her hands on her hips, she stretched her back. 'Tell Mary Ann Sanders they be kindly meant.'

'I'll fetch it.' Lizzie was already through the curtained archway that gave on to the cramped scullery.

'I wish she would come with us.' Deborah

341

watched the curtain fall back into place. 'The walk would be good for her and Thomas.'

Swinging the bracket with its soot-blackened kettle over the gleaming coals, Sadie shook her head. 'P'raps the lad be getting a bit much for her to carry to and fro. He be growing fast and it ain't as though Blakenhall were across the street. It be a fair walk, especially following the road.'

'But Lizzie would not have to carry him. There would be myself and Clay…'

'Clay!' Sadie gave a smothered chuckle. 'A man carryin' a babby! That would be a sight in Elmore and no mistake. Clay Gilmore would never hear the last of that. No, wench, the pair of you get along. Lizzie will come in her own good time.'

'But she so rarely goes beyond the door. It's almost as though she's afraid of what she might see.'

What she might see … or who? Sadie reached for her old teapot, the thought that so often troubled her held fast in her heart.

'It seemed after Thomas was born, that every-thing was going to be all right. Lizzie seemed almost her old self, and happy enough given the circumstances. But now she talks hardly at all and her smile is a thing of the past. What has happened to her? Why is she so unhappy … so afraid? It's not just my imagination, you must have seen it too, the change in her.'

The tea caddy with its painted scenes of gardens and women draped in colourful kimonos held in her hands, Sadie glanced quickly towards the scullery. 'Arrh, wench,' she admitted quietly, 'I've seen the change, but it be naught but the effect of birthing. Childbirth takes women in different ways. Some gets over it with no trace of bother but others … well, you see, young Lizzie for instance … they gets moody and acts as if the world be against them.'

'I don't think it's that with Lizzie,' Deborah answered, her own voice low. 'I think something has frightened her.'

'That be daft talk!' Sadie almost snapped. 'What could…'

'What be daft talk?' Basket in hand, Lizzie emerged from the scullery.

'All this cagmaggin' about not walking with Clay Gilmore.' Sadie spooned more tea into the pot, no trace of guilt for speaking a lie on her face.

'Are you still talking about that?' Lizzie rested the basket of food Sadie had packed on the table. 'Honestly, Deborah, folk would think it the greatest crime on earth the way you go on, and it isn't as if this were the first time you've walked alone with Clay.'

'I … I don't want people to talk.'

'Let the buggers do their worst.' Sadie snapped the tea caddy closed. 'While they be talkin' of you, they be givin' some other poor soul's name a rest. And if I knows anything at all of Clay Gilmore, he won't give a tinker's cuss for any gossip that lot cares to say. Get you along with the lad and be thankful. You could go a long way in the world and not find one of the same making. Clay be one in a million.'

'Sadie is right, Deborah.' Her hands resting on the handle of the basket, Lizzie did not look up.

343

'You can trust Clay, he would never hurt you, not like F–' She stopped suddenly, her fingers whitening as they closed convulsively about the bamboo handle. Then, her voice a whisper, added, 'Not like I was hurt.'

'Oh, Lizzie.'

Her whole heart in the cry Deborah caught the girl in her arms, feeling the dry sobs wrenching that thin body. Why was this happening? Lizzie was so kind and gentle; she had never done a moment's harm to anyone. It was all so unfair, so cruel.

'Go with Clay.' Against her shoulder Lizzie's voice shook with the same dry tears. 'He loves you, Deborah. Don't push him away, don't deny yourself the love he has to give. It will be a true love. He will never desert you, never break your heart. Marry him, Deborah. Marry him and love him as he loves you.'

'No, Lizzie, you're wrong.' The sudden tightening of her heart almost choking her, Deborah forced the words out. 'It's not me that Clay loves, it's...'

Pushing herself free of Deborah's arms Lizzie looked at her, tenderness brimming like tears in her soft brown eyes. 'No, Deborah, it is you who are wrong. Wrong to think that Clay is in love with me.'

'But you...'

Lizzie shook her head. 'No, Deborah, I am not in love with him nor have I been. Clay is a good man and a wonderful friend but the father of my child is the only man I will ever love and he is lost to me.'

'You cannot say that...'

A sad ghost-like smile touching her mouth, Lizzie's eyes took on a faraway look.

'I can,' she murmured. 'And I do. Thomas will never know his father and I will never have a husband. I accept that, it is punishment for my sin. But my son...' The tenderness in her eyes giving way to a fear that flamed bright as a torch, she grabbed Deborah's hands her grip biting in its sudden intensity. 'My son deserves no punishment, the sin was not his. Promise me, Deborah – promise me you will always care for my son?'

Looking deep into those tortured eyes she felt the cold touch of fear, a strong inexplicable fear that turned her blood to water. She wanted to smile, to say they would both care for the child, they would share the rearing of him together, but somehow she could not. Somehow the words would not come. Instead she could only whisper, 'I promise.'

The tea caddy still in her hands Sadie watched the two young women who shared her home. Two whom life had treated harshly. And one of them, she feared, would be treated more harshly still. Maybe it was her imagination but she feared for Lizzie Burton.

Chapter Twenty-four

Lizzie was not in love with Clay!

The April sunshine warm on her face, Deborah walked in silence, lost in the thoughts that had plagued her since leaving the house.

But Clay ... he loved Lizzie, he had made that obvious. His kindness towards her, his gentleness with both her and Thomas, it must be that he held a special affection for her. What would happen when he found she did not return his feelings?

'Why so silent?' At her side Clay wrestled with his own thoughts.

'I ... I was thinking about Lizzie.' Deborah's cheeks coloured under a warm flush, caught as she was by the question.

'What about her?'

Ahead of them a rabbit darted from the brush, alarmed by their approach. Deborah let her eyes follow its escape. She had to answer, but how ... how could she tell him the woman he loved did not love him?

'She ... she is so changed.' She stumbled over the words, searching for the next. 'I thought after Thomas was born she was much like she used to be. She would talk and smile. But now ... now she seems so altered, she is almost like a different person.'

'Lizzie has been through a lot,' he answered

quietly. 'It leaves its mark. Give her time, Deborah. Having a child cannot be easy for any woman.'

'That's what Sadie says. She thinks the change in Lizzie is just the effect of giving birth, that it will pass.'

'There you are then. Who are we to argue with Sadie Trent?'

Deborah heard the smile that accompanied his words but could not return it. Whether Sadie knew it or not there was more than that to Lizzie's unhappiness.

'I do not deny what Sadie says is true to a certain extent...'

Stepping in front of her Clay brought them both to a standstill, the smile he had tried to maintain slipping from his mouth.

'What is it, Deborah?' he asked quietly. 'What is it that is giving you no peace ... why won't you tell me?'

Trying to speak words that darted away as quickly as they formed, she faltered, 'I ... I don't know. Honestly, Clay, I don't know. Only I feel so scared...'

'Scared?' He frowned. 'You have no need to be scared, Deborah. I will never let anything harm you.'

'It's not for me.' She shook her head. 'I'm not afraid for myself, only for Lizzie.'

'But why ... why be scared for her?'

The worry kept so long inside bubbled to the surface and Deborah's face crumpled. Sinking to the ground, she buried her head in her hands, her reply coming brokenly.

'Because ... because there is something terrible ... it is hidden deep inside of her ... she will not say what it is, but I can feel it. Each time I look into her eyes I see its shadow and ... and it is so horrible. I fear it might turn her mind.'

Dropping to the ground beside her Clay pulled her gently to him, holding her, waiting patiently, putting no further question until the last of her tears was shed. Then, as she leaned quietly against his shoulder, he said, 'It's not the attack Abe Turley made on her, you told me yourself she was more or less over that, so what is it?'

'I wish I knew.' Drawing away from his hold, Deborah wiped her hands across her cheeks. 'I only know it began the day we went to church.' Slowly, without any interruption from him, she told the whole of the story; how Lizzie had looked towards the altar with fear on her face, the change that had taken place in her since that moment, her refusal to be parted from her son even for an hour.'

'Just now, as you arrived at the house, she was saying she would never marry. That not having a husband was punishment for her sin ... but that would be punishing you too, Clay.'

A puzzled frown bringing his brows together, he glanced at the girl beside him. 'How? How can Lizzie's not marrying be a punishment to me?'

Clenching her hands together, Deborah forced herself to answer: 'Because you love her.'

For a moment the only sound was that of a bee investigating the early blossoms of clover and kingcup nestling in the grass. She had not meant to say what she had. Deborah held her breath.

But he had not denied it.

'Yes, I love Lizzie.'

It was said gently but it cut into her heart with all the cruelty of a blade. What he had said that morning as the barge burned *had* been a slip of the tongue then. It was not her name he had meant to say but Lizzie's.

Beside her, calmly and quietly, Clay went on. 'I love Lizzie as I would a sister, anything I can do to help her I will, but I am not *in* love with her.'

Taking her chin in his hand he turned Deborah's face until he looked deep into her eyes. 'It is not Lizzie who has my heart, Deborah, it is you.'

'*I love you Deborah Hammond ... I love you with all my heart and soul!*'

The words sang in her heart and this time there was no doubt. He had not spoken the wrong name. Clay loved her.

Still holding her gaze with eyes that brimmed with emotion, he smiled. 'You have held it ever since I found you on the heath, and you will always hold it. I love you, Deborah. Whether you become my wife or not will have no bearing on it. I will always love you, nothing and no one will ever change that.'

Taking her clenched hands, he covered them with his own but still his eyes did not leave her face. 'If what I have said is offensive to you, then I apologise...'

'No.' She glanced up, the happiness in her eyes matching the tenderness in his. 'No, it is not offensive to me.'

He drew a long breath, the sound loud on the

quiet heath. 'Then I may hope – hope that one day you might come to love me?'

Her fingers relaxing, Deborah smiled into the face she had come to love so much. 'No, Clay,' she whispered. 'Why hope for what is yours already? I love you with all my heart.'

With a quick cry he caught her once more in his arms and as his lips settled on hers Deborah felt that never again would she know a moment so wonderful. But almost in that same moment she felt stricken with guilt that sent her pulling away from him. How could she have forgotten so quickly!

'Lizzie,' she said as he released her. 'What about Lizzie?'

'We will not abandon her.' Clay smiled at her. 'Nor young Thomas neither. They will never be without friends or someone to care for them as long as I live. Say you will marry me, Deborah, and if you wish Lizzie and the child can live with us.'

Marry him! Suddenly the joy inside her melted like snow in summer. How could she? How could she take such happiness whilst Lizzie had none? The answer lodged like a stone in her throat. She could not. She could not marry Clay Gilmore.

'They were all right, the lot of 'em?' Sadie's eyes asked a different question, but seated opposite her in the small living room Deborah avoided it.

'Yes, the twins are delighted with their new home, they dragged me all over it, and Molly and her mother were just as delighted if not quite so demonstrative.'

'Arrh, it seems it all turned out for the best. Something good comes out of a basket of rottenest fruit and there be none more rotten than the trade Florrie Marston were following. But that be all over and her doing a moonlight flit left a house that does just fine for Mary Sanders and the others. Though I ain't too sure you putting every penny you 'ave into it be such a good thing.'

'Florrie Marston's clientele could not have known of her illicit trade or they would never have continued to give her their custom. I know their tastes and, given the chance, I can build a business. Like I say the clientele is already established. That's as good as the battle won.'

'But if there were not a single customer you would have done just the same.' Sadie allowed herself a rare smile. 'I know you, Deborah Hammond. You 'ave a heart as soft as old Mother Bunney's fresh churned butter.' She shook her head. 'Every penny to rent a place for others to live in.'

'It isn't only my money.' Deborah defended her action in taking over the property at Blakenhall. 'Lizzie put hers in too, and so did Mrs Sanders. And, come to that, let's not forget to mention the share a certain Mrs Sadie Trent put into the venture.'

'That were naught but a few coppers compared to what you two gave,' Sadie said, not unkindly. ''Tis you and Lizzie put the bulk of it in, the Lord look kindly on you both.'

'You should see the place, Lizzie.' Deborah turned to her friend who sat sewing delicate glass bugle beads on to a jacket of midnight blue moiré silk. 'Molly and Mrs Sanders have worked really hard. They've made hangings and chair covers out of the pale green taffeta that Sadie sent and put them in the salon. Now it looks completely different and elegant.'

'I'm sorry I did not go to Blakenhall with you.' Lizzie looked up from her sewing, no hint of genuine interest in her empty eyes. 'But I will next time, you have my word.'

'Eh.' Sadie rested her hands on the satin she herself was sewing. 'Who would 'ave thought … you two wenches with a business all your own!'

'You would, Sadie Trent.' Throwing her arms about the older woman Deborah hugged her. 'If I remember correctly it was you said: "… in a year or two you pair could be opening your own fancy gown shop." That's what she said, isn't it, Lizzie?'

Trying very hard to show enthusiasm, Lizzie managed a smile. 'Her very words. I remember quite clearly her saying "… it will be your gowns, the ones you and Deborah have designed, your creations those women will hanker for. Open your own place and they will come to you."'

'I said all that?' Sadie chuckled as Deborah ceased her hugging and went to sit beside Lizzie. 'Well, if I did it were naught but the truth. The gentry will come and they will buy your gowns, you mark my words. They will come from all over to the Salon…' She hesitated. 'The Salon what? What name be you giving to this posh gown shop? It can't go on being called the Salon de Fleur Masson.'

'I had not thought. What will we call it, Lizzie?'

'Ze accent.' Lizzie lifted her shoulders in an exaggerated gesture. 'Zat I do not 'ave, *madame*.'

It was the first time the wench had laughed in months. Sadie watched as the two young women gave in to a fit of the giggles. Thank God whatever had been tormenting Lizzie seemed ready to give up its hold.

'I know … I know,' Deborah gasped. 'Elisa Burtonelli. We will call it the Salon Elisa Burtonelli.'

Lizzie's mouth opened in dismay but at least her eyes were smiling. 'We most certainly will not call the shop by that name! We will call it the Salon Debrina L'Ammondini.'

'How on earth do you two wenches dream such names up?' Sadie's heart warmed as giggles burst out afresh. 'But it 'as to be a fancy foreign-sounding name, the gentry like that. Don't matter who you really be so long as you sound continental.'

As one Deborah and Lizzie stopped giggling, both fastening their gaze on the older woman.

'Hmmm.' Deborah glanced at Lizzie. 'You think so?'

A twinkle at long last lighting her eyes Lizzie nodded thoughtfully as she turned her gaze towards Sadie. Leaving the needlework in her lap she lifted her hands, spreading the fingers as she turned them palm uppermost. Then, in a perfect imitation of Florrie Marston at her most imperious, tipped her head very slightly and said, *'Ah, oui, c'est magnifique.'*

'What are you daft pair going on about?' Sadie

looked from one face to the other.

'Why, the name of the shop.' Deborah's tone was innocent though her eyes betrayed mischief afoot. 'We have the perfect one, don't we, Lizzie?'

'Perfect.' She nodded.

'Then let's be hearing it,' Sadie demanded. 'Don't go keeping it to yourselves like spoilt kids with a bag of suck.'

'Well, it's not a bag of sweets, but it is a delightful name and one we like very much.'

'If you likes it that much, Lizzie Burton, then give a body a chance to 'ear it. Could be another will like it just as well.'

'We'd already decided on this name should Deborah and I ever have a gown shop of our own.' Glancing at the other girl, Lizzie waited for her nod of affirmation before going on. 'We discussed it a lot then finally settled on Maison Sadie.'

'What!' she exploded. 'Over my bloody dead body! It sounds like a knocking shop. You'll 'ave every prostitute for miles around flocking to your door! I don't give a bugger how long you discussed it, you can bloody well change it!'

'But we thought you would like it?' Deborah said, the picture of innocence as she looked at Sadie wide-eyed.

'Well, you can think again. Maison Sadie? What the hell do you think Elmore Green would have to say about that!'

'Oh, well,' Lizzie picked up her sewing, 'if you don't like that name we'll just have to go with the other.'

Eyeing them suspiciously, Sadie waited a

moment before asking. 'What other be that then?'

Head bent over the deep blue silk, Lizzie kept her tone matter-of-fact. 'Why, the Château de Tourante.'

'The Château...' Sadie almost burst with indignation. 'Where on earth do you two get such language from? I swear I never heard the like in all my life. It sounds as much like cussing as swearing. But I tell you this, you ain't calling no shop after me no matter what sort of fancy label you sticks on it. And that be enough said on the matter!'

Watching them fight against the giggles Sadie shook her head, her own sense of humour rapidly returning. It was a tonic as good as a pint of Joe Chapman's best ale to see young Lizzie smile again. Her own smile tugging her mouth she laid aside her sewing. 'It's to be hoped the running of that gown shop will bring you fewer worries than the choosing of its name,' Sadie commented.

'It need not.' It was Deborah who answered her. 'Molly and her mother are both good needle women and the twins are proving very helpful about the house. With them and you, together with Lizzie's designs, we cannot help but make a go of things.'

'I pray you be right, wench.'

'I am, Sadie, I know I am. Lizzie's designs are beautiful and the business, if it prospers, will provide security for her and for Thomas.'

Reaching for the poker in the hearth, Sadie raked ash from between the bars of the grate as she spoke.

'And what about you, wench, will it bring you what you want?'

'I have all I need.'

'That ain't what I asked.' Straightening, Sadie turned, her expression serious once more. 'I asked will it bring what you want? Will it bring happiness to your heart? And don't go telling me you have that already. Sadie Trent ain't given to calling folk a liar but that will be what I will call you if you says there be nothing troubling you, same as I would tell Clay Gilmore. There be something amiss between the two of you. Tell me to mind my own business if you will but don't go telling me I be wrong.'

'Is there something wrong, Deborah?' Lizzie was on her feet, the silk falling in a dark pool. 'Have you and Clay had a misunderstanding … you have not fallen out, have you?'

'No.' Deborah felt the misery at her refusal of Clay's offer sting with all its earlier ferocity. 'No, Clay and I had no argument.'

'Then what is it?' Throwing her arms about her friend, Lizzie was all sympathy. 'You can tell us, Deborah.'

Could she? Deborah closed her eyes. How could she say, she refused to marry Clay because Lizzie had said *she* would never marry? That would only add to the burden of guilt her friend already carried.

Her face resting against Lizzie's shoulder, she said quietly, 'Clay asked me to marry him and I refused.'

Lizzie pushed her to arm's length, incomprehension clouding her face. 'You refused! But why, Deborah ... why?'

The poker falling with a clatter in the hearth, Sadie too was perplexed. 'You refused Clay Gilmore? Why, wench?'

Every muscle straining, Deborah gave nonchalant shrug. 'Because I do not love him.'

For an instant Sadie's eyes locked with hers then she sat down, picking up her needlework. If the shop did not take off then Deborah Hammond could get a job at the theatre along of Elmore Road for that was as fine a bit of play acting as Sadie Trent had ever seen.

'Is that true, Deborah, you don't love him?' Lizzie looked troubled.

'Of course it 's true. Why should it not be?'

Still holding her shoulders, Lizzie looked deep into the other girl's eyes. 'Because of me,' she said quietly. 'Because you think that to marry while I do not would be hurtful to me.'

Deborah felt her heart jolt at the accuracy of Lizzie's insight. She could almost have read Deborah's mind. But even as her nerves tightened she forced herself to laugh again.

'That's nonsense, Lizzie.'

'Is it?' She dropped her hands and once more her lovely eyes darkened with pain. 'Is it, Deborah? Clay loves you and I know you love him. What else would make you refuse to marry him?'

'Well, I do *not* love him, so for once you are wrong, Miss Lizzie Burton.'

'It don't hurt to refuse a man once,' Sadie put in, smoothing over an awkward moment. 'It serves to fire his ardour. He'll ask again, be sure of that. Clay Gilmore ain't one for giving up easy, and if it be you 'ave made a mistake then you can rectify it with his next asking.'

'You will, won't you, Deborah?' Lizzie's eyes were imploring. 'You will accept Clay's offer?'

Her own gaze tender, Deborah took her friend's hand. 'I can only promise to think about it.'

Lizzie smiled. 'Then think hard, Deborah. Clay is a fine man. His sort are not found so easily as...'

Breaking off, she pulled her hand free and as she sat down Deborah could almost feel the emotion emanating from her.

As easily as the sort I found ... a man who would leave a girl to carry his child alone...

Was that what Lizzie had been about to say? She watched as her friend picked up the lovely silk jacket, head bent to hide the tears Deborah knew were filling her eyes.

'It be about time that babby were waking.' Sadie glanced at the clock, her matter-of-fact observation once more relieving the tension. 'He's gone long over his feed time, you'll be 'aving trouble with your breasts if he starts going past his times, the milk will clog and you will be sore.'

'I hadn't noticed the time.' Lizzie once more laid aside the jacket but she did not look up. 'I'll get him.'

'Let me.' Deborah glanced at the cradle in the corner. 'It's time I said hello to Sadie Trent's Godson.'

The beam on her face betraying her pleasure,

Sadie kept her voice tart. 'Arrh, well, when he does say hello mind his bottom. It will be good and wet by now.'

'Are you, young man?' Deborah smiled down at the child. 'Are you wet? Then it's a dry napkin for you before you eat.'

Folding back the covers Deborah touched a finger to the tiny hand and frowned. It was cold, very cold. Bending over the cradle she turned the child on to his back. The baby's lips were blue, his face waxen. Bending closer, she held her face to his, waiting for the warmth of his breath against her cheek.

Laying her hand on the little chest she held her own breath and suddenly the world stopped turning. There was no beat of his tiny heart. A scream of horror rising in her throat, she gripped the sides of the cradle.

Lizzie's child was dead.

Chapter Twenty-five

'She took my babby, stole him from his bed...'

Ginny Lennox shook off the restraining hands, her voice rising with renewed passion.

'It was her, I tell you, that bloody mad bitch! It was her took my lad. Ain't nobody's babby safe with her around. Her wants putting away, locking up in the lunatic asylum afore her kills another the way her killed her own!'

'Ain't no need to go talking like that, Ginny Lennox. Lizzie Burton's child died in its cradle, and your child be safe and well and no harm done.'

'No harm? No harm!'

The voice of Ginny Lennox rose to a screech as she faced the round figure of Sadie Trent, arms folded across her breasts, hands tucked beneath her black woollen shawl.

'You say it don't count as harm having a babby snatched from its home, from its own bed – I suppose you won't count it as harm when that mad bitch *kills* one of 'em!'

Drawing a deep breath, the swelling of her chest her only movement, Sadie looked coldly at the woman. 'Lizzie Burton has never hurt no child.'

'That be right enough.' A voice came from among the crowd of women who'd quickly assembled at the sound of raised voices. 'But her 'as taken a few, you can't deny that, Sadie Trent.'

'I can't and nor do I want to.' Sadie glanced in the direction of her accuser before looking back to the angry Ginny Lennox. 'But each time there has been no hurt to the child.'

'So far,' Ginny cut in maliciously, intent on being heard. 'But there has to be a first time for everything. What will you do then, Sadie Trent? What will your answer be then? How will you defend that crazy bugger once her kills a babby, eh? Tell me that. And you lot...' she sent a glance scudding over the faces of the assembled women '... ask yourselves whose kid it will be. Yours?' She jabbed a finger into the chest of one of the women. 'Or yours, Mary Tate? Or yours, Polly Turner? I can only tell you this – it will be one of them unless we do something now.'

'What Ginny says be true.' Polly turner stepped forward. 'Something should be done, Lizzie Burton be out of her head...'

'And you're going to be the one to do it, be that the way of it, Polly?' Sadie's arms were lowered slowly to her sides, a warning glint in her brown eyes. 'Well, think twice afore you start. You know very well what's happened to women who've tried taking on Sadie Trent. They haven't walked easy for many a month after.'

'I didn't mean for to threaten you, Sadie.' The woman stepped back hastily. Sadie Trent's temper was well known in the village. 'But we can't go on letting that wench run off with babbies.'

'They come to no harm, her want only to hold them. Her gives them back no sooner her be asked...'

361

'And what about when her don't want to give one back?' Ginny's voice rose again. 'What about when bloody mad Lizzie decides to hang on to the child her steals? What of the kid then? But that won't matter to you, will it, Sadie Trent? Nothing matters to you except mad Lizzie Burton.'

Ignoring the murmurs of the women huddled about the entry, Sadie stared coldly at the figure boldly stepping forward from the group, her flaming red hair dishevelled, several long strands escaping from their pins.

'Like your babby was of no matter to you, Ginny, while you was lying on your back underneath Henry Darby! The child was of no concern 'til the business in hand – or should I say in your belly – was finished. Same as every time you have some fancy man to entertain, which is more often than the rest of we have hot dinners.' Sadie heard the muted laughter and several quietly spoken murmurs of assent but her gaze stayed with the red-haired woman. 'You left that babby lying in a drawer out the front door while you was inside having that which got it. How do you think your husband will take to finding that out? What will he do when he discovers he's married to a whore?'

'You mind what you say!' Ginny's face flushed red as her hair.

'Oh, I will.' Sadie half smiled, arms folded again across her chest. 'I'll be careful to speak only the truth when I tell your Bert how come the son of Henry Darby, the one he thinks to belong to him, came to be in my house, not to mention how long the child was here afore you come to look for it. Enjoy *that*, Ginny Lennox. Enjoy the telling as much as you enjoyed coming here shouting your mouth off. As much as you enjoy whoring!'

Not waiting for an answer she disappeared into the house, emerging moments later with a baby swaddled in a grubby shawl.

Snatching the child from her, with not a look into its tiny face, Ginny's lips thinned and her eyes blazed.

'One day somebody will do for that mad bitch,' she snarled, 'and maybe they'll do for you too, Sadie Trent!'

'Oh, no! Not again!'

Deborah sank into a kitchen chair. She had felt so relieved coming back from The Poplars, so happy to have gained an order for another gown. The mistress there had been pleased with the blue taffeta and had added an extra half sovereign to the agreed seven pounds. The dress had taken Deborah and Sadie many long hours to sew, but coming back across Bullocks Field with that seven pounds ten shillings in her pocket, every long moment had seemed worth it.

'Yes, wench, again.' Sadie placed a cup of tea before her on the table. 'It were Ginny Lennox's child this time.'

Deborah groaned as she took the beaded linen cover from the milk jug. 'Did Ginny...'

'Oh, arrh, and then some.' Sadie nodded. 'Raised merry hell out there, gave the neighbours a fair treat.'

Her hand still on the milk jug, Deborah raised apologetic eyes. 'I'm sorry, Sadie...'

'Don't be.' The older woman grinned, showing teeth crooked from childhood. 'It gave me a fair treat an' all.'

'But Ginny...'

Taking the jug, Sadie added milk to both cups, the beads of green glass chinking against the pottery as she replaced the cover.

'I know. Ginny Lennox don't be one to smile and let things be, but her should have known better than to try her tricks on me. I told a thing or two her would have preferred kept quiet ... there'll be no more trouble from that quarter.'

No more trouble? Deborah dropped her glance to her cup. There had been nothing but trouble since Lizzie's child had been conceived, and since its death...

'What makes Lizzie the way she is?' She stared at the steaming liquid as if seeking the answer in its depths.

'That be a question we all ask.' Sadie stirred her own drink. But the answer? I think only the Lord has that. He has His reasons. Maybe in good time He will reveal what they be, then maybe again He will keep His own counsel. Whichever way, we can only care for her.'

'We should not be here,' Deborah answered softly. 'It isn't fair to you, dealing with this problem. I'll take Lizzie...'

'You will take her nowhere!' Sadie's mouth firmed, her hand bringing cup to saucer with an emphatic thump. 'I took you both in and here you will both stay. It will take more than the likes of Ginny Lennox to change my mind on that.'

'But what if Lizzie should harm a child?'

'There be no fear of that,' Sadie answered. 'You've seen her with them – the way she handles them so gently. Lizzie would never hurt a babby, I be willing to stake my life on that.'

'No.' Deborah shook her head. 'No, I don't believe she would, not intentionally. But who can tell what might happen in the future? She acts so strangely; one minute she's her old self, quite normal, and the next she seems to be in a world of her own, a world we know nothing of and one we cannot enter.'

Taking a sip from her cup Sadie stared into the fire, her answer taking a while to come. 'Who can tell the ways of the Lord? Seems He took part of her senses when her child died, but He wouldn't replace them with a desire to harm the babes of others. You can rest easy on that, wench. If hurt comes to any in Bloxwich it won't be any doing of Lizzie Burton's.'

'Do you think she will ever be well again?'

Sadie's sigh was heavy. 'The mind be a strange thing. No doctor can take a knife to it, no mother can place a poultice on it. The mending of it be beyond mortal man. We can only trust in the Lord to give healing. And one day He will, of that I am sure.'

'I hope you're right.' Deborah's mouth trembled. 'I hope with all my heart you are right.'

Later, watching the moonlight through the trees that bordered Bullocks Field, Deborah felt tears on her cheeks.

For all of Sadie's reassurances and her own

365

expressions of hope, doubt lay heavy in her heart. Lizzie showed no signs of recovering from the sickness that had stolen her mind; more and more often she was taking babies from their mothers, rocking them in her arms, crooning softly to them as if to her own child. But Lizzie's child was dead.

As if the thought called back the darkness of that awful time the moon slipped away, hiding its light behind a bank of cloud.

Why had the father of the child never turned up? Why had he deserted Lizzie? And Agnes Ridley – she had been so quick to condemn her, so swift to lay her sin before Cato Rawley who in turn had turned Lizzie directly from the only home she had known.

Deborah closed her eyes, pressing her lids hard down in an effort to close out a picture of her friend sitting in that kitchen, the housekeeper throwing insults at her bowed head; a woman who had herself committed the same sin – often. Why was it one could escape all blame while the other was made to suffer so? Where was heaven's justice in that?

'... *a dirty little slut ... a no good stinking little whore!*'

Deborah winced, remembering the venom behind those words. 'But it wasn't true,' she murmured into the darkness. 'What Lizzie did was wrong but she was no whore. She loved that man, whoever he was, the true wrong was his.' Lacing her fingers together she brought them to her lips, her voice a whisper in the silence. 'Lord grant that one day I will meet the man who wronged Lizzie. That one day I can tell him the harm he has done.'

But what good would that do? She opened her eyes, watching moonlight once more flood the tiny bedroom. It would not bring back Lizzie's dead child nor would it restore her senses. The fact was that he was free somewhere while Lizzie was bound by invisible chains, locked in the prison of her own mind. And he had turned the key.

And was Lizzie the only one? The thought brought fresh coldness to Deborah's heart. Was she the only girl he had betrayed or were there others suffering the same heartbreak?

It was so unfair. Fingers clenching the sheet, she stared at the light-bloomed window. 'I will find him, Lizzie,' she whispered aloud. 'I vow to you that I will find him, and when I do he will pay ... he will pay dearly.'

'I have told you, the woman was lying.' Leonie had listened to Cato's confession. 'You have no daughter by this Emmeline. Do you honestly think a pregnant serving girl would not say if she were having your child? Would not she at least demand you pay her off?'

Leonie Elliott smoothed the velvet of her lilac-coloured suit. It had taken time to choose just the right shade to set off the violet of eyes painted with extra care.

Cato Rawley had changed since that woman had spat out her secret. True he was as besotted with Leonie as before but after their love making he would lie silent, deep in his own private world.

367

'Forget that vixen,' Leonie went on. 'She hoped that lying with you, giving you what you wanted, would bring her to what *she* wanted: namely to become mistress of this house. She did not love you…'

Skirts rustling softly, every movement deliberate and provocative, the lovely figure crossed the room to press itself seductively against the man whose eyes drank greedily of its charms.

'She did not love you as I do.' The musical voice was low, whispered on perfumed breath. 'No woman can ever love you as I do, my darling. No woman can satisfy you in the same way. Forget the lie she told you, let me show you what real love is.'

Mouth partly open, violet eyes smoky with promise, Leonie lifted long slender fingers, cupping them to each side of Cato Rawley's face. Drawing his head slightly down, her soft lips fastened over his.

'Not here.' The full mouth still brushing his, Cato made to draw away, the movement so obviously half-hearted it was met with a low exultant laugh.

'Yes, my darling, here, right here.'

The touch of those lips, the perfumed sweetness of the body pressed close to him, drove all from his mind except the desire that filled it: the craving for the feel of flesh on flesh, the burning that set his loins throbbing. It was always like this with Leonie, it had been from the first. Nothing would ease his hunger for the promise of that body except the taking of it.

A soft groan his only reply, he stood while each

article of clothing was removed from him then watched the lilac velvet suit fall into a heap followed immediately by silken underwear.

'Not here, Leonie, we could be seen...'

His words cut off by that full laughing mouth, Cato trembled at the strength of the desire that swept through him. Tracing his mouth with a warm sweet tongue Leonie laughed again, a mocking yet bewitching sound like music from far away. Cato knew he should turn from it, get dressed, but the allure of that figure with its golden hair and beautiful face was too strong.

'Are you afraid of being seen, Cato?' Releasing him Leonie stepped backward, nakedness robed in the glow of sunlight streaming through the study window. 'Are you afraid of being seen making love to me?'

There was no one else in the house. He struggled with the lust filling his brain like a fog. The staff had all been dismissed by Agnes Ridley and he had engaged none since then, but even so the risk...

'Will I go Cato? Will I leave you?'

'No!' Arms rising almost of their own volition, he reached for the smiling figure. Bodies pressed close together, lips seeking lips as they dropped to the floor, Cato's reply was thick with passion. 'Never leave me, Leonie. Don't ever leave me.'

Father Philip Travers took the black hat held out to him by the housekeeper at the rectory.

'You really shouldn't be going out, 'tis such a damp morning.'

'My ministry must continue.' He smiled at the

plump comfortable figure.

'That be as it might, I ain't saying it shouldn't, but what I am saying is there be no need for you to go out on a day like this.'

Glancing skyward at storm clouds hanging thick and dark, he placed the hat on his head, pressing it down on a flurry of brown-gold curls.

'We can't let the promise of a little rain bring a stop to our work, Mrs Bailey.'

'A promise, is that what you call it?' Lila Bailey played a long look over the leaden sky. 'A downright threat is what I would call it.'

'Maybe it will clear.'

'And maybe it won't. Maybe the heavens will open an' you will get yourself soaked to the skin!'

His smile deepening, he shook his head slowly. 'Oh ye of little faith.'

'Faith nothing! You leave my faith out of this, Father Philip. 'Tis only common sense to see that rain is likely to come bucketing down any minute. You get yourself mightily soaked and take pneumonia and who is it will have the trouble of you? Lila Bailey, that's who!'

Smiling, the priest touched her elbow. 'If I promise to shelter should it rain, will that satisfy you?'

Lila Bailey looked hard at the man she secretly worshipped. 'I suppose it will have to, though I would rather you promised not to go out at all.'

'You worry too much, Mrs Bailey.'

Hearing his soft melodic laughter as he walked away, Lila Bailey felt the cold shiver she often felt when watching him leave the rectory; it was almost as if evil walked beside him. Keep him safe, she prayed silently. Lord keep him safe.

Lifting his face to the dank grey sky as the first drops of rain fell, Father Philip Travers smiled. Mrs Bailey might worry over his getting wet but he welcomed it. To get mightily soaked, as she put it, could only help his cause.

Waving away a hansom returning to Walsall he strode on. It had been something of a setback, Leonie Elliott being unable as yet to place any more of the convent girls. But a setback was all it would prove to be, a temporary hitch that would soon be put right. Until that time, he hunched his shoulders against the rapidly worsening downpour, he must try harder in other directions.

'Just look at you, Father! You be quite drenched.'

The young woman showing him to an upstairs sitting room frowned with concern. 'The mistress will go on at me something dreadful for not getting you out of them wet clothes and into some dry ones afore bringing you up.'

His smile teasing, he looked at the girl. 'And what is it you would have dressed me in? A cap and frilly apron look fine on you, but on me...' Pretty face colouring rapidly, the girl lowered her gaze shyly. 'You know what I mean, Father.'

'I do, Peggy, I do, and it was kindly meant. But really I will be all right, and promise I will not let your mistress give you one word of blame.'

Watching the girl bob a swift curtsey before leaving him alone with her mistress he remembered the one he had brought here from the convent of Little Sisters two years before. The

371

girl had been pretty enough for a different placing. It was a pity that a broken leg poorly set had left her with a limp.

But there were other girls in need of his help. Turning his almost violet eyes to the overdressed woman smiling up at him, Father Philip Travers reached for her hand. Other places ... other girls ... he would match one to the other.

Chapter Twenty-six

Six months. It had been six months since the death of her child and Lizzie had not once spoken his name.

Her heart cold inside her, Deborah thought back to that terrible time. She had not said, could not say those terrible words but Sadie had read them in her eyes. Hauling herself out of her chair she had come to the cradle but Lizzie had reached it before her, dread already on her face.

Deborah had tried to hold her back. She trembled at the memory. Tried to hold her away. But Lizzie would not be held. Finding an almost tigerish strength she had pushed them both away. Taking the baby from its bed she had smiled down at the still face, touched her lips to the closed eyelids. Without a word she had carried the tiny figure upstairs to her room and there, on her bed, she had nursed it all night; rocking back and forth she had crooned softly, face resting against the child's down-covered head.

And through the long hours they had sat with her, Sadie talking softly, gently trying to coax her into releasing the body. But Lizzie had not released it, their pleas seeming to have no power to penetrate her grief.

It had been the doctor who had taken the child from her. Sadie had sent for him the next morning. The child would need a death certificate, she had told Deborah quietly. There could be no arrangements made without one.

Lizzie had looked at him, eyes cold and dead as her child's body. This time she made no effort to keep him, made no move to push away Deborah's comforting hand, but simply stared as the little body was carried from the room.

There had been callers. On each of those awful days prior to the funeral women had called at the house, the same women who had decried Lizzie for immorality, coming now to give their condolences, show proper respect for the dead.

Her face drawn with sorrow, tired lines emphasising her lack of sleep, Sadie had received them, thanked them for their thoughtfulness, accept the tiny posies of wildflowers mothers had had their own children pick and carry to the house. She rested only when Lizzie slept from the draughts the doctor prescribed.

Even under their influence her sleep had been restless and rent by pitiful moans, the only sound in a house hushed in sorrow.

You should sleep too. Sadie had told Deborah a dozen times. But sleep had been evasive, teasing; settling on her eyes only to leave her minutes later. And even now sleep, deep sleep, was a blessing all too rarely given. Lying awake in her own room Deborah listened for any sound that would say Lizzie needed her, and in the quiet darkness would know that Sadie listened also.

Clay had come early on that final day. Sitting beside the fireplace, empty of its cheerful glow, the room shadowy behind curtains closed against the daylight, Lizzie had watched, silent and

374

unmoving, seeming not to hear Sadie's *'Come you away, wench.'* She watched as he nailed the lid on that tiny coffin.

It had been like being caught in some awful nightmare, a dream she could not wake from. Deborah felt her throat tighten as the memories came on, forcing themselves into her mind where time and again they had relived that day; relentlessly playing out their drama.

Close beside Lizzie, she had held the girl in her arms, trying to turn her away, to shield her from the sight of her son's body being closed inside that box. Deborah remembered how every sound of the hammer had caused her to shudder, shaking her body from head to foot until she had to press one curled fist against her mouth to stop herself from screaming. But through it all Lizzie had not moved. Still and silent, she had stood as if carved from stone.

'Come on, my little wench, it has to be done. The Lord will give you of His strength.'

Sadie had come to the other side of Lizzie and together they had held her as they followed the coffin from the house. Even now, months later, Deborah could not forget the look on Lizzie's colourless face as they walked to the church.

Beyond the entry that divided Sadie's house from the next, women had huddled together in a silent group. Shawls pulled low over their brows, they had crossed themselves as the coffin passed them by; old men on stools beside their garden gates, smoking clay pipes in the misty afternoon, removed their flat caps, resting on their chest as the three women wound their way behind the posy-strewn box carried in Clay's arms.

Then at last it was over. The brief service that would bring the child to its maker was finished, and only the posies set around the open grave marked his passing.

'I am the Resurrection and the Life, He who believeth in me...'

The words returned with brilliant clarity, but far from bringing the comfort they were meant to bestow, to ease the pain of suffering, they only sharpened it. How could she believe, how could any believe in mercy, in a God who could take away a beloved child, who could let Lizzie suffer so? Who eased her burden by closing away her mind.

It might have been better had Lizzie screamed and ranted, it might have tapped the grief locked inside her. But she had not, she had not even wept, not once in all this time.

It was not unknown, Doctor Wilson had said. He had been so kind, giving time talking to Sadie and herself, explaining that what had happened to Thomas was far from rare. That children, perfectly healthy children, sometimes died in their sleep for no apparent cause; that what had happened to Lizzie's son was no one's fault, no one was to blame.

It was like some awful nightmare. Deborah glanced at the girl walking beside her and felt again a sharp stab of anger and resentment that fate could be so cruel. The dreams faded when she woke, but the nightmare lived on.

The women had crossed themselves as the tiny body was carried past them, but in a matter of days the gossip and the sniping had begun again. Lizzie Burton had killed her own babby ... lay on the child in her own bed ... put the pillow over its face ... held her hand over its mouth ... on and on it had gone until it was shouted after Lizzie wherever she went; until finally it had overwhelmed her. That was when the new nightmares began, one that saw Lizzie taking other women's babies.

The first one had been an infant not yet a month old. She had walked into the house, the first smile since her own child's death curving her mouth. She had said nothing but simply carried the child to her place at the fireside, crooning softly as she rocked it back and forth.

Their questions had brought no reply. Only when Sadie turned back the tattered shawl to look at the tiny sleeping face had Lizzie smiled and said, *'Thomas is sleeping, we must not wake him.'*

And that was how it had gone on. One after another Lizzie would bring babies home, never hurting them, only rocking them tenderly in her arms. But day by day the women of the village had become more angry, snatching up their children when they saw her and rushing them into the house, slamming the door behind them.

Shock, the doctor had called it. It was shock had Lizzie behaving as she did. But that held no meaning for the women whose babies she took. They wanted no crazy wench walking the village. Who could tell when her would harm one of the babbies ... a body like her should be locked away in the insane asylum.

But Lizzie was not insane. Deborah glanced again at the girl singing softly at her side. She did all that Sadie or Deborah asked of her, only in this was she different.

Seeing Deborah's glance, Lizzie held up a doll wrapped in a piece of blanket. 'He likes being taken for a walk, Deborah.' She smiled innocently. 'Thomas likes being taken for a walk.'

Deborah's heart curled like a dry leaf. Sadie had taken Lizzie with her to Blakenhall. Passing the pawn shop there, Lizzie had picked up a doll from a basket of oddments set out on the pavement. Cradling it as she would a child, she had smiled at Sadie.

'That might be the answer,' Sadie had said when they returned. 'It be a terrible sight, I know, to see a grown woman nursing a tuppenny doll, but if it keeps her from taking other folks' babbies then we must accept it.'

'But for how long?' Deborah had asked. But Sadie had only shaken her head.

Lizzie had withdrawn into the safety of childhood, had been the doctor's explanation. Nursing the doll would help with her natural grieving, and sooner or later she would recover from the loss of her son.

But Lizzie was not recovering! Deborah ignored the shouts of a group of boys, their laughter as one of them folded his arms, crooning in cruel imitation of Lizzie. There was no change in her so far as could be seen. Every day she nursed the doll, talking to it, singing it to sleep as she would a living child, and every night she carried it up to her room, laying it in the

378

cradle Clay had made for Thomas.

Mad Lizzie, the village women called her, mad Lizzie who thinks a platter doll be a babby. And they made no effort to curb their children as they called after her in the street. 'Hey up, here be Mad Lizzie. How be your babby, Lizzie?'

But Lizzie only smiled. Now they did not leave her alone. Afraid of what might happen either Sadie or herself were always with her, their fear keeping them close beside her. But fear of what exactly? Ignoring the mutterings of women who turned their backs as they passed Deborah held her head high. Just what was it gave rise to this fear that stayed inside her, the same fear she saw in Sadie's eyes. Was it worry that Lizzie might regress to taking children from their mothers, worry of what the consequences of that might be?

Walking along, Lizzie hummed softly as she kissed the china head. Mad Lizzie! Deborah's heart twisted with pity. They were wrong, they were all wrong. Lizzie was not mad; it was just that life had dealt her so much sorrow she could not bear it. The pain was so great she had shut herself away where no more could reach her. Protected by the barrier in her own mind, she lived still with her son.

When dreams fade we have only reality. What reality would Lizzie face when her dreams finally faded?

Ahead of them, on the footpath that ran alongside Elmore Road, a young woman stood and watched them approach. Glancing at Lizzie, she flung her shawl tight about the child she held

379

in one arm, muttering as she hurried away in the opposite direction.

It was understandable. Deborah glanced once more at the girl beside her, oblivious to all except the doll cradled against her breast. She herself might well have acted in just that way were she in the woman's shoes. Might have been fearful for the safety of her own child, as protective of it as that young woman hurrying off down the street; but would she have been so cruel? Would her own attitude have been the same as the women who turned their backs on Lizzie, who saw only the strangeness of her behaviour and none of her pain? Some of those same women had lost babies of their own, buried them as Lizzie had buried hers. So why could they not understand? Why could they not see the torment behind her actions, the agony that had driven her to do what she had?

Lizzie was the same kindly gentle girl she had always been. She would never hurt a child so why had hers been taken from her? Why add so great a sorrow to that she had already suffered? These were questions Deborah and Sadie had discussed many a night after Lizzie was asleep but neither of them had found the answers.

And Clay. Deborah winced at the thought of the pain that lay beneath his smile. He had not mentioned marriage since that day they had gone together to the house at Blakenhall, but she knew from his touch, from the undisguised love whenever he looked at her, that he still hoped one day she would say yes.

But how could she? Wanting marriage to Clay

as much as she did it was even more forlorn a wish now than it had ever been. Lizzie needed her more each day, needed all of her love, and she would not go to Clay unless that could be his alone. Lizzie would have a home with them. He had repeated the promise he had given that day and Deborah knew he would keep it, but was it fair on him? Was it fair on any man to begin married life having to care for a woman with the mind of a child?

'He's asleep, Deborah.'

At her side Lizzie halted, drawing back the blanket to disclose the bland smiling china face.

'Look, he is fast asleep.'

Seeing those large brown eyes so peaceful now, Deborah felt her pity deepen.

'He wanted to go to the park but now he's asleep.' Lizzie pouted. 'Will I wake him, Deborah? He won't want to miss the park, it's so pretty.'

'No, Lizzie, don't wake him.' Deborah's throat closed as she fought the rising tears. 'Let him sleep. We'll go to the park later.'

'But he wanted to go now.'

'Yes, Lizzie, I know.' Hearing the truculence in her friend's voice, Deborah spoke gently. 'But first we decided we would buy the groceries Sadie wants, don't you remember? We said we would call at the shop and go home by way of the park. The baby will be awake by then...'

'Can I show him the flowers?'

Tears gathering, Deborah forced herself to smile.

'Of course you may.'

Her own smile bright, Lizzie kissed the hard cold face then gently drew the cover around the china head, murmuring softly, 'Did you hear that? Deborah says I may show you the flowers, but you have to be a good boy and not cry. I won't take you if you cry.'

Reaching the shop Deborah saw the two women already inside turn and stare through the window, one of them pointing to Lizzie as she said something to the man behind the counter. Perhaps she should take Lizzie straight home, leave her with Sadie and come back alone to buy the groceries.

Turning to speak to the girl she saw her seated on the wide stone step of the shop, her face pressed against that of the doll, rocking back and forth as she crooned to it. It would take only a few minutes to buy what Deborah had come for. Most likely the women would be pleased for her to be served before them. That way they could gossip after she and Lizzie were gone.

'Lizzie,' she said, 'I want you to stay where you are. I'll only be a few minutes. Stay there until I come out.'

Hesitating when the girl made no answer, she glanced again at the window. Three faces still watched her. Well, let them watch! Deborah lifted her head determinedly. 'Cagmaggers', Sadie called people like those. Women with no more to do with their time than gossip about other folk. Cagmaggers were best ignored. Glancing once more at Lizzie's bent head, she walked into the shop.

'How be that wench?' The older of the women

382

jerked her head sideways, indicating the spot where Lizzie sat.

'She is well, thank you.' Deborah felt her spine stiffen as her reply met with a derisive sniff.

The second woman, younger and heavily pregnant caught at her shawl with one hand, drawing it up on to her shoulders with a sharp authoritative movement. 'Well, is her? But then you be bound to say that, you and Sadie Trent. It ain't what the women in Elmore be saying.'

'You be right there, Cissie. They be saying that there wench ain't normal, her be weak in the 'ead.'

The younger of the two sniggered. 'Her ain't just weak in the 'ead, her be downright daft! Daft as any that can be found in the mad house, and that's where her should be. Locked up where her can't run off with another woman's babby.'

Placing the last of her purchases in her basket, Deborah counted several coins on to the counter. Nodding to the shopowner whose discomfiture showed on his bewhiskered face, she turned to the women, stood a little to one side of the small cluttered shop. Head high and eyes hard Deborah stared at first one and then the other of them.

'It is always beneficial to listen to the voice of the well informed,' she said icily. 'And you, it seems, are both authorities on the insane asylum. Is that because most of your relatives are there?'

'You watch your bloody mouth!' The younger of the two raised her fist threateningly.

Her glance steady, Deborah did not flinch. 'I advise you to watch yours. Things have a way of bouncing back.'

Her hand still raised, the woman glared, angry at Deborah's refusal to be intimidated. 'What do you mean by that?'

'Come away, Cissie.' The older woman caught the raised hand, drawing it down, a look bordering on fear crossing her tight features. 'Say no more. I know what her means. The sins of the parents be visited on the children. Say no more about that wench being soft in the 'ead 'case the one in your belly be born the same. Once a curse be laid it be laid and none can say the undoing of it. And you knows Sadie Trent as well as I does. It wouldn't be beyond her to take revenge. So leave it, I tells you. Say naught more lest you come to regret it.'

Behind the counter the grocer coughed, unsure how to handle the situation. To order any of them from his shop could only result in future loss of trade. Clearing his throat once more, he began tentatively, 'Now then, you women...'

'Thank you, Mr Riley you have been most helpful. I will call again next week.' Her head still high Deborah walked from the shop, pausing on the step to let her heart still its rapid beat.

How could those women say such things of Lizzie, how could they be so spiteful? Drawing a long calming breath, she turned to smile at the girl.

But the step was empty. Lizzie was gone!

Where? Where had she gone? Fighting the panic rising in her, Deborah fought to think clearly. She had told her to stay there on the step and, childlike, Lizzie always did as she was bid ... but this time she had not. But why had she chosen to move? Ice touching a spine still stiff from the encounter of minutes before, Deborah shivered as a further question drowned out the first. Had the decision to leave been of Lizzie's own making or had the choice been made by another? Had someone taken her away?

'Lizzie!' It was a sob on her lips. 'Oh, God, Lizzie, where are you?'

Hands and mouth trembling, Deborah forced herself to think. What had Lizzie said as they had walked together to the shop? Think, Deborah, think! One hand clasped vice-like about the handle of her basket, the other clenched into a tight ball, she forced her mind to travel back over the previous half hour.

'... *will I wake him, Deborah ... he won't want to miss the park...*'

The park! Deborah almost cried out. Lizzie must have got tired of waiting and gone to the park.

Boots rattling a tattoo on the setts of the road, ears deaf to the angry shout of a carter as she dashed in front of his horse, she began to run.

'Hey, Lizzie, let's see your babby!'

The catcalls and laughter swept along the street, meeting Deborah before she came in sight of the park.

'What be its name, Lizzie ... be it a chap or a wench? Let's 'ave a look...'

'Does it blart? Does its crying wake you in the night?'

'How often does it piddle its napkin?'

Breath tight in her lungs, a stitch gripping at

her side, Deborah ran on. The voices were not those of women but of children. And they were tormenting Lizzie.

'O' course it don't blart! Dolls can't cry nor piddle neither. That be no babby, Lizzie. Daft Lizzie ain't got no babby...'

'Daft Lizzie ... daft Lizzie ... daft Lizzie thinks a doll be a babby ... daft Lizzie...'

The chant ringing in her ears Deborah rounded the bend that gave a clear view of the wrought-iron railings that fenced the park, and there grouped before the tall gates saw several boys standing about a frightened Lizzie, the doll clutched tight in her arms.

'Give us it here.'

Still running as fast as the pain ripping through her side would allow, Deborah saw one lad reach for the doll. Snatching it away, he held it up in the air.

'Be this your babby?' he shouted as the others laughed. 'It be a pretty babby, don't it?'

A cry breaking from her lips, Lizzie reached for the doll.

'What? You wants it back?' The boy waved the doll out of reach of her fingers. 'Hey, lads, daft Lizzie wants her babby back. What say I give it 'er?'

A chorus of voices raised in answer, the boy held out the doll. 'Here you be, Lizzie, take your babby.'

Laughing he swung the doll once more, smashing the head to fragments against the iron gate.

'Lizzie... Oh, Lizzie, I'm so sorry.' The laughter of the boys still audible as they ran off, Deborah bent over to the kneeling girl, slowly picking up the fragments of painted china.

The pieces all collected, she allowed herself to be helped to her feet. The broken bits cradled in her hands, she stared at them.

'We will get you another ... another baby just as pretty.'

Her voice steady, Lizzie raised her head and as she smiled at Deborah her eyes were perfectly clear; all trace of blankness gone, understanding blazing in their depths.

'There's no need, Deborah,' she said quietly. 'It's over now.'

It was over. Slipping the calico night gown over her head, Deborah smoothed it down her body. Somehow a miracle had occurred. Instead of the smashing of the doll causing her grief, Lizzie had somehow been cured by it. Her mind was now back to normal. Perhaps one shock had counterbalanced the other, Deborah did not know, she only knew the happiness it had brought to herself and Sadie to have Lizzie speak and act like an adult once more. And she had talked for most of the afternoon and much of the evening, apologising for the trouble she had caused them, thanking them for the care they had taken of her and the love they had given her.

But not once had she spoken of her son. Reaching for the hair brush, Deborah drew it through hair freshly released from its pins. Not once had she spoken Thomas's name, nor that of the father.

'F...' Only once had Lizzie come close to

divulging his name, and only the first letter had passed her lips. 'F'. Deborah let the sound fall quietly. What name did it begin? Frederick … Francis?

Replacing the brush on the small table at the foot of her bed, she climbed between the sheets. How could she ever find out? For all her searching there had been no clue, no sign to such a man ever existing apart from Lizzie's child. It was a mystery she could not hope to solve. She had prayed that one day they would come face to face, that she could tell him what sort of creature he was to leave a girl in such a condition. But that, she realised, was not to be. It was sufficient that God in His mercy had restored Lizzie to her senses.

'*Thank the Almighty.*' Sadie had said after Lizzie had gone to bed, leaving them to talk together in the quiet kitchen. '*Thank the Almighty and leave the business of the father to Him. Say no more to Lizzie nor ask her no question, be only glad her be whole once more.*'

Whole? Would Lizzie ever be really whole again when part of her lay in the churchyard? Blowing out the candle, Deborah turned her face to the moon-filled window, watching the clouds outrace the wind. They were gone so soon, a fleeting mark upon the sky, a tiny shadow on the earth. 'Just as you were, Thomas,' she whispered, 'a tiny shadow upon the earth and then gone so quickly. But you gave us all so much joy, my little one, so much happiness. Especially your mother. She loved you so much, Thomas, so very, very much.'

And Lizzie would go on loving and remembering, she would have it no other way. But whole? Deborah closed her eyes against the familiar ache. What was it to feel whole? She had not felt that way since refusing Clay's proposal of marriage. How could she when her heart was no longer her own, when her soul was dead? She dragged through her days, slept fitfully at night, but through all the long hours the yearning for him, the knowing she could never give herself to him, cut her in two.

She woke with a start, not knowing the reason for the clutch of coldness in her stomach. Beyond the window the sky had donned the pearly grey of dawn. Deborah lay still, ears tuned to the rhythm of the sleeping house. Had there been a sound in its stillness? Had it reached into her sleeping brain, calling her back to wakefulness? But all was silent now. Perhaps it had been a fox calling to its mate? Lying on the pillows she tried to fall asleep again but the coldness in her stomach would not release its grip, nor the thought that there had been some sound, some movement within the house.

Had Lizzie called to her? Throwing back the bedcovers, her bare feet making no sound on the floor boards, she tiptoed to Lizzie's room.

Opening the door so carefully that it made no sound, she went to the bed. The pillows were dented and the sheets crumpled.

But Lizzie's bed was empty.

It was Clay who carried her home, the sodden night gown clinging to her thin body, trails of slime and water weed sticking in long tendrils to that once shining hair. He carried Lizzie past the women who had criticised and threatened her. Silent now they watched, holding tight to their children. He brought her to Sadie's house, laying her cold body on a door quickly brought in by two men. Then, without a word he left, leaving them to their tears.

It had been a week from Deborah's waking with fear cold and solid in her stomach, a week of dread, and then came heartbreak. Clay had been the one had found Lizzie floating in the canal.

Now Deborah looked at her grave, a single bunch of red roses laid on the freshly turned earth.

Sadie had wanted her to leave the room when Lizzie was returned to the house, leave the washing of her body to others, but Deborah had refused. Lizzie had been her true friend since their coming together at Portland House, she would not turn her back on that friendship. Sadie had accepted what she said and so together they had washed Lizzie. Then, without a word, Sadie had gone upstairs, returning moments later with a fall of white muslin, frothing in layers over her arms, reaching in soft folds to the floor.

'This were mine.' Sadie glanced at the delicate fabric cascading like spindrift over her arms. 'This were the gown I wore to my wedding. It were kept to be worn by the daughter that came after me. That child never came but the one I love as dearly as any child of my own body shall wear it now. Lizzie Burton never walked to the altar of the Lord robed as a bride, but she will walk into heaven dressed as one.'

Together, aided by the light of Sadie's glass-shaded oil lamps, they had dressed the body in the pretty muslin dress, fastening each of the tiny pink rosebud buttons that closed the neck and sleeves.

'...I will dress your hair with rosebuds...'

Eyes misty with memories of that terrible evening, Deborah recalled how those words had returned with startling clarity to her mind. Going out into the street she had walked to the park where, watched by its silent keeper, she had picked a handful of tiny pink rosebuds. Returning to the house she had fastened them in Lizzie's hair, now clean and shining once more.

And that was how Lizzie had left the house. Her face sweet with a smile, gowned in white, she had made her final journey and now, with her son, would lie for ever beneath the quiet earth.

'Rest in peace, Lizzie.' Her words no more than a whisper on the breeze Deborah turned away.

'...You have no daughter by this Emmeline...'

Slumped in a chair Cato Rawley stared at the logs burning in the stone fireplace.

The woman was lying.

But what if Agnes Ridley had not lied ... what if the words she had spat at him were true? Leonie had laughed at his concern, brushing the whole thing off as a figment of a sour woman's imagination, a ruse to get back at him for not holding to a promise only she thought he had made.

'Do you honestly think a serving girl would not say if she were having your child...?'

391

A log shifting in the fireplace filled the chimney with a shower of sparks that were gone as quickly as they came. As quickly as his peace of mind. Cato stared deep into the fire's heart.

Agnes Ridley's words, true or not, had plagued his mind from the moment he had heard them and always they remained, outweighing even Leonie's, leaving him uncertain.

He remembered Emmeline. In the empty hours since Leonie had left on one of her extended trips to London he had thought deeply of those snatched times with his mother's maid. She had been so pretty, with wide laughing eyes and tumbling hair he had loved to wind his fingers in. He remembered the photograph being taken by a university friend, who had come to the house for Easter, and how Cato had sworn him to secrecy; he remembered all these things but not once could he recall the girl asking for anything.

'... *would not at least demand you pay her off...*'

No. In his heart of hearts he did not believe the girl would have demanded that. He picked up the photograph from his desk, looking into those smiling eyes.

She had told him of the child she carried, told him it was his, but he had refused to believe her. Had accused her of trying to foist another man's bastard on to him. He had been so angry, shouting that she had lain willingly with him so why not with another? Who was to say which man had filled her belly? Then he had said she'd best leave, that she had no word but her own that he had lain with her, and did she really think his parents would believe her word over his?

She had gone quietly, saying nothing but that she wished to return home, never once making any demand. Turning the photograph, the faded words written there seemed to mock him.

You will never know our child, Cato...

But he had to. He rose to his feet, taking up the sheet of paper that had lain with the photograph on the desk. Shoving both into his pocket, he walked to the stables.

He had found the name in the household accounts ledger: Elizabeth Burton. Could she have been Emmy's child, Emmy's and his?

Setting his mount towards Elmore Green he let it walk on, his mind on the paper in his pocket. The man he had hired to find Emmeline Burton and her daughter – if such was the girl he had dismissed from his service – had quickly come up with results. Emmeline Burton had died of fever in the Sister Dora Hospital, Walsall. The child she'd had disappeared soon after, but apparently a girl by the name of Lizzie Burton now lived in Elmore Green.

Lizzie ... Elizabeth... It was Emmeline's name. But Burton! Yet Burton was not an uncommon surname, the girl living in Elmore Green was not bound to be the child of Emmy. But he had to know, to ask for himself the name of Emmy's husband and the name of the father of her child.

Chapter Twenty-seven

'Come you in...'

Sadie laid aside the sewing spread about her knees as Deborah opened the door to a tall spare man.

'Be you sure 'tis Sadie Trent you be wanting?' she asked.

Black silk hat in hand he glanced quickly around the small room that must serve them as kitchen and living quarters.

'Forgive my intrusion...'

''Tis no intrusion, 'cept if you comes from Florrie Marston.'

'Florrie Marston?'

Sadie watched his grey eyes carefully but saw no hint of recognition of the name she had spoken, only a slight bewilderment in his repetition of it. 'Seems you don't be from her.' She nodded to Deborah to close the door. 'So you be welcome in this house. Will you take a cup of tea?'

'Thank you but no.'

'Then what can Sadie Trent be doing for you?'

'I think...' He hesitated, glance going to Deborah.

'What you has to say can be said before us both.' Sadie glanced at Deborah. Her face had paled on seeing the visitor. 'Ain't nothing to be said in this house as Deborah Hammond can't listen to.'

Deborah Hammond. Disappointment or relief? Cato was not sure which he felt as he nodded politely towards the young woman swiftly clearing sewing from a chair.

'Mrs Trent, I have been given to believe you can help me...'

'Oh, arrh! And just who is it I be helping?'

'Forgive me.' Cato frowned. 'My name is Rawley, Cato Rawley.'

Cato Rawley! The room seemed to whirl around her and Sadie was back in her youth, with a young woman weeping in her arms. *'He did not believe me, Sadie, Cato did not believe the child is his.'* The words rang pitifully in her mind. And now he was here in her kitchen, Cato Rawley, the man who had destroyed her friend.

Pulling herself back from the past, Sadie stared coldly at the visitor, the pain of those long-gone days an ache in her throat.

'What brings you to my door?' Her tone clipped, she pointedly ignored his outstretched hand nor did she ask him to be seated. The sooner he was gone, the easier her heart would beat.

Glancing at the hat he passed from one hand to the other, Cato cleared his throat. There was an animosity in this woman he could almost taste, but for what reason? He did not even know her.

'Mrs Trent,' he began again. 'I am informed, and I believe reliably so, that a certain Elizabeth ... Lizzie Burton ... lives in this house.'

Lizzie? Deborah's nerves jarred. Why would Cato Rawley be looking for Lizzie? Was he ... could he be the father of Lizzie's child? Of course

395

not! Shock and fear brought a half laugh squeezing from her lips.

Feet set a little apart, arms folded across her breasts, Sadie glared at the man the very thought of whom had been like acid in her blood for almost twenty years. Eyes and voice hard as the flagstones they both stood on, she smiled icily.

'Then you should get yourself a better informant. The one you used ain't so reliable as you thought. If he told you there be a Lizzie Burton in this 'ouse then he told you false!'

'Please!' He glanced at Deborah then back at Sadie. 'I have no wish to harm the girl, but I have to find her.'

What for? So he could throw her out of the village as he had turned her out of his house? As he had turned away her mother? Sadie swallowed hard. There had been no way of proving that the girl who had come to her was Emmy's daughter, the name Burton was no real evidence of that. But she had known all the same. Watched the same turn of the head, the same quick smile, heard the same voice and looked into the same wide brown eyes. She had felt God's mercy in her heart, listened to the whisper of it in her soul. He had performed His miracle. He had returned Emmy's daughter to her and she had nursed the secret of it, said nothing to Deborah or the girl herself, telling her nothing of her mother or the man she claimed to be her baby's father. Sadie had not kept the secret out of spite but from a need to protect Lizzie, to shield her from further hurt, further rejection.

Her voice still hard, she said, 'You'll not find

her in this house. Like I told you, there be none of that name 'ere.'

Seeing the pain in features drawn and haggard despite the privileged life he led, Sadie felt a moment's hesitation, a lull in her hatred of him. He had been little more than a boy then, as Emmy had been no more than a girl. Perhaps he had been as frightened as she by what had happened; the only son of a rich influential family getting a love child by a servant girl. Perhaps he had later regretted turning his back on her. Perhaps he had told his parents and it was they who had forbidden him to search for her. But they were long gone from this earth and only now was he asking, only now searching for the child.

Hardening her heart, Sadie continued to stare at him.

'Perhaps you might have heard of her, know where I might look.' Reaching into his pocket he withdrew the photograph, holding it out to Sadie. 'She may have borne a resemblance to this girl. She ... she was her mother, Emmeline Burton. I believe Lizzie is my daughter.'

The bundle of cloth in her hands falling to the floor, Deborah gasped. Lizzie ... Cato Rawley's daughter! It was not true, it could not possibly be true. She had been brought from an institution like Deborah herself, Agnes Ridley had said so. But why would Cato Rawley be here, searching for a child taken from the workhouse? Glancing at Sadie she saw tears slide slowly down the old woman's face.

'I cared for her.' Sadie supported Deborah as she came to her side, leaning heavily against her.

397

'I cared for her after he turned from her. It was me went with Emmeline. We walked for days with hedgerows for a bed and sometimes only berries for food. There were few would give us work or a word of comfort. There was no place for whores, we were told. But Emmy was no whore. She knew no man before Cato Rawley, and none after him. I should know for 'twas me passed the long nights with her, shared the days. Me that helped birth her child and me brought her to that hospital where life passed from her body.'

'It's true,' Cato Rawley's face twisted. 'I did turn my back on Emmeline. She told me of the child she was carrying, vowed that it was mine, but I refused to believe her, refused to accept responsibility. But I swear I did not know she had given birth to it! After I told my father what had happened he assured me he would have the girl traced, make certain she and the child were well cared for. Then a few weeks later he told me she had miscarried the child naturally, but that he had given her enough money to provide her with a decent life. I believed him, Mrs Trent, I never had reason not to. My father had never lied to me before so why should he do so then?

'But recently my housekeeper, Agnes Ridley, told me Emmeline had indeed borne a child and that same child had been brought to my house as a servant, one I myself dismissed after she became pregnant. Did that girl come to this house? I beg you, tell me if she did.'

Lowering Sadie to a chair, Deborah turned to face the man for whom she had once worked. 'I do not know if the girl you once knew, this Emmeline Burton you speak of, was Lizzie's mother, but Lizzie herself was the maid you dismissed, Mr Rawley, and I was the other. I resigned that same night.'

'You were in service at Portland House?'

'Yes.' Deborah nodded. 'For many years. I was very young when my mother died. Mrs Ridley took me from the institution I had been taken to. At your home Lizzie and I became great friends.'

'Did she ... did she ever speak of her mother?'

Beside her Sadie sniffed, wiping her eyes on the hem of her long white apron as Deborah went on.

'She sometimes talked of a woman, but judging from the way she treated Lizzie, I cannot think she was her mother.'

'Then how ... how did this woman come to have the girl? Didn't you say, Mrs Trent, that you were with Emmeline when the child was born, with her when she died? Surely after such friendship you would not abandon the child?'

'And no more I did.' Sadie looked up through tear-damp eyes. 'You'd best sit down, Cato Rawley, for what I know will take more than a moment to tell.'

Sitting beside Sadie as Cato took a chair, Deborah listened, young hand held in old, as the whole story poured out.

'After finding the child gone, I searched and asked but none had seen or heard of her. The woman who claimed to be sister to Emmy disappeared like mist in the sun. That were when I come back 'ere to Elmore Green, and this be where Emmy's child returned to me.'

'Do you believe Lizzie is Emmeline Burton's daughter?' Cato asked when she'd finished.

Taking the photograph once more, Sadie touched the tip of one finger to the smiling face. 'I knowed it long afore you came to this house, long afore ever I saw this. Lizzie was the living, breathing image of her mother – may God forgive my never telling the wench I knew her! Yes, Cato Rawley. Lizzie Burton was the child of Emmy, the child of yourself, the child you refused to own.'

He leaned forward, his grey eyes holding an expression Sadie could not read. 'But I wish to own her now, Mrs Trent. I wish to give her my name, give her all that is rightfully hers, make up for the pain and heartache I caused. I want the world to know Lizzie is my daughter.'

A scornful laugh in her throat, Sadie shook her head. 'It be too late to make amends. You've come too late, Cato Rawley.'

'Please!' He turned his glance to Deborah and his eyes were alive with guilt. 'Please make her understand that I wish no harm to the girl. In God's name, please ask her to tell me where Lizzie is!'

'In God's name!' Suddenly all of Sadie's anger was back and her eyes glistened with condemnation. 'In God's name, you say! Then in His name I will tell you for it is with Him they all be. Emmy, Lizzie and the baby she bore. All three of them lie in consecrated ground, though Emmy be miles away in Walsall.'

'Dead!' It was just a whisper but the pain was

visible in Cato Rawley's drawn features. 'Lizzie too, and her son? She was carrying a child and I turned her away, just as I did her mother...'

'Lizzie did not blame you,' Deborah said quietly his obvious grief touching her heart. 'I don't really believe she would have blamed you had she known you were her father.'

'The man ... the baby's father.' Cato look up sharply. 'Who is he? What is his name?'

Deborah shook her head. 'I don't know, and neither does Mrs Trent. Lizzie would never say. She never said his name, only once beginning to, but all she said was the first letter: "F". We tried to find him, find out if he had made any search for Lizzie...'

'But you failed?'

'There was no trace of him.'

The hat falling from his hands, Cato dropped his head cradling his face in his palms. Silently the two women watched as he gave way to grief.

'I did not know,' he murmured more to himself than to them. 'I did not know and now they are dead. A daughter I lost without ever having known her and nothing of her left to cherish.'

Meeting Sadie's eyes, Deborah silently asked a question, one that was answered by the old woman's nod. Going quickly up the stairs, she came back with a sheaf of papers.

'Mr Rawley.' She waited until he'd lifted his head. 'Lizzie was very good at drawing. She designed many of the gowns we sew and the decorative beadwork we put on them. After ... after her death I found this among her drawings. There is no name on it but we think perhaps it is a representation of Thomas's father.'

'Thomas?'

'That was the name Lizzie gave her son.'

His brows knitting at the reply, Cato took the paper, looking at it for a long time.

'My two hearts.' He read aloud the words written across the foot of the drawing.

'It is Lizzie's writing,' Deborah said softly, watching the shades of emotion pass over his face. 'Two hearts. She must have meant her own and the one of the man in the drawing.'

'Did she?' His voice tight, Cato picked up the fallen hat then rose to his feet. When he looked at Deborah his eyes were once more cool and steady.

'Miss...?'

'Hammond.'

'Ah, yes.' He smiled apologetically. 'Miss Hammond. I know this will seem a lot to ask, especially in the face of my behaviour in the past, but may I keep this drawing as a keepsake, a memento of my daughter?'

It would be all he could ever have. He could not share in Lizzie as she and Sadie had done, find no relief in memories of her, feel no happiness for having known her. He would have none of that while she would have so much; Deborah could spare him this one thing.

A smile touching her mouth, she nodded assent.

At the door he turned to look back at Sadie, still sitting in her wooden chair. 'Thank you, Mrs Trent.' He smiled sadly. 'Thank you for giving them both what I did not – love and care.' Then to Deborah: 'If I can ever do anything to help you, Miss Hammond, please do not hesitate to ask. You were a good friend to my daughter, and you too have my thanks.'

The drawing in his hand, Cato Rawley left the house. Emmeline Burton was dead. His daughter was dead. But the man who had deceived her was not.

Was one any worse than the other? Was the man more to blame than he had been? They had both done wrong, both seduced a young girl then left her pregnant. Walking to where his horse stood tethered to a tree at the end of the street, Cato tried to reason with himself but all that came back to him was the same thought, over and over, like the waves beating against the shore.

His daughter dead and her child unnamed. There was not much he could do for her now except look for the man responsible.

And he would find him. By God, he would!

Giving his horse into the care of livery stables adjacent to Station Street, Cato strode into the railway station.

Walsall, Sadie Trent had told him yesterday, was where Emmeline had died, at the hospital in the centre of town. But the place where she had been laid to rest was called the Pleck. Maybe someone there might remember, might know this mysterious 'sister' of Emmeline's, be able to tell him who had stolen her child. It was many years and memories lost their edge, but for Emmy's sake he had to try.

Settled in a first-class compartment, empty but

for himself, he slid the drawing from his pocket, staring at it as he had for most of the week he'd had it. The face that smiled up at him was strikingly attractive; in a woman one would have called it beautiful. A perfectly shaped mouth; wide eyes that were slightly almond-shaped and deep with promise; hair that tumbled to the collar tinted with a paler shade where the light touched it. A handsome man indeed, one who might turn any head.

Leaving the train at Walsall he stood for a moment in the warm September sunshine, ignoring the calls of the driver of a hansom cab waiting in the street. He could go to the place Sadie Trent and Emmeline had found to live, but that could wait. First he would visit Emmy's grave in the churchyard of St Michael.

A nod to the hopeful driver had the hansom rolling to his feet. Giving the location, Cato settled back against the black leather upholstery.

The drive took only minutes. Alighting, he stared at the small building. Behind the lych gate, its wood discoloured by the black breath of countless coal pits and iron works, a spire rose tall and slender, standing guard over the church.

'Will I wait, sir?'

A shake of the head his refusal, Cato walked towards the low arched door, feet crunching on the well-worn track in the grass.

To either side of him headstones rose like the fingers of so many outstretched hands, as if each were trying to stop him from reaching the church. So many graves; some carefully tended with their tributes of flowers glowing in the sun, others bare and empty, their marker stones broken or falling over. That would be how Emmeline's was. Uncared for. Even in death she was rejected. But he would find her lonely resting place and there he would make his promise. The seducer of her child would pay his debt in full.

Staring at a small cross that rose from grass grown high, he read the name carved in its rotting wood: Emmeline Burton. For a moment that young face floated in his mind, the wide brown eyes staring at him, filled with pain.

'Yea, though I walk through the valley of the shadow of death I will fear no evil...'

Cato glanced over to where a side door in the church gave on to the churchyard. There, prayer book in hand, stood a priest. His white surplice gleamed and afternoon sunlight touched his bare head as he led a mourning procession towards an open grave.

'...they rod and thy staff they comfort me...'

The words floated over to Cato, accompanied by muffled sobs from a woman swathed in a black veil.

'The peace of God the Father Almighty...'

The priest raised his hand over the grave as the coffin was lowered into the ground.

Peace! Cato turned away. Where would be find peace ... in that church perhaps? Entering the main door he stood for a moment, his eyes adjusting to the shadows. Before him the aisle ran between plain wooden pews as it led to the altar.

Footsteps echoed on the stone-flagged floor Cato walked slowly forward. This was as good a place as any.

Chapter Twenty-eight

'Cato Rawley Lizzie's father!'

Sitting in Sadie's tiny living room, Clay Gilmore shook his head in disbelief.

'I could not believe it either.' Deborah smiled. She had repeated the story several times and with each telling Clay seemed as bewildered as before.

'But Lizzie worked in his house. How could he not know, not see who she was?'

'Eh, lad.' Sadie wagged her head to and fro. 'How many times do you think the gentry catches sight of a kitchen maid? They be kept out of sight like boils on a backside. To be caught above stairs when the master is about be asking for the sack.'

'I suppose you be right.'

'She is,' Deborah replied. 'In my ten years or so in that house, I hardly ever caught sight of the master. And Lizzie, I think, never saw him at all except for the time he dismissed her.'

'So he saw her then,' Clay countered. 'How come he did not recognise her? Sadie says her features were very like her mother's.'

Sadie shrugged her shoulders, turning to the fire. 'Memories fade, lad. They play many tricks as eyes grow old.'

'Hmmph!' Clay was clearly unconvinced. 'Were it that ... or were it Cato Rawley didn't want to recognise Lizzie? Didn't want his own lifestyle blighted by scandal?'

'He vowed he did not know about her. Said his father told him there had been a miscarriage, and that Lizzie's mother had been well provided for.'

'Arrh, and he settled for that!' Clay's tone was scathing. 'Tell me, Deborah, what kind of a man is it would not want to find out for himself?'

Reaching for the poker, Sadie stirred the fire coals then watched Clay as he fetched the bucket from the scullery to replenish the fire.

'Well, whatever the case it be all over now, lad. Arguing the toss over the rights and wrongs of it won't bring either of them back. Leave Cato Rawley to his regrets, if they be genuine as they seem, and leave Lizzie and her child to lie in peace.'

'Do you think Mr Rawley truly regrets not knowing Lizzie?' Deborah asked as Clay returned the bucket to its place beneath the scullery sink.

'Only the Lord can truly tell that, Deborah wench, and He don't always be given to letting folk know all they would like to. But Cato Rawley be nothing to us, best forget he ever was.'

That was easier to say than to do. In the sleepless hours of the night and in unguarded moments of her days Deborah often caught herself thinking of the morning he had called at the house. Of the expression that came over his face when he looked at that drawing. She could not tell him it was a sketch of the man who had hurt Lizzie so badly, but neither could she tell him it was not. To Cato Rawley the face had been unimportant; he wanted that drawing only as a

407

memento, perhaps as something to help relieve him of his own guilt.

'If you two be going to fetch my beer then you'd best get a move on or you'll have the knocker up banging on your window afore you be in bed, Clay Gilmore.'

'Will you listen to the woman?' He grinned, his good nature firmly back in place. 'What with my mother *and* Sadie Trent going on at me, it's a wonder I have any sense left at all.'

Throwing her shawl about her shoulders, Deborah picked up the jug standing ready on the dresser. Reaching the street, Clay at her side, they walked in silence. Drawing level with the park Deborah glanced over at the tall gates, their iron work like delicate lace against the purpling sky. The gates where those boys had tormented Lizzie, where they had smashed her doll's head and run away laughing. Unaware of the sob that escaped her lips, she covered them with one hand.

'She's gone, Deborah.' Gently Clay eased her hand away from her quivering mouth. 'Let her rest. Don't torment yourself with memories.'

'Oh, Clay! She was such a sweet girl, she never harmed anyone.'

Drawing her against him, he ignored the stare of an old woman passing on the other side of the street.

'I know,' he whispered, 'I know. Lizzie was one of the nicest girls, but you have to let go. You have to live your life and it can't be lived with your heart in the grave. Remember her by all means, yes, and love her. But not to the exclusion of all

408

others, Deborah. Leave room for someone else, someone to love you.'

Above her head he stared at the darkening sky, thoughts running silently through his mind.

Let me love you, Deborah. Let me love you.

Cato Rawley stared through the gathering shadows towards the altar, the gleam of the cross at its centre almost lost. He had sat there most of the afternoon and now it was evening. Soon it would be time for the priest to come back into his church, soon it would be time for Evensong, soon it would be time...

Moving only his hand he touched the pocket of his coat, feeling the drawing he had placed there, feeling the other thing he had brought with him from Portland House.

Somewhere to the left of the aisle a door creaked and a figure robed in black came to the altar. Having lit the candles placed to each side of it, the figure sank low on one knee.

In the body of the church Cato slipped from his pew.

'Two hearts.' His voice echoed around the almost empty church. 'My two hearts, that is what it says.'

The priest whirled round, his robe twisting about his legs.

'Here on this drawing.' Pulling the folded paper from his pocket, Cato let it fall open. 'That is what she wrote – my two hearts. Look at it, Father. Look at the words my daughter wrote.'

'I ... I don't understand.' His back to the flame-lit altar, the priest peered into the gloom.

'No ... you would not.' Cato walked closer, halting at the foot of three wide shallow steps that led up to the altar. 'Neither do I. But we will, we both will. Look at the picture, Father. Look at the eyes, the mouth, that small mark below the left eye. A handsome face, the face of a man with two hearts, one in his breast and one on his face. *Your* face, Father, *your* birthmark! "F", they said ... that was the letter they thought began the name of Lizzie's lover. But it was not "F". Oh, the sound was the same but it was no Frederick, no Francis, it was Philip.' Cato held up his hand, the drawing visible in the candles' light. 'This picture tells it all. *You* are the man who fathered Lizzie Burton's child.'

'You're wrong.' The priest came forward half a step.

'No, you were wrong to think you would not be discovered.' Cato laughed, a sound laced with despair. 'But our sins have a way of finding us out, don't they ... Leonie?'

'Cato, I can explain...'

'There's no need.' He laughed again. 'I knew what you were all along and I said nothing. I made love to you, totally bewitched by you. By your lovely mouth, your body, your golden wig. I was enchanted, caught in the web of my beautiful golden Satan. It didn't matter that you were a man, nor that you were a priest. I closed my eyes to all that you were. Even after the funeral of my wife, the funeral *you* conducted, I made love to you and felt no trace of sin, no stirring of remorse. But sooner or later we are called to account for our sins and we must pay for ours,

410

my too beautiful Leonie.'

'Cato, wait. Listen to me!' Philip Travers fought to keep desperation from his voice. 'No one knows. We will go to the continent as we planned. We will live there as man and wife. I love you, Cato…'

The drawing, loosed from Cato's hand, fluttered silently to the cold stone floor. 'And I loved you. God forgive the sinfulness of such love! That is why no one must ever know what you truly are: a man of God who made love to another man while at the same time seducing a young girl. I could take all that you were, my love, close my eyes to the evil that was my golden Satan, but sharing your love with another I cannot take.

'But you are right. No one but myself will ever know the truth behind the lovely Leonie – the truth of Father Philip Travers.'

Reaching into his pocket Cato withdrew the pistol he had taken from the drawer of his bedside table. Raising it level with his eyes, he pointed it at the heart-shaped birthmark.

Drawing a long breath he smiled at the figure outlined by the glow of the candles, the light shimmering over brown-gold hair.

'You hid one heart beneath a beauty patch, my lovely Leonie,' he said softly, 'the other beneath a priest's cassock. My beautiful golden Satan.'

'Cato!'

The cry was loud but the report of the gun was louder. Still smiling Cato watched the figure spin round, both hands flung across the altar, fingers closing convulsively about the cross.

Aiming the gun Cato fired once more into the back of the smashed head.

'Goodbye, my love.'

He laughed softly as he placed the barrel in his own mouth.

'Things are going well for you, Deborah.'

'Better than I ever dreamed they would, Clay.' She smiled. 'As Sadie says, the gentry know quality when they see it. But truly, I had not thought to win the custom we have.'

Bending, he plucked a blade of grass and twined it between his fingers as they walked across the heath.

'It was a kindly thing you did, putting every penny you had into a property to give a home to Mary Ann and her daughter.'

'It was no more than Sadie did for Lizzie and me. She shared everything she had with us.'

'Not quite the same.' Clay smiled yet his handsome face was not relaxed.

Glancing at him, Deborah felt the familiar tug at her heart. He would ask again, Sadie had said. But Clay had not asked her again, not since that day they had been to Blakenhall. He was still the same gentle, caring man, ever ready to help when he could, but not once had he spoken to her of the love she had refused.

'How not the same thing?' She glanced away across the stretch of empty heath.

'You had money, you and Lizzie both. You could have paid for lodgings anywhere.'

'Mary Ann had her wages and Molly had the few coins Martha Vines had given her. They could have paid for lodgings somewhere, at least for a few weeks. But they chose to put their money with mine so they could find a home the twins could share. Mary Ann's heart is like Sadie's, it has room in it for others.'

Beside her Clay walked in silence, studying the blade of grass as he twisted it between his fingers.

'And what of you, Deborah? How much room is there in your heart? I once said to you, love Lizzie but not to the exclusion of all others. I asked you to leave room for someone else, someone to love you. Can you do that, Deborah? Can you let someone else love you? Can you love them in return?'

Was he saying he loved her still?

Eyes green and soft as summer grass and shining with the love she had so long suppressed, Deborah smiled as finally he looked at her.

'I have a love, for several people,' she whispered, 'but it is not the same love I hold for one, there is a place in my heart for many people but only one commands it completely. Yes, Clay, I can love someone in return, love him as I have done since he found me one night on this heath.'

'Deborah!' Catching her elbows he stared down into her eyes, seeing at last the fullness of her love. 'Deborah, do you mean...'

'Yes.' She lifted her face to his. 'Yes, Clay, I love you. I love you with all my heart.'

A cry breaking from his lips, he crushed her to him his mouth closing over hers.

Later ... much later ... her hand in his as they walked towards the village, Clay looked down at the girl for whom he had yearned so long. 'What

413

will we tell Sadie?'

A smile painting her mouth, love gilding her eyes, Deborah replied instantly.

'We will tell her the name of the shop.'

Standing on tiptoe, she kissed his mouth.

'It will bear my husband's name.' She smiled. 'Gilmore.'

The publishers hope that this book has given you enjoyable reading. Large Print Books are especially designed to be as easy to see and hold as possible. If you wish a complete list of our books please ask at your local library or write directly to:

Magna Large Print Books
Magna House, Long Preston,
Skipton, North Yorkshire.
BD23 4ND

This Large Print Book for the partially sighted, who cannot read normal print, is published under the auspices of

THE ULVERSCROFT FOUNDATION

THE ULVERSCROFT FOUNDATION

... we hope that you have enjoyed this Large Print Book. Please think for a moment about those people who have worse eyesight problems than you ... and are unable to even read or enjoy Large Print, without great difficulty.

You can help them by sending a donation, large or small to:

**The Ulverscroft Foundation,
1, The Green, Bradgate Road,
Anstey, Leicestershire, LE7 7FU,
England.**
or request a copy of our brochure for more details.

The Foundation will use all your help to assist those people who are handicapped by various sight problems and need special attention.

Thank you very much for your help.